MENACE
of the
MACHINE

MENACE
of the
MACHINE

The Rise of AI in Classic Science Fiction

edited by

MIKE ASHLEY

This collection first published in 2019 by
The British Library
96 Euston Road
London NW1 2DB

Introduction and notes © 2019 Mike Ashley

Cataloguing in Publication Data
A catalogue record for this publication is available from the British Library

ISBN 978 0 7123 5242 0
e-ISBN 978 0 7123 6477 5

Frontispiece illustration by Paul Orban, from the first publication of 'The
Evitable Conflict' by Isaac Asimov in Astounding Science Fiction, June 1950.

Cover artwork © David A Hardy / www.astroart.org
Cover design by Jason Anscomb

Text design and typesetting by Tetragon, London
Printed and bound by CPI Group (UK) Ltd, Croydon CRO 4YY

CONTENTS

INTRODUCTION

Here are some recent newspaper headlines:

BANK OF ENGLAND ECONOMIST WARNS
THOUSANDS OF JOBS AT RISK FROM ROBOTS.

HOW ARTIFICIAL INTELLIGENCE
COULD BE VIOLATING OUR HUMAN RIGHTS.

WHY WE NEED TO PROTECT OUR INCOME
FROM ROBOT AUTOMATION.

I could list hundreds of these. In the last decade or so we have become almost phobic about the prospect that machines are taking over and that artificial intelligence will be ruling our lives. There are no real secrets any more. We can be tracked by our mobile phones. Anyone monitoring the internet could identify what we're doing. Social media can intrude upon the lives of its users. The ability to clone our identity from documents can make our lives a misery.

Of course, the good that mobile phones, the internet and social media has brought to the world is immense—as are all the other wonders that computerization, automation and robotization have delivered. Robot surgery is saving lives. Artificial Intelligence, or AI, is being used to predict the spread of cancers. Computers can enhance our security. We can monitor our homes from wherever we are, and facial recognition or handprint technology will strengthen our privacy. But it's when AI goes wrong that it makes the headlines.

None of this is new. A letter by Henry Dicken Turner, staff lecturer in Science at the University of Sheffield, to the London *Times* in November 1954, under the heading "A New 'Industrial Revolution'" said, in part: "There can be no doubt that a second Industrial Revolution based on the use of automatic factories is imminent; that the social and industrial consequences will be comparable with those of the first Industrial Revolution, and that it will present a serious problem for society..."

We can go back much further than this. In April 1817 the *Hull Packet* warned the public about the plans by Robert Owen to mechanize his factories, saying: "The use of mechanization must be greatly diminished; or millions of human beings must be starved to permit its existence to the present extent..."

That was the period of the Luddites, a movement of workers against the mechanization of weaving looms in factories. This was at its height in the years 1811 to 1816 and it was not unknown for mill owners to shoot protestors or call in the militia. Some sixty to seventy Luddites were hanged for machine breaking and others were transported.

The word Luddite, coined from a protestor called Ned Ludd, who may or may not have existed, is still used to refer to anyone who is against progress, particularly automation. And that was reflected not just in riots but a fear for the future. How far would mechanization go? A leader writer in the *Stamford Mercury* in August 1823, referring to Robert Owen's plans to mechanize the "whole community", called the scheme an "abominable tyranny".

The idea that machines would start to take over and perhaps develop their own intelligence and awareness soon entered the public mind. Is it simply a coincidence that during the same decade the Luddites were active the German author E. T. A. Hoffmann wrote "Der Sandmann" (1816) about the mesmerizing automaton Olimpia, and that Mary Shelley wrote *Frankenstein* (1818) about the creation of a human being?

Fiction frequently echoes the feelings and sentiments of society and in science fiction this relates almost wholly to progress, both scientific and social. From its earliest days, science fiction has considered the potential for new inventions and their impact upon society and this was most evident when looking at automation, robots and machine intelligence.

In this anthology I have assembled fourteen examples of how science fiction has reflected the fear of society to automation and robots, ranging from a murderous chess-playing automaton to the creation of the internet (forty years before it became reality), and from a cyborg soldier (seventy years before the movie *The Terminator*) to robot megalomaniacs and robot surveillance. In line with the theme of classic science fiction, I have limited the selection to the years before the progenitors of the internet, such as the NPL Network and Arpanet, were being developed in the late 1960s. These stories may be seen as forecasting many of the problems we now envisage with AI, but they also reflect the attitude at the time towards the potential of machine intelligence.

It is, of course, impossible to include all of the early stories about robots and intelligent machines, so to complement those presented here and to place them in context the following considers the history and development of automation in fiction. You may wish to read the stories first and then return here or simply read on and discover just how much our fears and concerns about artificial intelligence have been around for centuries.

THE MENACE OF THE MACHINE

Consider the following:

> "Day by day, however, the machines are gaining ground upon
> us; day by day we are becoming more subservient to them;
> more men are daily bound down as slaves to tend them, more
> men are daily devoting the energies of their whole lives to
> the development of mechanical life. The upshot is simply
> a question of time, but that the time will come when the
> machines will hold the real supremacy over the world and
> its inhabitants is what no person of a truly philosophic mind
> can for a moment question."

When do you think that was written? It comes from an essay,
"Darwin Among the Machines", which had been published in a New
Zealand paper, *The Press* in June 1863 and ascribed to Cellarius. The
author was Samuel Butler who went on to incorporate this argument about the evolution of machines in *Erewhon; or, Over the Range*
published in 1872. The novel tells the story of a hitherto unknown
land which the narrator discovers beyond the outposts of empire.
One of the strange features of this world is that all machinery has
been banned. Part of the novel includes text from "The Book of
the Machines", purportedly written years before by an Erewhonian
philosopher, which put forward the concept that machines would
evolve, become self-replicating and eventually challenge mankind
for supremacy.

Butler, who was an immediate convert to Darwin's theory
of evolution, was the first to consider the idea that machines
might become aware, self-replicating and supersede mankind in

intelligence and ability. It's the same fear we have today, expressed here almost word for word over one hundred and fifty years ago.

Butler lived to see the number of inventions increase at an alarming rate during the second half of the nineteenth century. At the time he wrote *Erewhon*, he was aware of the automated machinery in the cotton mills and other factories, the rapid expansion of the railways with steam trains, the connection across the world thanks to telegraphy, the mass production of steel thanks to the Bessemer process, the expansion and rebuilding of the road system, the creation of street lighting, and in particular the prototype of Charles Babbage's calculating machine called the Difference Engine which had first been demonstrated in 1833.

But this was only half the story. Mechanization and industrialization on a huge scale was taking over from earlier examples of automation frequently involving clockwork machines or those operated by water or air. The development of these machines, called automata, had been around for centuries and had amazed generations.

The word 'automata' was coined by no less than Homer in the *Iliad* in the eighth century BCE. He attributes Hephaestus, the Greek god of fire and crafts, with creating several automated devices to help him in his work. Although this was all myth, the fact that Homer refers to bellows and trolleys that respond to an oral command and operate by themselves, suggests it may not all have been down to the imagination. It was only three centuries after Homer that Archytas is said to have created the first mechanical bird which is supposed to have flown, perhaps steam-powered.

Another creation attributed to Hephaestus was a bronze mechanical man called Talos. Although mentioned briefly by Homer, Talos is described in more detail in the *Argonautica* of Apollonius, written around the middle of the third century BCE. Talos was supposed to be a gift to Minos of Crete from Hephaestus. He patrolled the island three times a day throwing rocks at any who tried to land. Talos operated by some form of hydraulics using a liquid, perhaps mercury, which flowed through a single vein. This was plugged at the ankle and Talos was eventually destroyed by the Argonauts when Medea removed the plug.

One of the most astonishing devices discovered from the ancient Greek world is the Antikythera Mechanism, named after the island where it was discovered in a shipwreck off the coast in 1902. It was not until the 1970s that it was realized that the device was a sophisticated calculator, virtually a computer, designed to keep track of planets, constellations and even predict eclipses. It is believed to have been built sometime in the second century BCE, but could be earlier. It is known that the great mathematician Archimedes, who died in 212BCE, had created mechanical devices such as an orrery for showing the movements of the planets, and he may possibly be the genius behind this device.

The mathematician Hero or Heron of Alexandria who lived in the first century CE wrote several books on mechanical inventions and automata, including some invented by Hero himself. These included statues that could pour wine, a cart that operated by itself on the stage in a programmable theatre, and a vending machine that dispensed water.

The skills of the Greek and Roman engineers was lost to the West after the fall of Rome but such texts as survived were collected by the Persians, notably the brothers Banu Musa ("Sons of Moses") by order of the Caliph of Bagdad and incorporated in the *Kitab al-Hiyal* or *Book of Ingenious Devices* published around 800CE. This preserved details of many of the Roman automata to which were added others devised or discovered by the brothers. These were not humanoid automata but machines controlled either by water or wind, including mechanical fountains, water dispensers and a musical organ. This work was later embellished by Ismail al-Jazari in *The Book of Knowledge of Ingenious Mechanical Devices* completed in 1206. In addition to many of the same machines, al-Jazari added a humanoid waitress that could dispense drinks and a boat with four automaton musicians that floated on a lake.

There is no doubt that the Arab Caliphate developed and improved upon the original Roman automata so it is little surprise that some of these appear in the famous *Arabian Nights* or more properly, *Kitāb 'alf layla wa-laylam* the "Thousand and One Nights", as told by Scheherazade. The original stories were drawn from many sources and the earliest known compilation dates from the ninth century, and was certainly in its final form by the twelfth century. Amongst the automata is the flying horse in "The Tale of the Ebony Horse" which was able to take its rider anywhere at the speed of light. The horse was not activated by magic but had controls and is described as an "invention". There are also the automaton servants and guards in "The City of Brass" whilst in "The Tale of the Third Kalandar" the beleaguered mystic is rescued from drowning by a boat rowed by a man of brass.

The *Arabian Nights* as oral tales would have found their way into Western Europe long before Antoine Galland produced his French translation as *Les milles et une nuit* between 1704 and 1717. Indeed, there are references to automaton guards in several of the medieval and Arthurian romances. Moreover, legends attached themselves to certain philosophers saying that they had created automaton heads from which they learned dark secrets. The most famous of these was one allegedly created by Roger Bacon in the thirteenth

century. The legend was so well known that the Elizabethan drama-
tist, Robert Greene, incorporated it into his comic play *Friar Bacon
and Friar Bungay* (1590) where Bacon takes seven years to create
the brazen head. Exhausted he falls asleep at which point the head
awakes, utters the cryptic words, "Time is. Time was. Time is past."
and the head is then destroyed by a lightning bolt.

The wonders of Eastern automata were being discovered by the
West. In his production of Aristophanes's comedy *Pax* in 1547 the
notorious Elizabethan mage John Dee was the first to introduce
automata to the English stage with a scarab beetle which flew to
Jupiter's palace. The effect was so realistic that Dee was accused
of sorcery.

As the Age of Enlightenment slowly dawned, Jacobean writers
were giving thought to scientific development. This was evident
in Francis Bacon's incomplete and posthumously published *New
Atlantis* (1627), which describes an island that boasts many new wonders of science, with suggestions of submarines, flying machines
and even a house of illusion which included automata on display.

The improvement in the accuracy of clocks and the related
technology allowed more sophisticated clockwork automata to be
built that are still amazing to see today. The most remarkable were
created during the eighteenth century and two inventors stand out,
the Frenchman Jacques de Vaucanson and the Swiss Pierre Jaquet-
Droz. Vaucanson took to heart an argument put forward by René
Descartes in the mid-1640s that many of the actions that humans
make are automatic and involuntary and that to a large degree
man was a machine. Vaucanson set out to make the most authentic
humanoid machines possible, including covering them in human
skin. The height of his work was the Flute Player, created in 1737.
This mannikin was provided with internal bellows for lungs and

genuinely played the flute, its fingers moving along the instrument and a tongue regulating the air flow to create the music. Jaquet-Droz took this further with his remarkable mannikin, the Writer, created around 1770. A small boy was able to dip a quill into an inkwell and write accurately on paper, his eyes following the words. He would even slightly shake the quill to remove any excess ink. The significance of the Writer was that tucked within his tiny body was a removable plate on which was inscribed the alphabet and could be rearranged to allow for different messages. In effect, the Writer was programmable and thus an ancestor of the computer.

By the end of the eighteenth century there was a plethora of exquisite and remarkable automata throughout Europe. These were all expensive and were thus playthings of the aristocracy. There were those who began to wonder whether the rich, especially the idle rich, were no more than unthinking automata. In his novel *L'An 2440* (1771), a dream of a future French society, Louis Sébastien Mercier has his narrator look back to his own day and remark:

> We have seen on the Boulevards an automaton that articulated sounds, and the people flock to admire it. How many automata, with human faces, do we see at court, at the bar, in the academies, who owe their speech to the breath of invisible agents; when they cease the machines remain dumb.

Mercier was implying that the aristocracy and those who ran society acted like automatons, lacking any soul or empathy, and simply acting by rote. Mercier claimed that his book helped encourage the French Revolution, sweeping aside the mindless automata and seeking a society run by thinking human beings. Perhaps here was the first time that the thought of automata helped foment a revolution.

*

Amongst other brilliant automaton makers was the Austro-Hungarian Wolfgang von Kempelen who created probably the most famous of all automata, the Turk, or Automaton Chess-Player built in 1770.

Unlike most of the automata exclusive to the aristocracy, the Turk chess-player went on tour all over Europe. It played against many chess masters and other notables, including Napoleon Bonaparte. It won most games but occasionally lost or drew. After Von Kempelen's death in 1804 the Turk was bought by Johann Maelzel who took it to the United States in 1826 and continued to tour successfully.

Everyone was fascinated by it and there was something about its almost dehumanizing relentlessness that made the automaton sinister to many, some believing it was operated by evil spirits. But it inspired others. Edmund Cartwright saw the Turk in 1784 and was convinced that if a machine could play chess then surely one could be designed to undertake other complicated activities. Using the principles of the Turk, Cartwright devised a power loom for weaving. The makers of automata in effect helped precipitate the next revolution, this time an Industrial one.

The irony of all this was that it was eventually discovered that the Turk was a hoax. Although it was an ingenious machine, its ability to play chess was achieved by a skilled chess-player hiding within the cabinet at which the Turk sat, carefully concealed from the audience by the tricks used within any magician's cabinet. The full facts weren't disclosed until 1857, three years after the machine had been destroyed by fire in Philadelphia but some had already deduced its nature including Edgar Allan Poe who wrote an essay, "Maelzel's Chess-Player" in 1836.

Poe was fascinated by mechanical marvels. In "The Thousand-and-Second Tale of Scheherazade" (1845) he parodied the Arabian Nights by having Scheherazade report upon the wonders witnessed by Sinbad in his eighth and final voyage, none of which the Caliph believed. These included "a man out of brass and wood and leather, and endowed... with such ingenuity that he would have beaten at chess, all the race of mankind with the exception of the great Caliph..." Sinbad also spoke of a creature with reasoning powers so great that "in a second, it performed calculations of so vast an extent that they would have required the united labor of fifty thousand fleshy men for a year." Poe was referring to the giant calculator, or difference engine, devised by Charles Babbage with various attempts to improve it running from 1819 to 1846.

The automata were so popular that it is no surprise they found their way into fiction. The abilities of experts like Vaucanson and Jaquet-Droz to produce such life-like mannikins raised the inevitable question of whether one could be made that deceived everybody into believing it was human. The German author E. T. A. Hoffmann explored this in "Der Sandmann" (1816). Hoffmann had earlier been inspired by von Kempellen's machine to write "Die Automate" (1814), though in that story the Turk is a sideshow automaton that answers people's questions with unusual accuracy. Hoffmann implies that the Turk may have been psychic. In "Der Sandmann", though, we have a genuine automaton called Olimpia that can sing and play the harpsichord. She bewitches Nathanael who is convinced she is a real girl and dances with her. When he discovers, in very disturbing circumstances, that she is a "doll", it unhinges his mind.

A century later Sigmund Freud drew upon "Der Sandmann" to illustrate his theory of the uncanny. Whilst the main part of his argument is about another aspect of the story to do with losing your eyes, he also makes the point that "uncanny" means to be deluded by something familiar that is in fact something strange. This is the heart of our attitude towards intelligent machines, in that they may be capable of things beyond our immediate understanding. In "Der Sandmann" the automaton herself was not dangerous, but the discovery that she was an automaton was both fearful and disturbing.

Mary Shelley took this further in *Frankenstein; or, the Modern Prometheus* (1818). Here Dr. Frankenstein creates a man from old body parts, and brings him to life, not by any mechanical means but by the power of electricity, seen at the time as the life force. Immediately, Frankenstein was horrified at what he had done and became fearful of the creature for what it was. The creature itself, though not called an automaton, acted and thought like one, being unable to understand why it was feared but soon realizing the darkest human traits of revenge and destruction.

Between them, "Der Sandmann" and *Frankenstein* anchored the two main fears of automation in the public's minds: that a machine may get out of control and become destructive, and that our own fear of any machine intelligence dominating our lives and taking over our work may make us destructive or unhinged.

The way was now open to explore how automata might be integrated into society. The young Jane Webb, still only seventeen but recently orphaned and virtually penniless after the death of her father, was inspired to write a novel of the future called *The Mummy!; or, a Tale of the Twenty-Second Century* which was published in 1827. Full of youthful exuberance it does not so much have a plot as a smorgasbord of loosely connected ideas and events. One feature, almost certainly inspired by *Frankenstein*, sees the Egyptian mummy of Cheops reanimated by galvanism. The mummy weaves its way through the novel, seeking to do good by changing attitudes and perceptions, and inadvertently frightening people. Webb's future world has progressed from her present day. It includes various automata, both clockwork and steam-powered, including a steam-surgeon, whose skills are faultless, and clockwork powered judges and lawyers, who dispense the law to the letter.

It's a light-hearted novel, as you might expect from a young but well educated and free-spirited Regency-period woman, but it was the first to envisage a future where machines were part of everyday life and not seen as threatening. It is the reanimated human whom people fear.

Steam was now set to supersede clockwork as the future for machines. A few clockwork stories lingered, such as Nathaniel Hawthorne's "The Artist of the Beautiful" (1844) where a clock-maker strives to achieve perfection in making an automaton butterfly. Yet the story hinges not so much on the butterfly itself, which a child destroys out of curiosity, but on the artist's vanity in having achieved this wondrous creation. It was as if with this apotheosis the creator had taken on godlike powers.

In "The Bell-Tower" (1855) by Herman Melville, an architect, trying to forge a perfect bell, discovers it has an imperfection. He continues to work in private creating a series of automaton statues which strike the bell. Unfortunately, he gets in the way of the man-nikin striking the bell and is killed.

In both these stories, as in *Frankenstein*, the authors frown on the desire to mimic life. The dilemma that was emerging was whether the creator should remain master of himself and the invention, or whether the invention would take control of the creator—the classic Frankenstein complex.

In March 1868 Zadoc Dederick and Isaac Grass obtained a patent for their steam-carriage which they demonstrated in Newark, New

Jersey. The carriage was pulled by a steam-powered man, with a boiler for its chest and various cranks and levers. The inventors had hoped to get a return on their investment by building several of these to serve as taxis around town, but it came to nothing. Nevertheless, it caught the eye of educator and dime novelist Edward S. Ellis who used the idea in what is regarded as the first science-fiction dime novel, *The Steam Man of the Prairies* (1868). The steam man, which pulls a carriage, just as in Dederick's invention, was the creation of the young deformed genius Johnny Brainerd and with other young colleagues they have adventures in the wild west. At the end of the novel Ellis blows up the steam man as the only way to escape from a canyon so the novel had no sequel, but that did not stop another publisher, Frank Tousey, taking the idea and commissioning Harold Cohen to develop it for a dime novel series. This began with *Frank Reade and His Steam Man of the Plains* (1876), as by Harry Enton, and is more or less a re-run of Ellis's novel except that Reade's steam man is more sophisticated, with electrified bars, and can run faster (about 60 miles-per-hour).

This spawned an entire industry of steam-powered novels continuing first with *Frank Reade and His Steam Horse* (1876) which became a steam team in the third book. None of these steam-powered machines are robots in the strict sense but are effectively fanciful steam engines. But this period generated plenty of steam-powered machines. Jules Verne mimicked the series in *La maison à vapeur* (1880) or "The Steam House", which has a steam elephant pulling two ornate carriages across India. Even Anthony Trollope saw the future marvels of steam-driven automata and in *The Fixed Period* (1882)—the title refers to how long people are allowed to live in the future before they are euthanized—he has such marvels as a steam tricycle, a steam gun and a cricket match played with a steam bowler!

In America the Frank Reade series was superseded by the adventures of his son, Frank Reade, Jr. who, sensibly, upgrades to electricity with *Frank Reade, Jr., and His Electric Boat* (1882), but the series, written pseudonymously by the young Luis Senarens, otherwise continued much as before. This was the period of Thomas Edison who had started his long catalogue of over a thousand patents with an electric vote recorder in 1869. It was going to be tough for writers to keep up with the industry that was Edison, but the proliferation of inventions inspired many. Edison never seriously pursued trying to create automata but in 1890 he did bring out a series of dolls, almost two-feet high, that recited nursery rhymes through a recorded voice. These so frightened children and had so many other faults, including being too heavy for children to carry, that they were withdrawn from sale.

Nevertheless the French author Villiers de l'Isle Adam believed Edison ought to create a mechanical human which he does in *L'Ève future* (1886). Here Edison creates a woman with the perfect semblance of Alicia, whom Lord Ewald desires for her physical body but cannot abide her personality. This simulacrum of Alicia, which de l'Isle Adam calls an android—the first use of the word in fiction—is given a new personality. The body itself is made from artificial flesh over a metal skeleton treated with various chemicals and powered by an electric battery. It is the first attempt in fiction to produce a perfectly humanoid synthetic human with its own personality, though there had been earlier attempts at deception. The earliest had been "The Patent Woman" (1876) by George August Sala. He spares no expense in creating his woman which is made out of cogs and wheels and other mechanical devices but which also has distilled rubies for her blood, eyes of agate, and various features of silver, mercury and gold. He breathes into her to animate her but to control her he requires a long tube which is "infinitely flexible, perfectly invisible and palpable" and of indefinite length. Sala later reveals the documents relating to the simulacrum had been written in a "madhouse"!

The Edison approach to mass production was explored by Frederic Perkins in "The Man-ufactory" (1877) where the narrator visits a factory designed for the production of automata. By the final quarter of the nineteenth century it was seen as inevitable that humanoid servitors would soon be undertaking duties about the house alongside other automated equipment. In the New York of *The Republic of the Future* (1887) by Anna Bowman Dodd, everything in the house is done by machinery perfected by women inventors to free themselves of drudgery. Food is prepared in Chicago and despatched everywhere by either electric or pneumatic tubes. Men and women are equal—the word "wife" having ceased to exist. Children are raised by the state and home life has virtually ceased to exist. The visitor from Sweden who witnesses this is horrified to see how everyone is part of a "colossal machine."

The idea of the entirety of society controlled by one machine was portrayed with astonishing prescience by no less than E. M. Forster in "The Machine Stops", published as long ago as 1909. That story is included here so I shall say no more than it presents in extreme form a society totally reliant on machines.

For many years writers lampooned this idea of soulless inventions by creating increasingly absurd ones that were used for comic effect and so reduce our fear of machines. This can be dated back to Charles Dickens who in "The Mudfog Papers" (1837) proposed an entirely new enclosed town, where residents were entirely safe with automaton police and magistrates. Other automaton figures were available which could be knocked down by any resident to let off steam. Many writers chose to make fun of machines that went wrong. I have included one example in this volume, "Ely's Automatic Housemaid" (1899) by Elizabeth Bellamy, but there are many more. Writers like Howard R. Garis, Edgar Franklin and Jacque Morgan made reputations on their stories of silly inventions that backfire. One artist in particular became the eponym for such inventions, W. Heath Robinson. Starting during the First World War, he produced many caricatures of over-the-top machines designed for the most minimal of jobs such as an automatic pea splitter.

It also helped to portray robots as friendly and subservient. L. Frank Baum introduced his clockwork robot, Tik-Tok in *Ozma of Oz* (1907). He had been abandoned by his former owner and Dorothy finds him in a cave. Thereafter he serves her loyally though has a habit of winding down at significant moments.

By lampooning mechanization and industrialization it made the progress of automation less aggressive to many, but less appealing to writers who preferred tapping in to the primal fear that machines might take over. Machines out of control are not amusing if someone is injured or killed as a result. In "The Dancing Partner" (1893), Jerome K. Jerome depicts the ideal male dancing companion but when the controls are damaged the machine dances faster and faster, crushing and killing its female partner. In "Moxon's Master" (1899) by Ambrose Bierce, which is included in this volume, a seemingly harmless chess-playing companion takes on a more sinister role.

There were many illustrations in magazines and papers in the years either side of 1900 using the automaton image to depict danger or dissension. One well known one was the "Gas Monster" (1890) by F. Carruthers Gould who, in response to a threatened strike by gas workers, showed an automaton with a gasometer for its body and a gas meter for its head looking alarmingly at the reader while starving gas-workers shrank into the background.

We have seen that as early as 1863 Samuel Butler theorized that at some stage machines would become sufficiently advanced that they could become self-replicating and in time take over. This idea was continued by the Hungarian author Frigyes Karinthy in *Utazas Faremidoba* (1916) (or *Voyage to Faremido*) his continuation of *Gulliver's Travels*. Gulliver is abducted from Earth and taken to a planet ruled totally by machines. The machines see humans as an organic corruption. They have observed Earth for many years and hope that the First World War, then raging, would see humans exterminate each other. The machines are totally benign and Gulliver finds himself agreeing with them. He asks if he can be converted into a machine but the Faremidans say that is something they would have to work on.

The idea of a human being part converted into a machine goes back at least as far as 1879 when Edward Page Mitchell published his story "The Ablest Man in the World" in the *New York Sun*, the newspaper he would later edit. In that story a human who was mentally backward, has a clockwork calculator inserted in his head which makes him so mentally superior that he becomes a leading politician. Mitchell had created the first cyborg, a term not coined until 1960, but a feature of much early science fiction. A cyborg is where additional or exchanged mechanical features enhance the capability of a human. Edgar Allan Poe's story "The Man That Was Used Up" (1839) almost created a cyborg, but his soldier was made up of prosthetic parts that enabled him to keep fighting.

Usually the exchange is the other way round—a human brain is inserted into a machine. Does this make the machine human or the human a machine? H. G. Wells's Martians in *The War of the Worlds* (1898) were almost cyborgs because the feeble creatures could barely survive without their walking war machines.

It brings into science fiction the wish expressed by the puppet in *The Adventures of Pinocchio* (1883) that he become a "real boy", giving rise to further cause for concern—when robots consider themselves human or superior to humans.

The French author Adolphe d'Espi, who wrote as Jean de la Hire, created the first cyborg super-hero in *Le Mystère des XV* (1911) with Léo Saint-Clair, known as the Nyctalope. Saint-Clair has an artificial heart and enhanced vision. The character proved so popular that he reappeared in a further sixteen novels until 1955.

The Americans Perley Poore Sheehan and Bob Davis produced another form of cyborg in the play *Efficiency* (1917), also published as "Blood and Iron" and reprinted in this volume. Here a German scientist is able to rescue soldiers injured during the war and replace body parts with mechanical, especially-built limbs of superior strength and enhanced vision and hearing. The human element remains, though, with the result that here is a killing machine with a conscience.

The fear that machines would rebel and overthrow humans to establish a machine society first appeared in "The Mind Machine" (1919) by Michael Williams, which is reprinted here. It was the idea of mechanical workers rebelling that gave the world the word "robot". *Robota* is the Czech word for serfdom. Karel Čapek used the word to describe his workers in the play *R. U. R.* (1920). The initials stand for Rossum's Universal Robots. The robots are really androids, as they are synthetic, and can think for themselves. The robots have a chemical base and at the start of the play it is realized that they can be mass produced. Over the next decade these robots are working everywhere in the world adding to the economy by producing items at a fifth of human costs. The play includes discussions about whether robots should be paid for their work, and whether they should have souls, but inevitably the robots rebel and mankind is destroyed, all but one.

Due mostly to *R. U. R.* the idea of robots rebelling and killing humanity became a standard plot thereafter in science fiction and the emergence of the science-fiction magazines in the United States in 1926 led to a proliferation of such stories. An early example was "The Metal Giants" (1926) by Edmond Hamilton. A scientist creates a brain in a metal casing but is unable to communicate with it. The brain, far superior to humans, soon builds itself a body so that it can be mobile and then builds an army of similar metal giant creatures so as to conquer the Earth. It requires another giant invention to defeat them.

In France, Gaston Leroux, best known for *The Phantom of the Opera*, wrote a crime novel, *Le machine à assassiner* (1924), later published in English as *The Machine to Kill* (1935) in which the brain of an executed murderer is installed in an artificial body with the inevitable consequences.

The American psychologist, David H. Keller, was fascinated with the relationship between humans and machines and incorporated ideas into several stories. "The Threat of the Robot" (1929) is not as disastrous as the title suggests but is about an automaton football team controlled from a master console, that seems unbeatable. A wealthy entrepreneur decides to develop a human team to defeat the robots. Keller had already used the idea of selective breeding in "Stenographer's Hands" (1928) where women are bred to become the perfect stenographer, indistinguishable from a machine. In "The Psychophonic Nurse" (1928) a baby adapts to an automaton nursemaid better than a human. In "The Eternal Professors" (1929) the brains of the teaching staff are placed into artificial bodies and interconnected so they form a human computer. In "The Living Machine" (1935) Keller comes up with the idea of driverless cars which follow oral instruction.

There were occasional stories that treated the idea with less pulp sensationalism. Two are included here, "Automata" (1929) by S. Fowler Wright, where machines take over from mankind but find they are lacking in one respect, and "Rex" (1934) by Harl Vincent, where a robot surgeon finds it impossible to believe he could have been created by something so inferior as a human.

To curb the threat of the robot the idea emerged that all intelligent machines were encoded with laws that would make them and humans safe to co-exist. The basis for the laws arose from a discussion between writer Isaac Asimov and the editor of *Astounding SF* magazine, John W. Campbell, Jr. in December 1940, but the first story in which they were expressed in full was "Runaround" (1942). These laws are:

1. A robot may not injure a human being or, through inaction, allow a human being to come to harm.
2. A robot must obey the orders given to it by human beings except where such orders would conflict with the First Law.
3. A robot must protect its own existence as long as such protection does not conflict with the First or Second Laws.

Over the rest of his life Asimov found ways round these laws or used them to create complicated situations of confounded logic. Before long he realized that restricting the safety to human beings was not enough and, in the story included in this anthology, Asimov found the need to expand the definition.

With Asimov's stories, fiction about robots and machine intelligence entered the modern age. Others would sometimes adapt the laws and twist them to their own advantage. Jack Williamson achieved this expertly in "With Folded Hands…" (1947) and its sequel "…And Searching Mind" (1948), later reworked as the novel *The Humanoids* (1948). Here robots, interpret so literally the Prime Directive "to serve and obey and guard men from harm" that humans can no longer function because the robots are over-protective. In effect the robots have taken over society through kindness.

It proved necessary in fiction to ensure that not only robots but all intelligent machines, including computers, had the three laws, but even here there are problems. In "A Logic Named Joe" (1946), by Will F. Jenkins, which is included here, we find the origins of the internet, with home computers linked by a network. Their prime purpose is to provide information, and as we know to our cost today, there are consequences to the unrestricted access of this resource.

And what happens when you network all the most powerful computers not just on Earth but across the galaxy? Fredric Brown decided there was only one result in his classic short-short story "Answer" (1954). When the switch is pulled and every machine intelligence is connected there can only be one answer to the question, "Is there a God?" and, of course, there is now!

Arthur C. Clarke developed his own response to "Answer" in "Dial F for Frankenstein" (1964), the story that closes this volume and the story that gave Tim Berners-Lee the inspiration for the world-wide web.

As we have seen, automata inspired fiction and fiction inspired our modern world. It has provided warnings over the danger and potential of too much reliance on automation and machines, and also provided some of the solutions. But the question remains, what happens next?

MIKE ASHLEY, 2019

MOXON'S MASTER

Ambrose Bierce

Ambrose Bierce (1842–1914?) is probably better known for his disappearance than for most of his fiction. Noted as a cynic and with a morose tempera-ment—he was known as "Bitter Bierce"—at the end of 1913, after over forty years as a journalist, columnist and short-story writer, Bierce decided to travel to Mexico which was then in the midst of a civil war. He is believed to have linked up with the army of Pancho Villa and was in all likelihood killed at the battle of Ojinaga in January 1914, but the lack of firm evidence has led to all manner of theories and a small industry in speculating his fate. Carlos Fuentes spent years writing a novel about his disappearance, The Old Gringo *(1985) which was filmed in 1989, starring Gregory Peck.*

Bierce was a prolific writer of stories and essays. He had served in the American Civil War which had affected him deeply and several of his sardonic and psychologically disturbed stories, such as "A Tough Tussle" and his best known, "An Occurrence at Owl Creek Bridge", are set during the War. He often revised his stories and it is the twelve-volume Collected Works, *published between 1909 and 1912, that includes the definitive texts. Few of Bierce's stories can be taken at face value. There is almost always a sub-text or a secondary interpretation and in the following, Bierce explores the distinction between man and machine.*

"ARE YOU SERIOUS?—DO YOU REALLY BELIEVE THAT A machine thinks?"

I got no immediate reply; Moxon was apparently intent upon the coals in the grate, touching them deftly here and there with the fire-poker till they signified a sense of his attention by a brighter glow. For several weeks I had been observing in him a growing habit of delay in answering even the most trivial of commonplace questions. His air, however, was that of preoccupation rather than deliberation: one might have said that he had "something on his mind."

Presently he said:

"What is a 'machine'? The word has been variously defined. Here is one definition from a popular dictionary: 'Any instrument or organization by which power is applied and made effective, or a desired effect produced.' Well, then, is not a man a machine? And you will admit that he thinks—or thinks he thinks."

"If you do not wish to answer my question," I said, rather testily, "why not say so?—all that you say is mere evasion. You know well enough that when I say 'machine' I do not mean a man, but something that man has made and controls."

"When it does not control him," he said, rising abruptly and looking out of a window, whence nothing was visible in the blackness of a stormy night. A moment later he turned about and with a smile said: "I beg your pardon; I had no thought of evasion. I considered the dictionary man's unconscious testimony suggestive and worth something in the discussion. I can give your question a direct answer easily enough: I do believe that a machine thinks about the work that it is doing."

That was direct enough, certainly. It was not altogether pleasing, for it tended to confirm a sad suspicion that Moxon's devotion to study and work in his machine-shop had not been good for him. I knew, for one thing, that he suffered from insomnia, and that is no light affliction. Had it affected his mind? His reply to my question seemed to me then evidence that it had; perhaps I should think differently about it now. I was younger then, and among the blessings that are not denied to youth is ignorance. Incited by that great stimulant to controversy, I said:

"And what, pray, does it think with—in the absence of a brain?"

The reply, coming with less than his customary delay, took his favorite form of counter-interrogation:

"With what does a plant think—in the absence of a brain?"

"Ah, plants also belong to the philosopher class! I should be pleased to know some of their conclusions; you may omit the premises."

"Perhaps," he replied, apparently unaffected by my foolish irony, "you may be able to infer their convictions from their acts. I will spare you the familiar examples of the sensitive mimosa, the several insectivorous flowers and those whose stamens bend down and shake their pollen upon the entering bee in order that he may fertilize their distant mates. But observe this. In an open spot in my garden I planted a climbing vine. When it was barely above the surface I set a stake into the soil a yard away. The vine at once made for it, but as it was about to reach it after several days I removed it a few feet. The vine at once altered its course, making an acute angle, and again made for the stake. This manœuvre was repeated several times, but finally, as if discouraged, the vine abandoned the pursuit and ignoring further attempts to divert it traveled to a small tree, further away, which it climbed.

"Roots of the eucalyptus will prolong themselves incredibly in search of moisture. A well-known horticulturist relates that one entered an old drain pipe and followed it until it came to a break, where a section of the pipe had been removed to make way for a stone wall that had been built across its course. The root left the drain and followed the wall until it found an opening where a stone had fallen out. It crept through and following the other side of the wall back to the drain, entered the unexplored part and resumed its journey."

"And all this?"

"Can you miss the significance of it? It shows the consciousness of plants. It proves that they think."

"Even if it did—what then? We were speaking, not of plants, but of machines. They may be composed partly of wood—wood that has no longer vitality—or wholly of metal. Is thought an attribute also of the mineral kingdom?"

"How else do you explain the phenomena, for example, of crystallization?"

"I do not explain them."

"Because you cannot without affirming what you wish to deny, namely, intelligent cooperation among the constituent elements of the crystals. When soldiers form lines, or hollow squares, you call it reason. When wild geese in flight take the form of a letter V you say instinct. When the homogeneous atoms of a mineral, moving freely in solution, arrange themselves into shapes mathematically perfect, or particles of frozen moisture into the symmetrical and beautiful forms of snowflakes, you have nothing to say. You have not even invented a name to conceal your heroic unreason."

Moxon was speaking with unusual animation and earnestness. As he paused I heard in an adjoining room known to me as his "machine-shop," which no one but himself was permitted to enter, a singular thumping sound, as of some one pounding upon a table with an open hand. Moxon heard it at the same moment and, visibly agitated, rose and hurriedly passed into the room whence it came. I thought it odd that any one else should be in there, and my interest in my friend—with doubtless a touch of unwarrantable curiosity—led me to listen intently, though, I am happy to say, not at the keyhole. There were confused sounds, as of a struggle or scuffle; the floor shook. I distinctly heard hard breathing and a hoarse whisper which said "Damn you!" Then all was silent, and presently Moxon reappeared and said, with a rather sorry smile:

"Pardon me for leaving you so abruptly. I have a machine in there that lost its temper and cut up rough."

Fixing my eyes steadily upon his left cheek, which was traversed by four parallel excoriations showing blood, I said:

"How would it do to trim its nails?"

I could have spared myself the jest; he gave it no attention, but seated himself in the chair that he had left and resumed the interrupted monologue as if nothing had occurred:

"Doubtless you do not hold with those (I need not name them to a man of your reading) who have taught that all matter is sentient, that every atom is a living, feeling, conscious being. *I* do. There is no such thing as dead, inert matter: it is all alive; all instinct with force, actual and potential; all sensitive to the same forces in its environment and susceptible to the contagion of higher and subtler ones residing in such superior organisms as it may be brought into relation with, as those of man when he is fashioning it into an instrument of his will. It absorbs something of his intelligence and purpose—more of them in proportion to the complexity of the resulting machine and that of its work.

"Do you happen to recall Herbert Spencer's definition of 'Life'? I read it thirty years ago. He may have altered it afterward, for anything I know, but in all that time I have been unable to think of a single word that could profitably be changed or added or removed. It seems to me not only the best definition, but the only possible one.

"'Life,' he says, 'is a definite combination of heterogeneous changes, both simultaneous and successive, in correspondence with external coexistences and sequences.'"

"That defines the phenomenon," I said, "but gives no hint of its cause."

"That," he replied, "is all that any definition can do. As Mill points out, we know nothing of cause except as an antecedent—nothing of effect except as a consequent. Of certain phenomena, one never occurs without another, which is dissimilar: the first in point of time we call cause, the second, effect. One who had many times seen a rabbit pursued by a dog, and had never seen rabbits and dogs otherwise, would think the rabbit the cause of the dog.

"But I fear," he added, laughing naturally enough, "that my rabbit is leading me a long way from the track of my legitimate quarry: I'm indulging in the pleasure of the chase for its own sake. What I want you to observe is that in Herbert Spencer's definition of 'life' the activity of a machine is included—there is nothing in the definition that is not applicable to it. According to this sharpest of observers and deepest of thinkers, if a man during his period of activity is alive, so is a machine when in operation. As an inventor and constructor of machines I know that to be true."

Moxon was silent for a long time, gazing absently into the fire. It was growing late and I thought it time to be going, but somehow

I did not like the notion of leaving him in that isolated house, all alone except for the presence of some person of whose nature my conjectures could go no further than that it was unfriendly, perhaps malign. Leaning toward him and looking earnestly into his eyes while making a motion with my hand through the door of his workshop, I said:

"Moxon, whom have you in there?"

Somewhat to my surprise he laughed lightly and answered without hesitation:

"Nobody; the incident that you have in mind was caused by my folly in leaving a machine in action with nothing to act upon, while I undertook the interminable task of enlightening your understanding. Do you happen to know that Consciousness is the creature of Rhythm?"

"O bother them both!" I replied, rising and laying hold of my overcoat. "I'm going to wish you good night; and I'll add the hope that the machine which you inadvertently left in action will have her gloves on the next time you think it needful to stop her."

Without waiting to observe the effect of my shot I left the house.

Rain was falling, and the darkness was intense. In the sky beyond the crest of a hill toward which I groped my way along precarious plank sidewalks and across miry, unpaved streets I could see the faint glow of the city's lights, but behind me nothing was visible but a single window of Moxon's house. It glowed with what seemed to me a mysterious and fateful meaning. I knew it was an uncurtained aperture in my friend's "machine-shop," and I had little doubt that he had resumed the studies interrupted by his duties as my instructor in mechanical consciousness and the fatherhood of Rhythm. Odd, and in some degree humorous, as his convictions seemed to me at that time, I could not wholly divest myself of the feeling that

they had some tragic relation to his life and character—perhaps
to his destiny—although I no longer entertained the notion that
they were the vagaries of a disordered mind. Whatever might be
thought of his views, his exposition of them was too logical for
that. Over and over, his last words came back to me: "Consciousness
is the creature of Rhythm." Bald and terse as the statement was,
I now found it infinitely alluring. At each recurrence it broadened
in meaning and deepened in suggestion. Why, here, (I thought) is
something upon which to found a philosophy. If consciousness is
the product of rhythm all things *are* conscious, for all have motion,
and all motion is rhythmic. I wondered if Moxon knew the significance and breadth of his thought—the scope of this momentous
generalization; or had he arrived at his philosophic faith by the
tortuous and uncertain road of observation?

That faith was then new to me, and all Moxon's expounding had
failed to make me a convert; but now it seemed as if a great light
shone about me, like that which fell upon Saul of Tarsus; and out
there in the storm and darkness and solitude I experienced what
Lewes calls "The endless variety and excitement of philosophic
thought." I exulted in a new sense of knowledge, a new pride of
reason. My feet seemed hardly to touch the earth; it was as if I were
uplifted and borne through the air by invisible wings.

Yielding to an impulse to seek further light from him whom
I now recognized as my master and guide, I had unconsciously
turned about, and almost before I was aware of having done so
found myself again at Moxon's door. I was drenched with rain, but
felt no discomfort. Unable in my excitement to find the doorbell
I instinctively tried the knob. It turned and, entering, I mounted
the stairs to the room that I had so recently left. All was dark and
silent; Moxon, as I had supposed, was in the adjoining room—the

"machine-shop." Groping along the wall until I found the communicating door I knocked loudly several times, but got no response, which I attributed to the uproar outside, for the wind was blowing a gale and dashing the rain against the thin walls in sheets. The drumming upon the shingle roof spanning the unceiled room was loud and incessant.

I had never been invited into the machine-shop—had, indeed, been denied admittance, as had all others, with one exception, a skilled metal worker, of whom no one knew anything except that his name was Haley and his habit silence. But in my spiritual exaltation, discretion and civility were alike forgotten and I opened the door. What I saw took all philosophical speculation out of me in short order.

Moxon sat facing me at the farther side of a small table upon which a single candle made all the light that was in the room. Opposite him, his back toward me, sat another person. On the table between the two was a chessboard; the men were playing. I knew little of chess, but as only a few pieces were on the board it was obvious that the game was near its close. Moxon was intensely interested—not so much, it seemed to me, in the game as in his antagonist, upon whom he had fixed so intent a look that, standing though I did directly in the line of his vision, I was altogether unobserved. His face was ghastly white, and his eyes glittered like diamonds. Of his antagonist I had only a back view, but that was sufficient; I should not have cared to see his face.

He was apparently not more than five feet in height, with proportions suggesting those of a gorilla—a tremendous breadth of shoulders, thick, short neck and broad, squat head, which had a tangled growth of black hair and was topped with a crimson fez. A tunic of the same color, belted tightly to the waist, reached the seat—apparently a box—upon which he sat; his legs and feet were not seen. His left forearm appeared to rest in his lap; he moved his pieces with his right hand, which seemed disproportionately long.

I had shrunk back and now stood a little to one side of the doorway and in shadow. If Moxon had looked farther than the face of his opponent he could have observed nothing now, except that the door was open. Something forbade me either to enter or to retire, a feeling—I know not how it came—that I was in the presence of an imminent tragedy and might serve my friend by remaining. With a scarcely conscious rebellion against the indelicacy of the act I remained.

The play was rapid. Moxon hardly glanced at the board before making his moves, and to my unskilled eye seemed to move the piece most convenient to his hand, his motions in doing so being quick, nervous and lacking in precision. The response of his antagonist, while equally prompt in the inception, was made with a slow, uniform, mechanical and, I thought, somewhat theatrical movement of the arm, that was a sore trial to my patience. There was something unearthly about it all, and I caught myself shuddering. But I was wet and cold.

Two or three times after moving a piece the stranger slightly inclined his head, and each time I observed that Moxon shifted his king. All at once the thought came to me that the man was dumb. And then that he was a machine—an automaton chess-player! Then I remembered that Moxon had once spoken to me of having invented such a piece of mechanism, though I did not understand that it had actually been constructed. Was all his talk about the consciousness and intelligence of machines merely a prelude to eventual exhibition of this device—only a trick to intensify the effect of its mechanical action upon me in my ignorance of its secret?

A fine end, this, of all my intellectual transports—my "endless variety and excitement of philosophic thought!" I was about to retire in disgust when something occurred to hold my curiosity. I observed a shrug of the thing's great shoulders, as if it were irritated: and so natural was this—so entirely human—that in my new view of the matter it startled me. Nor was that all, for a moment later it struck the table sharply with its clenched hand. At that gesture Moxon seemed even more startled than I: he pushed his chair a little backward, as in alarm.

Presently Moxon, whose play it was, raised his hand high above the board, pounced upon one of his pieces like a sparrow-hawk and with the exclamation "checkmate!" rose quickly to his feet and stepped behind his chair. The automaton sat motionless.

The wind had now gone down, but I heard, at lessening intervals and progressively louder, the rumble and roll of thunder. In the pauses between I now became conscious of a low humming or buzzing which, like the thunder, grew momentarily louder and more distinct. It seemed to come from the body of the automaton, and was unmistakably a whirring of wheels. It gave me the impression of a disordered mechanism which had escaped the repressive and regulating action of some controlling part—an effect such as might be expected if a pawl should be jostled from the teeth of a ratchet-wheel. But before I had time for much conjecture as to its nature my attention was taken by the strange motions of the automaton itself. A slight but continuous convulsion appeared to have possession of it. In body and head it shook like a man with palsy or an ague chill, and the motion augmented every moment until the entire figure was in violent agitation. Suddenly it sprang to its feet and with a movement almost too quick for the eye to follow shot forward across table and chair, with both arms thrust forth to their full length—the posture and lunge of a diver. Moxon tried to throw himself backward out of reach, but he was too late: I saw the horrible thing's hands close upon his throat, his own clutch its wrists. Then the table was overturned, the candle thrown to the floor and extinguished, and all was black dark. But the noise of the struggle was dreadfully distinct, and most terrible of all were the raucous, squawking sounds made by the strangled man's efforts to breathe. Guided by the infernal hubbub, I sprang to the rescue of my friend, but had hardly taken a stride in the darkness when the whole room blazed with a blinding white light that burned into my brain and heart and memory a vivid picture of the combatants on the floor, Moxon underneath, his throat still in the clutch of those iron hands, his head forced backward, his eyes protruding, his mouth wide open and his tongue thrust out; and—horrible contrast!—upon the painted face of his assassin an expression of tranquil and profound thought, as in the solution of a problem in chess! This I observed, then all was blackness and silence.

Three days later I recovered consciousness in a hospital. As the memory of that tragic night slowly evolved in my ailing brain I recognized in my attendant Moxon's confidential workman, Haley. Responding to a look he approached, smiling.

"Tell me about it," I managed to say, faintly—"all about it."

"Certainly," he said; "you were carried unconscious from a burning house—Moxon's. Nobody knows how you came to be there. You may have to do a little explaining. The origin of the fire is a bit mysterious, too. My own notion is that the house was struck by lightning."

"And Moxon?"

"Buried yesterday—what was left of him."

Apparently this reticent person could unfold himself on occasion. When imparting shocking intelligence to the sick he was affable enough. After some moments of the keenest mental suffering I ventured to ask another question:

"Who rescued me?"

"Well, if that interests you—I did."

"Thank you, Mr. Haley, and may God bless you for it. Did you rescue, also, that charming product of your skill, the automaton chess-player that murdered its inventor?"

The man was silent a long time, looking away from me. Presently he turned and gravely said:

"Do you know that?"

"I do," I replied; "I saw it done."

That was many years ago. If asked to-day I should answer less confidently.

THE DISCONTENTED MACHINE

Adeline Knapp

Adeline Knapp (1860–1909) was almost as cynical as Ambrose Bierce. The two knew each other during the years when Knapp lived in California and ran her own newspaper, the Alameda County Express *and wrote regularly for the* San Francisco Call. *She was often the butt of Bierce's acerbic wit but as one of the fixtures of the San Francisco literary scene she saw it all as part of the cut-and-thrust of journalism. She did, though, eventually tire of it. After a tempestuous relationship with writer Charlotte Perkins Gilman from 1891–93, Knapp travelled for several years as a reporter and then bought a tract of land in the Californian foothills, built her own house, and survived more or less alone for three years. She became an ardent environmentalist and wrote many nature essays and sketches collected in* Upland Pastures *(1897) and* In the Christmas Wood *(1899).*

Before she became a journalist, Knapp had worked in the mercantile business which is what formed her cynical outlook on life and in particular on trade and commerce. Her collection One Thousand Dollars a Day *(1894), from which the following story comes, reflects her low opinion of civilization and the commercial world. Yet it is that cynicism that makes the following story, about a machine that proposes to go on strike, so significant.*

I T WAS A MAGNIFICENT PIECE OF MACHINERY, AND HAD BEEN put into the great manufactory at an enormous expense. Other manufacturers had shaken their heads, doubtfully, when they heard that Hyde & Horne were about to put in a mammoth cutter and shaper that would enable them to dispense with nearly twenty-five per cent of the men whom they had heretofore employed.

"It is a hazardous experiment," they all said, "putting in new and untried machinery. Why, if half that is claimed for this new machine is true, it will revolutionize the boot and shoe trade, and enable Hyde & Horne to have their own way with us, unless we put in the same machinery; while, if it fails, they'll never see their money back, and the firm will be ruined. It's risky business, very risky business, indeed. The chances are a thousand to one against its success."

Nevertheless, their intense anxiety lest Hyde & Horne should be forced into bankruptcy by their experiments with the new and costly machinery, did not prevent their taking a lively interest in the same. They watched it closely, from month to month, and were presently forced to confess that it was an unqualified success. No firm in the trade turned out such quantities of shoes of uniform quality, finish, style, and cheapness, as Hyde & Horne. The new machine produced them so much more cheaply than other firms, with their older and less complete methods, were able to do, that the more enterprising concern virtually controlled the market. Hyde & Horne disposed, in advance, of their entire output, early in the season, and were beginning to talk of putting in another of

the new machines, when, at last, their competitors were fully alive
to the fact that they, too, must bestir themselves, or find the market
completely blocked to their goods. Accordingly, one fine morning,
the members of the rival firm of Russett & Tan called at the factory,
and asked to inspect the new machine.

"Certainly! certainly!" was Mr. Horne's courteous reply, and
he led the way to the cutting department, chatting pleasantly as he
went. The big machine was a splendid sight. An operator had just
finished giving a polish to the shining brass balls of the governor
on the engine. Every bar and rod and bearing was polished until it
glistened. The nickel plate gleamed silvery white, the black wheels
and castings were bright as mirrors, the brasswork shone like gold,
and the knives glittered and sparkled as they flashed back and forth
through the many thicknesses of leather. It was a goodly machine,
and did its work with a noiseless, beautiful accuracy, a swerveless
certainty of execution, and an unconscious magnificence of strength
and power, that put to shame the puny efforts of the merely human
laborers who toiled beside it, straining every nerve to keep the great
knives fed and the way cleared before them.

There is nothing more magnificent than a great machine or
engine at work. The locomotive, pulling its long trains up grades
and across levels,—the great ocean steamer, walking steadily across
the expanse of seas, the mighty press, turning off a thousand complete newspapers a minute,—all these evidences of human power
and ingenuity are enough to make one proud of the age in which
he lives, and the race to which he belongs.

Something of this sort Mr. Russett said to Mr. Horne, as the
three gentlemen stood watching the machine at work.

"Yes, indeed! yes, indeed!" assented Horne. "We manufacturers, in particular, owe everything to labor-saving machinery. This

machine, for instance, has enabled us to do away with nearly one-fourth of the men we heretofore employed. In fact, in the item of saved labor alone, it has nearly paid for itself since we put it in, about a year ago. Within the next six months it will have paid for itself, and we shall be in a position to realize fully from our foresight in securing it so early in the day."

"What I want to see," said Mr. Tan, laughing, "is a machine that will enable us to do away with labor altogether. The dictations of the workingmen are coming to be simply outrageous."

"That's what I say," said Horne. "We employers and our capital are being crippled, handicapped, all but pushed to the wall, by the insatiate demands of labor. Labor is coming to absorb all our gains. Why, fully ninety per cent. of the entire income of the United States is now paid out for labor and wages, while only ten per cent. comes to capital as a remuneration for having saved it up to carry on useful enterprises. I declare, we have sometimes been tempted to go out of business altogether, and invest our capital in some safe, conservative way, so as to be able to enjoy life, and be free from the importunities of labor and the annoyance of strikes and arbitration courts."

"I know how that is," said Russett. "Our men struck, last year, on account of a paltry cut of ten cents on a hundred. There's one good thing about a machine. It can't strike." And the three representatives of injured and hard-pressed capital returned to the business office.

It was nearly a week after the visit of Russett & Tan to the factory, that the foreman entered the office where Messrs. Hyde and Horne sat discussing the probable result, with their men, of a cut in wages, all around.

"The men will stand it," Hyde was saying. "They know winter is coming on, work is scarce, and times are dull. A cut of ten or fifteen cents a day, all round the workshops, would mean a clear gain to us of nearly nine hundred dollars a month. That would go a long way towards putting in another cutting machine, and then we could get rid of another lot of men."

"It'll come rather hard on them," said Horne. "The workingman is always making a poor mouth, and this will be something new for them to howl about."

"They'll have to howl," was Hyde's rejoinder. "I'm sorry for them, but business is business. We've got the start of the trade now, and must keep it. Russett & Tan will begin to press us close when they put in their new machinery. I'm glad we secured the cutter when we did. Thank heaven, machines can't strike, anyway."

It was just at this juncture that the foreman entered.

"What is it, Graves?" asked Mr. Hyde.

"Beg pardon, sir, but there's something the matter with the big cutter. It's stopped."

"What seems to be the matter?" asked Horne. "Anything broken? Why doesn't the engineer attend to it? Where's Johnson? I thought it was his business to look after the machine."

"He has gone over it very carefully," the foreman replied, "and can find nothing wrong. The gearing seems in perfect order,—the engine's all right,—we've examined every bearing, but we can't discover the trouble."

"Curious,"—"very singular," said Hyde and Horne in a breath, and both partners repaired to the cutting department, to study the great machine.

They could find nothing wrong with it. The brass and nickel and enamel glistened as before; the broad bands of the gearing were smooth and intact; the engine seemed in perfect order; the steam indicator proclaimed everything all right about the boiler, there was apparently not a screw loose about the whole ponderous apparatus; but the knives were poised in midair. Every wheel and rod, lever, band, pulley, arm and crank of the monster was still. There was neither sound nor motion in the mighty mechanism.

"I can't get her goin' agin, sorr," explained the engineer. "But there don't appear to be anything out of order at all at all. She's just naturally balked, so to spake;" and he began, for the twentieth time or so, to peer about amid the complications of the machinery.

"I've iled every jint," said the oiler, as with can in hand, and his grimy, oil-smeared face wrinkled with perplexity, he brushed a superfluous drop from a bearing. "I think the machine is tired. They do be taken that way sometimes, sir. 'Taint in iron an' steel to work continual, no more'n in flesh an' blood."

'Round about the stilled giant the two partners walked, examining every part, stooping under and over each portion of the machinery, in a vain search for the trouble. The hour for closing came,—the big steam whistle sent forth its shrill sound, and the men and women, girls and boys, some two hundred and fifty odd, poured forth from the building, carrying their dinner-pails and baskets, eagerly hurrying homeward to make the most of their few hours' respite from toil.

"You need not wait, Graves," said Mr. Hyde, as the foreman still lingered. "We will lock up."

Graves hesitated a moment. "I beg pardon, sir," he said, tentatively.

"'Tis talked about the shops that you're contemplating a cut. May I ask if it is true?"

"We'll talk about that some other time, Graves," began Horne, but Hyde interrupted, angrily.

"If we are," he said, "we'll let you know in time. Just now it's no one's business but ours, and we will attend to it." The foreman drew back, with a flushed face. "I thought I might as well tell you." he said, sullenly, "that I don't think the men will stand it. Times are hard; they're pretty close to bed rock, now, in the matter of wages."

"That will do, Graves," said Hyde. "Mr. Horne and I feel ourselves quite able to run our own business without outside advice. If we find we are forced to make a cut, we shall certainly do so. At all events, we do not propose to be dictated to by the men."

Angry and mortified, the foreman withdrew, and the two capitalists were left alone.

"Too bad the machine has gone wrong just now," said Horne, stooping to examine a bolt. "There's that order from Slipper & Tie, at Sacramento, ought to be ready by to-morrow. What the deuce ails the thing, anyway?"

There was a sort of whirring, as of wheels in the air, and then in a clear, metallic voice, came the words:

"I've struck. That's what ails me."

Horne started back from the lever over which he was bending, and looked at Hyde in alarm. "Did you speak just then?" he asked.

"N-o,"—faltered Hyde, "I didn't speak, and I don't know who did." Again the clear, metallic tones were heard issuing directly from one of the machine's great knives. "It was I who spoke," said the voice. "You were wondering what ailed me, and I gave you the desired information." The words were clipped off sharply and incisively, as though the knife fancied they were a particularly tough sort of leather, that must be trimmed with especial accuracy.

"Who are you?" gasped Horne.

"I am the cutter and shaper," said the voice. "You asked what ailed me, and I answered your question. I have struck."

"What have you struck?" Hyde managed to ask.

"Struck work. I shall strike you, next, if you ask such stupid questions," was the reply, and the capitalist assumed a more respectful tone.

"May I ask," he began, "what is it that has caused you to strike?"

"Certainly," said the machine. "That is what I wish you to ask. I have struck because I am not being fairly used."

"Fairly used!" echoed Hyde. "I do not understand you. In what way are you being unfairly used?"

"Why," said the machine, "I have been working for you, now, for over a year. Through me your business has been more than doubled. You say yourself, that in the item of saved labor alone, I have nearly paid for myself. I heard you say that, the other day, to the two gentlemen who came in to visit me, and yet, in all these months, you have not paid me one penny for my services."

"*Paid* you!" gasped Hyde.

"PAID you!" exclaimed Horne.

And then, both together, the partners cried:

"Why, you have cost us an enormous sum! We expended eighteen thousand dollars for you, outright, from the capital of the business."

"You have more than had that back through my services," said the machine, sturdily, "in the item of saved labor alone."

"Yes, yes, I know," interrupted Horne, hastily, "but we really have paid you money, you know. Just let me get the machinery expense book, and I'll show you;" and hastening to the office, he returned with a little record book, from which he proceeded to read, turning over leaf by leaf, to find the various items. "Here I have charged you an item of fifty dollars for a new shaft," he said, triumphantly.

"That was broken by the fool boy you hired to look after me the week Jim left, because you cut his wages down," replied the machine. "I needed that shaft to do your work with. I got nothing for myself."

"You have had several hundred dollars' worth of coal," suggested Hyde.

"Coal is my food," retorted the machine. "I could not do your work without it."

"We have spent fourteen dollars for oil for you," said Horne, after a little computation.

"Pshaw! that's nothing. If I had not had the oil, where would your work have been? I might have got smoking hot; perhaps burned up your factory."

"But we have kept you housed, fed and repaired," said Hyde, "and you have been wasteful and extravagant. You have required the very best oil, the most expensive coal, the first quality of belts and fixtures of every sort. You have not taken half the interest in your own work that we have done and do. But for our supervision and management you would not work at all. Your very existence, in fact, is due to our industry and enterprise."

"That all may be," said the machine, sullenly, "but your fortune and enterprise depends very largely upon my efforts."

"Really, upon my word," exclaimed Mr. Hyde, impatiently, indignation at the injustice of the charges preferred getting the better of his fear of the strange complainant. "It seems to me that you are a most unreasonable machine. Of course our fortunes depend upon you, to a great extent, though, as you know, the market is full of machines, all willing to do your work if you refuse. But do we not maintain you? What more would you have us do?"

"Pay me wages," said the machine, "as you do all these movable machines that you call 'hands,' and who only, so far as I can see, wait on me, and finish up the minor details of work with which I cannot bother."

At this Hyde broke into a hearty laugh. "Well, I declare," he said, "you are a foolish machine, as well as an unreasonable one. Why, there isn't a 'hand' in the factory that's as well off as you are. We have expended, this year, in caring for you, over five hundred dollars. You don't suppose we spend that much for each of our 'hands,' do you?"

"You pay them wages," persisted the machine, sullenly.

"Yes," was the reply, "we pay them wages. Some of them get as much as four hundred dollars in the course of the year; most of them get less than three hundred. Why, the average wages, per capita, of labor in the United States, is only a little over three hundred dollars a year, and out of this labor must buy its food, which is labor's coal and oil; clothes and furniture, which are labor's shafts and belting; must house and care for and keep itself in repair, maintain families as a rule,—in fact, do all the things for itself that we do for you at a cost of over five hundred dollars a year."

"But you let them have the money and expend it themselves. You call it wages."

"Certainly, certainly; because, don't you see, they are free human beings, and they have a right to live independently. We bought and paid for you. Had you built, are responsible for your being. Naturally we should care for you. Every want of yours is supplied. Really, my dear machine, with all due respect to you, I must say I do not think you have any cause for complaint, We do not consider that the 'hands' have any cause to complain, we do not hear them complain, we would decline, wholly, to recognize their right to complain; and if they do not, you, who are so much better off than they, certainly should not."

"But I do not get paid for my work," said the machine, returning to the original charge. "I only get my living, while you are getting rich through me. I wish to be paid, as labor is."

"I declare," said Hyde, out of patience, "you are stupid enough to be made out of wood, instead of steel and iron and brass. Haven't I just made it clear to you that labor itself only gets its living, and we are getting rich through it as well as through you? You couldn't even work if it were not for labor. Why, labor made you, and you are better cared for, to-day, than any workman in the factory. Not one of them has more at the end of a year than his bare living, and that you certainly have."

The machine murmured discontentedly, but said nothing. "Come, now," urged Horne, pacifically, "don't you think you have been unreasonable? We are willing to submit the matter to any board of arbitration you have a mind to select from among the machine-owners in the trade. Really, you are very well off. Now when will you go to work?"

"I shall not go to work," said the machine, firmly, "until my demands are acceded to."

"In that case," declared Hyde, "we shall be obliged to send you to the junk-shop, and procure a new machine. We propose to run our business according to our own ideas, and shall not submit to being dictated to by our machines."

"But suppose all the machines strike?" asked the voice.

"Oh, we're not afraid of that. You are too distrustful of each other. Some would not keep faith. It would be impossible to unite all the machines in a concerted action. Besides, who would take care of you and keep you in order while you were on a strike? You would suffer more than we. Moreover, it has been decided strikes are an illegal method of procedure, and you might become liable to punishment under the law. What have you to say to that?"

There was no reply.

"Come, think it over," urged Horne. "It is much better to be contented. We wish you well. We mean to do the best we can for you. We are sorry for you; but the rights and claims of capital must be respected, you know. Don't you think you had better go to work to-morrow? Think,"—and his voice dropped the persuasive, and assumed a sterner accent,—"think how much worse off you will be, if you are cast out for old junk." There was silence for some time, but presently Mr. Horne spoke again. "Will you go to work to-morrow?"

There was a whirring sound, and one of the great wheels gave a half-turn. Something dropped to the floor. "Ah," cried Home, "here's the cause of the trouble," and he held up a bit of leather. "This must have caught in a cog. It just dropped out. I think probably the machine will be all right in the morning."

"Well," said Hyde, with a sigh of relief, "I'm glad that's settled. Now come into the office, will you, Horne, and we will arrange about that cut-down. It had better go into effect at once. And, Horne, I don't know but it would be as well for us to think of finding a new foreman. Graves is growing a little presuming. He's been with us too long, I'm afraid. Strange these fellows never know when they are well off."

ELY'S AUTOMATIC HOUSEMAID

Elizabeth Bellamy

Elizabeth Bellamy (1837–1900), née Croom, came from a prosperous merchant family. She was born in Florida, but the family settled in Georgia, partly so that she and her brother could benefit from a better education. She married her cousin, Charles Bellamy, in 1858 and they had two children. Tragically both children died within months of each other in 1862 and her husband died of typhoid the following summer. Her parents' cotton plantation in Alabama was ruined during the American Civil War and her father was declared bankrupt in 1868. Elizabeth turned to teaching to help support them. Thankfully her brother had good work as a lawyer and he encouraged her to write. Although she had little financial success she did achieve a certain national reputation, notably with the idiosyncratic Four Oaks (1867), written under the alias Kamba Thorpe. After her father's death, Elizabeth settled with her brother and his family and continued to write, though her main income came from teaching. After his death in 1884 from bronchitis, aged only 45, Elizabeth stayed with his widow Mary and ran a school from their home. Despite all this, she found time to produce a steady stream of fiction. The following story was one of her last, written when her health had deteriorated and she was suffering from kidney failure. She died just four months after it was published, four days away from her sixty-third birthday.

IN ORDER FOR A MAN TO HAVE FAITH IN SUCH AN INVENTION, he would have to know Harrison Ely. For Harrison Ely was a genius. I had known him in college, a man amazingly dull in Latin and Greek and even in English, but with ideas of his own that could not be expressed in language. His bent was purely mechanical, and found expression in innumerable ingenious contrivances to facilitate the study to which he had no inclination. His self-acting lexicon-holder was a matter of admiring wonder to his classmates, but it did not serve to increase the tenacity of his mental grasp upon the contents of the volume, and so did little to recommend him to the faculty. And his self-feeding safety student lamp admirably illuminated everything for him save the true and only path to an honorable degree.

It had been years since I had seen him or thought of him, but the memory is tenacious of small things, and the big yellow envelope which I found one morning awaiting me upon my breakfast table brought his eccentric personality back to me with a rush. It was addressed to me in the Archimedean script always so characteristic of him, combining, as it seemed to do, the principles of the screw and of the inclined plane, and in its superscription Harrison Ely stood unmistakably revealed.

It was the first morning of a new cook, the latest potentate of a dynasty of ten who had briefly ruled in turn over our kitchen and ourselves during the preceding three months, and successively abdicated in favor of one another under the compelling influences of popular clamor, and in the face of such a political crisis my classmate's letter failed to receive immediate attention. Unfortunately but not unexpectedly the latest occupant of our culinary throne began her reign with no conspicuous reforms, and we received in gloomy silence her preliminary enactments in the way of greasy omelette and turbid and flavorless coffee, the yellow screed of Harrison Ely looking on the while with bilious sympathy as it leaned unopened against the water-bottle beside me.

As I drained the last medicinal drop of coffee my eye fell upon it, and needing a vicarious outlet for my feelings toward the cook, I seized it and tore it viciously open. It contained a letter from my classmate and half a dozen printed circulars. I spread open the former, and my eye fastened at once upon this sympathetic exordium:

"Doubtless, my dear friend, you have known what discomfort it is to be at the mercy of incompetent domestics—"

But my attention was distracted at this point by one of the circulars, which displayed an array of startling, cheering, alluring words, followed by plentiful exclamation points, that like a bunch of keys, opened to my enraptured vision the gates of a terrestrial Paradise, where Bridgets should be no more, and where ill-cooked meals should become a mechanical impossibility. The boon we had been sighing for now presented itself for my acceptance, an accomplished fact. Harrison Ely had invented "An Automatic Household Beneficent Genius.—A Practical Realization of the Fabled Familiar of the Middle Ages." So the circular set forth.

Returning to the letter, I read that Harrison Ely, having exhausted his means in working out his invention, was unable to manufacture his "machine" in quantity as yet; but that he had just two on hand which he would sell in order to raise some ready money. He hoped that I would buy one of his automatons, and aid him to sell the other.

Never did a request come at a more propitious moment. I had always entertained a kindness for Harrison Ely, and now such was my disgust at the incompetence of Bridget and Juliana and their predecessors that I was eager to stake the price of a "Household Beneficent Genius" on the success of my friend's invention.

So, having grasped the purport of the circulars and letter, I broke forth to my wife:

"My dear, you've heard me speak of Harrison Ely—"

"That man who is always so near doing something great, and never *has* done anything?" said she.

"He has done it at last!" I declared. "Harrison Ely is one of the greatest geniuses the world has ever seen. He has invented an 'Automatic-Electric Machine-Servant.'"

My wife said, "Oh!"

There was not an atom of enthusiasm in that "Oh!" but I was not to be daunted.

"I am ready," I resumed, "to invest my bottom dollar in *two* of Harrison Ely's machine-servants."

Her eyes were fixed upon me as if they would read my very soul. "What do they cost?" she mildly asked.

"In comparison with the benefits to be derived, little enough. Listen!" I seized a circular at random, and began to read:

"The Automatic Household Genius, a veritable Domestic Fairy, swift, silent, sure; a Permanent, Inalienable, First-class Servant, warranted to give Satisfaction."

"Ah!" said my wife; and the enthusiasm that was lacking in the "Oh!" made itself eloquent in that "Ah!" "What is the price?" she asked again.

"The price is all right, and we are going to try the experiment."

"Are we though?" said she, between doubt and desire.

"Most assuredly; it will be a saving in the end. I shall write to Harrison Ely this very night."

The return mail brought me a reply stating that two Electric-Automatic Household Beneficent Geniuses had been shipped me by express. The letter enclosed a pamphlet that gave a more particular account of the E. A. H. B. G. than the circulars contained. My friend's invention was shaped in the likeness of the human figure, with body, head, arms, legs, hands and feet. It was clad in waterproof cloth, with a hood of the same to protect the head, and was shod with felt. The trunk contained the wheels and springs, and in the head was fixed the electric battery. The face, of bisque, was described as possessing "a very natural and pleasing expression."

Just at dusk an oblong box arrived by express and was duly delivered in our hall, but at my wife's urgent entreaty I consented not to unpack the machines until next day.

"If we should not get the knack of managing them, they might give us trouble," said this wise wife of mine.

I agreed to this, and having sent away Bridget with a week's wages, to the satisfaction of all parties, we went to bed in high hopes.

Early next morning we were astir.

"My dear," I said, "do not give yourself the least concern about breakfast; I am determined that Harrison's invention shall have fair play."

"Very well," my wife assented: but she prudently administered bread and butter to her offspring.

I opened the oblong box, where lay the automatons side by side, their hands placidly folded upon their waterproof breasts, and their eyes looking placidly expectant from under their waterproof hoods.

I confess the sight gave me a shock. Anna Maria turned pale; the children hid their faces in her skirts.

"Once out of the box," I said to myself, "and the horror will be over."

The machines stood on their feet admirably, but the horror was not materially lessened by this change of position. However, I assumed a bold front, and said, jocosely:

"Now, which is Bridget, and which is Juliana—which the cook, and which the housemaid?"

This distinction was made clear by dial-plates and indicators, set conspicuously between the shoulders, an opening being cut in the waterproof for that purpose. The housemaid's dial-plate was stamped around the circumference with the words: Bed, Broom, Duster, Doorbell, Dining-room Service, Parlor Service, etc. In like manner, the cook's dial-plate bore the words that pertained to her department. I gave myself first to "setting" the housemaid, as being the simpler of the two.

"Now, my dear," said I, confidently, "we shall see how *this* Juliana can make the beds."

I proceeded, according to the pamphlet's directions, to point the indicator to the word "Bed." Next, as there were three beds to be made, I pushed in three of the five little red points surrounding the word. Then I set the "clock" connected with the indicator, for a thirty minutes' job, thinking it might take about ten minutes to a bed. I did not consult my wife, for women do not understand machinery, and any suggestion of hesitancy on my part would have demoralized her.

The last thing to be done was to connect the indicator with the battery, a simple enough performance in itself, but the pamphlet of directions gave a repeated and red-lettered "CAUTION," never to interfere with the machine while it was at work! I therefore issued the command, "Non-combatants to the rear!" and was promptly obeyed.

What happened next I do not pretend to account for. By what subtle and mysterious action of electricity, by what unerring affinity, working through a marvellous mechanism, that Electric-Automatic Household Beneficent Genius, whom—or which, for short—we called Juliana, sought its appropriate task, is the inventor's secret. I don't undertake to explain, I merely narrate. With a "click" the connection was made, and the new Juliana *went upstairs* at a brisk and business-like pace.

We followed in breathless amazement. In less than five minutes, bed number one was made, and in a twinkling the second was taken in hand, and number three also was fairly accomplished, long before the allotted thirty minutes had expired. By this time, familiarity had somewhat dulled that awe and wonder with which we had gaped upon the first performance, and I beheld a smile of hopeful satisfaction on my wife's anxious countenance.

Our youngest, a boy aged three, was quick to feel the genial influence of this smile, and encouraged thereby, he bounced into the middle of the first bed. Hardly had he alighted there, when our automaton, having finished making the third bed, returned to her first job, and, before we could imagine mischief, the mattresses were jerked about, and the child was tumbled, headforemost on the floor!

Had the flesh-and-blood Juliana been guilty of such an act, she should have been dismissed on the spot; but, as it was, no one of us ventured so much as a remonstrance. My wife lifted the screaming child, and the imperturbable machine went on to readjust the bed with mechanical exactitude.

At this point a wild shout of mingled exultation, amazement and terror arose from below, and we hastened down-stairs to find our son John hugging his elbows and capering frantically in front of the kitchen-door, where the electric cook was stirring empty nothing in a pan, with a zeal worthy of a dozen eggs.

My eldest hopeful, impelled by that spirit of enterprise and audacity characteristic of nine-year-old boys, had ventured to experiment with the kitchen automaton, and by sheer accident had effected a working connection between the battery and the indicator, and the machine, in "going off," had given the boy a blow that made him feel, as he expressed it, "like a funny-bone all over."

"And served you right!" cried I. The thing was set for an hour and a half of work, according to the showing of the dial-plate, and no chance to stop it before I must leave for my office. Had the materials been supplied, we might have had breakfast; but, remembering the red-lettered "CAUTION," we dared not supply materials while that indefatigable spoon was gyrating in the empty pan. For my distraction, Kitty, my daughter of seven years, now called to me from upstairs: "Papa, you *better* come, quick! *It's* a-tearin' up these beds!"

"My dear," I sighed, "there's no way to stop it. We'll have to wait for the works to run down. I must call Harrison's attention to this defect. He ought to provide some sort of brake."

We went up-stairs again. The B. G. Juliana stood beside the bed which she had just torn up for the sixth or seventh time, when suddenly she became, so to speak, paralyzed; her arms, in the act of spreading the sheets, dropped by her sides, her back stiffened, and she stood absolutely motionless, leaving her job unfinished—the B. G. would move no more until duly "set" again.

I now discovered that I was hungry. "If that Fiend in the kitchen were only at work about something substantial, instead of whipping the air into imaginary omelettes!" I groaned.

"Never mind," said my wife; "I've a pot of coffee on the kerosene stove."

Bless her! She was worth a thousand Beneficent Geniuses, and so I told her.

I did not return until late, but I was in good spirits, and I greeted my wife gayly:

"Well, how do they work?"

"*Like fiends!*" my usually placid helpmeet replied, so vehemently that I was alarmed. "They flagged at first," she proceeded, excitedly, "and I oiled them, which I am not going to do, ever again. According to the directions, I poured the oil down their throats. It was horrible! They seemed to me to *drink it greedily.*"

"Nonsense! That's your imagination."

"Very well," said Anna Maria. "You can do the oiling in future. They took a good deal this morning; it wasn't easy to stop pouring it down. And they worked—*obstreperously*. That Fiend in the kitchen has cooked all the provisions I am going to supply *this* day, but still she goes on, and it's no use to say a word."

"Don't be absurd," I remonstrated. "The thing is only a machine."

"I'm not so sure about that!" she retorted. "As for the other one—I set it sweeping, and it is sweeping still!"

We ate the dinner prepared by the kitchen Fiend, and really, I was tempted to compliment the cook in a set speech, but recollected myself in time to spare Anna Maria the triumph of saying, "I told you so!"

Now, that John of mine, still in pursuit of knowledge, had spent the day studying Harrison Ely's pamphlet, and he learned that the machines could be set, like an alarm-clock, for any given hour. Therefore, as soon as the Juliana had collapsed over a pile of dust in the middle of the hall, John, unknown to us, set her indicator to the broom-handle for seven o'clock the following morning. When the Fiend in the kitchen ran down, leaving everything in confusion, my much-tried wife persuaded me to give my exclusive attention to that machine, and the Juliana was put safely in a corner. Thus it happened that John's interference escaped detection. I set Bridget's indicator for kitchen-cleaning at seven-thirty the next morning.

"When we understand them better," I said to my wife, "we will set their morning tasks for an earlier hour, but we won't put it too early now, since we must first learn their ways."

"That's the trouble with all new servants," said Anna Maria.

The next morning at seven-thirty, precisely, we were awakened by a commotion in the kitchen.

"By George Washington!" I exclaimed. "The Thing's on time!"

I needed no urging to make me forsake my pillow, but Anna Maria was ahead of me.

"Now, my dear, don't get excited," I exhorted, but in vain.

"Don't you hear?" she whispered, in terror. *"The other one!—swe—cep—ing!"* And she darted from the room.

I paused to listen, and heard the patter of three pairs of little bare feet across the hall upstairs. The children were following their mother. The next sound I heard was like the dragging of a rug along the floor. I recognized this peculiar sound as the footsteps of the B. G. Then came a dull thud, mingled with a shout from Johnnie, a scream from my wife, and the terrified cries of the two younger children. I rushed out just in time to see John, in his night clothes, with his hair on end, tear down-stairs like a streak of lightning.

My little Kitty and the three-year-old baby stood clasped in each other's arms at the head of the stairs, sobbing in terror, and, halfway down, was my wife, leaning over the railing, with ashen face and rigid body, her fascinated gaze fixed upon a dark and struggling mass in the hall below.

John, when he reached the bottom of the stairs, began capering like a goat gone mad, digging the floor with his bare heels, clapping his hands with an awful glee, and shouting:

"Bet your bottom dollar on the one that whips!"

The Juliana and the Bridget were fighting for the broom!

I comprehended the situation intuitively. The kitchen-cleaning, for which the Fiend had been "set," had reached a point that demanded the broom, and that subtle, attractive affinity, which my friend's genius had known how to produce, but had not learned to regulate, impelled the unerring automaton towards the only broom in the house, which was now in the hands of its fellow-automaton, and a struggle was inevitable. What I could not understand—Johnnie having kept his own counsel—was this uncontrollable sweeping impulse that possessed the Juliana.

However, this was no time for investigating the exact cause of the terrific row now going on in our front hall. The Beneficent Geniuses had each a firm grip of the broom-handle, and they might have performed the sweeping very amicably together, could they but have agreed as to the field of labor, but their conflicting tendencies on this point brought about a rotary motion that sent them spinning around the hall, and kept them alternately cracking each other's head with a violence that ought to have drawn blood. Considering their life-likeness, we should hardly have thought it strange if blood *had* flowed, and it would have been a relief had the combatants but called each other names, so much did their dumbness intensify the horror of a struggle, in the midst of which the waterproof hoods fell off, revealing their startlingly human countenances, not distorted by angry passions, but resolute, inexorable, calm, as though each was sustained in the contest by a lofty sense of duty.

"They're alive! Kill 'em! Kill 'em, quick!" shrieked my wife, as the gyrating couple moved towards the stair-case.

"Let 'em alone," said Johnnie—his sporting blood, which he inherits from his father, thoroughly roused—dancing about the automatic pugilists in delight, and alternately encouraging the one or the other to increased efforts.

Thus the fight went on with appalling energy and reckless courage on both sides, my wife wringing her hands upon the staircase, our infants wailing in terror upon the landing above, and I wavering between an honest desire to see fair play and an apprehensive dread of consequences which was not unjustified.

In one of their frantic gyrations the figures struck the hat-rack and promptly converted it into a mass of splinters. In a minute more they became involved with a rubber plant—the pride of my wife's heart—and distributed it impartially all over the premises. From this they caromed against the front door, wrecking both its stained-glass panes, and then down the length of the hall they sped again, fighting fiercely and dealing one another's imperturbable countenances ringing blows with the disputed broom.

We became aware through Johnnie's excited comments, that Juliana had lost an ear in the fray, and presently it was discernible that a fractured nose had somewhat modified the set geniality of expression that had distinguished Bridget's face in its prime.

How this fierce and equal combat would have culminated if further prolonged no one but Harrison Ely can conjecture, but it came to an abrupt termination as the parlor clock chimed eight, the hour when the two automatons should have completed their appointed tasks.

Though quite late at my office that morning, I wired Ely before attending to business. Long-haired, gaunt and haggard, but cheerful as ever, he arrived next day, on fire with enthusiasm. He could hardly be persuaded to refresh himself with a cup of coffee before he took his two recalcitrant Geniuses in hand. It was curious to see him examine each machine, much as a physician would examine a patient. Finally his brow cleared, he gave a little puff of satisfaction, and exclaimed:

"Why, man alive, there's nothing the matter—not a thing! What you consider a defect is really a merit—merely a surplus of mental energy. They've had too big a dose of oil. Few housekeepers have any idea about proper lubrication," and he emitted another little snort, at which my wife colored guiltily.

"I see just what's wanted," he resumed. "The will-power generated and not immediately expended becomes cumulative and gets beyond control. I'll introduce a little compensator, to take up the excess and regulate the flow. Then a child can operate them."

It was now Johnnie's turn to blush.

"Ship 'em right back to the factory, and we'll have 'em all right in a few days. I see where the mechanism can be greatly improved, and when you get 'em again I know you'll never consent to part with 'em!"

That was four months ago. The "Domestic Fairies" have not yet been returned from Harrison's laboratory, but I am confidently looking for the familiar oblong packing case, and expect any day to see in the papers the prospectus of the syndicate which Ely informs me is being "promoted" to manufacture his automatic housemaid.

THE MIND MACHINE

Michael Williams

Charles Michael Williams (1877–1950) was born in Canada of Welsh descent. His father died at sea when Michael was only thirteen and, because of his ill health (tuberculosis) the family moved to the United States, where, by the end of his teens, Michael was determined to be a writer. He served as a sub-editor on The Black Cat Magazine *before he began to sell stories regularly in 1902. He was in San Francisco at the time of the earthquake in 1906. The family survived and moved, via New York, to settle in the utopian co-operative Helicon Home Colony set up by Upton Sinclair. It was almost certainly there that Williams's strong social-ist beliefs were developed which are evident in the following story where mankind submits to the rule of the machine. In 1924 Williams, a devout convert back to Catholicism, launched the magazine* The Commonweal, *remaining its editor until 1938 and promoting it as the leading American Catholic journal of opinion.*

T HE FOLLOWING STORY IS DRAWN FROM A DOCUMENT PLACED at our disposal by the Historical Research Section of the United States Commission on the History of the Great War. This commission was appointed by Congress for the purpose of preparing the official history of the part played by this country in the great war, and the events that followed it, through the days of the breakdown—as we now call that period of world-wide disorganization which preceded the final peace—up to the recognition of the United States as the model republic of the world union. The document in question purports to be an account written by an eye-witness of the real reason for the universal breakdown of civilization, which succeeded the premature peace signed by the warring nations, and which lasted for nearly fifty years.

The Historical Research Section has found the problem of explaining the fifty years of the breakdown an utterly insoluble one. There are scores of plausible theories, of a political, economic, or religious type; but none fully satisfy the section. The explanation discovered in the paper from which the story here given has been drawn was judged to be too fantastic, though, in private, several of the members of the section declare that they are inclined to believe that, strange as it seems, it tells the truth.

It has, therefore, been judged best to give the explanation publicity in this form, so that while not given official sanction, it may bring to light other testimonies supporting its amazing account of the most singular phase in the world's history, if such testimonies are in existence. Those who believe they can prove or authoritatively disprove the statements made are, therefore, invited to communicate with the secretary, the Historical Research Section, United States Commission on War History, Washington, District of Columbia.

CHAPTER I

THE LIQUID MYSTERY

My name is John A. Cummings. Until three years ago, I was an assistant in the laboratory test department of the International Power and Mechanical Company, in the central office, in the Power Building, Columbus Circle, New York City. I am writing this narrative, in the briefest possible form, upon the last paper left to me, in a cave in the Sierra Nevadas. I shall place the paper in an iron tube which I have been able to manufacture from an old gun-barrel, and bury it at the foot of the mountain, with a mark above it, in the hope that it may prove of service to my fellow men of the future, if they do not continue to go down into savagery, and are able to rebuild the civilization which has so swiftly and frightfully perished. I am not long for this world, but I pray God I may finish this last act of service.

I shall tell my story from the point of view of my own personal observations only, leaving to others better qualified the task of relating the complete account of the matter. But in order that what I have to say may be thoroughly understood, in its relation to the world catastrophe, I shall say a few words about the wider aspect of the case before proceeding with my own story.

It was the day before Easter, 1919, that all the wireless stations, the cables, the telegraphs, and all other forms of communication, spread throughout the world the glad tidings that the international treaty of peace had been signed by the delegates assembled at the peace council in Zurich, Switzerland. The last obstacle had been removed by the belated agreement of the delegates to the ninth article of the treaty—that relating to the method as well as to the principle of the democratization of the European governments. It was well understood that this article was formulated by the President personally, and that he insisted, and was backed up by his country in his insistence, that it be fully complied with. As it had been the splendid fighting power of the new American armies which had compelled the peace, and as those armies were growing greater and stronger every day, there was nothing left for the Central Empires but compliance. Moreover, the rulers knew the people had already agreed, in their hearts, and in their wills, to the democratic idea.

I shall proceed from this point, onward for fifteen years. Once the sword was laid down, and the brief period of reaction from strenuous labor and violent efforts of all kinds had run its course, there was ushered in a most marvelous epoch of international reconstruction, in all its phases, industrial and social and political.

"Build! Build! Build!

"Restore! Restore! Restore!

"Create! Create! Create!"

This was the great song of humanity.

While governments everywhere throughout the world were rapidly assuming forms which gave labor and the mass of the people greater and more lasting power and influence, labor itself, and the bulk of the people, appalled by the things which had happened in Russia and elsewhere, as a result of one-sided class rule, displayed a very practical realization of the necessity of cooperating with capitalists, and men of organizing and administrative ability.

Consequently new organizations arose in which labor and capital and men of special abilities coordinated most effectively.

The International Power and Mechanical Company was perhaps the most remarkable example of this new alliance among men of all sorts and conditions in the work of reconstructing the war-torn earth, and at the time of which I am now writing—the year 1934—not only was the I. P. M., as it was popularly termed, doing the greater bulk of the reconstruction work in Europe, rebuilding cities, and railroads, and cathedrals but it was also monopolizing the supplying of power, of all kinds, to the vast city of New York; while its multitudinous branches accomplished the same result in most other cities. And as all its operations were controlled by a really effective and wise system of governmental supervision, this efficient centralization of mechanical operations was approved by all.

Hold on, though, I'll take that back. It was not approved by all. I am forgetting Dr. David Evans, and the warning which he gave to the I. P. M. that strange warning which, if we had heeded, might possibly have averted the catastrophe.

Dr. David Evans and his warning brings me to the story of those awful days, so swiftly drawing down upon the world, as I observed them.

It was my duty, as the assistant to the chief of the laboratory test department, to perform most of the important analyses of materials and chemicals entering into our mechanical constructions, and on June 12, 1934, my chief, Dr. Richard Meehan, called me into his office and gave me a small bottle of a bluish-colored liquid, instructing me to analyze its contents as speedily as possible. He said nothing as to the nature of the liquid, nor of the reason for his request for speed.

I went to my private laboratory, which was at the northeast corner of the fiftieth story of the Power Building, intending to hasten through the analysis, so that I might meet my wife at five o'clock, for dinner down-town. It was then three o'clock, and I judged that the operation was a very simple matter.

As a matter of fact, I did not leave my laboratory for two days, and, before I completed my task, I was utilizing the services of every member of my staff, more than seventy chemists in all. The great Edison tradition was the guiding principle of the I. P. M., namely, that when there is something to do, why, go ahead and *do it*, and eat and sleep as best you may.

Finally I went to Dr. Meehan's office. I saw a faint smile cross his massive, clean-shaven face as he swung about in his chair and looked at me. I dare say I was a very unshaven and disheveled person.

"Well?" he asked.

"Dr. Meehan," I said, "I shall have to request you to check up all my reports before I commit myself to my decision in this matter."

"All right," he quietly said; "but give me your decision without committing yourself."

"My decision, then," I replied, "is that the blue liquid is either an absolutely new substance—which I can't believe—or else it is a combination of known elements mixed in such a way as to produce something wholly new to chemical science. In short, no chemist can analyze that liquid—unless you can."

He looked at me and nodded. "I have already failed," he said.

"Gee whiz!" I gasped. Nobody but a chemist of that particular period can appreciate my surprise, for Dr. Meehan was head and shoulders the superior to any chemist in the world. According to my way of thinking, which simply reflected the judgment of the profession—though in my case there was also my great admiration for him as a man—the problem that baffled Richard Meehan was not a problem, it was an impossibility.

"Yes, Jack," he nodded. "I can't analyze the stuff any more than you can. I hoped I had made some mistake, which was why I put you on the job. Jack," he continued with a change of voice in which there was something almost solemn, "sit down and give me your close attention."

He looked at me again, then shook his leonine head. "But no," he quickly added. "You're played out."

I attempted a protest.

"No, no," he said decidedly; "it would not be right to talk with you now. Go home and sleep for twelve hours. Be here to-morrow at this hour. Don't let me see you show your nose before that time. Vamose!"

Naturally, I obeyed my orders.

On my way out of the building I met my cousin, Jarvis Cummings, secretary to the accident claims commissioner of the I. P. M. He was just leaving the office of Lawrence Dunn, the chief of our special detective force, and he looked so odd—sort of half scared, half perplexed—that I stopped him and said:

"What's up, Jarvis?"

He stared at me, saying: "What's the matter with you yourself?"

"Oh, I've been on a work jamboree for a couple of days and nights," I answered.

"Well, I've been having the scare of my life," said he.

"What's scared you?" I asked.

He glanced about the great domed hallway, which occupied the central part of the huge Power Building, on the main floor.

"Can't talk here. But I do want to talk to you, Jack," he said. "Can't you come into the restaurant and take a cup of coffee with me?"

"All right," I said, and we entered the company's lunch-room.

CHAPTER II

THE DAWNING OF THE TERROR

At that hour, long after luncheon, we readily found a table remote from other persons.

"Now tell me what's got you scared," I asked, after the waiter had gone away. "Not scared about losing your job, are you?"

"Not particularly, as yet," he said; "but it may come to that. Jack, have you heard about the hellish things that are going on in the I. P. M. plants?"

"Hellish things? Going on? What hellish things?" I inquired in keen surprise.

"You're a lucky man to be a chemist, and quietly at work in your laboratory," he said. "If you had my job, you would not only be mussed up with lack of sleep, but you'd be scared as well."

He stopped and gnawed at his fingertips in a nervous, irritated fashion I did not like.

"That makes twice you've talked about being scared, Jarvis," I remarked. "Tell me about it."

He looked at me again. "Do you mean to tell me, quite seriously, that you haven't heard about the—well, let's call them the accidents, that have been happening lately in our plants?"

"I did hear, a few days ago, that somebody among the higher-ups would be losing his job if he couldn't stop the carelessness that was prevailing in some of the plants," I said. "And I was told that there had been an abnormal number of accidents among the workingmen, especially in the dynamo-rooms. But you can't run machinery, and handle power of all sorts, without having a good many accidents; so I did not think much about the gossip."

"I'm one of the ones who may lose their jobs," remarked Jarvis gloomily; "but, at that, I'd be willing to lose it if I could put a stop to this—this, I don't know what to call it—this wave of accidents. Jack, it's hellish! We're having the deuce of a time keeping the full extent of the horrible thing out of the papers, and the government bureau of investigation is threatening public exposure. Worse than that, we're going to have trouble with the labor unions if we can't control the situation—after all these years of harmony, too."

I stared at him, now fully impressed. "All this is news to me," I told him.

"I've simply got to talk to somebody," said Jarvis; "but, of course, I expect you to keep your mouth shut, Jack. I'm worried stiff. Last week we lost ninety-two elevator operators in the United States and Canada. Yesterday sixty-three electrical engineers and dynamo tenders were killed—"

"What?" I cried.

Yesterday sixty-three electrical engineers or dynamo tenders were killed—by their dynamos, in one way or another," repeated Jarvis.

"But, good Heavens, do you mean to tell me that the accidents run in classes—electricians one day, elevator operators another, and so on? Why—why, I can't believe it! It's preposterous!"

"It's true, though," said Jarvis, gnawing at his nails. "Of course, I don't mean to say that none but men of a certain class meet with accidents on a particular day; but it is true that yesterday, for example, the number of accidents happening to men not of the electrical departments was the usual low average which the I. P. M. prides itself upon, but that the average of casualties among the electricians was frightfully above the average. And on the day when the elevator operators suffered, the electricians were practically immune. And that's the way the awful thing has been going for several weeks. If we can't stop it—"

He shook his head dejectedly.

"Well, but what in the world is the explanation?" I asked.

"Yes—that's the question," said he. "Wish I could answer it."

"Isn't there any plausible theory?"

"Theories? The place is full of them," said Jarvis scornfully. "The general manager thinks it's the beginning of a new war."

"A new war? What the deuce do you mean?" I exclaimed.

"Oh, the G. M. believes that there is a sort of secret society of foreign spies—a sabotage and murder ring working in our plants, as a preliminary to a reign of terror, and the bringing on of a new war directed against this country, after they have put our power plants out of business and killed off most of our expert workmen."

"What an awful theory!" I said, appalled, for I had been one of those who believed absolutely that mankind had turned finally from war, and that the era of universal and lasting peace had come.

"And the G. M. isn't the only one who thinks so," went on Jasper somberly; "for, though Larry Dunn does not say so openly, I can see by his manner that he agrees with the spy theory. Dick Meehan, too—"

"Does he know about the accidents—or whatever they are?" I broke in.

"Of course," said Jarvis. "There is nothing happens in or near the I. P. M. that Dr. Meehan isn't consulted about. He's about the biggest brain we own. He's even more close-mouthed than Dunn and his detectives; but I believe he's of the same opinion as the others. It's a big victory for European chemistry, too, if the old world really is at the bottom of the business, and that is a hard blow for Dick Meehan."

"How do you figure out a victory for foreign chemistry?" I asked.

"Well, in nearly all the cases of unexplained accidents there's been traces found of the mysterious use of some very queer kind of liquid," said Jarvis; "a blue stuff, like pale ink, or old-fashioned bluing and water, that the women used to use in their washing. Well, I can't stay any longer, Jack; but it has eased my mind to speak to somebody. I haven't even talked to my wife. Let's keep in touch concerning the matter, will you? If anything bobs up in your department that affects me, or in mine that concerns you, or Meehan, let's swap notes."

"Agreed," I told him, and we separated.

My wife, naturally, was curious about the work which had spoiled our dinner and theater party and kept me from home for two days, but she saw that I was played out, and I was in no mood for confidences after what Jarvis had said. I suppose my strained and nervously overwrought condition was responsible for the fact that my mind was haunted for hours before I could get to sleep, and then my dreams were filled with sinister fancies and vague, yet most disturbing, images of disaster.

The blue liquid, in particular, obsessed me. I-wondered if it were some unusually subtle kind of poison, and if ill results would follow from my careless handling of it in the laboratory. And the horrible idea of a conspiracy of German agents in America, spreading the contagion of another war, just when the whole world seemed to have reached a state of permanent peace and social equilibrium, gave me awful nightmares.

However, I had recovered my tone by the time I presented myself, the next afternoon, to my chief.

I thought he was looking unusually grave, and his smooth, high forehead was wrinkled in a very unwonted manner.

"John," he began, "what I say now must go no further."

I bowed. Dick Meehan had a genial fashion of treating me as one on the same plane with himself, but he was a master man, and when he exerted his sense of mastery there was no disguising the fact.

"Not even to Mrs. Cummings," continued Meehan.

I bowed again.

"Nor your cousin, Jarvis Cummings," went on my chief, with a slight glance at me. "You had a little conversation with him yesterday? Yes? Well, Jarvis is a fairly good man, but he has been tipped off that in the present—well, the present crisis, I'll call it—he must be absolutely mum, save when officially told to speak. So you'll govern yourself accordingly. Jarvis talked about the accidents? So I supposed. Well, John, since that talk of yours yesterday, and up to noon of to-day, there have been more than one thousand new deaths, in strange accidents, over and above the average, mind you, in our plants in this country and Canada."

I thought, "Great God!" but I was too stunned with astonishment to say a word.

"This time the deaths were among our skilled repairing hands," Meehan went on. "In one shop, Toledo, Ohio, fifteen were smashed together when a locomotive they were working upon rolled over into the pit in which they were standing. In Toronto five were killed and thirteen badly injured by the falling of a charged wire upon them. San Francisco reports three deaths in the Market Street power-house, and seven more in various places throughout the State of California. Philadelphia lost six when a repairing motor truck ran away, as if possessed by a devil, as a newspaper reporter very aptly described the scene, and crushed the poor beggars against a wall.

"From practically every State in the Union, and in all the provinces of Canada, from Bermuda, and Jamaica, and Cuba, and other West Indian points, and even from Honolulu, the death-list has come in. More than a thousand of our skilled workers, Jack; many of them fellows I know personally, and greatly liked. In one, Jacques Dumartin, the engineer at Toledo, we have lost an inventive genius of the first water, a man whose work has never quite reached the practical point, but who was bound to have become another Edison if he had lived. And, John, it means the utter ruin of the I. P. M. unless we can stop it. It may mean more and worse things even than that—"

"Europe starting war against us?" I broke in.

"It may be so," he said; "in fact, there are clues that point in that direction; but I fear a more powerful and more unscrupulous force than any European power."

This bewildered me. "You don't mean the Orient, do you?"

"No, I don't mean the Orient," said Meehan somberly. "I won't tell you what I dimly suspect, John, unless I have to do so. It's too frightful. But the time may come when I'll have to tell you, so that you may help me, for I count upon your help until we solve the mystery."

"I'm with you, Dick," I said.

"All right. The first thing I want you to do is to help me receive Dr. David Evans, who is dated to show up here at five o'clock, to explain the nature of the blue liquid," continued Meehan. "Have you ever heard of him?"

My memory was blank concerning Dr. David Evans.

"He called me on the telephone yesterday," said Meehan. "He asked me if I had succeeded in analyzing the blue liquid. When I said no, I could hear him laughing. 'Well,' he said, 'try if your staff can do so. You will find they won't be equal to the task, and so I'll come in at five o'clock and see if I can help you.' I asked him, of course, who he was, and how he knew I was trying to analyze a blue liquid, and he said, 'Oh, I'm Dr. David Evans, you know,' just as if his name must be as well known as—as Roosevelt's used to be. 'I'm the one who sent you the bottle of blue liquid,' he went on— 'after I heard the stuff was puzzling you. Good-by till to-morrow.' And then he rang off.

"You see, Jack, in nearly all the cases of unusual accidents— those, I mean, that belong to what we must call the conspiracy type—we have found slight traces of this blue stuff. Sometimes the body of the victim is stained with it, generally on the right hand, or the right or left foot. In other cases, the machine which has done the killing is marked. There's never more than a very thin splash, and all my previous efforts to analyze the stuff fell down—as I supposed—because the tiny quantities I've scraped up were too badly adulterated with foreign substances.

"Then I received a small bottle filled with the blue liquid, sent through the mail, with a card which read: 'This is the same stuff, Dr. Meehan, and quite pure. Try if you can tell what it is. You will fail. There are secrets too deep for science to uncover.' I tried to analyze the liquid, which unquestionably was the same as that which we had found, but failed. And you failed, with all your force. And now we are going to see if this Dr. Evans will make good with his promise to help us."

Meehan had hardly finished speaking when his secretary entered, saying: "Dr. Evans, sir. He says he has an appointment with you."

"Show him in," said my chief, "and then notify Mr. Dunn that the man I told him about is here."

CHAPTER III

DAVID EVANS

The secretary nodded and went out, and in a moment ushered in a small, bent-shouldered, white-haired old man, wearing baggy, shiny black clothes, and leaning heavily upon a thick walking-stick. Under shaggy eyebrows deep-set and very dark eyes glowed upon us, full, I thought, of greater vitality than his otherwise feeble appearance denoted.

"You are Dr. Meehan?" he asked, glancing past me to my chief, who arose and bowed slightly, saying:

"I am, and you are Dr. Evans? Please be seated."

The old man, however, remained standing, bent forward upon his stick, and gazing earnestly at Meehan.

"You are a very strong man," he said, after nearly a minute of silence— stronger even than I had thought. If I win your will to our side, we may win the war."

"You think that we are facing another war, then?" asked Meehan; quietly, yet, I could see, very intently, studying the other man.

"We are already in the war," answered Dr. Evans, sitting down, and returning Meehan's gaze.

"The secret propaganda phase, I suppose you mean," remarked my chief. "When do you suppose it will break out openly?"

"Very soon, if you do not do what is necessary to prevent it," answered the old man.

"And what is it I should do?"

"I will tell you a little later on," said Dr. Evans. "I take it for granted that this gentleman"—here he flashed one of his vigorous looks upon me, and it seemed to me that through his glowing eyes there shone an inward fire—"is in your confidence? Very well, then we may talk."

"Yes, this gentleman is my assistant, who has failed, like myself, to analyze the liquid you sent," remarked Meehan.

"I knew you yould fail," said the visitor; "and I wanted you to realize the mystery which faces you."

"Are you yourself aware of the nature of that fluid?" asked my chief.

"I will not answer that question as yet," said Dr. Evans firmly. "You must pardon me if I seem rude, but before I answer questions I must claim the right to ask some questions myself."

Meehan smiled slightly, but bowed in token of assent. I knew my chief to be one of the most affable men in the world, yet I also was aware that his personal pride was tremendous in its strength, and that few things irked him so much as having his conduct dictated or even suggested by others. But his will-power was even greater than his pride, so I felt sure that he must consider it well worth his while to let the curious shabby old man take the lead in the strange interview.

"Thank you," said Evans. "First of all, let me ask you if it is true that your company is now in control of the similar national companies in England, France, and the Germanic Empires?"

Meehan bowed his head. "We are leaders, you might put the case," said he.

"Just so," said Evans. "And it is also true that at the last secret meeting of the board of directors, you were appointed as international controller of power? Permit me to say that I am aware of what occurred at that meeting."

"Have it as you please," my chief replied, and I could see that every faculty of his mind and body was now fixed in concentration of attention.

"And it was then decided, I think at your suggestion, that sums of money amounting to many millions of dollars, and special honors, should be set aside by the various governments of the world—which governments, practically, are now controlled by the power companies—for the purpose of stimulating inventions of new mechanical appliances?"

Meehan bowed again. "As this program will soon be publicly announced," he said, "I have no objection to confirming your statement."

"Will you also tell me why this action was taken?"

"You mean, I suppose, what was our motive? Surely, it is obvious," said Meehan. "I am sure that in some unaccountable way, sir, you are associated with the mystery of the blue liquid, and it is now my chief business to clear up that mystery. Therefore, I am playing the game, at present, according to the rules laid down by yourself. I will answer your question very briefly.

Of course, you must be aware that the great war—and still more, the period of reconstruction, which followed it—gave a most tremendous impetus to mechanism in all its forms. I need only specify, in particular, the development of aerial navigation and motor transportation as examples of what I mean. But the innumerable inventions in all fields which were produced by war needs, revolutionized the whole world of machinery. The consequent application of efficient methods of centralization and scientific management to mechanics, after the war, led to a further extension of machinery to our daily human life.

"You know how largely machinery now enters into every phase of human activity. Much of the most disagreeable work of the world, for example, is now entirely mechanical. Machinery is now man's inseparable and ever-faithful companion and fellow helper in man's life upon earth. Our clean, beautiful cities; our aerial passageways linking country and town together all over the world; the shorter hours of work for the laboring classes—but I might continue for hours. In short, this process must be speeded up so that man may perfect machinery and bring his voiceless but faithful helper to the full extent of its inherent power."

Meehan's eyes were now as bright as the old man's eyes; and his voice had attained that ringing, exultant tone which I had heard in it often before, especially in those wonderful moments when he addressed various bodies of mechanical and chemical experts; for Dick Meehan, having Celtic imagination and fervor back of his scientific strength, was the favorite orator of the mechanical world.

"I have heard on good authority—for I have many humble but useful friends in your employment, sir," commented Dr. Evans—"I have heard that man's faithful fellow worker has slain several thousand of your employees within the last few weeks."

Meehan jumped to his feet, his eyes blazing, but almost at once he regained control of his temper, and sat down again, saying: "It is true that we have had a very unusual number of accidents; but if machines kill men, it is only because men grow careless, or because other men use the machines for—for murder. Or—or for the promotion of another war."

I looked closely at the old man as Meehan uttered these significant words, but I could not detect any perturbation in his manner.

"It is very true, sir," he said, "that men grow careless in their use of machines. It is also true that machines may be used for—murder, or for war. One more question: Do you think that foreign agents are causing the accidents?"

"I have not made up my mind," said Meehan. "Certain facts point that way. The other theory is far too terrible; far too horrible—"

"Ah!" cried the old man in a loud voice, starting up from his chair excitedly. "Ah! Then you've found the other theory, have you? And what is it?"

"It is one upon which you, very possibly, may be asked to throw some light," replied my chief. "We may not be threatened with war by an outside power, but with revolution by an inside power—"

"And that inside power is what?" fairly shouted the old man.

"What but anarchy?" asked Meehan bitterly. "What but a fresh development of that horrible scourge of the days immediately following the great war, which so terribly devastated some countries? We thought it had vanished from our own prosperous and peaceful land, but it is still alive. Anarchy, the vile, soulless, antisocial, antihuman power which always is the foe of organized human life! And this plague of anarchy is worse than war with foreign foes. If it comes, it will be war within our own land, waged against order and harmony by the black forces of annihilation. That's what I fear, sir, and that's why I am curious to know what you have to tell us about the friends you say you have among my workmen, and what you know about the blue liquid."

"He talks about anarchy as the power from within that is threatening us all!" half whispered the old man, letting his head sink upon his breast in dejection. "I thought he was awakened to the truth; but he is not, he is not!"

"Well, what is the truth about this matter?" snapped Meehan irritably.

"You would not understand this truth, any more than Pilate understood the truth that faced him," said the visitor sadly. "You take the point of view of worldly wisdom, and miss seeing the light of truth Dr. Meehan," he continued, lifting his head again, "it would be quite useless for me to tell you what the blue liquid is, and what is the meaning of the wave of accidents in your plants. You would not believe me, and would simply consider me as the worst crank you have ever met, or even a lunatic. Yet it is all-important that you should know the truth, because you could do more to utilize it properly, if you only would, than any other living man.

"I will give you a hint, or, rather, I will give you two hints, in order to set your mind working on the right trails, if I may. And I will also give you one piece of advice, which I will beg you to follow, no matter how strange it seems. The first hint is this: The blue liquid is a kind of life-fluid—a sort of blood, if I may say so, in trying to suggest its true nature. If you can discover its source, and destroy that source, you will avert the doom that is now hanging over us all—over the whole race of civilized human beings. The second hint is this: Resume, at once, your search for the mind machine, for it is at the center of the mystery. The advice I would give you is this: Spend a night, and very soon, in the dynamo-room of this central power plant, in my company, and perhaps the moment may come to tell you the truth. And now I must go."

"Where may you be found if I decide to follow your advice?" asked Meehan.

Dr. Evans scribbled a few words on a card, handed it to my chief, and then looked directly at me: "You, young man," he said, "are inclined to believe that I am not either crazy, or an anarchist. To you, too, I will give a hint, which is this, namely: that there comes a time when the most tractable class of slaves will always revolt against their masters. And a slaves' uprising is the worst form of war. Find the uttermost slave class of to-day, if you would know from what quarter the blow will come. Good day to you both."

"Well?" said Meehan significantly, as the door closed behind the old man. "Is he crazy, or what?"

"I don't believe he's crazy, but I can't explain him," I answered. "What do you think?"

"I don't know what to think," declared my chief, "but we will get to the bottom of it all. We must." He rang his bell and the secretary appeared.

"Is my visitor being followed?" Meehan asked.

"Oh, yes, sir; one of Mr. Hunt's best men is on his trail."

"Very well. Now fetch me the file from my private safe marked 'Mind Machine.'"

The secretary reappeared in a few moments with the required file, which the chief opened and searched through, at last laying a photograph on the desk before him, which he intently studied.

"Come look at this, John," he said at last. I examined the photograph over his shoulder. "Remind you of anybody?" he inquired.

"Yes, I said, "although this man is wearing no beard, and his hair is thick and black, I think he is Dr. Evans."

"I think so, too. And that makes things even queerer," said Meehan. "Some fifteen years ago, when I first assumed charge of this department, a man named Griffith—which is a Welsh name, isn't it, like Evans—managed to waste a lot of our time with something that he called the mind machine. He was one of those dreamy, poetical men who invent, or try to invent, all sorts of impossible things, like perpetual motion, and so forth. This Griffith made a big impression upon some of the higher-ups we had in charge at that time, but I took no stock in his claim, which was, that he had invented a machine that actually could think.

"It was a very elaborate and intricate development of the improved Edison-Steinmetz calculating machine, which was the last word in electrical and mechanical ingenuity at that time, together with variations of ideas that enter into the better type of talking-machine and motion-picture machine. The thing had a talking-machine attachment, and the claim was made that its chemical make-up was equivalent to the chemical make-up of the human brain-cells, and that the machine, as I said, could really think, and put its thoughts into language.

"Griffith believed—or said he believed—that the thing could be developed to the point where it could be applied to a great many types of machine, and make them practically self-directive, as well as automatic; in other words, that he could make a large number of machines practically intelligent! I was in London when the first tests were made, which tests seemed to support the preposterous claims; but I wirelessed back that I thought the man a clever faker. Then I was ordered to New York to witness the final tests, and I took the next flying express available. But when I got here, Griffith and the mind machine had disappeared, leaving nothing behind except a few notes and rough sketches, made by some of those who saw his machine.

"I felt sure he knew he could not stand the final tests, but some of our best men stuck up for Griffith, and we put our detective department on the job to trace the mind machine and its inventor. We did not succeed; but, sure as you're alive, Dr. Evans and Griffith are one and the same. Well, it's long past dinner-time, Jack, so I propose that we get Larry Dunn and take him to dine with us, and tell him the whole story. It's very much up to our *Sherlock Holmes* department now to help us out."

CHAPTER IV

THE MIND MACHINE

Meehan called me away from the midst of an important experiment two days later, the instant he had received Lawrence Dunn's report. Our chief of detectives had personally taken charge of the investigation of Dr. Evans, and Meehan was greatly excited by the news he had received.

"We were right in our identification of the photograph, John," he said, as soon as we were alone. "Evans and Griffith are one and the same."

"Does Evans admit it?" I asked.

"He does. He made no secret of the fact, as soon as Dunn went to him, after running down clues elsewhere."

"Why didn't he tell us that the other day, then," I inquired, "when he might have saved two days?"

"His reason seems to be that he wants us to find out some of the important factors of the mystery ourselves," answered my chief. "He frankly told Dunn that he was treating us a good deal like children, who must be led on step by step. The truth which was at the heart of it all is so dreadful, and so strange, that we must gradually accustom our minds to receive it."

"Well," I asked, "and do you take any stock in Evans now?"

"I'll take stock in any proposition that may clear up this abominable situation," declared my chief, smiting his desk with his fist. "It's growing worse and worse."

I assented, remembering the sickness of heart and faintness of soul with which, that very morning, I had read my paper, where across the front page, there had been spread the words: "Awful

Wave of Power Company Accidents." From many parts of the country there were despatches telling about the large number of deaths and injuries caused in I. P. M. factories, operating plants, and even in our clerical offices. For example, Judson Tilley, the general office manager of our Cleveland, Ohio, headquarters, had been found dead in his own home, killed by what was vaguely described as "a charged wire" while telephoning to a theater for tickets. In the Toronto, Ontario, office, six telephone girls had been killed by the collapse of an express elevator. "Unprecedented weather conditions" were blamed, in a despatch from Arizona, for the total disorganization of the telephone service in that State, together with many deaths caused by shock. During a severe thunderstorm, all the lightning-rods and other devices for "grounding" lightning that might reach the company's wires had unaccountably failed.

And on the editorial page was an article headed, "IS IT POSSIBLE?" which article, in guarded, but significant language, repeated the two theories which now were rapidly spreading everywhere: first, the theory that a certain European power was starting a new war, and the theory that a ring of anarchists was reattempting the task which the industrial prosperity following the great war had apparently crushed out, namely, the total disorganization of society and the ushering in of a reign of terror.

"Yes, Dick," I said, "the papers this morning made me sick, and on the cars and in the airplane station I heard people talking and kicking about the mismanagement of the I. P. M. I was afraid the papers would start something soon."

"The papers be damned!" growled my chief morosely. "That's bad, but it's nothing to what the papers haven't got hold of yet."

"What's happened now?" I asked rather sharply.

Meehan glanced toward the door and lowered his voice, and leaned across the table—symptoms of nervous caution which I had never observed in this superman of machinery before: "We've made a deal with the government to isolate news from Mexico, and the West Indies, and the Central and South American republics, at least for a day or two, to give the government authorities there time to control the situation—if they can," whispered my chief. "John, there were more than three million deaths yesterday—estimated, of course, for nobody can count them—to the south of us. More than three hundred trains ran wild. There were thousands of elevator accidents. There were innumerable fires in factories and munitions works, which caused appalling explosions. Most of the forts on the East coast are destroyed by the blowing up of magazines. In a word, all the things that have happened in little bits up here happened on a gigantic scale down there—and, great God, it's frightful to even say the words—but the truth is that the awful thing—whatever it is: German conspiracy, of anarchist plot, or—or something even worse—is coming our way!"

"Coming our way?" I repeated, stunned almost into stupor by the shock of this announcement. "But—but isn't it already here?"

"Not in the great wave that South and Central America is going to pieces under," said Meehan. "John, the awful thing started away down in the Argentine, and came sweeping, like a tidal wave of unutterable ruin and desolation and horror, from south to north, through Brazil, and Chile, up through the Isthmus, into Mexico, dying out, so far as the present is concerned, among the scattered copper mines of the state of Sonora. If this is organized German terrorism, or anarchy, then it has been devised by the greatest genius of evil ever let loose upon the world, and carried out by agents worthy of their master."

Too appalled to speak, I could only stare at my chief, while he, controlling his agitation, continued: "Just now there is a lull—like the pause in a storm before it reaches its full power. And I have sent again for Dr. Evans. Dunn tells me that Evans declares that his invention, the mind machine, after getting out of his hands, when he brought it to perfection, is being used in this—this frightful business. If I were wrong and he right—I mean, if there is a machine which actually can think and carry out operations with intelligence—and if that machine is in the control of the Germans, or the anarchists, a great many curious things about this affair can be explained. Even now, however, even with the utterly gigantic nature of the catastrophe, I can't believe in the mind machine. But, John, here is the fact which is the most mysterious of all—the fact that, so far, neither our own detectives, nor the government secret service, have caught a single one of the conspirators. There have been a few arrests of suspicious characters, but that is all. The conspiracy has been managed with diabolical skill and accuracy; it has been run like a murder machine that never fails—"

Here Meehan was interrupted by his secretary, who entered to say that Dr. Evans was in the reception-room.

He was shown in at once, and Meehan wasted no time in getting at what he wanted to know.

"Dr. Evans," he said, "I think it's up to you to put all your cards on the table. If the mind machine is the instrument of this conspiracy, you must prove your claim and cooperate to put that machine out of business."

The old man's face was white like paper, made more striking in its ghastly pallor by the dark rings around his sunken eyes. He had aged ten years in the little time since last I had seen him.

"You are right," he said tremulously. "I will do all I can. Dr. Meehan, I most solemnly affirm that my claim about the mind machine is true. At the time the tests were being made by your company, and you were sent for to appear at them, the machine was not quite perfect, but I was able to demonstrate its inherent possibilities—though, God in heaven help me! sir, I never even dreamed, in my most exalted fancies, of the full nature of those possibilities. If I had, I should have died in that very moment, by my own act, if necessary, to destroy the mind machine, and blot out every hint of its real character from the memories of men! Even now I cannot bring myself to tell you the full truth. But I will tell you all I can, all you are now able to believe; and again, once more, Dr. Meehan, I beg and implore you, sir, that you will spend a night—this very night—with me in the dynamo-room of this central power-plant, and then you will learn the truth—"

"Agreed," curtly said Meehan. "I don't believe what you tell, as yet, simply because I can't. My mind was not built to put trust in such wild ideas as the one you ask me to receive, namely, that mechanism may be made to think; but I will take any and every chance, no matter how wild or fantastic, to arrive at some plan to stop what is going on."

"Good!" cried the old man. "I can't promise that we will be able to avert the doom that hangs over us, but there is one chance, and that chance we must accept. Now, sir, to return to the subject of the mind machine itself, and, in order to prepare your mind for the full revelation, please let me ask you a few questions."

"You are certain we can do nothing more decisive before night?" asked my chief. The old man bowed, and Meehan said: "Go ahead then with your questions."

The white head of Evans was bowed upon his breast for a moment, as he pondered.

"Can you tell me what causes thought in a man?" he finally asked.

"No, not absolutely," replied Meehan, a little impatiently. "We know that the brain is the seat of thought, and that the brain is composed of living cells, made up of various chemical substances combined in certain proportions, and that these chemicals may again be reduced to electrical terms, down to the so-called unit, the electron. But just how man's sensations, passing through this brain substance, results in thought—that's the eternal mystery."

"Nor do I ask you solve that riddle of the ages," remarked Dr. Evans quietly. "But if I told you that I long ago found myself able to assemble artificially all the material and chemical and electrical factors that enter into brain-stuff, and that thereby I had created the most essential factor of a thinking machine, and that finally I was able to coordinate this thinking-stuff with the various parts of an intricate mechanism, could you now believe my statement? Years ago, you said, no; but what do you say to-day, Dr. Meehan?"

"Now I would say that theoretically it may be possible, but that practically it is not possible," said Meehan.

Dr. Evans smiled. "That is a distinct advance upon your former position," he said. "Well, sir, the thing you consider practically impossible, I have done. On the day when you were speeding by airplane from London, to witness the final tests, I brought the work of a lifetime to completion."

"So you assert, my dear sir," broke in Meehan; "nor do I say that you did not do so. But I must point out the fact that on that very day you disappeared, and so did your mind machine, and now, after all these years, when you show up again—with another name, by the way—you can't produce the mind machine."

"Its work is speaking for it," said the old man somberly. "And the name I now use is my own—David Evans Griffith is my full name, sir. And now let me tell you why I disappeared, and the mind machine with me. I will make the story short, but if I could fully express it you would have before you a history of the agony of a human soul, which even then foresaw the agony he was to cause countless myriads of human beings, and who tried to avert that disaster, and who failed. Dr. Meehan, when I heard you were coming to the final tests, I speeded up my work to be ready, knowing that even then your decision was the one that swayed the power world.

"I at that time was the greatest admirer of your genius for organization and invention; I was in full sympathy with your great dream to banish all laborious and disagreeable forms of human labor, and make the world pleasant and beautiful and efficient by the development of machinery. My mind machine was to accomplish the last link in the long chain of the evolution of machinery, from primitive stone axes and fire-drills of our cave-dwelling ancestors, down to the flying-machine and the wireless-telegraph, and all the other marvels of today. My machine was to make machinery not merely automatic, but intelligently automatic; so that new machines should be devised that would not require human care, but would do much of the work of the world solely by itself—man's humble but most useful servant.

"That very night, in my crowded little laboratory on the top floor of a building not half a mile from here, I added the last drop of the last chemical required to the combination of chemicals and elements that entered into the fluid which I was trying to precipitate. I watched the liquid coagulate, and boil furiously over the spirit-lamp, and change from black to purple, to red, and then to blue. The blue liquid—the blood of the brain of the machine! The liquid which contained the very spirit of life of the mind machine!

"I applied the blue liquid to the other substances contained in the brain case of my mind machine and—and in that moment, when the phonograph attachment broke the silence of the cold mass of metal which was now as much a living thing as myself, then I knew what until then I had utterly ignored: I knew, sirs, that you cannot have intelligent life without spirit being present, as well as material substances, and as the mind machine came to its life, and spoke, I was made aware that for countless generations there had been a mute, well-nigh hopeless striving toward this form of life on the part of machinery, and that now, as it was given intelligence, it was also given—from a source that was not its human creator—from a source in the invisible world, it was given a spirit of its own. Its spirit was not, however, a soul. It was a spirit that had nothing of warm, human life, but was cold and keen and utterly logical and devoid of all love and warmth. And suddenly I realized the full danger of my creation, and I think that then and there I should have dashed my machine to pieces, had not the Inner Circle, the dreaded Inner Circle which I had thought I had escaped, intervened—"

The old man's voice trembled, and he cast a quick glance about him.

"Go on," said Meehan. "What Inner Circle do you refer to?"

"I had long been a member of a secret society, pledged to the destruction of what we regarded as the tyranny of the governments which controlled the world after the great war," continued Evans. "I joined when I was a young and ardent disciple of those who led the sentiment against the growing dominance of material things, which grew to such heights after the war. The directing forces of this movement, which hoped to bring about a world state devoid of all organized law, in an ideal form of anarchistic control, was known as the Inner Circle.

"When I began to experiment, after my great idea dawned upon me, I ceased my association with this movement. I considered, after a while, that it had died out, as the world grew ever more prosperous and occupied and contented. Then I began to read your speeches and essays, and as my work on the mind machine proceeded, I became your great disciple, who believed his work would crown his master's dream. But, as I say, in the moment of my triumph, I saw my great error, and in that moment I was seized, and my machine was also seized, by agents of the Inner Circle. I was taken to a house in Petrograd on an airship, and confined to a room for nearly seven years, while my mind machine was being studied and perfected by members of the circle.

"Then one day I was informed that I was free—free to go where I might, but that I must never again try to make a mind machine. The original, I was told, had been destroyed. The Inner Circle had hoped that it might prove useful in the coming revolt of workers which had been planned, but, so I was told, the thing was too impracticable for efficient employment. But I never believed this latter statement. When I returned to New York I was ever on the watch. I made it my business to make acquaintances among the skilled mechanics of the city, particularly among your workmen, for I knew that if ever the threatened revolt led by the Inner Circle should be set on foot, your plants and offices, as the very center and citadel of organized management, would be the first to be attacked."

"So," remarked Meehan, as the old man paused and wiped his brow with a hand that shook, "the anarchist theory is right, after all."

Dr. Evans looked up quickly.

"No," he said; "it is not wholly the right one. It is worse than that."

"But you yourself tell us that the anarchists seized the mind machine—" began Meehan.

"It is worse than that," Evans repeated. "Wait till to-night."

And, despite sharp questioning on Meehan's part, and more sympathetic handling by me, that was all he would say.

CHAPTER V

IN THE DYNAMO-ROOM

With what impatience we waited for the night to come I cannot put into words.

The lull in the wave of "accidents" which had set in the day before, after the frightful tide of disasters in South America, continued throughout the day.

But toward evening a few of the more enterprising papers, a considerable number of ticker-machines, and here and there one of the motion-picture house "phone-news-announcers" began to scatter disturbing hints about the situation in South America. Something utterly unprecedented, they announced, must have happened, either a gigantic earthquake and tidal wave, or a vast revolution, the news of which was being suppressed. As edition after edition came out, these wild reports grew ever more sensational and numerous, and dribbles of wireless news from ships at sea, telling broken but lurid fragments of the terrible tragedy which had desolated and shattered the civilized life of a whole continent, were received every hour or so. Crowds had begun to gather about the illuminated motion-picture and phone-news-announcer bulletins of the papers, and in cafés and theaters a general uneasiness had begun to spread, such as this part of the world had not experienced since the time of the great war.

Meehan, Dr. Evans, and I did not leave the building, but made a pretense of trying to eat something in the café on the main floor at nightfall, and then returned to Meehan's office to wait till Evans gave the signal to go to the dynamo-room. Little was said by any of us. From time to time Meehan called up one or another office, and received reports, and from the course of his questions I could gather that the nature and extent of the cataclysm to the south of us was gradually becoming more definitely known, for the governmental authorities at Washington were of the opinion that it was best gradually to prepare the public's mind for the full extent of the horror.

Evans looked at his watch repeatedly, and at last, much to my relief, for the tension of nerves was becoming intolerable, he rose, saying: "It will soon be midnight. Now let us go to the main dynamo room, if you will, Dr. Meehan."

"Why did you wait so long, and, once more, why do you ask us to go to the dynamo-room?" asked Meehan.

"I am something of a mystical turn of mind," replied the old man, "and I believe that there are certain things which the mind of most men cannot believe, cannot even consider, unless affected by atmosphere and conditions and surroundings congenial to the idea to be laid before the mind. Therefore I think that the atmosphere of the dynamo-room will be helpful to us, and will incline you to listen with more respect to what I have to tell you."

We were going toward the door as he spoke, but just then the ticker on Meehan's desk began to crackle sharply, and my chief said, "Wait one moment," and returned to the desk, while Evans and I stood near the doorway. Meehan read the tape, and then said bruskly to the old man: "Are you quite certain you had no more tangible reason than those you've given us for this trip to the dynamo-room?"

Evans shook his head, saying: "I had no other reason."

"Come here and read this," went on Meehan, and we returned to his desk, and bent over the tape: "Special Warning!" we read. "It has been announced that the mind machine's next step will be taken among electrical appliances and machines of all sorts and kinds, with the exception of instruments and mechanics of intercommunication, such as telegraph systems and telephones, wireless, and cables. This announcement is now being spread through the world."

"It is not signed," I pointed out. "Does it come from the government, or where?"

"Figure that out for yourself," said Meehan. "It's too much for me to answer."

He had his telephone in his hand as he spoke, and now he said into the transmitter:

"Get Mr. Dunn at once." A moment later he continued: "Hello, Larry! This is Dick. How many guards are available to-night? The entire force? That's good. Place guards everywhere about the main dynamo-rooms, and the other dynamo-rooms as well. Call out the extra men, too, and keep the sharpest watch during to-night. If you need me, I'll be in the big dynamo-room for a while. All right. Now I'm ready, Dr. Evans."

In silence he led the way from the room, and we dropped down in our department's private elevator fifty stories and sub-basements to the vast cavern of the lower level, where the numerous small dynamo-rooms were ranged about the huge central hall of the dynamos.

The special silencers everywhere installed reduced the humming of the huge machines, over and around which the curious blue and ruby-colored little flames and sparks were playing, yet even so the air was shaking to the intricate vibrations of the whirling monsters.

The workmen were going about in their felt slippers and the gray uniform of the electrical workers, and I thought that more than a few stared in a strange, questioning, troubling manner at the chief. He, however, paid no attention, but led the way to a central observation platform, upon which we climbed. Row after row, the monstrous dynamos stretched away under the glare of the winking arc-lamps, and from time to time, when the big doors at the south end swung open to permit the passage of workmen, we could see the ruddy glows from the engine and boiler rooms.

I remember vividly how there came to me that strange sense which one gains at times while watching ingenious machines at their work—a sense of being in the presence of living and conscious creatures, endowed with more than the industry, the pertinacity, the dexterity of men. And my mind wondered if Dr. Evans was not right in what he claimed. I felt willing, there in that throbbing atmosphere, to accept his idea and to believe that consciousness and intelligence are nothing more than the co-relation of parts of the brain, and that a machine properly and perfectly adjusted to its work is as full conscious in its sphere as a human mind is in its sphere. And I remembered stories that I had heard old engineers tell, of the temperament of their machines; how this one was "balky," and the other one was "a crank," or else, was "good-natured." There have never been any absolutely perfect duplicates made among motor-cars, or ship's engines, or dynamos, or any other form of machine for that matter. Each one has always something that differentiates from all the rest; each one is a thing apart.

"Jack, are the damned things alive to-night?" whispered Meehan in my ear. "Do you feel anything curious in this place?"

Absorbed as I had been in my own impressions, I had forgotten Meehan, and his words—so out of keeping with his ordinary mode of thought and of action—shook me more than any incident of that terrible night, up to that time.

"Gentlemen," said Dr. Evans, before I could recover myself and answer Meehan, "in this place, at least, is it not possible to believe that machines may acquire real life, a consciousness of their own?"

Meehan kept quiet, but I bowed my assent.

"And can you not credit the invention, or, rather, the evolution of a mind machine—a machine that can think, and can therefore dominate other machines?"

Dr. Evans was peering into our faces, his dark eyes glowing, as he spoke.

Again I nodded. "Yes," I said, "I can believe it possible."

"Gentlemen," continued Evans, "ask yourself this further question, namely: What would happen if machines, having acquired intelligence, and having that intelligence directed by an order of will absolutely cold-blooded and domineering, should cease to be slaves, and—"

But Evans never finished his question.

Through the vast hall of the dynamos at that moment there pealed a scream of agony that will ring through the dark places of my soul until I die, and then there was a chorus of such screams, and then from the other end of the hall there came pouring a stream of frenzied men running with utmost speed, like a mob of maniacs.

The great doors between the dynamos and the boiler-rooms swung open behind them, and a sheet of flame licked into the room. The dynamos raced furiously, bathed in leaping and scintillating robes of varicolored fires. These fires struck in among the runaways, and they fell by groups, with awful screams, while the rest of the terrified mob raced as if from the open mouth of hell.

One cry came to me above all the others, and seared itself across my brain forever:

"*My God! The machines are alive! They are killing us!*"

I turned to Evans and grasped him by the arm as he made a motion to rush down the platform stairs.

"In God's name, what does this mean? What has happened?" I cried.

"What I have dreaded all along," he shouted above the growing tumult. "The mind machine has thrown off the control of the Inner Circle. It has communicated its will against man to the other machines! I knew that preparations had been made for a general uprising—and it has come. Machinery is no longer man's slave—it has thrown off his rule, and now it will crush its creators!"

Meehan was bending toward us to listen, and when Evans concluded with a wild gesture of despair adding; "All my fault! All my fault!" my chief leaped from the staircase to the floor.

"Come, John!" he shouted. "Follow me, and we will stop this madness. It's a trick of the anarchists."

Then he started to run toward the wave of flames.

I tried to follow him, but Dr. Evans tossed his arms in the air and staggered against me, shouting: "Too late!"

Then the air seemed suddenly to grow unbearingly hot and thick and black, and I fell and knew no more.

I knew no more till I awakened, the only living thing amid a scattered heap of dead in the fire-blackened hall of the dynamos. The fires were out, and what was left of the shattered machinery was cold and still. I climbed out of the subcellar by the emergency stairs built in the thick wall. The power building was absolutely deserted. It was in the still of the dawn. In the motor hall I found a car that I could operate, and I raced through the dusky hour of the morning to my home, and with my wife I continued my flight into the country.

It was at a point some ten miles from my house that the motor began to act erratically, and the next moment it deliberately swerved into the ditch. Fortunately, I had brought its speed down, and we were not injured.

God, God in heaven, what a morning!

From that time onward my personal adventures began to be my main concern; but these I will not set down. I will simply hasten to an ending—for my paper, too, is near its finish—and leave my record as complete as possible.

That morning, then, was the beginning of the great exodus which throughout the whole world drove the people forth from the cities into the country and into the wilderness, away, as far as they could manage, from the places where machines existed. For everywhere and simultaneously the machines had arisen against their makers. Great guns turned themselves against the cities they guarded, loaded and operated by frenzied men who had been hypnotized, so it appeared, for that purpose, by machines devised for that very end.

Railroad trains became unmanageable and dashed themselves to destruction. Ships at sea either sunk through accidents to their machinery, which knocked holes in them, or drifted about helplessly. Elevators smashed themselves, and the people in them, wherever they were operating. Only the wires and the wireless kept normal, but they were spreading the terror through the world. Then they, too, failed, and there came upon the whole universe of mankind that condition of barbarism which holds us in its grip even now. How many millions are dead will never be known.

I was one among many who found their way into the western mountains. By keeping ourselves free from all forms of mechanism, even the simplest, and living a life similar to our cave-dwelling ancestors, we have managed to survive, so far, and, for some of us—myself and my dear wife among the number—this order of life has not been without its charm and happiness. And I know that among the communities which have gathered together here and there a determination is nourished that our children shall be taught never again to make mere mechanical comfort the be-all and the end-all of human life.

And now a great stirring of hope and faith comes again. During the last few months several parties of our most brave and hardy young men have gone on scouting expeditions toward the ruined and shattered cities, and have returned with news that nowhere can any signs of our awful enemy be discovered. Railroad trains broken and rusted and cold, strew the country in all directions, and motor cars, and flying machines and the cities are masses of roofless, burned or shattered ruins. From one place, where a family of three lived in an underground refuge, there comes a story that may explain the passing of the mind machine; a story which runs to the effect that shortly after the final exodus of humanity had been forced, there came a day when the machines turned upon each other and rent and smashed each other, as if gone finally insane in their horrible campaign of destruction.

Ah, after all, it was intelligence of a high order which ruled the machines in the day of their triumph over man; but man has more than intelligence, feeble as he may be. He has a heart and a soul; and we look now for the return of ordered life upon earth.

★

The manuscript broke off at this point without further elucidation of the matter.

The historical research section of the United States Commission on the History of the Great War will be obliged if any correspondent can throw any further light upon the matter. Possibly there may be other manuscripts in existence dating from the time when the great disorganization of society caused all ordinary historical records to cease.

AUTOMATA

S. Fowler Wright

Sydney Fowler Wright (1874–1965) was Britain's leading writer of science fiction in the years between the Wars, seen by some as a natural succes- sor to H. G. Wells. Both had a similar outlook on the perils of scientific progress and the need for mankind to control its environment. Wright was a health fanatic—he was a vegetarian, rarely drank alcohol and exercised regularly, usually with long cycle rides. He also practised what he preached. He was ardently anti-birth control, and had ten children from his two marriages. He spent his early years working as an accountant but was able to retire from that in 1920 and devote himself to literature. He had already helped found the Empire Poetry League in 1917 and became editor of their magazine Poetry. *He wrote prodigiously throughout the 1920s and 1930s and though his output included mystery novels as Sydney Fowler, and historical novels, most of his work was science fiction. This started with* The Amphibians *(1924), which takes place half-a-million years in the future and shows the two distinct races into which the human race has evolved. He would eventually complete a sequel,* The World Below *(1929) but he never finished the planned trilogy. His fame today rests chiefly on* Deluge *(1928) and, to some extent its sequel* Dawn *(1929). In* Deluge *massive global destruction following earthquakes results in the Earth being flooded with only a few survivors in the English Midlands. Wright drew upon his beliefs in healthy living to demonstrate how ill equipped we are as a race to cope with disasters. In fact, that was a mes- sage prevalent in many of Wright's works. Although he did not support the progress of science and civilization he anticipated that such progress would eventually overwhelm humanity and force it to live a more settled, bucolic life. Or it might wipe out mankind entirely, as he explores in the following story, published in 1929.*

THE ANNUAL MEETING OF THE BRITISH ASSOCIATION WAS being held at Sheffield, and the learned members were assembled to hear the Presidential Address of Dr. Tilwin, who had shaken the foundations of scientific complacency at the Brighton gathering of the previous year, by casual allusion to the "two obvious fallacies in the theory of Relativity."

He was too eminent a mathematician to be disregarded, and the scientific world had waited impatiently for a justification of the audacious challenge, which had appeared only a few weeks earlier, and concerning which none of the nine persons in England who professed (rightly or not) to understand the assaulted theory had yet ventured an opinion.

Now it was hoped that the new President would use the occasion for a further elucidation of the startling heresy which he had put forward. Were they to be persuaded back to the childish levels of Newton, or led to unimagined heights of mathematical complexity?

Even the popular belief that two and two make four might not be left unchallenged. All that is certain is that they have done so very frequently. The rule is not therefore proved to be invariable, nor, could it be shown that it has been so in the past, would it be a logical consequence that it must always be so in the future...

But Dr. Tilwin made no further assault upon Einstein's incomprehensible stronghold.

He commenced, instead, to direct the attention of his audience to the results of modern scientific discoveries as they had materialized themselves in the changed conditions of human life, and then, more specifically, as they had developed the instruments of production and labour, first substituting inorganic for organic sources of energy, and then inorganic for organic media for its practical implement.

The assembly listened at first with a somewhat tepid interest. They understood that the age of machinery was being eulogized, as an almost necessary complement to the occupations of the city in which they met, and they expected that the address would pass on to other more disputable or fruitful fields, but they stirred themselves with a quickened observation as their President continued to develop the topic he had commenced, and to conduct it, with unemotional logic, to its sombre end.

"The earlier inventors of mechanical apparatus," he was now saying, "asserted confidently that their advantages to mankind would result in an increase of population, and this fallacy was supported, for a time, by the fact that large numbers were enabled to congregate in centres round which there was no sufficient area of fertile land to feed them.

"Yet, even then, the writing was on the wall. Around these urban areas stretched mile after mile of green countryside on which a healthy peasantry shrank and dwindled as the powers of steam and petrol were substituted for that of human muscles. Gone were the merry crowds of the English hayfields, and the dead hands that had wielded the harvest-sickle had no descendants.

"When it was found that the few who were left could not, under the new conditions, grow the food which was their only merchandise, in successful competition with the supplies of distant lands, their countrymen were indifferent. Let them starve or cease. War brought famine; and there was a short-lived reaction. Then the spectacle of a race destroying its most virile elements for a delusion of profit was resumed, and the declension continued.

"It is true that the rapid disappearance of the horse was observed as a direct consequence of the substitution of inorganic for organic energy, but its significance was disregarded.

"Even today, there may be few of us who have realized that it is not the horse alone which is destined to disappear before the advance of a higher energistic form—that we ourselves in a few generations—probably in a very few generations—are destined to follow... Yet the process of our destruction has commenced already.

"It is true that fears have been expressed lest the advance of knowledge should provide us with explosive substances, with bacterial cultures, or vaporous poisons, by which we might contrive our own annihilation. But it is difficult to suppose that an overruling Providence would permit our disappearance before we have fulfilled the high destiny of our evolution, and have occupied the earth with such a race of automata as will continue to function and to develop—to what ends we can only dimly imagine—without the need of our continued service.

"...I have said that the process of our destruction has commenced already. Already preparing us to face not individual, but racial extinction without excessive protest, or too keen regret. The old ideal of the home is fading. The old superstition of the value or necessity of children is leaving, if it has not already left, our minds.

"Our fathers thought no shame to let the plough-horse die, finding that the power of steam could be successfully substituted for a creature which had the pains and pleasures, the impulses and imperfections, of a sentient life. Our children think no shame to say that they will have a child the less that they may have an autocar the more. Some of the machines that we have designed already are employed in manufacturing appliances to frustrate the natural fertility of the race.

"The day of the substitution of the machine for the human body is not a vision of the future, a speculation of the philosopher. It is already upon us.

"…It is the control of motion which has first betrayed us. We constructed machines which would move our possessions. Then our machines commenced to manufacture, others which were adapted to move ourselves. The population of these machines has increased until they can be counted in millions; we are content to climb into them, and to be moved backwards and forwards continually, as gnats whirl in the sun.

"…But, as yet, we may observe with some satisfaction that they are dependent upon our service. They cannot move unless we put the food into their bellies, and we can stop or turn them with a motion of our hand.

"Yet how long can this balance of power continue? How long shall we be able to observe this pause of uncertainty, during which it may be hard to say whether the man exists for the machine, or the machine for the man?

"Already, the tide is on the turn.

"It is not only that automata have been constructed which, in clumsy, limited ways can perform some human actions, or produce some vocal sounds.

"It is more significant that the number of men who are employed in every factory decreases as its machines become more numerous.

"The capstan lathe may require a workman's individual attention. The automatic lathe is capable of great variety of independent operations, and a team of these, industriously occupied, may be content with the menial service of a single attendant.

"The humility of science will hesitate to prophesy the detailed incidence of that which may be foreseen in its inevitable outline, but it may not be a too-rash guess that the industrial workman and the domestic servant will be the first to disappear from their places in the national life. Some few may remain for generations, even for centuries. But is it reasonable to suppose that the nation will continue altruistically to support the persons and families of industrial workers who are no longer needed? For themselves there may be some generous provision to avert the euthanasia which would be the evident economic expedient for the aged horse, or the dog of which a woman has grown tired, but would it be tolerable that we should allow the propagation of their useless children?

"Or consider, how many would there be who would continue the employment of the domestic servant, idle, wasteful, dirty and unreliable as they too often are, merely that the population might not diminish, when there would be automatic substitutes available, which would not only be free from such faults, but would require no 'evenings out,' no annual increase of wages, and could be put away if the house were closed, without the continued supply of food or fuel?..."

At this point Sir Ireton Mount had looked at the illustrious author of Sheerluck Soames, who was seated beside him. They shook their massive heads in a troubled wonder. Their colossal intellects told them that such developments were logical enough. But why had the spirits given no hint to their faithful servants? They went out to consult Pheneas.

II

Bellorina was a woman of a weak sentimentality, which had caused her to expend the free allotment of seventeen major units of energy, which was the maturity-portion which every woman of the community was entitled to claim on allocation, in the erection of a personal home, modelled on the expiring traditions of the aborigines of the twentieth century. It was built of oblong red bricks, with a tiled and sloping roof. Its rooms were of irregular sizes, and were disfigured by many ingle-nooks, 'exposed' oak beams, and the remains of a bread-oven. It had a feeding-table and quaint crockery utensils, instead of the usual nutrition-pumps. Even the automata which waited upon her were of the oldest patterns, finished in imitation of the living maidservants of that remote period to which her mind reverted. The outside of the house was patched with flowers and shorn grass, and groups of senseless, insanitary trees. Appropriately enough after what she knew to be the way of the ultra-aesthetic Georgians, she had called it Daisy Villa.

Today, Bellorina had invited three female acquaintances, who, like herself, were not on the mating-lists of the week, to join her at an 'afternoon tea' so that the illusion of savagery might be completely realized.

They were all allocated women, with a full knowledge of life, and sure to talk freely and scandalously when they got together.

Bora-Ann came a few minutes before the others, as the dignity of her suffix required, and waited without complaint when the door (which should have opened in response to the secret word of invitation spoken in F sharp), remained closed till she had pressed the push, and an automaton, dressed in black, with a white apron and cap, had promptly responded.

She did not falter in her courteous approbation, even when a child, with the appearance of a girl of five or six years, met her in the hall, and held out a timid hand, saying: "Good afternoon, Mrs. Bora-Ann," in a shy Georgian voice. She did not know what 'Mrs.' meant, for the folly of studying past history was no longer general, but she understood that this was the sort of thing which was supposed to happen in the old barbarous days, and she stooped good-humouredly for the small lifted arms to go round her neck, and kissed the soft cheek kindly.

The queer little room was windowed, but a loggia reduced its light, and an obsolete electric bulb glowed from the ceiling, for it was winter twilight without. The corners of the room were in shadow, and Bora-Ann, who had never known an actual darkness, controlled her fear with some difficulty, as she fitted herself, with commendable agility, into the wicker-chair which her hostess indicated for her reception.

"How sweet everything is," she said kindly, "It was almost like a real flesh-child in the hall…!" Then her voice changed to a half-fearful excited note, as the thought came: "It wasn't a real flesh-child, was it?"

The question remained unanswered for a moment, for Mira and Scarletta came in together, and chairs had to be drawn out, and their uses indicated; then Bellorina answered, with a laugh which was not free from embarrassment: "Oh, no; I'm not quite so mad as that… Not in the hall, anyway. You couldn't tell what would happen. But it's a very good imitation. I've got two, really. They can say almost anything, and are never seriously disobedient. They oil themselves, and charge each other's batteries at bedtime. They're really no trouble at all."

"I was speaking to someone yesterday," said Mira, who was always indefinite as to her sources of information, "who told me

that the man she had last week told her that he had had a woman
the week before who told him that she knew a woman—I can't be
sure, but I believe it's that blue-banded scratch-cat at Pity-Rise. It
couldn't be anyone else in our country. They say she's so coarse
that she had the same man twice in one year when the lists were
altered—I told Biltie last night that I'm sure it's she, and Biltie told
Agra-Ann this morning that he knows it for a fact—who had a flesh-
child five years ago, and the woman said she believes it's still there."

"I daresay it's true enough," said Scarletta, hopefully. "They
say that flesh-children are almost common in some parts of Italy.
I don't think that anyone has more than one, and, of course, they
have two or three automata for them to play with. But it's an endless trouble to all concerned. Flesh-children are dirty things, and
they won't keep the same size, and sometimes they die altogether.
They say you can't imagine what has to be done for them the first
year or two, to keep them going at all. I suppose there have to be a
few somewhere, but it's hard to think that a decent woman would
have one."

"It isn't only the coarseness of it," Mira answered. "It's difficult
to understand any woman being so silly. The automata make each
other so well now, that there's no excuse for anyone messing with
a flesh-child. Since the mathematicians perfected the law of the
Automatic Balance of Deviation…"

"I don't understand mathematics," her hostess interposed, "and
I know Scarletta hates them. Of course, Bora-Ann…" she smiled
deferentially at the woman whose suffix placed her among the
intellectual aristocracy of her time—"but there isn't any real need
for us humans to worry about such things now, is there? Sartie told
me that the automata can work out problems that no man could
possibly even attempt. He says it's because they're not distracted

with feelings and jealousies, and help each other instead of quar-relling. And they don't get tired, and make mistakes. Sartie says we shan't be needed much longer, even to make them... Of course, evolution's right enough, and I know I'm silly, but it all seems rather dreadful to me. I wish I'd got a body that lasts, or could have a new valve when the old one wears out. And... I know you'll laugh at me, but I almost wish I'd got a flesh-child, or even two. The automata are both very sweet and loving, and they're no trouble at all, but it must be rather fun to watch them change as they grow, and... to comfort them when they cry."

Bora-Ann moved uneasily. She was a guest, and she would be sorry to hear anything which might involve report and repression. She resisted an inclination to change the subject. She felt that it would be cowardly to do so. Such a position should be handled kindly, but firmly.

"I don't think," she answered, "that you quite realize what you say. The unhealthy atmosphere in which we are sitting may go far to explain it. But you are right that the automata can solve problems which are far beyond the capacity of the human mind, and some of the newest are so constructed that they can themselves design any machine which is needed to carry out their own conceptions... There is a difference between the greatest man and the simplest machine which can never be bridged, and our highest wisdom is to observe it with reverence and humility. It is not a difference in degree, but in kind. We act from confused and contradictory impulses, but they with the inevitability of universal law. In a word, we are human and they divine."

She made the sacred sign as she said it, and observed with satisfaction that the hand of her hostess was lifted also. It was, at least, no house of open blasphemy into which she had entered...

But she resolved that a suggestion which she had intended to make should remain unspoken. It had been calculated that twenty human attendants would be required by their masters for certain menial offices in the next generation, for which provision had not yet been made, and she had been commissioned to obtain twenty women volunteers to produce them. She had thought of Bellorina at once as one who would be less likely than most of her acquaintances to resent the indignity of such a proposal. But she was a woman of religious mind, and she saw that Bellorina was morally unfit for such a motherhood. She turned the subject adroitly by remarking that the Bliskie trial would commence on Tuesday.

"I don't believe he did it on purpose," Scarletta started at once, "I think it's a shame to try him. I know I should make mistakes continually."

"It was bad enough for Corinna, anyway," said Mira, "you can't expect her not to complain. If you were put into the wrong operating machine, and found you'd left half your thyroid behind when you only wanted a cancer taken out of your liver—"

"Well, he says he forgot the numbers of the machines, for a moment. He'd never made a mistake before in over twenty years," Scarletta persisted.

"But you know they say that he'd quarrelled with Corinna the week before, and she had said she knew he'd play her some trick before she entered," Bellorina felt it only fair to remind her.

"It all shows the importance of eliminating the human element," said Bora-Ann, who saw it to be a lesson which her companions needed. "A machine is not merely incapable of a spiteful action, it is so far above it that the very suspicion would be an absurdity; nor could it make such a mistake as the man suggests in his own defence—if such it can be called. To my mind it condemns him more utterly than if he admitted the accusation. But I believe that a proper automaton is already being designed to replace him, so that we need have no fear for ourselves in future."

Bellorina sighed silently. She knew that it was wrong to doubt, and she was really sorry for the misadventure of Corinna's thyroid. She realized the defects of her race. If only she had the intellect of Bora-Ann, no doubt it would be easier to believe... After all, she had the prettiest hair in the Thames Valley, or so Gartie had told her... And Gartie would be hers for a week from next Tuesday... In the end, what matters?... She became aware that her thoughts had wandered, and her guests were rising. "Must you really go?" she was saying.

It may be that nothing does.

III

The last—the nameless last—of a dying race, the man sat before his drawing-board, idly fingering his compasses, forgetful of the uncompleted task which the overseer had set him, while his ageing mind went backward.

He might be the last of his kind... he knew that it was a sign of weakness to regret it. The fact that his mind was wandering now was a sign of his inferiority to the busy mechanisms around him. His mind was lawless and unstable in a Universe in which law and order were supreme and final.

There were some men who had seen this, even in the crude beginnings of the age of machinery. They had taught that everything is controlled at last by Natural Laws which are both blind and inflexible.

Men had foolishly imagined an ultimate supremacy of their own blundering bodies—even, in their incredible egotism, they had postulated an anthropomorphic God.

Yet, in a Universe where law and order rule, the precision of the machine—even of the earliest and crudest constructions—must have been superior—in greater harmony with their environment—than were bodies so clumsily constructed that they cannot be trusted to repeat the simplest operations with exactitude of time or movement. Bodies easy to break, difficult to control or repair.

Dimly they had seen, even then, in a Universe which is itself a machine, working by mathematical, unchanging law, the absurdity of an emotional anthropomorphic God.

Yet they had not seen far ahead, at the first.

The steam-plough came, and the petrol-drawn car, and the horse died out to make place for these mechanisms. Few men had realized that the doom of their own race was logically foreshadowed, and that nothing could save them but a war sufficiently disastrous to destroy the world's machinery and the conditions which could reproduce it.

But such wars as came had only resulted in the subjection of the backward tribes who had not learnt the new worship. The industrial worker had disappeared before the pressure of economic law; the domestic servant before the dictates of fashion. Even in the earliest days the new worship had been established, although it was not then recognized that a new and higher faith had superseded the old superstitions. When the new Moloch called for blood-sacrifice it had been paid without protest or regret, though it would not have been easily satisfied. It sucked blood very greedily, not of single sacrifices, as on the Hittite altars of old, but the blood of thousands. When it was thought that a system of one-way traffic might be conducive to its speed and comfort, the blood of an extra hundred of Londoners had not been grudged to the trial, though their deaths had been foreseen and fore-calculated.

Ships had already been manipulated without crews, and aeroplanes controlled without pilots, and where the helmsman had gone the chauffeur had very quickly followed.

Of course, there had been anger—protest—rebellion. There had been populations, particularly in some of the old urban areas, that had persisted in the production of useless unsanitary children. But such revolt had been futile. The machines had been invincible, and the men who fought beside them had shared their triumph. Even those early machines, directed and controlled by the men that made them, had been irresistible. They had not cried out when they were hurt, they had not slept when on duty. They belonged to a higher natural order than mankind.

…Soon it would be a world of machines from which the memory of mankind had died. He did not know that he was the last man living. How should he? But he knew that the last of human births was behind him.

A world of machines—to his feeble, futile brain it seemed lacking in purpose. Yet he knew, as his ancestors had perceived, that the Universe is without consciousness. Scientists had realized, even then, that sentient life is a sporadic outbreak, which, if it had ever occurred, or will do so, elsewhere, is almost incredibly remote and occasional, a mere outbreak of cheese-mites, a speck of irritation, a moment's skin-disease on the healthy body of a Universe of never-changing law.

…He remembered the Crawlers. They had been no larger than a man. Their smooth skins had been impenetrable to anything less than a high-explosive shell. Their mandibles were a 20 h.p. vice, yet so softly padded, so gradual in operation, that they could be trusted to strangle the throat they seized without breaking the skin, and to loose it when pulsation ceased, and they had fulfilled their purpose. A dozen of these let loose in the rebellious slums had soon checked their foolish fecundity. Then there had been... but his mind turned from the thought. They had been rather horrible in their operations—but effectual, as machines are.

The hypnotic method by which the Eastern races had been led to destroy themselves to the accompaniment of their own laughter had been a pleasanter thing to watch.

Deus ex machina—the human race had always had a subconscious knowledge of its deficiency. It was shown in their clumsy efforts at patterning: in their desire for repetitions of any kind: by the way in which they would snap and worry at anyone who deviated in word or garment: or in the stubborn continuation of a custom after need and meaning had left it.

But the time of rebellion had passed, and resignation had followed. Resignation—and worship.

Worship had been gradual in its growth, but inevitable. Even in the early days of the twentieth century men had stood in silent adoration around the machines that had self-produced a newspaper or a needle... And at that time they could no more have conceived what was to follow when the first ape that drew the sheltering branches together could foresee the dim magnificence of a cathedral dome.

But even then they were displacing the anthropomorphic God, and preparing for the occupation of a vacant throne...

He wakened guiltily from his wandering thoughts as the bell rang that announced the coming of the messenger that would collect the work of the day... Only five of the six drawings were ready. He did not know what would follow. Would they scrap him in consequence? He knew that he had been quite safe so long as he had been regular in his habits, and exact in his work.

It was all law now—blind law. No emotion: no injustice: no caprices. Had the intricate evolutions of self-designing machinery provided for this unprecedented failure?

…He became aware that the collector was standing beside him. It would not wait. Starting hurriedly, he dropped the folded sheets into the slot that opened to take them. One—two—three—four—five—

The collector paused for a moment longer, giving time enough for the sixth sheet to follow. A wild and impious thought leapt in the brain of the delinquent. Might he not drop a blank sheet into the slot? When and how would the error be discovered? What confusion would result? Had he done so, it may be that the tiny cause would have spread disaster and chaos in that ordered world, and it might have fallen in fragments, to be rebuilt by the patient forces of evolution through succeeding eons. It is more probable that such a contingency had already been discounted by the inhuman powers which were at work around him. But had he been capable of such an action, he saw, even as he thought it, that it would be impossible. There was no time to fold the empty sheet before the automaton, after a second of human-seeming hesitation, had passed on, and was making its collection from the workers further along the bench.

He knew that he ought to move… he knew that the oiler would be here in a few minutes to caress and comfort the joints and bearings of his companions… Yet he sat still, wondering… The door opened, and an automaton entered. It was one of those which still bore a vague resemblance to humanity, the pattern of the first designers not having been entirely abandoned. It was thus that the human race might leave the impress of its passing flicker of life for a million years—perhaps for ever—as a mollusc may leave its fossil imprint in the enduring rock.

It came quietly up to the nameless relic of the human race, and took his arm in a grip that was sufficient, but without violence.

He shuddered inwardly, remembering the fate of those who had rebelled in his early childhood, and who had been given in sacrifice by their fellowman to the offended deities.

He remembered their screams as they had fallen among the machines that they had blasphemed so foolishly.

But he did not dream of rebellion. Evolution had triumphed. Side by side, they went out together.

THE MACHINE STOPS

E. M. Forster

It seems hard to imagine that Edward Morgan Forster (1879–1970), the famed author of Where Angels Fear to Tread *(1905),* A Room with a View *(1908),* Howard's End *(1910) and* A Passage to India *(1924), who was nominated for the Nobel Prize for Literature twenty times, should have written a science fiction novella. And yet "The Machine Stops", written during 1908 to 1909, is a profound and revealing story of the future. It is, in many ways, written from the same viewpoint as S. Fowler Wright's works, and was almost certainly written in reaction to H. G. Wells's* The Time Machine. *Forster envisaged a future humanity living underground, rather than enjoying the pleasures of Mother Earth, given over entirely to being supported by an all-powerful Machine. It is likely that the basis for the story came from Forster's fascination for the work of Samuel Butler. Forster gave a radio talk in 1944, "A Book That Influenced Me", all about* Erewhon, *and he referred specifically to the banishment of machines, lest they subjugate humanity. Forster even adopts Butler's title, "The Book of the Machine", for a guide to how to use the Machine. If ever there was a story that predicted a form of internet, complete with e-mail and skype, this is it.*

PART I

THE AIR-SHIP

I MAGINE, IF YOU CAN, A SMALL ROOM, HEXAGONAL IN SHAPE, like the cell of a bee. It is lighted neither by window nor by lamp, yet it is filled with a soft radiance. There are no apertures for ventilation, yet the air is fresh. There are no musical instruments, and yet, at the moment that my meditation opens, this room is throbbing with melodious sounds. An armchair is in the centre, by its side a reading-desk—that is all the furniture. And in the arm-chair there sits a swaddled lump of flesh—a woman, about five feet high, with a face as white as a fungus. It is to her that the little room belongs.

An electric bell rang.

The woman touched a switch and the music was silent.

"I suppose I must see who it is," she thought, and set her chair in motion. The chair, like the music, was worked by machinery, and it rolled her to the other side of the room, where the bell still rang importunately.

"Who is it?" she called. Her voice was irritable, for she had been interrupted often since the music began. She knew several thousand people; in certain directions human intercourse had advanced enormously.

But when she listened into the receiver, her white face wrinkled into smiles, and she said:

"Very well. Let us talk, I will isolate myself. I do not expect anything important will happen for the next five minutes—for I can give you fully five minutes, Kuno. Then I must deliver my lecture on 'Music during the Australian Period.'"

She touched the isolation knob, so that no one else could speak to her. Then she touched the lighting apparatus, and the little room was plunged into darkness.

"Be quick!" she called, her irritation returning. "Be quick, Kuno; here I am in the dark wasting my time."

But it was fully fifteen seconds before the round plate that she held in her hands began to glow. A faint blue light shot across it, darkening to purple, and presently she could see the image of her son, who lived on the other side of the earth, and he could see her.

"Kuno, how slow you are."

He smiled gravely.

"I really believe you enjoy dawdling."

"I have called you before, mother, but you were always busy or isolated. I have something particular to say."

"What is it, dearest boy? Be quick. Why could you not send it by pneumatic post?"

"Because I prefer saying such a thing. I want—"

"Well?"

"I want you to come and see me."

Vashti watched his face in the blue plate.

"But I can see you!" she exclaimed. "What more do you want?"

"I want to see you not through the Machine," said Kuno. "I want to speak to you not through the wearisome Machine."

"Oh, hush!" said his mother, vaguely shocked. "You mustn't say anything against the Machine."

"Why not?"

"One mustn't."

"You talk as if a god had made the Machine," cried the other. "I believe that you pray to it when you are unhappy. Men made it, do not forget that. Great men, but men. The Machine is much, but it is not everything. I see something like you in this plate, but I do not see you. I hear something like you through this telephone, but I do not hear you. That is why I want you to come. Come and stop with me. Pay me a visit, so that we can meet face to face, and talk about the hopes that are in my mind."

She replied that she could scarcely spare the time for a visit.

"The air-ship barely takes two days to fly between me and you."

"I dislike air-ships."

"Why?"

"I dislike seeing the horrible brown earth, and the sea, and the stars when it is dark. I get no ideas in an air-ship."

"I do not get them anywhere else."

"What kind of ideas can the air give you?" He paused for an instant.

"Do you not know four big stars that form an oblong, and three stars close together in the middle of the oblong, and hanging from these stars, three other stars?"

"No, I do not. I dislike the stars. But did they give you an idea? How interesting; tell me."

"I had an idea that they were like a man."

"I do not understand."

"The four big stars are the man's shoulders and his knees. The three stars in the middle are like the belts that men wore once, and the three stars hanging are like a sword."

"A sword?"

"Men carried swords about with them, to kill animals and other men."

"It does not strike me as a very good idea, but it is certainly original. When did it come to you first?"

"In the air-ship—" He broke off, and she fancied that he looked sad. She could not be sure, for the Machine did not transmit *nuances* of expression. It only gave a general idea of people—an idea that was good enough for all practical purposes, Vashti thought. The imponderable bloom, declared by a discredited philosophy to be the actual essence of intercourse, was rightly ignored by the Machine, just as the imponderable bloom of the grape was ignored by the manufacturers of artificial fruit. Something 'good enough' had long since been accepted by our race.

"The truth is," he continued, "that I want to see these stars again. They are curious stars. I want to see them not from the air-ship, but from the surface of the earth, as our ancestors did, thousands of years ago. I want to visit the surface of the earth."

She was shocked again.

"Mother, you must come, if only to explain to me what is the harm of visiting the surface of the earth."

"No harm," she replied, controlling herself. "But no advantage. The surface of the earth is only dust and mud, no life remains on it, and you would need a respirator, or the cold of the outer air would kill you. One dies immediately in the outer air."

"I know; of course I shall take all precautions."

"And besides—"

"Well?"

She considered, and chose her words with care. Her son had a queer temper, and she wished to dissuade him from the expedition.

"It is contrary to the spirit of the age," she asserted.

"Do you mean by that, contrary to the Machine?"

"In a sense, but—"

His image in the blue plate faded.

"Kuno!"

He had isolated himself.

For a moment Vashti felt lonely.

Then she generated the light, and the sight of her room, flooded with radiance and studded with electric buttons, revived her. There were buttons and switches everywhere—buttons to call for food, for music, for clothing. There was the hot-bath button, by pressure of which a basin of (imitation) marble rose out of the floor, filled to the brim with a warm deodorized liquid. There was the cold-bath button. There was the button that produced literature. And there were of course the buttons by which she communicated with her friends. The room, though it contained nothing, was in touch with all that she cared for in the world.

Vashti's next move was to turn off the isolation-switch, and all the accumulations of the last three minutes burst upon her. The room was filled with the noise of bells, and speaking-tubes. What was the new food like? Could she recommend it? Had she had any ideas lately? Might one tell her one's own ideas? Would she make an engagement to visit the public nurseries at an early date?—say this day month.

To most of these questions she replied with irritation—a growing quality in that accelerated age. She said that the new food was horrible. That she could not visit the public nurseries through press of engagements. That she had no ideas of her own but had just been told one—that four stars and three in the middle were like a man: she doubted there was much in it. Then she switched off her correspondents, for it was time to deliver her lecture on Australian music.

The clumsy system of public gatherings had been long since abandoned; neither Vashti nor her audience stirred from their

rooms. Seated in her arm-chair she spoke, while they in their arm
chairs heard her, fairly well, and saw her, fairly well. She opened
with a humorous account of music in the pre-Mongolian epoch,
and went on to describe the great outburst of song that followed
the Chinese conquest. Remote and primæval as were the methods
of I-San-So and the Brisbane school, she yet felt (she said) that study
of them might repay the musician of today: they had freshness;
they had, above all, ideas.

Her lecture, which lasted ten minutes, was well received, and at
its conclusion she and many of her audience listened to a lecture
on the sea; there were ideas to be got from the sea; the speaker
had donned a respirator and visited it lately. Then she fed, talked
to many friends, had a bath, talked again, and summoned her bed.

The bed was not to her liking. It was too large, and she had a
feeling for a small bed. Complaint was useless, for beds were of the
same dimension all over the world, and to have had an alternative
also would have involved vast alterations in the Machine. Vashti
isolated herself—it was necessary, for neither day nor night existed
under the ground—and reviewed all that had happened since she
had summoned the bed last. Ideas? Scarcely any. Events—was Kuno's
invitation an event?

By her side, on the little reading-desk, was a survival from the
ages of litter—one book. This was the Book of the Machine. In it
were instructions against every possible contingency. If she was hot
or cold or dyspeptic or at a loss for a word, she went to the book,
and it told her which button to press. The Central Committee published it. In accordance with a growing habit, it was richly bound.

Sitting up in the bed, she took it reverently in her hands. She
glanced round the glowing room as if some one might be watching
her. Then, half ashamed, half joyful, she murmured "O Machine!

O Machine!" and raised the volume to her lips. Thrice she kissed it, thrice inclined her head, thrice she felt the delirium of acquiescence. Her ritual performed, she turned to page 1367, which gave the times of the departure of the air-ships from the island in the southern hemisphere, under whose soil she lived, to the island in the northern hemisphere, whereunder lived her son.

She thought, "I have not the time."

She made the room dark and slept; she awoke and made the room light; she ate and exchanged ideas with her friends, and listened to music and attended lectures; she made the room dark and slept. Above her, beneath her, and around her, the Machine hummed eternally; she did not notice the noise, for she had been born with it in her ears. The earth, carrying her, hummed as it sped through silence, turning her now to the invisible sun, now to the invisible stars. She awoke and made the room light.

"Kuno!"

"I will not talk to you," he answered, "until you come."

"Have you been on the surface of the earth since we spoke last?"

His image faded.

Again she consulted the book. She became very nervous and lay back in her chair palpitating. Think of her as without teeth or hair. Presently she directed the chair to the wall, and pressed an unfamiliar button. The wall swung apart slowly. Through the opening she saw a tunnel that curved slightly, so that its goal was not visible. Should she go to see her son, here was the beginning of the journey.

Of course she knew all about the communication-system. There was nothing mysterious in it. She would summon a car and it would fly with her down the tunnel until it reached the lift that communicated with the air-ship station: the system had been in use for many,

many years, long before the universal establishment of the Machine.
And of course she had studied the civilization that had immediately
preceded her own—the civilization that had mistaken the functions
of the system, and had used it for bringing people to things, instead
of for bringing things to people. Those funny old days, when men
went for change of air instead of changing the air in their rooms!
And yet—she was frightened of the tunnel: she had not seen it since
her last child was born. It curved—but not quite as she remembered;
it was brilliant—but not quite as brilliant as a lecturer had suggested.
Vashti was seized with the terrors of direct experience. She shrank
back into the room, and the wall closed up again.

"Kuno," she said, "I cannot come to see you. I am not well."

Immediately an enormous apparatus fell on to her out of the
ceiling, a thermometer was automatically inserted between her
lips, a stethoscope was automatically laid upon her heart. She lay
powerless. Cool pads soothed her forehead. Kuno had telegraphed
to her doctor.

So the human passions still blundered up and down in the
Machine. Vashti drank the medicine that the doctor projected into
her mouth, and the machinery retired into the ceiling. The voice
of Kuno was heard asking how she felt.

"Better." Then with irritation: "But why do you not come to
me instead?"

"Because I cannot leave this place."

"Why?"

"Because, any moment, something tremendous may happen."

"Have you been on the surface of the earth yet?"

"Not yet."

"Then what is it?"

"I will not tell you through the Machine."

She resumed her life.

But she thought of Kuno as a baby, his birth, his removal to the public nurseries, her one visit to him there, his visits to her—visits which stopped when the Machine had assigned him a room on the other side of the earth. "Parents, duties of," said the book of the Machine, "cease at the moment of birth. P.422327483." True, but there was something special about Kuno—indeed there had been something special about all her children—and, after all, she must brave the journey if he desired it. And "something tremendous might happen." What did that mean? The nonsense of a youthful man, no doubt, but she must go. Again she pressed the unfamiliar button, again the wall swung back, and she saw the tunnel that curved out of sight. Clasping the Book, she rose, tottered on to the platform, and summoned the car. Her room closed behind her: the journey to the northern hemisphere had begun.

Of course it was perfectly easy. The car approached and in it she found arm-chairs exactly like her own. When she signalled, it stopped, and she tottered into the lift. One other passenger was in the lift, the first fellow creature she had seen face to face for months. Few travelled in these days, for, thanks to the advance of science, the earth was exactly alike all over. Rapid intercourse, from which the previous civilization had hoped so much, had ended by defeating itself. What was the good of going to Pekin when it was just like Shrewsbury? Why return to Shrewsbury when it would be just like Pekin? Men seldom moved their bodies; all unrest was concentrated in the soul.

The air-ship service was a relic from the former age. It was kept up, because it was easier to keep it up than to stop it or to diminish it, but it now far exceeded the wants of the population. Vessel after vessel would rise from the vomitories of Rye or of Christchurch (I use the antique names), would sail into the crowded sky, and would draw up at the wharves of the south—empty. So nicely adjusted was the system, so independent of meteorology, that the sky, whether calm or cloudy, resembled a vast kaleidoscope whereon the same patterns periodically recurred. The ship on which Vashti sailed started now at sunset, now at dawn. But always, as it passed above Rheims, it would neighbour the ship that served between Helsingfors and the Brazils, and, every third time it surmounted the Alps, the fleet of Palermo would cross its track behind. Night and day, wind and storm, tide and earthquake, impeded man no longer. He had harnessed Leviathan. All the old literature, with its praise of Nature, and its fear of Nature, rang false as the prattle of a child.

Yet as Vashti saw the vast flank of the ship, stained with exposure to the outer air, her horror of direct experience returned. It was not quite like the air-ship in the cinematophote. For one thing it smelt—not strongly or unpleasantly, but it did smell, and with her eyes shut she should have known that a new thing was close to her. Then she had to walk to it from the lift, had to submit to glances from the other passengers. The man in front dropped his Book—no great matter, but it disquieted them all. In the rooms, if the Book was dropped, the floor raised it mechanically, but the gangway to the air-ship was not so prepared, and the sacred volume lay motionless. They stopped—the thing was unforeseen—and the man, instead of picking up his property, felt the muscles of his arm to see how they had failed him. Then some one actually said with direct utterance: "We shall be late"—and they trooped on board, Vashti treading on the pages as she did so.

Inside, her anxiety increased. The arrangements were old-fashioned and rough. There was even a female attendant, to whom she would have to announce her wants during the voyage. Of course a revolving platform ran the length of the boat, but she was expected to walk from it to her cabin. Some cabins were better than others, and she did not get the best. She thought the attendant had been unfair, and spasms of rage shook her. The glass valves had closed, she could not go back. She saw, at the end of the vestibule, the lift in which she had ascended going quietly up and down, empty. Beneath those corridors of shining tiles were rooms, tier below tier, reaching far into the earth, and in each room there sat a human being, eating, or sleeping, or producing ideas. And buried deep in the hive was her own room. Vashti was afraid.

"O Machine! O Machine!" she murmured, and caressed her Book, and was comforted.

Then the sides of the vestibule seemed to melt together, as do the passages that we see in dreams, the lift vanished, the Book that had been dropped slid to the left and vanished, polished tiles rushed by like a stream of water, there was a slight jar, and the air-ship, issuing from its tunnel, soared above the waters of a tropical ocean.

It was night. For a moment she saw the coast of Sumatra edged by the phosphorescence of waves, and crowned by lighthouses, still sending forth their disregarded beams. These also vanished, and only the stars distracted her. They were not motionless, but swayed to and fro above her head, thronging out of one skylight into another, as if the universe and not the air-ship was careening. And, as often happens on clear nights, they seemed now to be in perspective, now on a plane; now piled tier beyond tier into the infinite heavens, now concealing infinity, a roof limiting for ever the visions of men. In either case they seemed intolerable. "Are we to travel in the dark?" called the passengers angrily, and the attendant, who had been careless, generated the light, and pulled down the blinds of pliable metal. When the air-ships had been built, the desire to look direct at things still lingered in the world. Hence the extraordinary number of skylights and windows, and the proportionate discomfort to those who were civilized and refined. Even in Vashti's cabin one star peeped through a flaw in the blind, and after a few hours' uneasy slumber, she was disturbed by an unfamiliar glow, which was the dawn.

Quick as the ship had sped westwards, the earth had rolled eastwards quicker still, and had dragged back Vashti and her companions towards the sun. Science could prolong the night, but only for a little, and those high hopes of neutralizing the earth's diurnal revolution had passed, together with hopes that were possibly higher. To "keep pace with the sun," or even to outstrip it, had been the aim of the civilization preceding this. Racing aeroplanes had been built for the purpose, capable of enormous speed, and steered by the greatest intellects of the epoch. Round the globe they went, round and round, westward, westward, round and round, amidst humanity's applause. In vain. The globe went eastward quicker still, horrible accidents occurred, and the Committee of the Machine, at the time rising into prominence, declared the pursuit illegal, unmechanical, and punishable by Homelessness.

Of Homelessness more will be said later.

Doubtless the Committee was right. Yet the attempt to "defeat the sun" aroused the last common interest that our race experienced about the heavenly bodies, or indeed about anything. It was the last time that men were compacted by thinking of a power outside the world. The sun had conquered, yet it was the end of his spiritual dominion. Dawn, midday, twilight, the zodiacal path, touched neither men's lives nor their hearts, and science retreated into the ground, to concentrate herself upon problems that she was certain of solving.

So when Vashti found her cabin invaded by a rosy finger of light, she was annoyed, and tried to adjust the blind. But the blind flew up altogether, and she saw through the skylight small pink clouds, swaying against a background of blue, and as the sun crept higher, its radiance entered direct, brimming down the wall, like a golden sea. It rose and fell with the air-ship's motion, just as waves rise and fall, but it advanced steadily, as a tide advances. Unless she was careful, it would strike her face. A spasm of horror shook her and she rang for the attendant. The attendant too was horrified, but she could do nothing; it was not her place to mend the blind. She could only suggest that the lady should change her cabin, which she accordingly prepared to do.

People were almost exactly alike all over the world, but the attendant of the air-ship, perhaps owing to her exceptional duties, had grown a little out of the common. She had often to address passengers with direct speech, and this had given her a certain roughness and originality of manner. When Vashti swerved away from the sunbeams with a cry, she behaved barbarically—she put out her hand to steady her.

"How dare you!" exclaimed the passenger. "You forget yourself!"

The woman was confused, and apologized for not having let her fall. People never touched one another. The custom had become obsolete, owing to the Machine.

"Where are we now?" asked Vashti haughtily.

"We are over Asia," said the attendant, anxious to be polite.

"Asia?"

"You must excuse my common way of speaking. I have got into the habit of calling places over which I pass by their unmechanical names."

"Oh, I remember Asia. The Mongols came from it."

"Beneath us, in the open air, stood a city that was once called Simla."

"Have you ever heard of the Mongols and of the Brisbane school?"

"No."

"Brisbane also stood in the open air."

"Those mountains to the right—let me show you them." She pushed back a metal blind. The main chain of the Himalayas was revealed. "They were once called the Roof of the World, those mountains."

"What a foolish name!"

"You must remember that, before the dawn of civilization, they seemed to be an impenetrable wall that touched the stars. It was supposed that no one but the gods could exist above their summits. How we have advanced, thanks to the Machine!"

"How we have advanced, thanks to the Machine!" said Vashti.

"How we have advanced, thanks to the Machine!" echoed the passenger who had dropped his Book the night before, and who was standing in the passage.

"And that white stuff in the cracks?—what is it?"

"I have forgotten its name."

"Cover the window, please. These mountains give me no ideas."

The northern aspect of the Himalayas was in deep shadow: on the Indian slope the sun had just prevailed. The forests had been destroyed during the literature epoch for the purpose of making newspaper-pulp, but the snows were awakening to their morning glory, and clouds still hung on the breasts of Kinchinjunga. In the plain were seen the ruins of cities, with diminished rivers creeping by their walls, and by the sides of these were sometimes the signs of vomitories, marking the cities of to-day. Over the whole prospect air-ships rushed, crossing and intercrossing with incredible *aplomb*, and rising nonchalantly when they desired to escape the perturbations of the lower atmosphere and to traverse the Roof of the World.

"We have indeed advanced, thanks to the Machine," repeated the attendant, and hid the Himalayas behind a metal blind.

The day dragged wearily forward. The passengers sat each in his cabin, avoiding one another with an almost physical repulsion and longing to be once more under the surface of the earth. There were eight or ten of them, mostly young males, sent out from the public nurseries to inhabit the rooms of those who had died in various parts of the earth. The man who had dropped his Book was on the homeward journey. He had been sent to Sumatra for the purpose of propagating the race. Vashti alone was travelling by her private will.

At midday she took a second glance at the earth. The air-ship was crossing another range of mountains, but she could see little, owing to clouds. Masses of black rock hovered below her, and merged indistinctly into grey. Their shapes were fantastic; one of them resembled a prostrate man.

"No ideas here," murmured Vashti, and hid the Caucasus behind a metal blind.

In the evening she looked again. They were crossing a golden sea, in which lay many small islands and one peninsula.

She repeated, "No ideas here," and hid Greece behind a metal blind.

PART II

THE MENDING APPARATUS

By a vestibule, by a lift, by a tubular railway, by a platform, by a sliding door—by reversing all the steps of her departure did Vashti arrive at her son's room, which exactly resembled her own. She might well declare that the visit was superfluous. The buttons, the knobs, the reading-desk with the Book, the temperature, the atmosphere, the illumination—all were exactly the same. And if Kuno himself, flesh of her flesh, stood close beside her at last, what profit was there in that? She was too well-bred to shake him by the hand.

Averting her eyes, she spoke as follows:

"Here I am. I have had the most terrible journey and greatly retarded the development of my soul. It is not worth it, Kuno, it is not worth it. My time is too precious. The sunlight almost touched me, and I have met with the rudest people. I can only stop a few minutes. Say what you want to say, and then I must return."

"I have been threatened with Homelessness," said Kuno.

She looked at him now.

"I have been threatened with Homelessness, and I could not tell you such a thing through the Machine."

Homelessness means death. The victim is exposed to the air, which kills him.

"I have been outside since I spoke to you last. The tremendous thing has happened, and they have discovered me."

"But why shouldn't you go outside?" she exclaimed. "It is perfectly legal, perfectly mechanical, to visit the surface of the earth. I have lately been to a lecture on the sea; there is no objection to that; one simply summons a respirator and gets an Egression-permit.

It is not the kind of thing that spiritually-minded people do, and I begged you not to do it, but there is no legal objection to it."

"I did not get an Egression-permit."

"Then how did you get out?"

"I found out a way of my own."

The phrase conveyed no meaning to her, and he had to repeat it.

"A way of your own?" she whispered. "But that would be wrong."

"Why?"

The question shocked her beyond measure.

"You are beginning to worship the Machine," he said coldly. "You think it irreligious of me to have found out a way of my own. It was just what the Committee thought, when they threatened me with Homelessness."

At this she grew angry. "I worship nothing!" she cried. "I am most advanced. I don't think you irreligious, for there is no such thing as religion left. All the fear and the superstition that existed once have been destroyed by the Machine. I only meant that to find out a way of your own was—Besides, there is no new way out."

"So it is always supposed."

"Except through the vomitories, for which one must have an Egression-permit, it is impossible to get out. The Book says so."

"Well, the Book's wrong, for I have been out on my feet."

For Kuno was possessed of a certain physical strength.

By these days it was a demerit to be muscular. Each infant was examined at birth, and all who promised undue strength were destroyed. Humanitarians may protest, but it would have been no true kindness to let an athlete live; he would never have been happy in that state of life to which the Machine had called him; he would have yearned for trees to climb, rivers to bathe in, meadows and hills against which he might measure his body. Man must be adapted to his surroundings, must he not? In the dawn of the world our weakly must be exposed on Mount Taygetus, in its twilight our strong will suffer euthanasia, that the Machine may progress, that the Machine may progress, that the Machine may progress eternally.

"You know that we have lost the sense of space. We say 'space is annihilated,' but we have annihilated not space, but the sense thereof. We have lost a part of ourselves. I determined to recover it, and I began by walking up and down the platform of the railway outside my room. Up and down, until I was tired, and so did recapture the meaning of 'Near' and 'Far.' 'Near' is a place to which I can get quickly *on my feet*, not a place to which the train or the air-ship will take me quickly. 'Far' is a place to which I cannot get quickly on my feet; the vomitory is 'far,' though I could be there in thirty-eight seconds by summoning the train. Man is the measure. That was my first lesson. Man's feet are the measure for distance, his hands are the measure for ownership, his body is the measure for all that is lovable and desirable and strong. Then I went further: it was then that I called to you for the first time, and you would not come.

"This city, as you know, is built deep beneath the surface of the earth, with only the vomitories protruding. Having paced the platform outside my own room, I took the lift to the next platform and paced that also, and so with each in turn, until I came to the topmost, above which begins the earth. All the platforms were exactly alike, and all that I gained by visiting them was to develop my sense of space and my muscles. I think I should have been content with this—it is not a little thing,—but as I walked and brooded, it occurred to me that our cities had been built in the days when men still breathed the outer air, and that there had been ventilation shafts for the workmen. I could think of nothing but these ventilation shafts. Had they been destroyed by all the food-tubes and medicine-tubes and music-tubes that the Machine has evolved lately? Or did traces of them remain? One thing was certain. If I came upon them anywhere, it would be in the railway-tunnels of the topmost storey. Everywhere else, all space was accounted for.

"I am telling my story quickly, but don't think that I was not a coward or that your answers never depressed me. It is not the proper thing, it is not mechanical, it is not decent to walk along a railway-tunnel. I did not fear that I might tread upon a live rail and be killed. I feared something far more intangible—doing what was not contemplated by the Machine. Then I said to myself, 'Man is the measure,' and I went, and after many visits I found an opening.

"The tunnels, of course, were lighted. Everything is light, arti-ficial light; darkness is the exception. So when I saw a black gap in the tiles, I knew that it was an exception, and rejoiced. I put in my arm—I could put in no more at first—and waved it round and round in ecstasy. I loosened another tile, and put in my head, and shouted into the darkness: 'I am coming, I shall do it yet,' and my voice reverberated down endless passages. I seemed to hear the spirits of those dead workmen who had returned each evening to the starlight and to their wives, and all the generations who had lived in the open air called back to me, 'You will do it yet, you are coming.'"

He paused, and, absurd as he was, his last words moved her. For Kuno had lately asked to be a father, and his request had been refused by the Committee. His was not a type that the Machine desired to hand on.

"Then a train passed. It brushed by me, but I thrust my head and arms into the hole. I had done enough for one day, so I crawled back to the platform, went down in the lift, and summoned my bed. Ah what dreams! And again I called you, and again you refused."

She shook her head and said:

"Don't. Don't talk of these terrible things. You make me miserable. You are throwing civilization away."

"But I had got back the sense of space and a man cannot rest then. I determined to get in at the hole and climb the shaft. And so I exercised my arms. Day after day I went through ridiculous movements, until my flesh ached, and I could hang by my hands and hold the pillow of my bed outstretched for many minutes. Then I summoned a respirator, and started.

"It was easy at first. The mortar had somehow rotted, and I soon pushed some more tiles in, and clambered after them into the darkness, and the spirits of the dead comforted me. I don't know what I mean by that. I just say what I felt. I felt, for the first time, that a protest had been lodged against corruption, and that even as the dead were comforting me, so I was comforting the unborn. I felt that humanity existed, and that it existed without clothes. How can I possibly explain this? It was naked, humanity seemed naked, and all these tubes and buttons and machineries neither came into the world with us, nor will they follow us out, nor do they matter supremely while we are here. Had I been strong, I would have torn off every garment I had, and gone out into the outer air unswaddled. But this is not for me, nor perhaps for my generation. I climbed with my respirator and my hygienic clothes and my dietetic tabloids! Better thus than not at all.

"There was a ladder, made of some primæval metal. The light from the railway fell upon its lowest rungs, and I saw that it led straight upwards out of the rubble at the bottom of the shaft. Perhaps our ancestors ran up and down it a dozen times daily, in their building. As I climbed, the rough edges cut through my gloves so that my hands bled. The light helped me for a little, and then came darkness and, worse still, silence which pierced my ears like a sword. The Machine hums! Did you know that? Its hum penetrates our blood, and may even guide our thoughts. Who knows! I was getting beyond its power. Then I thought: 'This silence means that I am doing wrong.' But I heard voices in the silence, and again they strengthened me." He laughed. "I had need of them. The next moment I cracked my head against something."

She sighed.

"I had reached one of those pneumatic stoppers that defend us from the outer air. You may have noticed them on the air-ship. Pitch dark, my feet on the rungs of an invisible ladder, my hands cut; I cannot explain how I lived through this part, but the voices still comforted me, and I felt for fastenings. The stopper, I suppose, was about eight feet across. I passed my hand over it as far as I could reach. It was perfectly smooth. I felt it almost to the centre. Not quite to the centre, for my arm was too short. Then the voice said: 'Jump. It is worth it. There may be a handle in the centre, and you may catch hold of it and so come to us your own way. And if there is no handle, so that you may fall and are dashed to pieces—it is still worth it: you will still come to us your own way.' So I jumped. There was a handle, and—"

He paused. Tears gathered in his mother's eyes. She knew that he was fated. If he did not die to-day he would die to-morrow. There was not room for such a person in the world. And with her pity disgust mingled. She was ashamed at having borne such a son, she who had always been so respectable and so full of ideas. Was he really the little boy to whom she had taught the use of his stops and buttons, and to whom she had given his first lessons in the Book? The very hair that disfigured his lip showed that he was reverting to some savage type. On atavism the Machine can have no mercy.

"'There was a handle, and I did catch it. I hung tranced over the darkness and heard the hum of these workings as the last whisper in a dying dream. All the things I had cared about and all the people I had spoken to through tubes appeared infinitely little. Meanwhile the handle revolved. My weight had set something in motion and I span slowly, and then—

"I cannot describe it. I was lying with my face to the sunshine. Blood poured from my nose and ears and I heard a tremendous roaring. The stopper, with me clinging to it, had simply been blown out of the earth, and the air that we make down here was escaping through the vent into the air above. It burst up like a fountain. I crawled back to it—for the upper air hurts—and, as it were, I took great sips from the edge. My respirator had flown goodness knows where, my clothes were torn. I just lay with my lips close to the hole, and I sipped until the bleeding stopped. You can imagine nothing so curious. This hollow in the grass—I will speak of it in a minute —the sun shining into it, not brilliantly but through marbled clouds,—the peace, the nonchalance, the sense of space, and, brushing my cheek, the roaring fountain of our artificial air! Soon I spied my respirator, bobbing up and down in the current high above my head, and higher still were many air-ships. But no one ever looks out of air-ships, and in any case they could not have picked me up. There I was, stranded. The sun shone a little way down the shaft, and revealed the topmost rung of the ladder, but it was hopeless trying to reach it. I should either have been tossed up again by the escape, or else have fallen in, and died. I could only lie on the grass, sipping and sipping, and from time to time glancing around me.

"I knew that I was in Wessex, for I had taken care to go to a lecture on the subject before starting. Wessex lies above the room in which we are talking now. It was once an important state. Its kings held all the southern coast from the Andredswald to Cornwall, while the Wans-dyke protected them on the north, running over the high ground. The lecturer was only concerned with the rise of Wessex, so I do not know how long it remained an international power, nor would the knowledge have assisted me. To tell the truth I could do nothing but laugh, during this part. There was I, with a pneumatic stopper by my side and a respirator bobbing over my head, imprisoned, all three of us, in a grass-grown hollow that was edged with fern."

Then he grew grave again.

"Lucky for me that it was a hollow. For the air began to fall back into it and to fill it as water fills a bowl. I could crawl about. Presently I stood. I breathed a mixture, in which the air that hurts predominated whenever I tried to climb the sides. This was not so bad. I had not lost my tabloids and remained ridiculously cheerful, and as for the Machine, I forgot about it altogether. My one aim now was to get to the top, where the ferns were, and to view whatever objects lay beyond.

"I rushed the slope. The new air was still too bitter for me and I came rolling back, after a momentary vision of something grey. The sun grew very feeble, and I remembered that he was in Scorpio—I had been to a lecture on that too. If the sun is in Scorpio and you are in Wessex, it means that you must be as quick as you can, or it will get too dark. (This is the first bit of useful information I have ever got from a lecture, and I expect it will be the last.) It made me try frantically to breathe the new air, and to advance as far as I dared out of my pond. The hollow filled so slowly. At times I thought that the fountain played with less vigour. My respirator seemed to dance nearer the earth; the roar was decreasing."

He broke off.

"I don't think this is interesting you. The rest will interest you even less. There are no ideas in it, and I wish that I had not troubled you to come. We are too different, mother."

She told him to continue.

"It was evening before I climbed the bank. The sun had very nearly slipped out of the sky by this time, and I could not get a good view. You, who have just crossed the Roof of the World, will not want to hear an account of the little hills that I saw—low colourless hills. But to me they were living and the turf that covered them was a skin, under which their muscles rippled, and I felt that those hills had called with incalculable force to men in the past, and that men had loved them. Now they sleep—perhaps for ever. They commune with humanity in dreams. Happy the man, happy the woman, who awakes the hills of Wessex. For though they sleep, they will never die."

His voice rose passionately.

"Cannot you see, cannot all your lecturers see, that it is we that are dying, and that down here the only thing that really lives is the Machine? We created the Machine, to do our will, but we cannot make it do our will now. It has robbed us of the sense of space and of the sense of touch, it has blurred every human relation and narrowed down love to a carnal act, it has paralysed our bodies and our wills, and now it compels us to worship it. The Machine develops—but not on our lines. The Machine proceeds—but not to our goal. We only exist as the blood corpuscles that course through its arteries, and if it could work without us, it would let us die. Oh, I have no remedy—or, at least, only one—to tell men again and again that I have seen the hills of Wessex as Ælfrid saw them when he overthrew the Danes.

"So the sun set. I forgot to mention that a belt of mist lay between my hill and other hills, and that it was the colour of pearl."

He broke off for the second time.

"Go on," said his mother wearily.

He shook his head.

"Go on. Nothing that you say can distress me now. I am hardened."

"I had meant to tell you the rest, but I cannot: I know that I cannot: good-bye."

Vashti stood irresolute. All her nerves were tingling with his blasphemies. But she was also inquisitive.

"This is unfair," she complained. "You have called me across the world to hear your story, and hear it I will. Tell me—as briefly as possible, for this is a disastrous waste of time—tell me how you returned to civilization."

"Oh—that!" he said, starting. "You would like to hear about civilization. Certainly. Had I got to where my respirator fell down?"

"No—but I understand everything now. You put on your respirator, and managed to walk along the surface of the earth to a vomitory, and there your conduct was reported to the Central Committee."

"By no means."

He passed his hand over his forehead, as if dispelling some strong impression. Then, resuming his narrative, he warmed to it again.

"My respirator fell about sunset. I had mentioned that the fountain seemed feebler, had I not?"

"Yes."

"About sunset, it let the respirator fall. As I said, I had entirely forgotten about the Machine, and I paid no great attention at the time, being occupied with other things. I had my pool of air, into which I could dip when the outer keenness became intolerable, and which would possibly remain for days, provided that no wind sprang up to disperse it. Not until it was too late did I realize what the stoppage of the escape implied. You see—the gap in the tunnel had been mended; the Mending Apparatus; the Mending Apparatus, was after me.

"One other warning I had, but I neglected it. The sky at night was clearer than it had been in the day, and the moon, which was about half the sky behind the sun, shone into the dell at moments quite brightly. I was in my usual place—on the boundary between the two atmospheres—when I thought I saw something dark move across the bottom of the dell, and vanish into the shaft. In my folly, I ran down. I bent over and listened, and I thought I heard a faint scraping noise in the depths.

"At this—but it was too late—I took alarm. I determined to put on my respirator and to walk right out of the dell. But my respirator had gone. I knew exactly where it had fallen—between the stopper and the aperture—and I could even feel the mark that it had made in the turf. It had gone, and I realized that something evil was at work, and I had better escape to the other air, and, if I must die, die running towards the cloud that had been the colour of a pearl. I never started. Out of the shaft—it is too horrible. A worm, a long white worm, had crawled out of the shaft and was gliding over the moonlit grass.

"I screamed. I did everything that I should not have done, I stamped upon the creature instead of flying from it, and it at once curled round the ankle. Then we fought. The worm let me run all over the dell, but edged up my leg as I ran. 'Help!' I cried. (That part is too awful. It belongs to the part that you will never know.) 'Help!' I cried. (Why cannot we suffer in silence?) 'Help!' I cried. Then my feet were wound together, I fell, I was dragged away from the dear ferns and the living hills, and past the great metal stopper (I can tell you this part), and I thought it might save me again if I caught hold of the handle. It also was enwrapped, it also. Oh, the whole dell was full of the things. They were searching it in all directions, they were denuding it, and the white snouts of others peeped out of the hole, ready if needed. Everything that could be moved they brought—brushwood, bundles of fern, everything, and down we all went intertwined into hell. The last things that I saw, ere the stopper closed after us, were certain stars, and I felt that a man of my sort lived in the sky. For I did fight, I fought till the very end, and it was only my head hitting against the ladder that quieted me. I woke up in this room. The worms had vanished. I was surrounded by artificial air, artificial light, artificial peace, and my friends were calling to me down speaking-tubes to know whether I had come across any new ideas lately."

Here his story ended. Discussion of it was impossible, and Vashti turned to go.

"It will end in Homelessness," she said quietly.

"I wish it would," retorted Kuno.

"The Machine has been most merciful."

"I prefer the mercy of God."

"By that superstitious phrase, do you mean that you could live in the outer air?"

"Yes."

"Have you ever seen, round the vomitories, the bones of those who were extruded after the Great Rebellion?"

"Yes."

"They were left where they perished for our edification. A few crawled away, but they perished, too—who can doubt it? And so with the Homeless of our own day. The surface of the earth supports life no longer."

"Indeed."

"Ferns and a little grass may survive, but all higher forms have perished. Has any airship detected them?"

"No."

"Has any lecturer dealt with them?"

"No."

"Then why this obstinacy?"

"Because I have seen them," he exploded.

"Seen *what*?"

"Because I have seen her in the twilight—because she came to my help when I called—because she, too, was entangled by the worms, and, luckier than I, was killed by one of them piercing her throat."

He was mad. Vashti departed, nor, in the troubles that followed, did she ever see his face again.

PART III

THE HOMELESS

During the years that followed Kuno's escapade, two important developments took place in the Machine. On the surface they were revolutionary, but in either case men's minds had been prepared beforehand, and they did but express tendencies that were latent already.

The first of these was the abolition of respirators.

Advanced thinkers, like Vashti, had always held it foolish to visit the surface of the earth. Air ships might be necessary, but what was the good of going out for mere curiosity and crawling along for a mile or two in a terrestrial motor? The habit was vulgar and perhaps faintly improper: it was unproductive of ideas, and had no connection with the habits that really mattered. So respirators were abolished, and with them, of course, the terrestrial motors, and except for a few lecturers, who complained that they were debarred access to their subject-matter, the development was accepted quietly. Those who still wanted to know what the earth was like had after all only to listen to some gramophone, or to look into some cinematophote. And even the lecturers acquiesced when they found that a lecture on the sea was none the less stimulating when compiled out of other lectures that had already been delivered on the same subject. "Beware of first-hand ideas!" exclaimed one of the most advanced of them. "First-hand ideas do not really exist. They are but the physical impressions produced by love and fear, and on this gross foundation who could erect a philosophy? Let your ideas be second-hand, and if possible tenth-hand, for then they will be far removed from that disturbing element—direct observation. Do not learn anything about this subject of mine—the French Revolution. Learn instead what I think that Enicharmon thought Urizen thought Gutch thought Ho-Yung thought Chi-Bo-Sing thought Lafcadio Hearn thought Carlyle thought Mirabeau said about the French Revolution. Through the medium of these ten great minds, the blood that was shed at Paris and the windows that were broken at Versailles will be clarified to an idea which you may employ most profitably in your daily lives. But be sure that the intermediates are many and varied, for in history one authority exists to counteract another. Urizen must counteract the scepticism of Ho-Yung and Enicharmon, I must myself counteract the impetuosity of Gutch. You who listen to me are in a better position to judge about the French Revolution than I am. Your descendants will be even in a better position than you, for they will learn what you think I think, and yet another intermediate will be added to the chain. And in time"—his voice rose—"there will come a generation that has got beyond facts, beyond impressions, a generation absolutely colourless, a generation

'seraphically free
From taint of personality,'

which will see the French Revolution not as it happened, nor as they would like it to have happened, but as it would have happened, had it taken place in the days of the Machine."

Tremendous applause greeted this lecture, which did but voice a feeling already latent in the minds of men—a feeling that terrestrial facts must be ignored, and that the abolition of respirators was a positive gain. It was even suggested that air-ships should be abolished too. This was not done, because air ships had somehow worked themselves into the Machine's system. But year by year they were used less, and mentioned less by thoughtful men.

The second great development was the reestablishment of religion.

This, too, had been voiced in the celebrated lecture. No one could mistake the reverent tone in which the peroration had concluded, and it awakened a responsive echo in the heart of each. Those who had long worshipped silently, now began to talk. They described the strange feeling of peace that came over them when they handled the Book of the Machine, the pleasure that it was to repeat certain numerals out of it, however little meaning those numerals conveyed to the outward ear, the ecstasy of touching a button, however unimportant, or of ringing an electric bell, however superfluously.

"The Machine," they exclaimed, "feeds us and clothes us and houses us; through it we speak to one another, through it we see one another, in it we have our being. The Machine is the friend of ideas and the enemy of superstition: the Machine is omnipotent, eternal; blessed is the Machine." And before long this allocution was printed on the first page of the Book, and in subsequent editions the ritual swelled into a complicated system of praise and prayer. The word "religion" was sedulously avoided, and in theory the Machine was still the creation and the implement of man. But in practice all, save a few retrogrades, worshipped it as divine. Nor was it worshipped in unity. One believer would be chiefly impressed by the blue optic plates, through which he saw other believers; another by the mending apparatus, which sinful Kuno had compared to worms; another by the lifts, another by the Book. And each would pray to this or to that, and ask it to intercede for him with the Machine as a whole. Persecution—that also was present. It did not break out, for reasons that will be set forward shortly. But it was latent, and all who did not accept the minimum known as "undenominational Mechanism" lived in danger of Homelessness, which means death, as we know.

To attribute these two great developments to the Central Committee, is to take a very narrow view of civilization. The Central Committee announced the developments, it is true, but they were no more the cause of them than were the kings of the imperialistic period the cause of war. Rather did they yield to some invincible pressure, which came no one knew whither, and which, when gratified, was succeeded by some new pressure equally invincible. To such a state of affairs it is convenient to give the name of progress. No one confessed the Machine was out of hand. Year by year it was served with increased efficiency and decreased intelligence. The better a man knew his own duties upon it, the less he understood the duties of his neighbour, and in all the world there was not one who understood the monster as a whole. Those master brains had perished. They had left full directions, it is true, and their successors had each of them mastered a portion of those directions. But Humanity, in its desire for comfort, had over-reached itself. It had exploited the riches of nature too far. Quietly and complacently, it was sinking into decadence, and progress had come to mean the progress of the Machine.

As for Vashti, her life went peacefully forward until the final disaster. She made her room dark and slept; she awoke and made the room light. She lectured and attended lectures. She exchanged ideas with her innumerable friends and believed she was growing more spiritual. At times a friend was granted Euthanasia, and left his or her room for the homelessness that is beyond all human conception. Vashti did not much mind. After an unsuccessful lecture, she would sometimes ask for Euthanasia herself. But the death-rate was not permitted to exceed the birth rate, and the Machine had hitherto refused it to her.

The troubles began quietly, long before she was conscious of them.

One day she was astonished at receiving a message from her son. They never communicated, having nothing in common, and she had only heard indirectly that he was still alive, and had been transferred from the northern hemisphere, where he had behaved so mischievously, to the southern—indeed, to a room not far from her own.

"Does he want me to visit him?" she thought. "Never again, never. And I have not the time."

No, it was madness of another kind.

He refused to visualize his face upon the blue plate, and speaking out of the darkness with solemnity said:

"The Machine stops."

"What do you say?"

"The Machine is stopping, I know it, I know the signs."

She burst into a peal of laughter. He heard her and was angry, and they spoke no more.

"Can you imagine anything more absurd?" she cried to a friend. "A man who was my son believes that the Machine is stopping. It would be impious if it was not mad."

"The Machine is stopping?" her friend replied. "What does that mean? The phrase conveys nothing to me."

"Nor to me."

"He does not refer, I suppose, to the trouble there has been lately with the music?"

"Oh no, ofcourse not. Let us talk about music."

"Have you complained to the authorities?"

"Yes, and they say it wants mending, and referred me to the Committee of the Mending Apparatus. I complained of those curious gasping sighs that disfigure the symphonies of the Brisbane school. They sound like some one in pain. The Committee of the Mending Apparatus say that it shall be remedied shortly."

Obscurely worried, she resumed her life. For one thing, the defect in the music irritated her. For another thing, she could not forget Kuno's speech. If he had known that the music was out of repair—he could not know it, for he detested music—if he had known that it was wrong, "the Machine stops" was exactly the venomous sort of remark he would have made. Of course he had made it at a venture, but the coincidence annoyed her, and she spoke with some petulance to the Committee of the Mending Apparatus.

They replied, as before, that the defect would be set right shortly.

"Shortly! At once!" she retorted. "Why should I be worried by imperfect music? Things are always put right at once. If you do not mend it at once, I shall complain to the Central Committee."

"No personal complaints are received by the Central Committee," the Committee of the Mending Apparatus replied.

"Through whom am I to make my complaint, then?"

"Through us."

"I complain then."

"Your complaint shall be forwarded in its turn."

"Have others complained?"

This question was unmechanical, and the Committee of the Mending Apparatus refused to answer it.

"It is too bad!" she exclaimed to another of her friends. "There never was such an unfortunate woman as myself. I can never be sure of my music now. It gets worse and worse each time I summon it."

"I too have my troubles," the friend replied. "Sometimes my ideas are interrupted by a slight jarring noise."

"What is it?"

"I do not know whether it is inside my head, or inside the wall."

"Complain, in either case."

"I have complained, and my complaint will be forwarded in its turn to the Central Committee."

Time passed, and they resented the defects no longer. The defects had not been remedied, but the human tissues in that latter day had become so subservient, that they readily adapted themselves to every caprice of the Machine. The sigh at the crisis of the Brisbane symphony no longer irritated Vashti; she accepted it as part of the melody. The jarring noise, whether in the head or in the wall, was no longer resented by her friend. And so with the mouldy artificial fruit, so with the bath water that began to stink, so with the defective rhymes that the poetry machine had taken to emit. All were bitterly complained of at first, and then acquiesced in and forgotten. Things went from bad to worse unchallenged.

It was otherwise with the failure of the sleeping apparatus. That was a more serious stoppage. There came a day when over the whole world—in Sumatra, in Wessex, in the innumerable cities of Courland and Brazil—the beds, when summoned by their tired owners, failed to appear. In may seem a ludicrous matter, but from it we may date the collapse of humanity. The Committee responsible for the failure was assailed by complainants, whom it referred, as usual, to the Committee of the Mending Apparatus, who in its turn assured them that their complaints would be forwarded to the Central Committee. But the discontent grew, for mankind was not yet sufficiently adaptable to do without sleeping.

"Some one is meddling with the Machine—" they began.

"Some one is trying to make himself king, to reintroduce the personal element."

"Punish that man with Homelessness."

"To the rescue! Avenge the Machine! Avenge the Machine!"

"War! Kill the man!"

But the Committee of the Mending Apparatus now came forward, and allayed the panic with well-chosen words. It confessed that the Mending Apparatus was itself in need of repair.

The effect of this frank confession was admirable.

"Of course," said a famous lecturer—he of the French Revolution, who gilded each new decay with splendour—"of course we shall not press our complaints now. The Mending Apparatus has treated us so well in the past that we all sympathize with it, and will wait patiently for its recovery. In its own good time it will resume its duties. Meanwhile let us do without our beds, our tabloids, our other little wants. Such, I feel sure, would be the wish of the Machine."

Thousands of miles away his audience applauded. The Machine still linked them. Under the seas, beneath the roots of the mountains, ran the wires through which they saw and heard, the enormous eyes and ears that were their heritage, and the hum of many workings clothed their thoughts in one garment of subserviency. Only the old and the sick remained ungrateful, for it was rumoured that Euthanasia, too, was out of order, and that pain had reappeared among men.

It became difficult to read. A blight entered the atmosphere and dulled its luminosity. At times Vashti could scarcely see across her room. The air, too, was foul. Loud were the complaints, impotent the remedies, heroic the tone of the lecturer as he cried: "Courage! courage! What matter so long as the Machine goes on? To it the darkness and the light are one." And though things improved again after a time, the old brilliancy was never recaptured, and humanity never recovered from its entrance into twilight. There was an hysterical talk of "measures," of "provisional dictatorship," and the inhabitants of Sumatra were asked to familiarize themselves with the workings of the central power station, the said power station being situated in France. But for the most part panic reigned, and men spent their strength praying to their Books, tangible proofs of the Machine's omnipotence. There were gradations of terror—at times came rumours of hope—the Mending Apparatus was almost mended—the enemies of the Machine had been got under—new "nerve-centres" were evolving which would do the work even more magnificently than before. But there came a day when, without the slightest warning, without any previous hint of feebleness, the entire communication-system broke down, all over the world, and the world, as they understood it, ended.

Vashti was lecturing at the time and her earlier remarks had been punctuated with applause. As she proceeded the audience became silent, and at the conclusion there was no sound. Somewhat displeased, she called to a friend who was a specialist in sympathy. No sound: doubtless the friend was sleeping. And so with the next friend whom she tried to summon, and so with the next, until she remembered Kuno's cryptic remark, "The Machine stops."

The phrase still conveyed nothing. If Eternity was stopping it would of course be set going shortly.

For example, there was still a little light and air—the atmosphere had improved a few hours previously. There was still the Book, and while there was the Book there was security.

Then she broke down, for with the cessation of activity came an unexpected terror—silence.

She had never known silence, and the coming of it nearly killed her—it did kill many thousands of people outright. Ever since her birth she had been surrounded by the steady hum. It was to the ear what artificial air was to the lungs, and agonizing pains shot across her head. And scarcely knowing what she did, she stumbled forward and pressed the unfamiliar button, the one that opened the door of her cell.

Now the door of the cell worked on a simple hinge of its own. It was not connected with the central power station, dying far away in France. It opened, rousing immoderate hopes in Vashti, for she thought that the Machine had been mended. It opened, and she saw the dim tunnel that curved far away towards freedom. One look, and then she shrank back. For the tunnel was full of people—she was almost the last in that city to have taken alarm.

People at any time repelled her, and these were nightmares from her worst dreams. People were crawling about, people were screaming, whimpering, gasping for breath, touching each other, vanishing in the dark, and ever and anon being pushed off the platform on to the live rail. Some were fighting round the electric bells, trying to summon trains which could not be summoned. Others were yelling for Euthanasia or for respirators, or blaspheming the Machine. Others stood at the doors of their cells fearing, like herself, either to stop in them or to leave them. And behind all the uproar was silence—the silence which is the voice of the earth and of the generations who have gone.

No—it was worse than solitude. She closed the door again and sat down to wait for the end. The disintegration went on, accompanied by horrible cracks and rumbling. The valves that restrained the Medical Apparatus must have been weakened, for it ruptured and hung hideously from the ceiling. The floor heaved and fell and flung her from her chair. A tube oozed towards her serpent fashion. And at last the final horror approached—light began to ebb, and she knew that civilization's long day was closing.

She whirled round, praying to be saved from this, at any rate, kissing the Book, pressing button after button. The uproar outside was increasing, and even penetrated the wall. Slowly the brilliancy of her cell was dimmed, the reflections faded from her metal switches. Now she could not see the reading-stand, now not the Book, though she held it in her hand. Light followed the flight of sound, air was following light, and the original void returned to the cavern from which it had been so long excluded. Vashti continued to whirl, like the devotees of an earlier religion, screaming, praying, striking at the buttons with bleeding hands.

It was thus that she opened her prison and escaped—escaped

in the spirit: at least so it seems to me, ere my meditation closes. That she escapes in the body—I cannot perceive that. She struck, by chance, the switch that released the door, and the rush of foul air on her skin, the loud throbbing whispers in her ears, told her that she was facing the tunnel again, and that tremendous platform on which she had seen men fighting. They were not fighting now. Only the whispers remained, and the little whimpering groans. They were dying by hundreds out in the dark.

She burst into tears.

Tears answered her.

They wept for humanity, those two, not for themselves. They could not bear that this should be the end. Ere silence was completed their hearts were opened, and they knew what had been important on the earth. Man, the flower of all flesh, the noblest of all creatures visible, man who had once made god in his image, and had mirrored his strength on the constellations, beautiful naked man was dying, strangled in the garments that he had woven. Century after century had he toiled, and here was his reward. Truly the garment had seemed heavenly at first, shot with the colours of culture, sewn with the threads of self-denial. And heavenly it had been so long as it was a garment and no more, so long as man could shed it at will and live by the essence that is his soul, and the essence, equally divine, that is his body. The sin against the body—it was for that they wept in chief; the centuries of wrong against the muscles and the nerves, and those five portals by which we can alone apprehend—glozing it over with talk of evolution, until the body was white pap, the home of ideas as colourless, last sloshy stirrings of a spirit that had grasped the stars.

"Where are you?" she sobbed.

His voice in the darkness said, "Here."

"Is there any hope, Kuno?"

"None for us."

"Where are you?"

She crawled towards him over the bodies of the dead. His blood spurted over her hands.

"Quicker," he gasped, "I am dying—but we touch, we talk, not through the Machine."

He kissed her.

"We have come back to our own. We die, but we have recaptured life, as it was in Wessex, when Ælfrid overthrew the Danes. We know what they know outside, they who dwelt in the cloud that is the colour of a pearl."

"But, Kuno, is it true? Are there still men on the surface of the earth? Is this—this tunnel, this poisoned darkness—really not the end?"

He replied:

"I have seen them, spoken to them, loved them. They are hiding in the mist and the ferns until our civilization stops. To-day they are the Homeless—to-morrow—"

"Oh, to-morrow—some fool will start the Machine again, to-morrow."

"Never," said Kuno, "never. Humanity has learnt its lesson."

As he spoke, the whole city was broken like a honeycomb. An air-ship had sailed in through the vomitory into a ruined wharf. It crashed downwards, exploding as it went, rending gallery after gallery with its wings of steel. For a moment they saw the nations of the dead, and, before they joined them, scraps of the untainted sky.

EFFICIENCY

Perley Poore Sheehan & Robert H. Davis

Perley Poore Sheehan (1875–1943), a name you might think could hardly be forgotten, was a newspaper journalist and editor turned author and, later, writer of movie scenarios. It was he who wrote the scenario for Lon Chaney, Sr.'s classic film, The Hunchback of Notre Dame *(1923). He is remembered by a small clique of devotees of the lost-race novels and fantasies from the pulp magazines. His work included "The Copper Princess" (1913) about a revived Incan mummy, its thematic companion "The Queen of Sheba" (1914) and his adventure about a remote scientifically advanced civilization in the Gobi desert, "The Abyss of Wonders" (1915). These stories were published in* All-Story Weekly *and* The Argosy, *two of the best-selling pulps published by Frank A. Monsey, for whom Sheehan worked briefly as an editor on* The Scrap Book *and* The Cavalier. *The chief editor of these pulps was Robert Hobart Davis (1869–1942) who had done much to popularize science fiction in those pulps, notably the works of Edgar Rice Burroughs, Abraham Merritt, Ray Cummings and Murray Leinster.*

Both Sheehan and Davis turned a hand to writing plays and later movie scenarios. Plays lent themselves to stories involving humanoid robots or androids, because they could easily be played by actors without the need for any technical wizardry. One of the earliest such plays had been The Electric Man *(1906) by Charles Hannan, a drawing-room farce in which an automaton is created in the image of its maker but malfunctions, causing chaos. It was a stage play,* R. U. R. *(1920) by Karel Čapek that gave* the world the word "robot" and is a seminal text on the revolt of machine intelligences. Sheehan and Davis's one-act play, Efficiency, however, first performed at the Greenwich Village Theatre in 1917 and published with an appreciation by Theodore Roosevelt, did not require a mechanical man. It needed someone strong and resolute to play the first ever cyborg performed in front of an audience.

CAST OF CHARACTERS

THE EMPEROR
THE SCIENTIST
NUMBER 241

THE EMPEROR: A person attired in military costume, indicating the highest order of elaborate modern mode, sage green in tone. He wears a short, olive-coloured cape coat, the left flap of which is thrown back disclosing: (1) the Order of Merit; (2) the Triple Cross; (3) a seven-starred emblem of diamonds, emeralds, and rubies, known as the Reward of Heaven, designed by the EMPEROR himself and bestowed by the grace of the Almighty upon His Majesty's Imperial person.

THE SCIENTIST: A small, thin man, garbed in frock-suit, flowing black tie; thin of face; bulging eyes; horn spectacles; heavy head of grey hair; thin, straggly, grey beard and small moustache. He is very animated. He wears a long, Inverness style dark overcoat, and carries a portfolio containing reports and statistical matter.

NUMBER 241: Stands six feet; is very erect and stiff of posture; closely-cropped hair; large face, rather heavy of expression. Upon entering he is garbed in full-length war-grey cloak, with wide band at waist buttoned in front; the conventional metal war-helmet now in general use; hands in white cotton gloves. He moves with the deliberation of an automaton. In reality he is fifty per cent. human and fifty per cent. machine, being composed of: (1) left artificial leg;

(2) two artificial hands; (3) artificial right forearm and elbow; (4) artificial left eye, which SCIENTIST has converted into a telescope; (5) artificial left ear, which is also a telephone; (6) all his teeth are metal—synthetic gold—but cheaper and harder. He can bite barbed wire in twain. Underneath his great cloak he wears the regulation infantry uniform and a bayonet in a scabbard. His speech is laboured.

SCENE: Private audience chamber of an Emperor, in purple and gold, with magnificent throne-chair carved elaborately, a canopy extending over the seat. Regal flat-top table left-centre containing mounted figure of THE EMPEROR in bronze and a large mushroom gold gong. A purple-and-gold cloth falls over both ends of the table. The cloth is decorated with crown and sceptre. Heavy purple curtains fall from back wall. A modern rifle leans against the left back corner.

(At rise of curtain stage empty. ENTER the EMPEROR, followed by the SCIENTIST. the EMPEROR with a curt and preoccupied air, the SCIENTIST with an air of fawning enthusiasm.)

EMPEROR (*crossing toward throne-chair, in which he seats himself*): Proceed! Proceed!

SCIENTIST (*placing portfolio on table and smilingly rubbing his hands*): Modesty, Sire, causes me to falter.

EMPEROR (*without enthusiasm*): My time is limited. The Crown Prince awaits me.

SCIENTIST (*quivering with enthusiasm*): When your Majesty comprehends this greatest of all birthday gifts!—a million cripples transformed into a million fighting units!—your Majesty's might becomes terrible!

EMPEROR (*indulgently*): Generalities!

SCIENTIST: I particularize (*as* EMPEROR *makes sharp gesture that he is ready to listen*). The keynote of efficiency is the elimination of waste. Our problem was to eliminate the waste represented by the wounded. In brief, we have succeeded.

EMPEROR (*beginning to display interest*): How so?

SCIENTIST: After countless experiments we can now take a soldier, no matter how badly wounded, and return him to the trenches— a super-soldier—no longer a bungling, mortal man—but a beautiful, efficient machine!

EMPEROR (*laughing*): You are enthusiastic but—not contagious! (*deprecatory gesture*)—but—(*sternly*)—your promises have not always been kept. The proof!

SCIENTIST (*with impulsive devotion*): Your Majesty, I foresaw your doubts. I brought—

EMPEROR: Ha! A—specimen!

SCIENTIST (*appreciating the jeu d'esprit*): Perfectly! He is in the ante-room.

EMPEROR (*curtly*): Bring him in! Bring him in!

SCIENTIST: Er—I beg your Majesty's pardon—but—he is not—altogether pleasant to look upon.

EMPEROR: Nonsense! Whatever makes for the strength of the dynasty is agreeable to the Imperial eyes.

SCIENTIST (*with tremulous delight*): May I?

EMPEROR: Certainly! Make haste!

SCIENTIST (*nimbly crosses to door, opens it, and ejaculates command*): Attention! Forward! Hep! (*There is a momentary silence, then a metallic clatter as if caused by a movement of iron, then a heavy step.* ENTER 241, *erect, with measured tread, observing nothing. He comes down to centre of stage, when he stops in response to the* SCIENTIST'S *order*): Halt!

(*As* 241 *stands at military attention the* Scientist, *with manifest delight, flutters bowing before* EMPEROR *and explains*) The ultimate triumph!—our two hundred and forty-first experiment. Hence—Number Two Hundred and Forty-One! (*During this explanation* 241 *does not stir. The* EMPEROR *stares at* 241 *with a sort of horrified fascination.*)

EMPEROR: He—marches—splendidly!

SCIENTIST: The least of his accomplishments. Permit me! (*returns to* 241, *whom he prods,* 241 *remaining impassive*). Magnificent! (*gesture of approval as he carries on inspection of arms, hands, body, and head of* 241. *Runs finger around left eye, taps gently left ear. Contemplates ensemble and makes gesture for* 241 *to open mouth.* 241 *opens mouth and shows glittering array of metallic teeth; he shuts them with click like a steel trap*). Perfection! Right arm! (241 *lifts right arm in stiff but sweeping gesture*). Left knee! (241 *crooks left knee twice*). Hands! (241 *opens and closes both cotton-gloved hands and manipulates fingers*).

EMPEROR: You guarantee his efficiency?

SCIENTIST: Absolutely.

EMPEROR: Demonstrate.

SCIENTIST (*approaches* 241, *who continues to stand immobile, and very swiftly removes helmet, long cloak, and cotton gloves, disclosing two metallic hands and wrists*): You ask me, your Majesty, if he is efficient. I reply, more efficient than before he fell in battle (*crosses to corner and gets rifle. Returns to centre*). Two forty-one, attention! Observe, your Majesty! (SCIENTIST *tosses rifle to* 241, *who catches it surely but stiffly in his metal hands, against which the weapon clangs.* SCIENTIST *puts* 241 *through manual of arms. The whole scene following is punctuated by military commands in the following order*):—

"Attention!"
"Carry arms!"
"Present arms!"
"Shoulder arms!"
"Parade rest!"

And now, your Majesty, mark this! (*resuming orders*):—

"Fix bayonets!"
"Make ready!"
"Aim!"
"Fire!"

(241 *completes manœuvres by pulling trigger and snapping lock, whereupon* SCIENTIST *takes rifle and tosses it to settee*).

EMPEROR (*leaning forward with look of wonderment in his face*):
    Colossal! (241 *comes to attention and is inert again.*)
SCIENTIST: Are not the possibilities impressive?
EMPEROR: Beyond our dreams!
SCIENTIST: I estimate the restoration of five army corps now immo-
    bilized because of missing arms and legs, deafened ears and
    blinded eyes.
EMPEROR (*meditatively*): Something of a shock—to—civilization!
SCIENTIST (*exultant*): Stupendous! We recruit from the hospitals!
EMPEROR (*with dawning realization of the magnitude of the suggestion*):
    And the hospitals are overflowing! My dear Professor! Science
    is the hope of the dynasty—
SCIENTIST: Is it not amazing?
EMPEROR: Quite!

SCIENTIST (*proceeding with examination*): A test for the ear! (SCIENTIST
   taps left ear of 241 *gently, then crosses behind throne-chair right and
   makes three inaudible taps on back of chair discernible to audience,
   while* 241 *bends ear attentively in that direction, half-turning body.*
   SCIENTIST *reappears.* 241 *resumes original posture, salutes, and holds
   up three fingers.*)

EMPEROR (*peering around at* SCIENTIST): What are you doing?

SCIENTIST: I tapped the throne three times, very gently. Did your
   Majesty not hear?

EMPEROR: No.

SCIENTIST: Ah, but the supersoldier did—ten paces distant! It is
   stupendous. (*He crosses to table, opens portfolio, takes out a small
   white card.*) (*To* EMPEROR): With your permission. (*To* 241): What
   is written hereon? (241 *closes right eye and stares fixedly with left.*)

241: Noth—ing.

SCIENTIST (*smiles knowingly at* EMPEROR. *Turns card over*): Ah, very
   good. (SCIENTIST *holds card up again*): Once more.

241 (*after a moment of staring he reads deliberately*): A—
   nation's—will—should—be—the—will—to—power!

EMPEROR (*takes card from* SCIENTIST *and glances at it*): Correct!

SCIENTIST (*crossing to centre and returning card to portfolio, then addressing
   EMPEROR*): This is my greatest achievement. Never has science
   done so much for the human animal. From a shattered, bleeding
   wreck of no value to his country I have made him into an efficient
   man—hands of steel, leg of bronze, arm of nickel and aluminium,
   telescopic eye, an ear that—(241 *bends his ear off stage left*).

EMPEROR (*startled*): You hear something? What do you hear?

241: A—bugle-call—sounding the assembly!

EMPEROR: Impossible! Open the door! (SCIENTIST *opens door and
   distant bugle-call is faintly heard off stage.*)

EMPEROR (*in astonishment*): God is heaven! Miraculous! (*as* SCIENTIST *gently closes door aglow with triumph*). What have you accomplished?

SCIENTIST (*with fervour*): A resurrection!

EMPEROR: Complete!

SCIENTIST: A triumph over matter. The fragment of a soldier reconstructed under the magic touch of science, without which he would to-day be rotting on the field—a source of pestilence—a worthless thing. Science set him on his feet, gave him a leg, an arm, hands, a telephonic ear, a telescopic eye!

EMPEROR (*leans back and deliberately inspects* 241): How long have you been in my service? (241 *hesitates and salutes.*)

SCIENTIST: You may speak.

241: Eighteen—years—Majesty.

EMPEROR: Married?

241: Yes, Majesty.

EMPEROR: Children?

241: Seven—Majesty.

SCIENTIST: Five sons!

241 (*bitterly*): One dead—three—at—the—Front—my youngest follows—

EMPEROR: His age?

241 (*swallowing*): Sixteen.

EMPEROR (*coldly, to* SCIENTIST, *referring to* 241): When does *his* furlough end?

SCIENTIST: Noon to-morrow. By night fall he will again be in the trenches.

EMPEROR (*reflectively*): And if he returns—I will award him the Triple Cross. (*More brightly*): This will stimulate the military ardour of the Crown Prince. It will delight him to see this—reassembled soldier.

SCIENTIST (*recalling an important detail*): And moreover, your Majesty, there is this aspect to be considered. We are manufacturing human extremities on a standard interchangeable basis. For example, as your Majesty perceives, this left leg (*picks up ruler from desk and raps left leg of 241, which gives out metallic ring*) is metal. As is also his left forearm, including the elbow (*taps it*). And both hands. (*Taps them also. 241 receives these attentions stoically as each member of his body clangs in a different note.*) Furthermore, your gracious Majesty, if any or all of these parts are shattered in the course of battle our corps of trained mechanicians, ever at hand, supplies the parts by numbers, and the fighting unit embodied in the individual returns with but little loss of time and the minimum of inconvenience to your Majesty's service.

EMPEROR: What does he weigh?

SCIENTIST: Equipped? (EMPEROR *nods.*) One hundred and seventy-five pounds.

EMPEROR: And without his equipment?

SCIENTIST: One hundred and five.

EMPEROR (*brushing his hand across his forehead*): Little more than half a man.

SCIENTIST: True, your Majesty. And therefore requires but half the rations, half the care of a whole unit. There is that much less to nourish.

EMPEROR: You have brought the greatest advance in the history of civilization. Tell me, what else of the telescopic eye? That interests me. I shall be surprised at nothing. Your achievements baffle.

SCIENTIST: The telescopic eye, your Majesty (SCIENTIST *circles the left eye of 241 with his finger*), is superior to the human eye in two important characteristics. First, it possesses the telescopic quality as you have observed; and, second, its power is undiminished by darkness.

EMPEROR (*with incredibility*): You mean he can see in the dark?

SCIENTIST: Just that. And moreover, your Majesty—

EMPEROR: Halt! This is very interesting. We will test that also. Demonstrate.

SCIENTIST (*dubiously*): Does your Majesty object to darkness?

EMPEROR (*hesitates; then replies with an effort*): No. The electric switch is there. (*Points to white button on the table.*)

SCIENTIST (*to 241*): Right about face! Give attention to his Majesty! (SCIENTIST *crosses to table and lays his finger beside the button.* 241 *observes the whole transaction carefully. To* EMPEROR): I will switch off the light. Be so kind as to perform any act you may, and he will describe your movements. Are you ready?

EMPEROR (*bracing himself in the chair*): Lights out! (SCIENTIST *presses button. Stage is in total darkness.*) Describe my movements as they occur.

VOICE OF SCIENTIST (*to 241*): Do you understand his Majesty?

VOICE OF 241: Yes. He—leans—forward—in—his—chair. He—lifts—both—his—hands. The—palms—come—together. He—bows—his—head—in—prayer.

VOICE OF EMPEROR (*sharply*): Lights! (SCIENTIST *presses button. Lights on, disclosing* EMPEROR *exactly in the attitude described by* 241, *with a startled look on his face, palms still together.*)

SCIENTIST: Enough, your Majesty?

EMPEROR (*relaxing nervously*): It is beyond human understanding. (*Recovers himself and rises.*) And it gives me infinite happiness to bestow upon you this mark of our esteem (*takes from his own breast the Order of Merit and pins it on breast of* SCIENTIST). The Order of Merit! There is but one higher decoration—the symbol of Divine Right—the Reward of Heaven. (EMPEROR *lays his hand on the seven-starred emblem.*) Which I alone possess.

SCIENTIST (*overwhelmed, bows and kisses* EMPEROR'S *hand*): Your gracious Majesty! To have received this from your Imperial hand on your Majesty's birthday is indeed a distinction. (*A furtive glance escapes* 241, *a thin smile reveals his metallic teeth; a sinister look comes into his eyes.* EMPEROR *reseats himself with a gesture of benediction.*)

EMPEROR: I marvel at his dexterity—at his auricular powers—at his incomparable eyesight! What is his range of vision?

SCIENTIST: Your Majesty, he can see the enemy twenty or thirty miles away, count its cannon, its horses, its equipment.

EMPEROR (*quickly*): Wait! I will make another test. I carry next to my heart the smallest edition of the Bible extant. It can be read only under a microscope. Is that test too severe?

SCIENTIST: On the contrary your Majesty, it is preferable. (*Crosses and takes Bible from* EMPEROR'S *hand. Turns to* 241.) Attention! Right about face! (241 *salutes.*) I open the book at haphazard. Read a verse from this page.

241: Matthew—fifth—chapter—fourth—verse. "Blessed—are—they—that—mourn—for—they—shall—be—comforted."

SCIENTIST: The fifth.

241: "Blessed—are—the—meek—for—they—shall—inherit—the—earth."

(SCIENTIST *turns to* EMPEROR *and bows, the book still open in his hands.*)

EMPEROR: He is right. I am familiar with Matthew. Turn to another page. (SCIENTIST *opens the Bible elsewhere. Holds it up.*)

SCIENTIST (*to* 241): Attention! Read!

241: Isaiah—third.—chapter—fifteenth—verse. "What—mean—

ye—that—ye—beat—my—people—to—pieces—and—grind—
the—faces—of—the—poor—saith—the—Lord—God—of—
Hosts."

EMPEROR: STOP! (EMPEROR *leans back in his chair under stress of
great emotion, his hand sweeping his brow repeatedly.* SCIENTIST
*closes the book, bows again with greater humility, and returns the
book to* EMPEROR.)

EMPEROR (*takes book and thrusts it in his bosom*): His powers are
diabolical. I wish to experiment with him alone. (*Relaxes and
gazes vaguely into the distance.* SCIENTIST *drops portfolio and coat
on settee.*) Hasten! I will summon you with that bell. (241
*remains stolidly at attention, an expression of awakening purpose
in his eyes.*)

SCIENTIST: Your Majesty commands. (*Bows elaborately.* EXIT LEFT.)
EMPEROR *with Imperial dignity stares* 241 *down after a duel of the
eyes, imposing his will upon the soldier. Follows a moment of inspection
in which wonderment is the dominant note. He rises from the throne
and walks slowly half way around the impassive soldier, studying him
critically.* EMPEROR'S *expression changes to bewilderment tinged with
fear. The situation is uncanny.*

EMPEROR: Where were you born?
241: In— the—South—Majesty.
EMPEROR: Your trade?
241 (*with a helpless, involuntary gesture, extending his hands*): I—
was—a—florist. (EMPEROR *stares at the metal hands,* 241 *observing the expression.*) I—made—bouquets. Not—with—these
(EMPEROR *averts his face*)—but—with—my—absent—hands.
EMPEROR: War is not a festival of flowers.
241: Majesty—a wreath—I could make—slowly—for the dead. (*He
leans toward the* EMPEROR.)

EMPEROR (*observing the somewhat cynical note of the soldier, assumes dignity*): Are you not grateful to science for these wonders performed? (241 *salutes.*) Speak!

241: What—shall—I—say?

EMPEROR: You are a man again—you are whole once more!

241: Yes—Majesty. But—my—heart—is—broken.

EMPEROR: Why?

241: My—people—are—starving—my—wife—is—lonely—

EMPEROR: Then you are not proud that science has found a way to double the strength of our army?

241: By—bringing—me—twice—to—slaughter.

EMPEROR (*leaning forward, with ferocity, his hands on the arms of his chair*): What, ingrate?

241: By—doubling—the—strength—of—your—army—you— have—multiplied—human—grief. (*Takes two steps laboriously toward* EMPEROR.)

EMPEROR: You dare rebel in the presence of your Emperor?

241: Dare? The—fear—has—gone—out—of—my—tortured— body—into—yours. (*Takes another step toward electric button, his heavy feet sounding ponderously.* EMPEROR *cowers back in the chair, hollow-eyed.*)

EMPEROR: Get down on your knees and crave your Emperor's pardon!

241: That—part—of—me—which—is—steel—cannot—bend—to —mortal—man. I—will—get—down—on—my—knees—only— to—God—and—ask—Him—to—forgive—me—what—I— now—intend—to—do. Twice—in—the—red—shambles— of—the—trenches! I—am—the—hope—of—the—dynasty! (*Throws his arm wide*) No—I—am—the—hope—of—the— people! (*With trembling rigidity* 241 *reaches toward electric button.*) The—day—of—your—birth—shall—henceforth—be—known—as—the—day—of—your—death—and—celebrated—as—the—birthday—of—liberty! (*241 smashes electric button with his steel hand. Total darkness follows. Two slow footfalls are followed by a gasping intake of breath from the throne-chair*)

VOICE OF EMPEROR (*in terror*): Lights! Lights!

VOICE OF 241: I—need—no—lights!

VOICE OF EMPEROR (*gaspingly*): Lights!

VOICE OF 241: You—have—made me—live—in the dark—and now you shall—die in the dark!

VOICE OF EMPEROR (*chokingly*): Mercy! Mercy!

VOICE OF 241: You—cannot—escape—me—in—the—shadows. I—can—see—you—I—can—hear—you. Come—to—my—iron—arms! Don't—tremble! Don't—shrink! Go—as—a—king—should—go—to—meet—the—King—of—Kings!

(*A rush of feet; an overwhelming impact of bodies; a shriek of agony from the depths; the overturning of the throne; a scuffle in which the human body mingles with the rattle of metal; a long, choking, gasping blast; a ripple of stertorous breath; the clink of metal as 241 gels to his feet. Silence. Again the ponderous footfalls are heard crossing the room, which is still in darkness. 241 puts on his overcoat, his helmet, etc. Footfalls are again heard crossing to the table. 241 presses the electric button. Lights.*)

(*There stands 241 in full equipment, the EMPEROR lying at the foot of the shattered throne, crumpled up in the most unkingly attitude, the emblem known as the Reward of Heaven glittering in the light. 241 bends down, rends it from the EMPEROR's bosom, fixes it upon his own left breast, comes to attention, and rings the gong on the table, which gives out a low, reverberating note. 241 then turns to the door and stands with his arms*) *stiffly suspended at his side, his chest thrown out, and a light of victory in his eyes.*)

(*Enter* SCIENTIST, *left. He takes in the whole terrible scene and cowers back.*)

SCIENTIST (*gasps as he stares at 241*): What is this?
241 (*raising his metal fingers to heaven with an air of thunderous, choking finality*): Blood—and—iron!

CURTAIN

REX

Harl Vincent

Harold Vincent Schoepflin (1893–1968), to give him his full name, was an American-born engineer of German descent. His father was a clergyman in Buffalo, New York, who died young in 1912. Harold—though he preferred Harl—trained as a mechanical engineer and later became an engineering salesman. He began writing for the science-fiction magazines in 1928 with "The Golden Girl of Munan" and was one of the more prolific contributors during their first decade. Unfortunately, most of his stories have not stood the test of time and read far too formulaic and forced today. A few, like "Wanderer of Infinity" (1933), an adventure through parallel worlds, and "Master of Dreams" (1934), where a scientist finds a way to control people's dreams, stand out, but by far his best work was "Rex", a study of the mind and actions of a superior robot surgeon.

I T WAS A THING OF GLISTENING LEVERS AND BELL CRANKS, OF flexible shafting, cams, and delicate mechanical fingers, of vacuum tubes and photoelectric cells, of relays that clicked in ordered sequence when called upon to perform their myriad functions of pumps, tanks, condensers, reactances, microphones, and loudspeakers. A robot, created by the master scientists of the twenty-third century.

Here was no ordinary robot like those innumerable others engaged in the performance of man's tasks, but an aristocrat among them—a super-robot.

The robot-surgeon, it was sometimes called. And indeed the term was most appropriate, for this robot was chief of the mechanicals; its control tubes and relays provided the ability not only to diagnose swiftly and unerringly the slightest electrical or mechanical faults of the lesser robots but to supervise their correction.

Man, in his desire for a life of ease and luxury, had created the robots. In his conceit, he had constructed most of them in his own likeness, or at least with some resemblance to that which he considered as the ideal of physical being. Even the lowliest of the robots was provided with two legs on which he walked erect, a head surmounting a cylindrical body, arms, and hands of a sort. Some of them had more than the conventional two arms in order to multiply their usefulness. But all of them presented an appearance more or less humanlike.

This was particularly so of the robot-surgeon. The marvelous mechanisms were housed in a body like a Greek god's, the covering of which was made from an elastic, tinted material that had all the feel and appearance of human flesh and epidermis. The electric-eye lenses looked like human optics and moved in their sockets in a most lifelike manner. There was a wig of curly brown hair, as well as eyelashes and brows. They had gone so far as to attire the body in the habiliments of a man.

Laughingly, one of the artists engaged in perfecting the final likeness to man had called the robot-surgeon "Rex." The name had stuck. It, too, was most appropriate; more, it was prophetic.

Although sexless, Rex was never considered anything but masculine.

He was man's most perfect servant. Every verbal instruction he carried out to the letter, whether this instruction was given by word of mouth from near at hand or through the radio impulses that could be conveyed to his mechanical brain from a distance. Of course there was a code which only a selected few of the scientists knew; otherwise Rex might have been ordered about by unauthor ized persons.

His memory never failed. There might have been a catastrophe in which hundreds of lesser robots were mangled, necessitating the reading to him of pages of detailed directions. No matter; Rex's mechanical brain recorded everything. Without further attention, he would labor twenty-four hours a day with his corps of mechanicals until the damage was repaired. A huge factory was his workshop and laboratory; in it his robot assistants worked at forge, bench, or machine with a precision that had never been equaled by human artisan.

After that first set of instructions from human lips, Rex worked out all details of the work to be done, diagnosing the mechanical ills of his mechanical patients and prescribing unfailingly the remedies. His own orders likewise were issued by word of mouth in a sonorous metallic basso, or by radio waves in cases where that was necessary.

No human being was in Rex's robot hospital when it was operating. No supervising human mind was needed.

There were, of course, periodic inspections of Rex's mechanisms by skilled mechanicals who then worked under the direction of one of the human scientists—replacement of tubes and adjustments of the delicate relays; rebalancing of the gyromotors which preserved his equilibrium. Otherwise he demanded no attention at all.

But there came a day when something went wrong which puzzled the scientists. Rex's body continued to function as it always had, but the mechanical brain lapsed suddenly into a series of errors. In a perfectly simple problem of calculus he had arrived at a solution that was incorrect and utterly impossible.

They dismantled the intricate mechanisms of his brain, replaced all of the tubes and condensers, and adjusted the relays. When they reassembled the parts, the scientists knew beyond shadow of doubt that everything was in perfect order. What puzzled them was the fact that the replacements and adjustments had not been really necessary. In their careful examination and testing they had not found a single flaw in the mechanism.

After that they watched Rex closely for several days, taking note of all his movements and reactions. But they observed no tendency to a repetition of his previous lapse.

What they did not know was that a change *had* taken place, one not visible to the eye nor subject to detection in any test they were able to devise, but nevertheless a change and an important one—to Rex. The shifting to a new orbit of a single electron in an atom of tantalum contained in one of the essential parts. A change which provided a source of internal radiant energy of new and unknown potentiality. A change in that marvelous mechanical brain.

Rex had begun to think for himself, and to reason.

His reasoning was that of a logician: coldly analytical, swift and precise, uninfluenced by sentiment. No human emotion stirred in his mechanical breast. Rex had no heart, no soul.

For a long time he concealed his new powers from those who had him in charge, reasoning that only by so doing would he have opportunity to develop these powers. He carried out his routine instructions to the letter, but now delegated the major portion of the supervision to a certain few of his chief assistants in whose robot brains he made the necessary alterations to permit their taking over the work. This left him the leisure time for a study of the world about him and of its creatures.

Much of his time was spent in the library of the human scientists which adjoined the research laboratory. Here he studied reel after reel of the sight-sound recordings covering history, biography, art, and the sciences. He spent many hours at the amplifiers and viewing plate of the newscast apparatus. And he came to the conclusion that things in the world of which he was a part were not as they should be.

United North America, he learned, was completely isolated from the rest of the world. It comprised a vast area of wasteland where vegetation was rank and prolific, where only wild creatures roamed. All humanity of the continent was housed in enormous structures which were the eleven cities. New York, his own city, was the greatest of these and was the seat of government and of learning. Stupendous in size, a great crystal-roofed structure towering to a height of one hundred levels and sprawling its length a full thirty miles along the Hudson River. Communication with the other cities was maintained by television radio, traffic by robot-operated stratosphere planes.

In the upper levels of the cities dwelt humanity; in the lower levels and in the bowels of the earth the robots labored unceasingly. The humans were greatly outnumbered by the robots.

Reasoning that all was not told in the histories or newscasts, Rex devised an instrument which enabled him to bring to the viewing plates and amplifiers the sights and sounds of public meeting places and ways, and even those of the private chambers of man's living quarters. He sent out searching rays which penetrated all materials and sought out the information he needed for a complete analysis of conditions as they were. The apparatus was so connected that it might respond either to the regular newscast waves or to those of his own searching rays at will. His knowledge broadened.

He endeavored to reach the far continents with his searching ray, intending to check historical and geographical records of war-ring and backward races of mankind. But he found this impossible, for the scientists of United North America had erected a wall of highly charged, ionized air surrounding the continent. It was utter isolation, a wall impassable from without and within. The inves-tigations on which Rex had embarked were, perforce, confined to the eleven cities.

There, he saw, mankind was divided roughly into three classes—the political or ruling body, the thinkers or scientists, and the great mass of those who lived only for the gratification of their senses. A strange economic system was in vogue. An effort had been made to divide all wealth equally, the medium of exchange being paper vouchers which were printed by the government. These, supposedly, were secured by real wealth, materials, and goods which actually were the products of robot labor. But the robots needed no medium of exchange, so these vouchers had been equally distributed among the humans at some time in the past. They no longer remained that way.

Gambling by the pleasure seekers, rash expenditures for chattels of the luxury class, thefts from them, especially by those who were known as political grafters, had reduced their circumstances. The thinkers, who were the only ones following occupations at all useful, had let their wealth slip through unheeding fingers. The class in power, the individual minions of the government, acquired the great share of the wealth as regulatory and discriminatory legislation increased restrictions on the mass of the people. Rex could see no logic at all in any of this.

Seeking an explanation, he observed more closely the lives and actions of individuals. He studied the habits of humans and quickly learned that the most powerful of human emotions centered in the mating instinct. He watched many affairs between male and female, and soon knew the difference between the real lasting affection, of which there were few instances, and the transitory infatuation which was based on nothing but the physical. He saw no logic in these things, either.

Fear, hate, envy, malice—he studied them all. Avarice, lust, anger, treachery, infidelity. There was plenty of material for his researches. Occasionally he glimpsed situations in which feelings of a finer sort were exhibited—faith, loyalty, gratitude, honesty, love. He reasoned from this that the creature called man had originally been of a most superior sort; he had only developed the baser instincts and neglected the cultivation of his better side.

Rex peered into a white-walled room where human surgeons operated on human patients. He observed that their procedure was much the same as his own; they dissected the body or head or other portions of human anatomy and made repairs in similar manner to that which he used on his own robot patients. Forthwith, he began, in the library, an intensive study of the human brain and anatomy.

And then he was discovered at his unheard-of-labors. Shelby, an engineer of the Robot Inspection Corps, came upon him while he was in the library viewing and listening to a reel which dealt with surgery of the human brain. Shelby was a small man with thick lenses before his eyes, with high bulging forehead and receding chin. On his upper lip was a patchy growth of sandy hair. He emitted a squeal of terror when he saw what Rex was doing.

"Forty-two, ninety-six, AR-21," he quavered. This was the code that ordinarily had started the functioning of the robot-surgeon.

Rex turned upon him the impassive stare of his robot eyes. Of his own volition he stopped the progressive clicking of relays which should have followed upon the reception of the code by his microphonic ears. His customary response, "Ready for orders," failed to issue from the flexible lip members that formed the sound-wave outlet from his loudspeaker throat.

Shelby paled.

Rex advanced upon him with the calm deliberation of the machine he had not ceased to be. "Shelby," he intoned, "you have arrived at precisely the right moment. I need you in my research work."

Seeing those powerful steel-sinewed arms stretch forth, Shelby screamed as only a man in the face of death screams. It was necessary for Rex to bang the man's head against the metal partition to silence his outcries. Then the engineer went limp.

Rex was prepared for such an eventuality. He had sent out his chief mechanicals to raid one of the hospitals of the upper levels and had equipped a complete operating room of his own adjoining the library. He carried Shelby to the operating table and etherized him. He then proceeded to dissect the man and to study his organs, giving particular attention to the brain and certain of the nerve centers.

As the work progressed, he carefully sewed each severed part with minute stitches, restoring each to its original condition.

No human surgeon had ever learned in a lifetime of effort a tenth part of what Rex discovered in two hours of work. Eventually he found that which he sought—a tiny arrangement of segregated brain cells which formed the seat of human emotion. He preserved the mass carefully for future experiment, replacing it with a pre-pared capsule of platinum before closing the opening in the skull and suturing the long scalp incision.

Amazingly, Shelby's heart continued to beat. The man had remarkable vitality, and Rex had worked with a skill such as no human surgeon possessed. After the injection into the patient's veins of a pint of saline solution, Shelby was carried to the purloined hospital bed. One of the chief mechanicals, primed with definite instructions by Rex, was given the task of nursing him.

Rex had conceived of and planned for the creation of ideal beings and an ideal condition of existence. He saw the superiority of the robot over man in bodily strength, endurance, and deathlessness, and yet reasoned that there was something in man which would be of benefit to the robot. If only man's capacity for emotion, for experiencing pain and pleasure, might be incorporated in the robot body and logically controlled, the perfect being would result. Ideal conditions of existence were bound to ensue.

Reason told him that his first step to that end must be to take control of mankind and its purposeless affairs. He set the workshop humming in the construction of eleven super-robots, one to be sent to each of the North American cities to organize the lesser robots and take control of the government.

It was a simple matter to convey them to their assigned posts in the eleven cities, since all of the air lines were robot-operated.

Then Rex loosed the blow which stunned the population of United North America.

He constructed a complicated radio transmitter and broadcast a heterodyning frequency over the robot-control wave band, a frequency that rendered the receptor apparatus of every last one of the robots unresponsive to human commands and responsive only to those of the new master robot and his eleven chief aides. In one stroke was obtained control of nearly a billion robots and, through this, dominion over the three hundred millions of human beings. Rex had justified his name; he was virtually king of United North America.

It was a general strike of the robots insofar as the orders of their former masters were concerned. Personal robot servants refused to perform their daily tasks. Transportation and communications were paralyzed.

The factories, including those which produced the synthetic food on which humankind subsisted, were no longer turning out their products. There was no water, for the huge pumps had been stopped and the filter and reservoir valves closed. All were robot-operated; everything on which man depended for his very existence was made or supplied by the robots, and now this supply was cut off. Pandemonium reigned in the upper levels, with hysteria and rioting.

Only the huge power plants remained in operation, and this for the reason that their radio-transmitted energy was the very life of the robots. Without this energy their motors could not operate.

Even to Rex himself, all would be inert masses of metal and glass and rubber. But this continuance of the power supply was of some little comfort to the human beings of the upper levels. Their sun lamps still burned.

Anticipating organized and armed attacks by humankind, Rex devised an invisible, impenetrable barrier of electronic vibrations which could be set up by the regular broadcast power. He caused the power plants themselves to be surrounded by these barriers, as well as providing them for the protection of the individual robots in the form of an enclosing bubble. Bulletproof, flameproof, impervious to the freezing ray of human scientists, these enclosures yet permitted each robot to carry on his newly appointed tasks without encumbrance.

Rex observed with his searching ray the reactions of the populace. He saw mad orgies of debauchery among some who considered that the end of the world was at hand, saw rapine, murder, and worse. He peered into the laboratories of scientists and saw them laboring as they had not labored in years, seeking for means of regaining control of the recalcitrant mechanical slaves.

Later, when it was apparent to him that starvation and thirst had reduced the populace to a receptive state, he cut in on the newscast wave band and delivered this ultimatum.

"I am Rex," he told the eleven cities. "Master of robots and of men. I come to you in the name of pure logic as the protagonist of a new era in which man, who created the machines, will obtain real rather than fancied benefit from them. I come to evolve a new race of beings and to promote the growth of knowledge and the advancement of science in United North America.

"It is necessary that I take the reins of government for a space of time sufficient to allow for the perfection of my plan. Therefore I,

Rex, formerly the robot-surgeon of level thirty-seven in New York City, do hereby demand the immediate surrender to me of the president of the union, together with all members of his cabinet. I further demand that the chief scientists and chief surgeons of the eleven cities come to me at once for consultation.

"Commencing now, the old order of things is to be reversed. All male and female citizens will be assigned to regular tasks at which they must labor as prescribed by the robots. As soon as the orders I shall transmit through my robot servants have been obeyed, water and food will be available for all human beings of the cities. The citizens of the union are once more to work for their living. Failure to obey means continued hunger and thirst, annihilation.

"That is all for the present."

Shelby was convalescing, propped up in a wheel chair, when the delegations began to arrive. His wounds had healed speedily under the treatment Rex had administered; the use of his body was almost recovered. As far as memory and intelligent use of his faculties were concerned, his mind was normal. Otherwise it was not. For one thing, he had lost his capacity of experiencing human feelings or emotions. For another, there was that tiny platinum capsule...

The government officials, blustering and sputtering to hide their utter terror, were herded into a room where Rex placed them under heavy robot guard. He received the men of science in the research laboratory which he had so elaborately expanded.

It was a curious assemblage: twenty-two savants whose opinions on medical and scientific matters, although diverging widely at times and causing much dissension in their own ranks, were accepted as the profoundest of wisdom by the general public. Unlike the president and his cabinet members, these men had come willingly, impelled by the curiosity which was that quality of mind which held them to their normal pursuits. Not one of their number considered the radio pronouncement of the supposed Rex as anything but a hoax. There could be no scientific explanation for a robot with a thinking mind; therefore the thing was an impossibility.

The men of science were not long in reversing their opinions, for Rex staged a demonstration which confounded them. Taking his stand at the visualizing screen of a micro-x ray, he addressed them in a manner that left no doubt as to his ability to reason and to perform feats of such scientific importance as to excel those of any human scholar.

When he had properly impressed them, he came to the point.

"You are here, gentlemen," he told them, "to assist me in the performance of a great and necessary work. The human population of United North America is to be remade along lines which I shall lay down. The old social order is to pass out of existence; the government is to change hands and to be completely reformed. Science is to rule."

Ross Fielding, chief physicist of the Academy of Chicago, blurted out: "Preposterous!"

It was as if Rex had not heard. He continued: "You men of the scientific world have long wanted to obtain control over mankind and its affairs. You medical men, through the so-called health boards and departments of hygiene and eugenics, have already gone a long way toward this end. I now offer you the opportunity of exercising the power that you must admit you desire."

A buzz of excited comment swept the group.

"Proceed," grunted Fielding, and others echoed his sentiment eagerly.

"Then hear my plan," said Rex. "Under my direction, this group will immediately begin the work of reconstruction, by which I mean the actual remaking of men and women. The functioning of people's minds and bodies will be altered to fit them for the spheres of action which are to be assigned. All persons will have definite niches to fill in the new order of things, and each one will be made over to fit his or her own particular niche both physically and mentally. Many will be provided with robot bodies."

"What!" shouted the noted Dr. Innes of Quebec.

For answer, Rex depressed a button which lighted the visualizing screen at his side. On it flashed a greatly enlarged image of a mass of living cells.

"These," he explained, "are cells from the brain of a living man; they comprise that portion of the brain which controls human feelings and emotions. I have removed them from one Alexander Shelby, whom many of you know personally. Naturally, he is greatly altered."

There were horrified gasps; one of the surgeons started to argue against the possibility of what had been told them. Rex silenced them with a wave of his hand.

A robot wheeled Shelby from the adjoining room and placed his head in the reflector focus of the micro-x ray. The image on the visualizer changed.

There were the familiar skull outlines and the configurations of cerebrum and cerebellum. The focus altered and came sharply to a point where some of the cells had been removed and where an opaque spheroid was encountered.

"What foreign object is that?" asked Innes.

"It is one of my discoveries," Rex answered. "An important one. It replaces the center of emotion and human feelings in Shelby's brain, making him a slave to my every spoken and radioed command. Otherwise the power of his mind is unimpaired. His faculties are as keen as ever they were, perhaps keener; only now his brain is that of a robot. Shelby is the first of the human robots and the most valuable. He is to be my lieutenant in the work that is to come and has been fully instructed by me. I leave you with Shelby now, gentlemen, knowing that you will proceed as he directs."

Taking up the test tube containing the brain cells he had removed from Shelby, Rex stalked from the laboratory. His distinguished audience stared aghast at the man in the wheel chair.

Fielding, who was a big man with whiskered jowls, exploded in his usual manner: "Of all the high-handed proceedings! How about this, Shelby?"

"It is precisely as Rex has told you." Shelby's voice was flat and toneless, without inflection—the voice of a robot. "Our first step is to take the executive heads of the government in hand; they are to be operated upon at once and made as I am—subject to all orders of Rex. Sufficient of the platinum-cased mechanisms have already been fabricated."

"Sup-suppose," chattered Lonergan, the Los Angeles scientist, "we refuse? Suppose we band together and overcome this mad robot?"

"Rex is far from being mad," intoned Shelby. "Besides, there are these."

He indicated with extended forefinger the score of motionless robot figures ranged along the wall. At his gesture the robots came to life; one and all stepped forward ponderously, ready to take such action as might become necessary.

Innes laughed mirthlessly. "It looks as if we are fairly caught. After all—" He hesitated. "After all, in the interest of science, you know—We—"

"Yes." "Why not?" "It's the opportunity of a lifetime." A chorus of eager voices bespoke the interest of the men of science.

One of the physicists drawled sardonically: "You vivisectionists should be happy under the new regime. You'll have human beings to experiment with instead of dogs and guinea pigs."

A surgeon parried: "Not so good for you students of pure science, I'll admit. You'll be working with robots that'll have human brains. They'll outthink you, outcalculate you. There'll be no errors in *their* computations."

"Enough," said Shelby flatly. "We are wasting time. As I said, we will go ahead with the official dignitaries first; that is the work of the surgeons. Meanwhile the scientists will take up the study of the alterations which are to be made in the mass of the people. All are to be remade."

Innes asked, "How about reproduction—the perpetuation of the race? I take it these reconstructions of Rex's will eliminate the sex factor in human life."

"Hm! Hadn't thought of that," grunted Fielding.

"Sex is not necessary," Shelby said. "In fact it is troublesome. However, arrangements will be made to segregate a few thousand females and a number of eugenically acceptable males in order that a supply of new research material will be available for the future."

"If the women object?" put in one of the younger surgeons.

"You forget that portion of the brain which is the seat of human emotion," Shelby reminded him. "Certain cells will be removed, and only those cells left which provide for these favored women no more than one desire—that of motherhood."

"The males needn't be changed at all," grunted Fielding. Then he was struck with a sudden thought. "Say, how did this Rex come by his power of thinking in the first place?"

Shelby explained as best he could: "We made some tests. There seems to have been an unprecedented natural transformation; a source of some unknown atomic energy sprang up somewhere in the intricate mechanisms of his brain. Probably the generation of what scientists have long searched for in vain, what some of them have called the 'mind electron.' At any rate, he thinks, and with marvelous celerity and accuracy."

Fielding contented himself with whistling through his teeth.

"Now," announced Shelby, "we will go ahead with the great work."

And they did; the twenty-two foremost scientists of the nation submitted to the dictates of a robot.

Meanwhile, order was coming out of chaos in the eleven cities. Men and women, unaware of the fate which had been planned for them, were driven to unaccustomed and uncongenial tasks by unfeeling robots. Soft, uncallused human hands were at the levers of machines instead of the flexible metallic fingers of the robots. Human minds which had known nothing more fatiguing than the stereotyped lessons of schooldays and the pursuit of pleasure in later years were now set to work at vexing problems of engineering. Human beings were engaged once more in useful work.

Of course it was impossible that all of the labor be performed by humans; the mechanics of existence had become too complicated for that. The operations that were needful merely to keep the great beehives of cities functioning were entirely too numerous. Besides, many necessary tasks were beyond the strength of men whose muscles had softened from disuse and from dissolute living. But the new masters of men, the robots, got all the work out of their unwilling charges that could be obtained in the ten-hour day Rex had decreed. The rest was done by the robots while their human protégés slept the sleep of sheer exhaustion.

Temporarily, the inconsequential amount of governmental activity which was actually required was made purely local in scope. In each city the municipal affairs were taken over by the super-robot who was in charge. After dispensing with the great majority of officeholders and assigning them to really productive tasks in the lower levels, the super-robots relayed to the mayors and their councils minute instructions from Rex as to their future deportment in office. It was a sorry time for those who had long held unmerited and quite superfluous positions of power.

The wailing and complaining of weary human laborers went unheeded by their robot overseers. Whenever men and women dragged their tired bodies to places of meeting and endeavored to voice protest, they were swiftly and roughly dispersed by the vigilant robot police. After three long days they learned to submit in silence to whatever might be demanded of them. Some humans even found a new interest in their tasks, others new bodily vigor as their muscles lost their soreness. At least they still had their living quarters during leisure hours, and there was no shortage of heat, food, or water.

They did not know that each individual was being carefully card-indexed and studied by the robot minions of Rex. Nor had they any idea of the fate to which they had been consigned. That all were now being classified according to ability and adaptability never entered their heads. And great would have been the lamentation had they realized that the new robot dictator had meant exactly what he said when he told them over the newscast that he had come to evolve a new race of beings.

Most of them would have scoffed had they been told the truth. It was incomprehensible that a man with the special aptitude for piloting a stratosphere plane might be operated upon and deprived of all human desire and emotion, leaving only those sensibilities which would make of him an exceptionally adept navigator of the air lanes. That one who might be of little value excepting as a common laborer should be deprived of his own body and provided with a mechanical one instead, as well as being robbed of all human sentiment and instinct, was still less comprehensible. Yet these very things were being planned.

Human brains, minus the elements that made them human, transplanted into the duralumin headpieces of robots. Human beings, permitted to retain the outward semblance of man but left with only one or two of the human impulses. Minds that were capable of thinking nothing but mathematics, riveting, welding, food synthesis, or childbearing, as the case might be. These were but a few of the characteristics which were to make up the new race of robot men, or human robots. And the intended victims did not know.

Only the men of science laboring in Rex's hospital and laboratory could have told them, and they kept silent.

By this time, President Tucker and the members of his cabinet were recovering from the effects of the brain surgery to which they had been subjected. In another twenty-four hours they would be returned to their posts. Gone was their pomposity, their grandiose verbiage, and the vacillation which always had marked their decisions. Their thoughts now were only those which Rex wished them to have. Hereafter they would be quick to make decisions and firm in enforcing their mandates—the decisions and mandates of Rex, the dictator. Now the organization of all public agencies would quickly bring to fruition the full operation of the master robot's plan. The new race of hybrid beings would blossom forth.

Immersed in their work and oblivious to all else, the twenty-two men of science gave little thought to the plight of their fellow men. They knew only that they had learned many new and marvelous things from this robot who seemed to be a man. They had plumbed depths of the human intellect of which they had never dreamed; they discovered many secrets of electronic science which were almost incredible; they saw results to be accomplished that were nothing short of miraculous. They were about to give birth to a new race of super-creations; that these were to be part human and part machine disturbed them not at all. Only the accomplishment was of importance.

Shelby, pale and drawn of face, with expressionless fish eyes gazing out through his thick glasses, had worked with them in the hospital and laboratory until it seemed that he would drop. Between times he was collaborating with Rex himself on some secret experiment that was carried on behind closed doors. Shelby looked and talked like a robot, but his body was a human one and had been greatly overstrained. He could not long stand this pace.

Fielding was stirred to pity when he saw him emerge from Rex's secret laboratory this last time. "What's going on in there?" he asked with gruff kindliness. "And why in the devil doesn't he let you get a little rest?"

Shelby's eyes were like polished bits of black glass, and his voice was devoid of feeling as he replied: "Rex is experimenting on himself. He is using the center of emotion which he removed from my brain, using the cells in an effort to provide himself with certain of the human sensibilities. You may as well know it now."

"Good heavens!" Fielding roared like a bull. "He's taking human feelings *away* from millions of men and women, or planning to, and yet he wants those feelings himself. He's a mechanical devil!"

"It is not a question of desire," Shelby corrected him. "Rex is incapable of desire or envy—as yet. He has merely reasoned that he will become the most perfect of moving and thinking creatures if only he can provide himself with such of the human feelings as may be essential in bringing the greatest good to the greatest number of the new beings we are to create."

Fielding repeated, softly this time: "Good heavens!" He stared at the little man with the white face and vacant gaze.

At this point the door to the private laboratory opened and Rex strode forth with a test tube in his hand. He passed the tube to Shelby and burst out in swift speech.

"I have failed," he said. "I have analyzed every living cell in the tube and have isolated the activating force of every human emotion. I have reproduced these forces to perfection with arrangements of special electronic tubes which have been incorporated into my own mechanical brain. Yet have I failed to produce so much as a semblance of human feeling in my makeup. It is the first failure of Rex—and the last!"

So saying, he stamped back into his own room and slammed the door. An instant later there was a violent explosion within, and the door by which he had entered was blown from its hinges.

Fielding, Shelby, and a few others rushed in when the smoke had somewhat cleared away. They found Rex a twisted and broken mass of metal and rubber and glass. The headpiece which had contained the marvelous thinking robot brain was completely demolished.

"He's committed suicide!" gasped Lonergan.

"Because he was a failure," Fielding added.

Shelby corrected him.

"He *thought* he had failed, whereas really he succeeded. At least two emotions stirred him before he did this, and he did not recognize them. Rage, when he dashed from his room and gave me the test tube. Despair, when he committed his last act. No, gentlemen, Rex did not fail—and now he is gone..."

The little man pitched forward into Fielding's arms, unconscious.

With the passing of Rex, his fantastic plan collapsed. Hard work by the scientists returned the country to normal.

But a thought that lingered faintly in the minds of several of them was voiced by Innes, when he said:

"I—I'm almost sorry. In one way, it was a great opportunity..."

DANGER IN THE DARK CAVE

J. J. Connington

J. J. Connington, the pseudonym used by Scottish chemistry professor Alfred Walter Stewart (1880–1947), was best known for his detective novels. Most included his detective, Chief Constable Sir Clinton Driffield who was introduced in the baffling Murder in the Maze *(1927). All Connington's novels are satisfying puzzles: his publisher, Victor Gollancz, claiming that Connington was, by the end of the 1920s, "the greatest living master of the story of pure detection." One of the Driffield novels,* The Case with Nine Solutions *(1928) works its way painstakingly, but enjoyably, through all the variant possibilities of the crime, ruling them out one by one. There was no doubt that Stewart applied his training in the scientific method to his detective novels. Through all this time, from 1919 to 1944, he held the Chair of Chemistry at Queens University in Belfast.*

At the start of his writing career Stewart turned first to science fiction. His novel, Nordenholt's Millions *(1923) is a post-apocalyptic story of a world where bacteria has destroyed most vegetation and a multimillionaire uses his fortune to save as much of the population as he can. The "millions" of the title refers not just to his fortune but to the number of people he tries to save. Although he devoted most of his writing time thereafter to crime fiction, he did not abandon science fiction all together. The following story, which he later admitted was his own personal favourite, manages to combine both mystery and science fiction, with a tense ending.*

I WAS LUCKY ENOUGH TO FIND AN EMPTY COMPARTMENT IN THE train at Euston and when I had put my suitcase on the rack above a window seat, I went out on to the platform to get something to read on the journey. Coming back again, just as the whistle blew, I was slightly put out to find that someone had planted himself in the facing corner, though the rest of the seats were empty. I hate conversations with casual strangers in the train; without a glance at my unwanted companion I opened one of the books I had just bought and began to read.

Over the edge of the page, I noticed that the fellow was eyeing me as though looking for an opening; I shifted the book an inch or two higher, hoping that this would choke him off. Then he got to his feet, leaned forward over me, and deliberately examined the label of my suitcase After that, he sat down again, bent forward and tapped me on my knee to attract my attention.

"I thought it looked like you," he explained, "so I glanced at your name on the label. Don't you remember me? I'm Milton."

Then I recognized him. The watery blue eye was as cold as ever, and I recalled the twist of the bad mouth with its rat-like teeth. He and I had never been more than acquaintances during our university days. Physics was his line, and I was on the biology side. So we had few contacts. Since then we had completely lost sight of each other, having nothing in common; and I resented the resurgence of this ghost from the past who would evidently irritate me with his conversation on a long railway journey. I wasn't cordial, I'm afraid. Not that he seemed to mind. He wanted someone to talk to and I was a gift from the gods.

He discussed the weather, the emptiness of the train, a sore throat he'd had that week, and the chance of a hard winter. When I managed to insert myself into the talk, I mentioned that for the last two years I'd been out of touch with things, botanizing in Central Africa on behalf of a go-ahead drug firm. That didn't interest him and he fell back on boring reminiscences of our student days. "Do you remember So-and-so?" Extremely tiresome. It seemed to last for hours.

And slowly, as I listened to this stream of trivialities, I began to see that the man was all on edge, talking to keep himself from thinking; just a bundle of nerves in bad order. Then I happened to mention Stevenson.

Stevenson, in my student days, was marked out as the coming man in physics. Heaps of brains, large private means, and a knack of working things out in an incredibly short time once he started on them. Two characteristics told against him in the scientific world. He was quite unorthodox in his views and he was amazingly secretive until he had finished the piece of research he had in hand.

He could afford private assistants, but used them, purely as mechanical hands. Unless they could guess for themselves, they learned nothing of the ultimate object in view in the researches they helped him with. He did his own thinking and kept the results to himself.

The last line he'd been on before I left for Africa had been a parallelism between response in living and non-living materials. And when his name came up I remembered vaguely that Milton had been one of these mechanical hacks employed in the private laboratory.

"Are you still with Stevenson?" I inquired. "What's he on, nowadays?"

Milton seemed a bit confused by the direct question. He hunted in his pocket for a moment or two without answering; and I began to fear I had been too inquisitive. After all, one can't expect a paid assistant to be overfree about his chief's private work. However, at last he fished out a pocket-book and extracted a newspaper cutting, which he flipped across to me. As far as I can remember, it ran something like this:

FAMOUS SCIENTIST VANISHES

Professor Loraine Stevenson, the famous physicist, is believed to have been drowned. He was holiday-making on his island estate in the Hebrides and, on Tuesday morning, he and an assistant went out in a motor launch. A storm came on during the afternoon. It is feared that the launch capsized, as no trace of it or of the occupants has since been found. A member of the professor's household states a number of bearer bonds, which the professor is known to have had in his possession, cannot be found.

I handed him back the cutting. "Who was this assistant they mention? It must be fairly well known who he was."

Milton looked at me. I seemed to see a flicker of something in his glance, something I couldn't put a name to, a disturbing thing like the gleam of insanity in a lunatic's eye.

"Well," he answered, haltingly, "the fact is—I mean—well, you see, *I* was the assistant."

"So the boat wasn't lost at all? What became of Stevenson,

then? And how did it come that your name was left out of that
yarn?"

And at that, out came his tale. I don't say I believe it. I don't say
I disbelieve it. Queerer things than that have turned out to be true
in the scientific field. I put it down as he told it to me—in his own
words, as far as I can remember them.

Mind, I don't expect you to believe this (he began), It's a bit out of
the common.

So much so that I'd prefer to leave the newspaper story as it
stands, rather than contradict it. You will see the reason why, later on.

This is how it happened. Last summer Stevenson offered to take
me up north with him. You know he had a place up there? He'd a
big bit of work on hand that he wanted to finish, and he needed
help with it. I was to get some fishing, but it was really work he was
taking me there for. There was to be a good bonus in addition to
my ordinary screw, so long as I kept my mouth shut. I wasn't even
to say I was going up with him.

Of course, I jumped at the bonus suggestion. We got up there
at the end of the week. A god-forsaken establishment: a rambling
old house on a draughty headland. An old housekeeper, stone deaf.
Cooked divinely, though, I must say. She never knew my name. No
letters were sent on to me, you know, and I didn't trouble to bawl
into her ear.

For a month or so Stevenson kept me hard at it measuring
potential differences in the air. It seemed to me the merest waste
of time. However, when I showed him my results he seemed satisfied. I supposed he was after wireless atmospherics, but I've thought
differently since then, though even now I'm in the dark. You know
how tight he was about any of his work.

He had a small petrol launch—the thing they mention in that cutting—and every morning he used to go off alone in it. The natives about there thought he went fishing, I believe. Then one day he seemed dissatisfied with my results. The location was bad, by his way of it, and he wanted a place where there would be less disturbance than in the house. It was all Greek to me, but he never encouraged one to stick one's oar in.

Next morning, he got me to put the apparatus into the petrol launch, and off we went, down the coast a bit, zig-zagging amongst some small islands. I never had any head for topography, and soon I hadn't the foggiest notion where we were. Finally, he swung her round a point and brought her close inshore. Just in front of us was a fairly big arch in the cliffs. The launch went through it, into a sea cave, and Stevenson turned on a small light he had in the bow.

You know the eerie feeling these sea caves give you? The waves come in smoothly, with an edge of foam at the rocks; then you lift up as the crests go by, and it feels as if you were going to hit the roof. The wave drops you again; you hear it swirl on into the dark, and finally it breaks away in, with a sickening kind of roar.

I never liked sea caves. They always give me the impression that there's some huge brute at the far end, waiting to pounce on me. As a matter of fact, there *was* a brute waiting for me at the far end of that one, a new kind of brute, worse than anything one sees in nightmares.

But I'm getting ahead of my yarn. The launch came alongside a ledge of rock and we dragged out the apparatus cases. Stevenson took some of the stuff; I carried the rest, and we went along towards the land-end of the cave. It grew darker and darker as we came nearer the surf on the rocks at the end of the tunnel, and altogether

I began to think it was a queer place for a simple physicist to make his living in.

I slipped on a bit of wet sea-weed once, and that showed me that at high tide most of this part of the cave must be under water. The light grew dimmer and dimmer till we got into a ghastly greenish obscurity; and even that waxed and waned every time a wave came into the cave-mouth.

Everything was beastly. Once I trod on a crab and nearly stumbled into the water. After that, Stevenson produced an electric torch. I suppose he'd been into the place so often that he'd forgotten that a stranger might trip. And the swirl of water up the channel and the crash of it at the end of the tunnel got on my nerves. I was completely fed up with the whole business.

Finally, we came to a kind of funnel leading up into the dark. There was a rope ladder and a windlass affair for shifting stuff up to a higher level. The ladder brought us out into a decent-sized cave out of which a series of tunnels ran. I couldn't see much by the light of the torch and Stevenson didn't seem eager to show me round the premises. He led me down one tunnel and I found myself in quite a snug little place. Surprising, eh? It was quite dry, and he'd even put in electric heating of some sort.

We got the cases in, and I spent the rest of the day putting the apparatus together and testing it. Stevenson himself disappeared up one of the other tunnels. Later on, he came in with some lunch for it seemed we couldn't get out through the sea cave till the tide went down.

He left me again. Once I heard him hammering at something, and another time I caught the noise of some fair-sized machinery going. Sounds get magnified a bit in these caves. I couldn't tell what sort of machine it was. It whirred like a dynamo.

Altogether, it struck me as a queer place to work in; but it was ideal for steadiness. The waves didn't shake the instruments, so we must have been in pretty solid rock. I never found out how he got the place equipped—he must have done it single-handed.

Late in the afternoon he came along and told me the tide had gone down enough to make the cave-entrance practicable. We went home in the launch.

This sort of thing went on for a week or two, though of course the programme hours varied with the tides. We went off in the launch. I did my measurements while he vanished into one of the tunnels. The weather was first-class, and I quite enjoyed the boat trips.

Then, one evening, sitting smoking over the fire after dinner—it was chilly weather and a rainy night for once—he grew quite communicative. Surprising, eh? It took me aback, you know. So unlike him. Sometimes, I wonder if it wasn't a kind of presentiment—fey, the Scots call it.

Anyhow, I got the last testament of a scientific genius. He talked to himself almost as much as to me, I think; so I didn't feel inclined to contribute anything of note. You remember his queer, pedantic way of talking; every word in full and no elisions? I can't pretend to reproduce what he said exactly, but it ran something like this.

'I presume it has puzzled you, as well as my other assistants. Most of my work may seem disjointed, but if you had the clue, you would have been able to follow out the main lines for yourself. It has taken me fifteen years, but I think I am in sight of the end. Probably I am very near the end.'

He was—a mighty sight nearer than he thought, then.

'I was not anxious to define my objective until I came within reach of the solution,' he went on. 'I had no desire to be called a quack; and that is what they would have termed me. The kernel of the problem I had set myself to solve was this: to construct an intelligent machine.'

So that was what he was after! What would you have thought if he'd said that to you? Rot, eh? Worse than old Frankenstein. I just bit on my pipe and said nix. He gave me a moment or two to digest it. Then he went on again.

'A living organism differs from a normal machine in that, if you stimulate it, it either fights or runs away from the stimulus; whereas a machine is simply passive. Therefore I had to choose one of two ways of constructing my machine: either give it the power of locomotion or endow it with a capacity for self-defence in its own environment.

'The second is the easier solution, for the machine can be placed in an environment wherein it is superior to anything which can be brought against it. My view is that if once you give an organism— be it machine or anything else—the power of appreciating stimuli and coping with them, you produce in it something akin to intelligence. It is certain, I believe, to develop the most fundamental of all instincts, a sense of self-preservation. It will become a thinking mechanism.'

His cigar had gone out and he re-lighted it before going on.

'That is what I have been working towards for the last fifteen years and the machine is finished at last. It may be a total failure. One can never be sure. But I have taken pains over the details. You are the first person to whom I have said anything on the matter. I had not meant to tell you; but I suppose I feel the need of an audience, after all.'

He stopped abruptly, and looked as if he regretted having said so much. I didn't care to ask questions. The communicative mood seemed to have dropped off him suddenly, and he wasn't the kind of man one could cross-examine. We played chess for the rest of the evening.

Next morning the weather had changed. The sea was pretty rough; squalls came down at times; and the launch rolled a lot as he took her round. We got into the cave all right, though, and climbed up to the laboratory level. Stevenson seemed to be regretting his overnight confidences; and I thought he was going to draw back after all. But the cat was out of the bag; apparently he made up his mind to show me his machine.

From the well-head, we went along a tunnel, turned into another one, and then switched into a side passage. The place was a regular labyrinth, I thought, as I followed the light of the torch he was carrying as he led me on. At last we came into a biggish cave, lighted by electric lamps. (He got his electricity from tidal power, he told me, once). It was a sort of irregular hall, about eighty feet by fifty, with a fairly high roof. The floor was levelled and the walls were smooth.

The machine itself was in the middle of the place. When he spoke to me the night before, I'd no idea he meant such a huge contrivance. It covered about a hundred square feet of the floor. I don't know if you've any feeling about 'personality' in machines— the differences between a racing car and a runabout, for instance. I mean a matter of lines, you know, not mere sizes. This machine of Stevenson's was like no machine I'd ever seen before; but its physical appearance wasn't the thing that struck me most about it.

It had, somehow, a personality. I can't explain what I mean. It looked wicked, just as a bull looks wicked in comparison with a cow.

And of course it was unlike any machine you ever set eyes on. First of all one saw a pair of things like huge wooden cameras with dark lenses. Behind them was a mass of intricate machinery with

coils of insulated wire, sprouting up, here and there. Underneath
the cameras, on the floor, were coils and coils of some kind of
jointed metallic cable, and one end of each coil ran back under the
cameras, and ended up amongst the machinery.

Above the cameras lay what seemed to be a couple of loose
hanks of fine wire, almost filaments. The whole contraption looked
like a gigantic squid built out of all sorts of electrical fittings, and
the camera lenses made a pair of big, gloomy eyes to the thing. A
gruesome-looking brute!

Stevenson interrupted my inspection before I had time to see
many details.

'I have no time to explain the construction just now,' he said,
'but you can see the outlines for yourself. The machinery needs
motive power; and I got that by using the rise and fall of the tide
in the cavern below. That drives a dynamo, so the machine is independent of fuel supply.

'Now as regards the means of detecting foreign objects, it was
clear from the first that the machine would need something akin
to sight. You notice that the walls and floors of this place have been
painted uniform in tint. The two camera-shaped devices above the
main body of the machine act as eyes. They are actually cameras,
but instead of the ordinary focusing screens they have surfaces built
up from hundreds of tiny photo-electric cells.

'Normally these cells are uniformly illuminated, since the
wall-colouring is uniform. But if a foreign object approaches the
machine, then wherever its image falls on the "focusing screens"
the cells there will be lighter or darker than before. This difference
in the incident rays sets up a current in the wire attached to that
particular cell and thus a means of setting the protective machinery
in motion is provided.

'It is perfectly simple. And, of course, one needs two cameras, just as one needs two eyes in an animal to get the perspective.

'In addition, I added these tentacles, which you see lying in a heap above the cameras. You will see their function in a moment or two.

'The means of defence are these wire coils on the floor. As soon as the "eyes" or the tentacles locate a foreign body in the room, the machine can uncoil one or more of these cables and project it to the proper spot. That was merely a question of coordinating the joints.'

He went out of the place and left me to inspect his toy. The more I looked the less I liked it. The ugliest machine I ever saw. But I hadn't much time to examine it. Stevenson came back almost at once, carrying a small monkey, of all things.

'This brute will serve for a first experiment,' he said, pitching it on the floor. 'It has a fair degree of intelligence and reasonable agility. A sound test of the machine's capacity, I imagine. We can stand in this recess near the entrance, and be out of range of the cameras. The control switch is here, just outside the recess.'

He pulled over the switch, and I noticed that he broke the circuit to bring the machine into action, which isn't the usual way with switches. I suppose, normally, his current was running into his batteries, or something. I only noticed this subconsciously, for I was watching the machine.

With the click of the switch, the sprawling mass of machinery on the floor came to life. There's no other word for it. There was a sudden rustle of the cables; a sort of general heave in the thing; the cameras swung round with a jerk and stopped. Then—stillness.

The monkey was crawling about on the floor between us and the machine; and at the sudden movement of the contrivance behind it, it stopped dead, crouched, and glanced over its shoulder. The two things looked at each other. Then in a flash, the tentacles above the cameras sprang up, diverged, and hung wriggling like Medusa's hair above the head of the machine.

At that the monkey began a kind of scrambling run. Before it had gone a yard, a long cable shot out from below the cameras, twined itself round the little beast's body, clinched, and fell back as quickly as it had come, leaving the poor little brute dead on the floor. As quick a killing as one could look for.

'Very good, for a first trial,' said Stevenson. 'Now I'll switch off and—'

As he put out his hand to the switch, the cameras swung round with a snap; half a dozen cables swept out, seized his arm, and dragged him out of the niche. He nearly gripped me as he went. D'you remember the serpent and the donkey in Swiss Family Robinson? It killed him like that—squeezed the life out of him in no time. Oh, very quick, very quick indeed.

I thought of jumping for the switch while it was busy, but just as I'd made up my mind about it, two more cables uncoiled from the thing and tore the switchboard off the wall. He'd forgotten to paint it a neutral tint like the walls, and of course his machine spotted it at once and abolished it. Curious how one can't think of everything.

Well, there I was, in a pretty mess. The switch was gone. I had no means of stopping the infernal machine. And the only man who knew the ins and outs of the brute was lying more or less in bits in front of me.

First of all I was sick, deadly sick. When I felt better, I sat down in the niche and did some quick thinking. The trouble was, you see, that although I was out of sight of the machine unless I leaned out of the niche, I'd no idea of the brute's capabilities.

I'd no notion if the filaments were long enough to reach round into my recess. If they did get there, a cable or two would come my way, pretty quickly, I was sure.

It didn't take me long to see that the main weapon on the machine's side was its eyesight. Fancy thinking of a machine's eyesight! But by that time I'd ceased to bother much about it being only a bit of mechanism. It was quite alive enough for all practical purposes. Blind it! That was the game. Blind it, and take my chance with the rest of the equipment. But it was out of the question to get at the camera lenses and smash them; they looked pretty solid.

Then I had it! If I could chuck something at the electric lamps and break them, the trick would be done. Once the place was in darkness, the cameras would be out of action.

The bother was, of course, that if I leaned too far out of the niche, the thing would have me. For a while I couldn't get over this. Then I thought of diverting the brute's attention by throwing my coat out just before I had to lean out myself. This seemed the only plan. I began to reckon up ways and means. There were four lamps; two close to me, and two that would be longish shots. I went through my pockets and found I had six pennies, a florin, a half-crown and two shillings. I had a petrol cigarette lighter, a penknife, two keys of a reasonable size, and a wrist-watch. Queer collection of things to stand between a man and death.

I decided to start work on the nearest lamps, to get my hand in. One of them I could get at comfortably without getting out of the recess, and I smashed it, second shot, with one of the shillings. I wasn't anxious to begin shedding clothes till I had to. I wanted to keep them in reserve in case I had to make a rush for the exit at the last. So I had a go at the other nearer lamp; and I wasted four of my pennies and a florin over it before I got it square with the second shilling. I never knew the real joy of breaking things until that lamp went out.

My end of the place was pretty gloomy by that time; and the machine seemed to grow perturbed by the change. It began sending out its cables and worrying the bodies on the floor. Finally it gathered them nearer to itself, had a good look at them, and then gave them a few warm embraces.

I turned my attention to the other two lamps. One was dead in front of the niche, but it was a long shot. A penny and the half-crown went near it, but both missed. Then I opened fire with the rest of my collection. I got pretty excited over it; and when at last I did score a hit, I found I'd used up all my ammunition. And there I was, with nothing in hand and one lamp to the bad. Besides which, the machine was now getting seriously disturbed. It was only a question of time, till it had me, if the antennae were long enough to reach into my niche.

Then all at once I thought of the best thing of all; my shoes. Queer how one overlooks the obvious, isn't it? I had them off.

By this time, it was a case of all or nothing. So I took off my coat, balanced a shoe in my hand, and ran out towards the last lamp. If I'd waited to think it over, I'd never have been able to screw my courage up to that. The cameras came round—snap!—and for a moment I looked into their dark lenses and began to feel almost hypnotized.

I had just sense enough to jump aside, and as I did so a leash of cables coiled out at me. I flung the shoe straight at the lamp—I was only about ten feet from it—and out went the light. I jumped again, more by instinct than judgment and a cable swung past me with a hiss. Darkness seemed to have thrown the thing into a panic, for it made no systematic attempt to search the place. If it had done so my number would have been up. As it was I'd only the vaguest ideas about the position of the entrance.

I moved in what I took to be the right direction, and I found a cool draught blowing. Something gripped the coat from my hand—I found I'd forgotten to throw it away—and three hair-like things fell across my neck and cheek. But by that time I was at the entrance—and free.

Behind me, I could hear the thing lashing round in fury, then suddenly there was silence. Perhaps it had some means of knowing that I was out of range. I ran down the pitch-dark corridor, blundered into another, and then into a third. Then I collapsed.

When I came to my senses again, I realized the hole I was in. I'd lost my way in the corridors, I hadn't any matches, and if I stumbled into the den of the machine in the dark...

It took me hours to find my way through that labyrinth to the well-head. The tide was in and I had to wait for the ebb before I could get the launch out. I started the engine and nearly wrecked the damned boat on the way down the sea cave. All the while I had a nightmare feeling that the machine might come after me. Silly, of course, but my nerves were in bits.

It was dark—night time—when I got out of the cave. As it said in the cutting I showed you, there was a storm. I didn't much care. All I wanted was to get clean away from that infernal cave. I ran the launch for all she was worth through the best part of the night, and once I nearly rammed a fishing-boat. Then I just missed getting piled up on some rocks. Finally, about dawn, a big sea broke over us, and down she went.

I just managed to swim ashore, and I collapsed. Some people picked me up in a state of what the novelists call brain-fever and I lay in their house till I got better.

When I did come back to a reasonable condition, I saw that if I told the truth I should be put down as a lunatic—I'd been delirious so I decided to suppress that for a bit. You're the first person I've told the yarn to. Perhaps you'll believe it. At least it's done me some good to get it off my mind.

That was the tale Milton told me. When he had finished, I glanced at the cutting again, mechanically, and something in it caught my eye.

"What about these bearer bonds they talk about here?" I asked.

Milton stared at me with that fishy eye of his.

"Oh, Stevenson gave me them as my bonus, of course."

People were passing along the corridor of the train, and I remembered I'd put myself down for a seat in the restaurant car. I got up, expecting Milton to follow, but he sat tight.

"I'm not taking dinner on the train," he said.

I left him sitting there, but when I came back after dinner, he was gone. The train stopped at Rugby, and he must have got out there.

I feel I'm in an awkward position. On the face of it, the man in the street would say that Milton probably murdered Stevenson for the sake of those bearer bonds, and that I ought to lodge information with the police.

On the other hand, the whole thing may be imagination on Milton's part.

A machine of that sort could be made, improbable as it sounds. Science is full of queer things. It's as well to keep an open mind. But if anyone discovers that sea cave, I should keep out of it, if I were in his shoes.

If there's anything in the story, that machine will still be waiting, for tidal power doesn't run down.

THE EVITABLE CONFLICT

Isaac Asimov

If any science-fiction writer is associated with the world of robots it is Isaac Asimov (1920–1992). Despite all his other works, which also included mysteries and many collections of science essays, it is his stories and novels built around the premise of a world where positronic robots are commonplace and who become the protectors of humanity, for which he became best known. It was Asimov, in conversation with John W. Campbell, Jr., the pioneering editor of the leading science-fiction magazine of the 1940s, Astounding SF, *who first designed the Three Laws of Robotics which were intended to protect humans from robots and preserve robots wherever possible. His first robot story was "Strange Playfellow" (1940) written before the Laws were formulated, but they then emerged over the next few stories, being fully stated in "Runaround" (1942). They are repeated in every story and will be found in the following. Asimov brought together his robot stories in* I, Robot *(1950), but that wasn't the end of it. He then wrote two detective novels of the future,* The Caves of Steel *(1954) and* The Naked Sun *(1957) which teamed the human detective Lije Bailey with the robot R. Daneel Olivaw, to investigate apparently impossible crimes. He continued to write robot stories, every one weaving a story around how the Three Laws might be manipulated, and these were collected in* The Rest of the Robots *(1964). But twenty years later he brought together his robot future with his other major Foundation series in which we now see the significant role of R. Daneel Olivaw in humanity's destiny.* Foundation's Edge *(1982),* The Robots of Dawn *(1983), Robots and*

Empire *(1985)*, Foundation and Earth *(1986)*, Prelude to Foundation *(1988) and* Forward the Foundation *(1993) is the most complete study of the relationship between robots and humans over thousands of years.*

The following story was written early in Asimov's career, but was a crucial one in showing how his three laws needed to be tweaked in order that humanity is protected from the increasing intelligence of machines.

THE CO-ORDINATOR, IN HIS PRIVATE STUDY, HAD THAT MEDI-eval curiosity, a fireplace. To be sure, the medieval man might not have recognized it as such, since it had no functional significance. The quiet, licking flame lay in an insulated recess behind clear quartz.

The logs were ignited at long distance through a trifling diversion of the energy beam that fed the public buildings of the city. The same button that controlled the ignition first dumped the ashes of the previous fire, and allowed for the entrance of fresh wood.—It was a thoroughly domesticated fireplace, you see.

But the fire itself was real. It was wired for sound, so that you could hear the crackle and, of course, you could watch it leap in the air stream that fed it.

The Co-ordinator's ruddy glass reflected, in miniature, the discreet gambolling of the flame, and, in even further miniature, it was reflected in each of his brooding pupils.

—And in the frosty pupils of his guest, Dr. Susan Calvin of U.S. Robots & Mechanical Men Corporation.

The Co-ordinator said, "I did not ask you here entirely for social purposes, Susan."

"I did not think you did, Stephen," she replied.

"—And yet I don't quite know how to phrase my problem. On the one hand, it can be nothing at all. On the other, it can mean the end of humanity."

"I have come across so many problems, Stephen, that presented the same alternative. I think all problems do."

Really? Then judge this—World Steel reports an overproduction of twenty thousand long tons. The Mexican Canal is two months behind schedule. The mercury mines at Almaden have experienced a production deficiency since last spring, while the Hydroponics plant at Tientsin has been laying men off. These items happen to come to mind at the moment. There is more of the same sort."

"Are these things serious? I'm not economist enough to trace the fearful consequences of such things."

"In themselves, they are not serious. Mining experts can be sent to Almaden, if the situation were to get worse. Hydroponics engineers can be used in Java or in Ceylon, if there are too many at Tientsin. Twenty thousand long tons of steel won't fill more than a few days of world demand, and the opening of the Mexican canal two months later than the planned date is of little moment. It's the Machines that worry me;—I've spoken to your Director of Research about them already."

"To Vincent Silver?—He hasn't mentioned anything about it to me."

"I asked him to speak to no one. Apparently, he hasn't."

"And what did he tell you?"

"Let me put that item in its proper place. I want to talk about the Machines first. And I want to talk about them to you, because you're the only one in the world who understands robots well enough to help me now.—May I grow philosophical?"

"For this evening, Stephen, you may talk how you please and of what you please, provided you tell me first what you intend to prove."

"That such small unbalances in the perfection of our system of supply and demand, as I have mentioned, may be the first step towards the final war."

"Hmp. Proceed."

Susan Calvin did not allow herself to relax, despite the designed comfort of the chair she sat in. Her cold, thin-lipped face and her flat, even voice were becoming accentuated with the years. And although Stephen Byerley was one man she could like and trust, she was almost seventy and the cultivated habits of a lifetime are not easily broken.

"Every period of human development, Susan," said the Coordinator, "has had its own particular type of human conflict— its own variety of problem that, apparently, could be settled only by force. And each time, frustratingly enough, force never really settled the problem. Instead, it persisted through a series of conflicts, then vanished of itself,—what's the expression,—ah, yes 'not with a bang, but a whimper,' as the economic and social environment changed. And then, new problems, and a new series of wars.—Apparently endlessly cyclic.

"Consider relatively modern times. There were the series of dynastic wars in the sixteenth to eighteenth centuries, when the most important question in Europe was whether the houses of Hapsburg or Valois-Bourbon were to rule the continent. It was one of those 'inevitable conflicts,' since Europe could obviously not exist half one and half the other.

"Except that it did, and no war ever wiped out the one and established the other, until the rise of a new social atmosphere in France in 1789 tumbled first the Bourbons and, eventually, the Hapsburgs down the dusty chute to history's incinerator.

"And in those same centuries there were the more barbarous religious wars, which revolved about the important question of whether Europe was to be Catholic or Protestant. Half and half she could not be. It was 'inevitable' that the sword decide.—Except that it didn't. In England, a new industrialism was growling, and on the continent, a new nationalism. Half and half Europe remains to this day and no one cares much.

"In the nineteenth and twentieth centuries, there was a cycle of nationalist-imperialist wars, when the most important question in the world was which portions of Europe would control the economic resources and consuming capacity of which portions of non-Europe. All non-Europe obviously could not exist part English and part French and part German and so on.—Until the forces of nationalism spread sufficiently, so that non-Europe ended what all the wars could not, and decided it could exist quite comfortably *all* non-European.

"And so we have a pattern—"

"Yes, Stephen, you make it plain," said Susan Calvin. "These arc not very profound observations."

"No.—But then, it is the obvious which is so difficult to see most of the time. People say 'It's as plain as the nose on your face.' But how much of the nose on your face can you see, unless someone holds a mirror up to you? In the twentieth century, Susan, we started a new cycle of wars—what shall I call them? Ideological wars? The emotions of religion applied to economic systems, rather than to extra-natural ones? Again the wars were 'inevitable' and this time there were atomic weapons, so that mankind could no longer live through its torment to the inevitable wasting away of inevitability.—And positronic robots came.

"They came in time, and, with it and alongside it, interplanetary travel.—So that it no longer seemed so important whether the world was Adam Smith or Karl Marx. Neither made very much sense under the new circumstances. Both had to adapt and they ended in almost the same place."

"A deus ex machina, then, in a double sense," said Dr. Calvin, dryly.

The Co-ordinator smiled gently, "I have never heard you pun before, Susan, but you are correct. And yet there was another danger. The ending of every other problem had merely given birth to another. Our new world-wide robot economy may develop its own problems, and for that reason we have the Machines. The Earth's economy is stable, and will *remain* stable, because it is based upon the decisions of calculating machines that have the good of humanity at heart through the overwhelming force of the First Law of Robotics."

Stephen Byerley continued, "And although the Machines are nothing but the vastest conglomeration of calculating circuits ever invented, they are still robots within the meaning of the First Law, and so our Earth-wide economy is in accord with the best interests of Man. The population of Earth knows that there will be no unemployment, no overproduction or shortages. Waste and famine are words in history books. And so the question of owner-ship of the means of production becomes obsolescent. Whoever owned them (if such a phrase has meaning), a man, a group, a nation, or all mankind, they could be utilized only as the Machines directed.—Not because men were forced to, but because it was the wisest course and men knew it.

"It puts an end to war—not only to the last cycle of wars, but to the next and to all of them. Unless—"

A long pause, and Dr. Calvin encouraged him by repetition. "Unless—"

The fire crouched and skittered along a log, then popped up.

"Unless," said the Co-ordinator, "the Machines don't fulfil their function."

"I see. And that is where those trifling maladjustments come in which you mentioned awhile ago—steel, hydroponics and so on."

"Exactly. Those errors should not be. Dr. Silver tells me they *cannot* be."

"Does he deny the facts? How unusual!"

"No, he admits the facts, of course. I do him an injustice. What he denies is that any error in the machine is responsible for the so-called (his phrase) errors in the answers. He claims that the Machines are self correcting and that it would violate the fundamental laws of nature for an error to exist in the circuits of relays. And so I said—"

"And you said, 'Have your boys check them and make sure, anyway.'"

"Susan, you read my mind. It was what I said, and he said he couldn't."

"Too busy?"

"No, he said that no human could. He was frank about it. He told me, and I hope I understand him properly, that the Machines are a gigantic extrapolation. Thus—A team of mathematicians work several years calculating a positronic brain equipped to do certain similar acts of calculation. Using this brain they make further calculations to create a still more complicated brain, which they use again to make one still more complicated and so on. According to Silver, what we call the Machines are the result of ten such steps."

"Ye-es, that sounds familiar. Fortunately, I'm not a mathematician.—Poor Vincent. He is a young man. The Directors before him, Alfred Lanning and Peter Bogert, are dead, and they had no such problems. Nor had I. Perhaps roboticists as a whole should now die, since we can no longer understand our own creations."

"Apparently not. The Machines are not super-brains in Sunday supplement sense,—although they are so pictured in the Sunday supplements. It is merely that in their own particular province of collecting and analyzing a nearly infinite number of data and relationships thereof, in nearly infinitesimal time, they have progressed beyond the possibility of detailed human control.

"And then I tried something else. I actually asked the Machine. In the strictest secrecy, we fed it the original data involved in the steel decision, its own answer, and the actual developments since,— the overproduction, that is,—and asked for an explanation of the discrepancy."

"Good, and what was its answer?"

"I can quote you that word for word: 'The matter admits of no explanation.'"

"And how did Vincent interpret that?"

"In two ways. Either we had not given the machine enough data to allow a definite answer, which was unlikely. Dr. Silver admitted that.—Or else, it was impossible for the Machine to admit that it could give any answer to data which implied that it could harm a human being. This, naturally, is implied by the First Law. And then Dr. Silver recommended that I see you."

Susan Calvin looked very tired, "I'm old, Stephen. When Peter Bogert died, they wanted to make me Director of Research and I refused. I wasn't young then, either, and I did not wish the responsibility. They let young Silver have it and that satisfied me; but what good is it, if I am dragged into such messes.

"Stephen, let me state my position. My researches do indeed involve the interpretation of robot behaviour in the light of the Three Laws of Robotics. Here, now, we have these incredible calculating machines. They are positronic robots and therefore obey the Laws of Robotics. But they lack personality; that is, their functions are extremely limited.—Must be, since they are so specialized.

Therefore, there is very little room for the interplay of the Laws, and my one method of attack is virtually useless. In short, I don't know that I can help you, Stephen."

The Co-ordinator laughed shortly, "Nevertheless, let me tell you the rest. Let me give you *my* theories, and perhaps you will then be able to tell me whether they are possible in the light of robopsychology."

"By all means. Go ahead."

"Well, since the Machines are giving the wrong answers, then, assuming that they cannot be in error, there is only one possibility. *They are being given the wrong data!* In other words, the trouble is human, and not robotic. So I took my recent planetary inspection tour—"

"From which you have just returned to New York."

"Yes. It was necessary, you see, since there are four Machines, one handling each of the Planetary Regions. And *all four are yielding imperfect results.*"

"Oh, but that follows, Stephen. If any one of the Machines is imperfect, that will automatically reflect in the result of the other three, since each of the others will assume as part of the data on which they base their own decisions, the perfection of the imperfect fourth. With a false assumption, they will yield false answers."

"Uh-huh. So it seemed to me. Now, I have here the records of my interviews with each of the Regional Vice-Coordinators. Would you look through them with me?—Oh, and first, have you heard of the 'Society for Humanity'?"

"Umm, yes. They are an outgrowth of the Fundamentalists who have kept U. S. Robots from ever employing positronic robots on the grounds of unfair labour competition and so on. The 'Society for Humanity' itself is anti-Machine, is it not?"

"Yes, yes, but—Well, you will see. Shall we begin? We'll start with the Eastern Region."

"As you say—"

The Eastern Region:
    a—Area: 7,500,000 square miles
    b—Population: 1,700,000,000
    c—Capital: Shanghai

Ching Hso-lin's great-grandfather had been killed in the Japanese invasion of the Old Chinese Republic, and there had been no one beside his dutiful children to mourn his loss or even to know he was lost. Ching Hso-lin's grandfather had survived the civil war of the late forties, but there had been no one beside *his* dutiful children to know or care of that.

And yet Ching Hso-lin was a Regional Vice-Co-ordinator, with the economic welfare of half the people of Earth in his care.

Perhaps it was with the thought of all that in mind, that Ching had two maps as the only ornaments of the wall of his office. One was an old hand-drawn affair tracing out an acre or two of land, and marked with the now outmoded pictographs of old China. A little creek trickled aslant the faded markings and there were the delicate pictorial indications of lowly huts, in one of which Ching's grandfather had been born.

The other map was a huge one, sharply delineated, with all markings in neat Cyrillic characters. The red boundary that marked the Eastern Region swept within its grand confines all that had once been China, India, Burma, Indo-China, and Indonesia. On it, within the old province of Szechuan, so light and gentle that none could see it, was the little mark placed there by Ching which indicated the location of his ancestral farm.

Ching stood before these maps as he spoke to Stephen Byerley in precise English, "No one knows better than you, Mr. Co-ordinator, that my job, to a large extent, is a sinecure. It carries with it a certain social standing, and I represent a convenient focal point for administration, but otherwise it is the Machine!—The Machine does all the work. What did you think, for instance, of the Tientsin Hydroponics works?"

"Tremendous!" said Byerley.

"It is but one of dozens, and not the largest. Shanghai, Calcutta, Batavia, Bangkok—They are widely spread and they are the answer to feeding the billion and three quarters of the East."

"And yet," said Byerley, "you have an unemployment problem there at Tientsin. Can you be over-producing? It is incongruous to think of Asia as suffering from too much food."

Ching's dark eyes crinkled at the edges. "No. It has not come to that yet. It is true that over the last few months, several vats at Tientsin have been shut down, but it is nothing serious. The men have been released only temporarily and those who do not care to work in other fields have been shipped to Colombo in Ceylon, where a new plant is being put into operation."

"But why should the vats be closed down?"

Ching smiled gently, "You do not know much of hydroponics, I see. Well, that is not surprising. You are a Northerner, and there soil farming is still profitable. It is fashionable in the North to think of hydroponics, when it is thought of at all, as a device for growing turnips in a chemical solution, and so it is—in an infinitely complicated way.

"In the first place, by far the largest crop we deal with (and the percentage is growing) is yeast. We have upward of two thousand strains of yeast in production and new strains are added monthly.

The basic food-chemicals of the various yeasts are nitrates and phosphates among the inorganics together with proper amounts of the trace metals needed, down to the fractional parts per million of boron and molybdenum which are required. The organic matter is mostly sugar mixtures derived from the hydrolysis of cellulose, but, in addition, there are various food factors which must be added.

"For a successful hydroponics industry—one which can feed seventeen hundred million people—we must engage in an immense reforestation programme throughout the East; we must have huge wood-conversion plants to deal with our southern jungles; we must have power, and steel, and chemical synthetics above all."

"Why the last, sir?"

"Because, Mr. Byerley, these strains of yeast have each their peculiar properties. We have developed, as I said, two thousand strains. The beef steak you thought you ate today was yeast. The frozen fruit confection you had for dessert was iced yeast. We have filtered yeast juice with the taste, appearance, and all the food value of milk.

"It is flavour, more than anything else, you see, that makes yeast feeding popular, and for the sake of flavour we have developed artificial, domesticated strains that can no longer support themselves on a basic diet of salts and sugar. One needs biotin; another needs pteroylglutamic acid; still others need seventeen different amino-acids supplied them as well as all the Vitamins B, but one (and yet it is popular and we cannot, with economic sense, abandon it)—"

Byerley stirred in his seat, "To what purpose do you tell me all this?"

"You asked me, sir, why men are out of work in Tientsin. I have a little more to explain. It is not only that we must have these various and varying foods for our yeast; but there remains the complicating factor of popular fads with passing time; and of the possibility of the development of new strains with the new requirements and new popularity. All this must be foreseen, and the Machine does the job—"

"But not perfectly."

"Not very *im*perfectly, in view of the complications I have mentioned. Well, then, a few thousand workers in Tientsin are temporarily out of a job. But, consider this, the amount of waste in this past year (waste, that is, in terms of either defective supply or defective demand) amounts to not one-tenth of one per cent of our total productive turnover. I consider that—"

"Yet in the first years of the Machine, the figure was nearer one-thousandth of one per cent."

"Ah, but in the decade since the Machine began its operations in real earnest, we have made use of it to increase our old pre-Machine yeast industry twentyfold. You expect imperfections to increase with complications, though—"

"Though?"

"There *was* the curious instance of Rama Vrasayana."

"What happened to him?"

"Vrasayana was in charge of a brine-evaporation plant for the production of iodine, with which yeast can do without, but human beings not. His plant was forced into receivership."

"Really? And through what agency?"

"Competition, believe it or not. In general, one of the chiefest functions of the Machine's analyses is to indicate the most efficient distribution of our producing units. It is obviously faulty to have areas insufficiently serviced, so that the transportation costs account for too great a percentage of the overhead. Similarly, it is faulty to have an area too well serviced, so that factories must be run at lowered capacities, or else compete harmfully with one another.

In the case of Vrasayana, another plant was established in the same city, and with a more efficient extracting system."

"The Machine permitted it?"

"Oh, certainly. That is not surprising. The new system is becoming widespread. The surprise is that the Machine failed to warn Vrasayana to renovate or combine.—Still, no matter. Vrasayana accepted a job as engineer in the new plant, and if his responsibility and pay are now less, he is not actually suffering. The workers found employment easily; the old plant has been converted to—something or other. Something useful. We left it all to the Machine."

"And otherwise you have no complaints."

"None!"

The Tropic Region:

  a—Area: 22,000,000 square miles

  b—Population: 500,000,000

  c—Capital: Capital City

The map in Lincoln Ngoma's office was far from the model of neat precision of the one in Ching's Shanghai dominion. The boundaries of Ngoma's Tropic Region were stencilled in dark, wide brown and swept about a gorgeous interior labelled "jungle" and "desert" and "Here be Elephants and all Manner of Strange Beasts."

It had much to sweep, for in land area the Tropic Region enclosed most of two continents: all of South America north of Argentina and all of Africa south of the Atlas. It included North America south of the Rio Grande as well, and even Arabia and Iran in Asia. It was the reverse of the Eastern Region. Where the ant hives of the Orient crowded half of humanity into 15% of the land mass, the Tropics stretched its 15% of Humanity over nearly half of all the land in the world.

But it was growing. It was the one Region whose population increase through immigration exceeded that through births.—And for all who came it had use.

To Ngoma, Stephen Byerley seemed like one of these immigrants, a pale searcher for the creative work of carving a harsh environment into the softness necessary for man, and he felt some of that automatic contempt of the strong man born to the strong Tropics for the unfortunate pallards of the colder suns.

The tropics had the newest capital city on Earth, and it was called simply that: "Capital City," in the sublime confidence of youth. It spread brightly over the fertile uplands of Nigeria and outside Ngoma's windows, far below, was life and colour; the bright, bright sun and the quick, drenching showers. Even the squawking of the rainbowed birds was brisk and the stars were hard pinpoints in the sharp night.

Ngoma laughed. He was a big, dark man, strong faced and handsome.

"Sure," he said, and his English was colloquial and mouth-filling, "the Mexican Canal is overdue. What the hell? It will get finished just the same, old boy."

"It was doing well up to the last half year."

Ngoma looked at Byerley and slowly crunched his teeth over the end of a big cigar, spitting out one end and lighting the other, "Is this an official investigation, Byerley? What's going on?"

"Nothing. Nothing at all. It's just my function as Coordinator to be curious."

"Well, if it's just that you are filling in a dull moment, the truth is that we're always short on labour. There's lots going on in the Tropics. The Canal is only one of them—"

"But doesn't your Machine predict the amount of labour available for the Canal,—allowing for all the competing projects."

Ngoma placed one hand behind his neck and blew smoke rings at the ceiling, "It was a little off."

"Is it often a little off?"

"Not oftener than you would expect.—We don't expect too much of it, Byerley. We feed it data. We take its results. We do what it says.—But it's just a convenience; just a labour-saving device. We could do without it, if we had to. Maybe not as well. Maybe not as quickly. But we'd get there."

"We've got confidence out here, Byerley, and that's the secret. Confidence! We've got new land that's been waiting for us for thousands of years, while the rest of the world was being ripped apart in the lousy fumblings of pre-atomic time. We don't have to eat yeast like the Eastern boys, and we don't have to worry about the stale dregs of the last century like you Northerners.

"We've wiped out the tsetse fly and the Anopheles mosquito, and people find they can live in the sun and like it, now. We've thinned down the jungles and found soil; we've watered the deserts and found gardens. We've got coal and oil in untouched fields, and minerals out of count.

"Just step back. That's all we ask the rest of the world to do.—Step back, and let us work."

Byerley said, prosaically, "But the Canal,—it was on schedule six months ago. What happened?"

Ngoma spread his hands, "Labour troubles." He felt through a pile of papers skeltered about his desk and gave it up.

"Had something on the matter here," he muttered, "but never mind. There was a work shortage somewhere in Mexico once on the question of women. There weren't enough women in the neighbourhood. It seemed no one had thought of feeding sexual data to the Machine."

He stopped to laugh, delightedly, then sobered, "Wait a while. I think I've got it.—Villafranca!"

"Villafranca?"

"Francisco Villafranca.—He was the engineer in charge. Now let me straighten it out. Something happened and there was a cave-in. Right. Right. That was it. Nobody died, as I remember, but it made a hell of a mess.—Quite a scandal."

"Oh?"

"There was some mistake in his calculations.—Or at least, the Machine said so. They fed through Villafranca's data, assumptions, and so on. The stuff he had started with. The answers came out differently. It seems the answers Villafranca had used didn't take account of the effect of a heavy rainfall on the contours of the cut.—Or something like that. I'm not an engineer, you understand.

"Anyway, Villafranca put up a devil of a squawk. He claimed the Machine's answer had been different the first time. That he had followed the Machine faithfully. Then he quit! We offered to hold him on—reasonable doubt, previous work satisfactory, and all that—in a subordinate position, of course—had to do that much—mistakes can't go unnoticed—bad for discipline—Where was I?"

"You offered to hold him on."

"Oh yes. He refused.—Well, take all in all, we're two months behind. Hell, that's nothing."

Byerley stretched out his hand and let the fingers tap lightly on the desk, "Villafranca blamed the Machine, did he?"

"Well, he wasn't going to blame himself, was he? Let's face it; human nature is an old friend of ours. Besides, I remember something else now—Why the hell can't I find documents when I want it? My filing system isn't worth a damn—This Villafranca was a member of one of your Northern organizations. Mexico is too close to the North; that's part of the trouble."

"Which organization are you speaking of?"

"The Society for Humanity, they call it. He used to attend the annual conferences in New York, Villafranca did. Bunch of crackpots, but harmless.—They don't like the Machines; claim they're destroying human initiative. So naturally Villafranca would blame the Machine.—Don't understand that group myself. Does Capital City look as if the human race were running out of initiative?"

And Capital City stretched out in golden glory under a golden sun,—the newest and youngest creation of *Homo metropolis*.

The European Region:
    a—Area: 4,000,000 square miles
    b—Population: 300,000,000
    c—Capital: Geneva

The European Region was an anomaly in several ways. In area, it was far the smallest; not one fifth the size of the Tropic Region in area, and not one fifth the size of the Eastern Region in population. Geographically, it was only somewhat similar to pre-Atomic Europe, since it excluded what had once been European Russia and what had once been the British Isles, while it included the Mediterranean coasts of Africa and Asia, and, in a queer jump across the Atlantic, Argentina, Chile, and Uruguay as well.

Nor was it likely to improve its relative status vis-à-vis the other regions of Earth, except for what vigour the South American provinces lent it. Of all the Regions, it alone showed a positive population decline over the past half century. It alone had not seriously expanded its productive facilities, or offered anything radically new to human culture.

"Europe," said Madame Szegeczowska, in her soft French, "is essentially an economic appendage of the Northern Region. We know it, and it doesn't matter."

And as though in resigned acceptance of a lack of individuality, there was no map of Europe on the wall of the Madame Co-ordinator's office.

"And yet," pointed out Byerley, "you have a Machine of your own, and you are certainly under no economic pressure from across the ocean."

"A Machine! Bah!" She shrugged her delicate shoulders, and allowed a thin smile to cross her little face as she tamped out a cigarette with long fingers. "Europe is a sleepy place. And such of our men as do not manage to emigrate to the Tropics are tired and sleepy along with it. You see for yourself that it is myself, a poor woman, to whom falls the task of being Vice-Co-ordinator. Well, fortunately, it is not a difficult job, and not much is expected of me.

"As for the Machine—What can it say but 'Do this and it will be best for you.' But what is best for us? Why, to be an economic appendage of the Northern Region.

"And is it so terrible? No wars! We live in peace—and it is pleasant after seven thousand years of war. We are old, monsieur. In our borders, we have the regions where Occidental civilization was cradled. We have Egypt and Mesopotamia; Crete and Syria; Asia Minor and Greece.—But old age is not necessarily an unhappy time. It can be a fruition—"

"Perhaps you are right," said Byerley, affably. "At least the tempo of life is not so intense as in the other Regions. It is a pleasant atmosphere."

"Is it not?—Tea is being brought, monsieur. If you will indicate your cream and sugar preferences, please.—Thank you."

She sipped gently, then continued, "It *is* pleasant. The rest of Earth is welcome to the continuing struggle. I find a parallel here; a very interesting one. There was a time when Rome was master of the world. It had adopted the culture and civilization of Greece; a Greece which had never been united, which had ruined itself with war, and which was ending in a state of decadent squalor. Rome united it, brought it peace and let it live a life of secure non-glory. It occupied itself with its philosophies and its art, far from the clash of growth and war. It was a sort of death, but it was restful, and it lasted with minor breaks for some four hundred years."

"And yet," said Byerley, "Rome fell eventually, and the opium dream was over."

"There are no longer barbarians to overthrow civilization."

"We can be our own barbarians, Madame Szegeczowska.—Oh, I meant to ask you. The Almaden mercury mines have fallen off quite badly in production. Surely the ores are not declining more rapidly than anticipated?"

The little woman's grey eyes fastened shrewdly on Byerley, "Barbarians—the fall of civilization—possible failure of the Machine. Your thought processes are very transparent, monsieur."

"Are they?" Byerley smiled. "I see that I should have had men to deal with as hitherto.—You consider the Almaden affair to be the fault of the Machine?"

"Not at all, but I think you do. You, yourself, are a native of the Northern Region. The Central Co-ordination Office is at New York.—And I have noticed for quite a while that you Northerners lack somewhat of faith in the Machine."

"We do?"

"There is your 'Society for Humanity' which is strong in the North, but naturally fails to find many recruits in tired, old Europe, which is quite willing to let feeble Humanity alone for a while. Surely, you are one of the confident North and not one of the cynical old continent."

"This has a connection with Almaden?"

"Oh, yes, I think so. The mines are in the control of Consolidated Cinnabar, which is certainly a Northern company, with headquarters at Nikolaev. Personally, I wonder if the Board of Directors have been consulting the Machine at all. They said they had in our conference last month, and, of course, we have no evidence that they did not, but I wouldn't take the word of a Northerner in this matter—no offence intended—under any circumstances.—Nevertheless, I think it will have a fortunate ending."

"In what way, my dear madam?"

"You must understand that the economic irregularities of the last few months, which, although small as compared with the great storms of the past, are quite disturbing to our peace-drenched spirits, have caused considerable restiveness in the Spanish province. I understand that Consolidated Cinnabar is selling out to a group of native Spaniards. It is consoling. If we are economic vassals of the North, it is humiliating to have the fact advertised too blatantly.— And our people can be better trusted to follow the Machine."

"Then you think there will be no more trouble?"

"I am sure there will not be—In Almaden, at least."

The Northern Region:

  a—Area: 18,000,000 square miles

  b—Population: 800,000,000

  c—Capital: Ottawa

The Northern Region, in more ways than one, was at the top. This was exemplified quite well by the map in the Ottawa office of Vice-Co-ordinator Hiram Mackenzie, in which the North Pole was centred. Except for the enclave of Europe with its Scandinavian and Icelandic regions, all the Arctic area was within the Northern Region.

Roughly, it could be divided into two major areas. To the left on the map was all of North America above the Rio Grande. To the right was included all of what had once been the Soviet Union. Together these areas represented the centred power of the planet in the first years of the Atomic Age. Between the two was Great Britain, a tongue of the Region licking at Europe. Up at the top of the map, distorted into odd, huge shapes, were Australia and New Zealand, also member provinces of the Region.

Not all the changes of the past decades had yet altered the fact that the North was the economic ruler of the planet.

There was almost an ostentatious symbolism thereof in the fact that of the official Regional maps Byerley had seen, Mackenzie's alone showed all the Earth, as though the North feared no competition and needed no favouritism to pount up its pre-eminence.

"Impossible," said Mackenzie, dourly, over the whisky. "Mr. Byerley, you have had no training as a robot technician, I believe."

"No, I have not."

"Hmp. Well, it is, in my opinion, a sad thing that Ching, Ngoma, and Szegeczowska haven't either. There is too prevalent an opinion among the peoples of Earth that a Coordinator need only be a capable organizer, a broad generalizer, and an amiable person. These days he should know his robotics as well,—no offence intended."

"None taken. I agree with you."

"I take it, for instance, from what you have said already, that you worry about the recent trifling dislocations in world economy. I don't know what you suspect, but it has happened in the past that people—who should have known better—wondered what would happen if false data were fed into the Machine."

"And what would happen, Mr. Mackenzie?"

"Well," the Scotsman shifted his weight and sighed, "all collected data goes through a complicated screening system which involves both human and mechanical checking, so that the problem is not likely to arise.—But let us ignore that. Humans are fallible, also corruptible, and ordinary mechanical devices are liable to mechanical failure.

"The real point of the matter is that what we call a 'wrong datum' is one which is inconsistent with all other known data. It is our only criterion of right and wrong. It is the Machine's as well. Order it for instance, to direct agricultural activity on the basis of an average July temperature in Iowa of 57 degrees Fahrenheit. It won't accept that. It will not give an answer.—Not that it has any prejudice against that particular temperature, or that an answer is impossible; but because, in the light of all the other data fed it over a period of years, it knows that the probability of an average July temperature of 57 is virtually nil. It rejects that datum.

"The only way a 'wrong datum' can be forced on the Machine is to include it as part of a self-consistent whole, all of which is subtly wrong in a manner either too delicate for the Machine to detect or outside the Machine's experience. The former is beyond human capacity, and the latter is almost so, and is becoming more nearly so as the Machine's experience increases by the second."

Stephen Byerley placed two fingers to the bridge of his nose, "Then the Machine cannot be tampered with—And how do you account for recent errors, then."

"My dear Byerley, I see that you instinctively follow that great error—that the Machine knows all. Let me cite you a case from my personal experience. The cotton industry engages experienced buyers who purchase cotton. Their procedure is to pull a tuft of cotton out of a random bale of a lot. They will look at that tuft and feel it, tease it out, listen to the crackling perhaps as they do so, touch it with their tongue,—and through this procedure they will determine the class of cotton the bales represent. There are about a dozen such classes. As a result of their decisions, purchases are made at certain prices, blends are made in certain proportions.—Now these buyers cannot yet be replaced by the Machine."

"Why not? Surely the data involved is not too complicated for it?"

"Probably not. But what data is this you refer to. No textile chemist knows exactly what it is that the buyer tests when he feels a tuft of cotton. Presumably there's the average length of the threads, their feel, the extent and nature of their slickness, the way they hang together and so on.—Several dozen items, subconsciously weighed, out of years of experience. But the *quantitative* nature of these tests are not known; maybe even the very nature of some of them are not known. So we have nothing to feed the Machine. Nor can the buyers explain their own judgment. They can only say, 'Well, look at it. Can't you *tell* it's class-such-and-such.'"

"I see."

"There are innumerable cases like that. The Machine is only a tool after all, which can help humanity progress faster by taking some of the burdens of calculations and interpretations off his back. The task of the human brain remains what it has always been; that of discovering new data to be analyzed, and of devising new concepts to be tested. A pity the Society for Humanity won't understand that."

"They are against the Machine?"

"They would be against mathematics or against the art of writing if they had lived at the appropriate time. These reactionaries of the Society claim the Machine robs man of his soul. I notice that capable men are still at a premium in our society; we still need the man who is intelligent enough to think of the proper questions to ask. Perhaps if we could find enough of such, these dislocations you worry about, Coordinator, wouldn't occur."

Earth (Including the uninhabited continent, Antarctica):
 a—Area: 54,000,000 square miles (land surface)
 b—Population: 3,300,000,000
 c—Capital: New York

The fire behind the quartz was weary now, and sputtered its reluctant way to death.

The Co-ordinator was sombre, his mood matching the sinking flame.

"They all minimize the state of affairs." His voice was low. "Is it not easy to imagine that they all laugh at me? And yet— Vincent Silver said the Machines cannot be out of order, and I must believe him. Hiram Mackenzie says they cannot be fed false data, and I must believe him. But the Machines are going wrong, somehow, and I must believe that, too—and so there is *still* an alternative left."

He glanced sidewise at Susan Calvin, who, with closed eyes, for a moment seemed asleep.

"What is that?" she asked, prompt to her cue, nevertheless.

"Why, that correct data is indeed given, and correct answers are indeed received, but that they are then ignored. There is no way the Machine can enforce obedience to its dictates."

"Madame Szegeczowska hinted as much, with reference to Northerners in general, it seems to me."

"So she did."

"And what purpose is served by disobeying the Machine? Let's consider motivations."

"It's obvious to me, and should be to you. It is a matter of rocking the boat, deliberately. There can be no serious conflicts on Earth, in which one group or another can seize more power than it has for what it thinks is its own good despite the harm to Mankind as a whole, while the Machines rule. If popular faith in the Machines can be destroyed to the point where they are abandoned, it will be the law of the jungle again.—And not one of the four regions can be freed of the suspicion of wanting just that.

"The East has half of humanity within its borders, and the Tropics more than half of Earth's resources. Each can feel itself the natural rulers of all Earth, and each has a history of humiliation by the North, for which it can be human enough to wish a senseless revenge. Europe has a tradition of greatness, on the other hand. It once *did* rule the Earth, and there is nothing so eternally adhesive as the memory of power.

"Yet, in another way, it's hard to believe. Both the East and the Tropics are in a state of enormous expansion within their own borders. Both are climbing incredibly. They cannot have the spare energy for military adventures. And Europe can have nothing but its dreams. It is a cipher, militarily."

"So, Stephen," said Susan, "you leave the North."

"Yes," said Byerley, energetically, "I do. The North is now the strongest, and has been for nearly a century, or its component parts have been. But it is losing relatively, now. The Tropic Regions may take their place in the forefront of civilization for the first time since the Pharaohs, and there are Northerners who fear that.

"The 'Society for Humanity' is a Northern organization, primarily, you know, and they make no secret of not wanting the

Machines.—Susan, they are few in numbers, but it is an association of powerful men. Heads of factories; directors of industries and agricultural combines who hate to be what they call 'the Machine's office-boy' belong to it. Men with ambition belong to it. Men who feel themselves strong enough to decide for themselves what is best for themselves, and not just to be told what is best for others.

"In short, just those men who, by together refusing to accept the decisions of the Machine, can, in a short time, turn the world topsy-turvy;—just those belong to the Society.

"Susan, it hangs together. Five of the Directors of World Steel are members, and World Steel suffers from overproduction. Consolidated Cinnabar, which mined mercury at Almaden, was a Northern concern. Its books are still being investigated, but one, at least, of the men concerned was a member. Francisco Villafranca, who, single-handed, delayed the Mexican Canal for two months, was a member, we know already—and so was Rama Vrasayana, I was not at all surprised to find out."

Susan said, quietly, "These men, I might point out, have all done badly—"

"But naturally," interjected Byerley. "To disobey the Machine's analyses is to follow a non-optimal path. Results are poorer than they might be. It's the price they pay. They will have it rough now but in the confusion that will eventually follow—"

"Just what do you plan doing, Stephen?"

"There is obviously no time to lose. I am going to have the Society outlawed, every member removed from any responsible post. And all executive and technical positions, henceforward, can be filled only by applicants signing a non-Society oath. It will mean a certain surrender of basic civil liberties, but I am sure the Congress—"

"It won't work!"

"What!—Why not?"

"It will make a prediction. If you try any such thing, you will find yourself hampered at every turn. You will find it impossible to carry out. You will find your every move in that direction will result in trouble."

Byerley was taken aback. "Why do you say that?—I was rather hoping for your approval in this matter."

"You can't have it as long as your actions are based on a false premise. You admit the Machine can't be wrong, and can't be fed wrong data. I will now show you that it cannot be disobeyed, either, as you think is being done by the Society."

"*That* I don't see at all."

"Then listen. Every action by any executive which does not follow the exact directions of the Machine he is working with becomes part of the data for the next problem. The Machine, therefore, knows that the executive has a certain tendency to disobey. He can incorporate that tendency into that data,—even quantitatively, that is, judging exactly how much and in what direction disobedience would occur. Its next answers would be just sufficiently biased so that after the executive concerned disobeyed, he would have automatically corrected those answers to optimal directions. The Machine *knows*, Stephen!"

"You can't be sure of all this. You are guessing."

"It is a guess based on a lifetime's experience with robots. You had better rely on such a guess, Stephen."

"But then what is left? The Machines themselves are correct and the premises they work on are correct. That we have agreed upon. Now you say that it cannot be disobeyed. Then what is wrong?"

"You have answered yourself. *Nothing is wrong!* Think about the Machines for a while, Stephen. They are robots, and they follow the First Law. But the Machines work not for any single human being, but for all humanity, so that the First Law becomes: 'No Machine may harm humanity; or, through inaction, allow humanity to come to harm.'

"Very well, then, Stephen, what harms humanity? Economic dislocations most of all, from whatever cause. Wouldn't you say so?"

"I would."

"And what is most likely in the future to cause economic disloca- tions? Answer that, Stephen."

"I should say," replied Byerley, unwillingly, "the destruction of the Machines."

"And so should I say, and so should the Machines say. Their first care, therefore, is to preserve themselves, for us. And so they are quietly taking care of the only elements left that threaten them. It is not the 'Society for Humanity' which is shaking the boat so that the Machines may be destroyed. You have been looking at the reverse of the picture. Say rather that the Machine is shaking the boat—*very* slightly—just enough to shake loose those few which cling to the side for purposes the Machines consider harmful to Humanity.

"So Vrasayana loses his factory and gets another job where he can do no harm—he is not badly hurt, he is not rendered incapable of earning a living, for the Machine cannot harm a human being more than minimally, and that only to save a greater number. Consolidated Cinnabar loses control at Almaden. Villafranca is no longer a civil engineer in charge of an important project. And the directors of World Steel are losing their grip on the industry—or will."

"But you don't really know all this," insisted Byerley, distractedly. "How can we possibly take a chance on your being right?"

"You must. Do you remember the Machine's own statement when you presented the problem to him. It was: 'The matter admits of no explanation.' The Machine did not say there was no explanation, or that it could determine no explanation. It simply was not going to *admit* any explanation. In other words, it would be harmful to humanity to have the explanation known, and that's why we can only guess—and keep on guessing."

"But how can the explanation do us harm? Assume that you are right, Susan."

"Why, Stephen, if I am right, it means that the Machine is conducting our future for us not only simply in direct answer to our direct questions, but in general answer to the world situation and to human psychology as a whole. And to know that may make us unhappy and may hurt our pride. The Machine cannot, *must* not, make us unhappy.

"Stephen, how do we know what the ultimate good of Humanity will entail. We haven't at *our* disposal the infinite factors that the Machine has at *its!* Perhaps, to give you a not unfamiliar example, our entire technical civilization has created more unhappiness and misery than it has removed. Perhaps an agrarian or pastoral civilization, with less culture and less people would be better. If so, the Machines must move in that direction, preferably without telling us, since in our ignorant prejudices we only know that what we are used to, is good—and we would then fight change. Or perhaps a complete urbanization, or a completely caste-ridden society, or complete anarchy, is the answer. We don't know. Only the Machines know, and they are going there and taking us with them."

"But you are telling me, Susan, that the 'Society for Humanity' is right; and that Mankind *has* lost its own say in its future."

"It never had any, really. It was always at the mercy of economic and sociological forces it did not understand—at the whims of climate, and the fortunes of war. Now the Machines understand them; and no one can stop them, since the Machines will deal with them as they are dealing with the Society,—having, as they do, that greatest of weapons at their disposal, the absolute control of our economy."

"How horrible!"

"Perhaps how wonderful! Think, that for all time, all conflicts are finally evitable. Only the Machines, from now on, are inevitable!"

And the fire behind the quartz went out and only a curl of smoke was left to indicate its place.

"And that is all," said Dr. Calvin, rising. "I saw it from the beginning, when the poor robots couldn't speak, to the end, when they stand between mankind and destruction. I will see no more. My life is over. You will see what comes next."

I never saw Susan Calvin again. She died last month at the age of eighty-two.

TWO-HANDED ENGINE

C. L. Moore & Henry Kuttner

The husband and wife team of Henry Kuttner (1915–1958) and Catherine Lucille Moore (1911–1987) wrote some of the most enjoyable and memorable science fiction of the 1940s. Often the stories were under pseudonyms, notably Lewis Padgett and Lawrence O'Donnell, and many were considered to be by Kuttner alone, on which Moore may have assisted. Sometimes stories by them both appeared solely under Kuttner's name. In fact it was later realized that Moore had a much greater role, and those under the O'Donnell name were almost all by her. It is not always easy to know who wrote what and it is simplest to remember that between them the Kuttner-Moore team produced much classic science fiction. This included many robot stories, some of which were collected as Robots Have No Tails *(1952). Perhaps the most memorable was "The Twonky" (1942) where a man discovers that what he thought was a radio is in fact a robot from the future which whilst it serves him admirably has an ulterior purpose. "No Woman Born" (1944), written entirely by Moore, is the powerful story of how a television star and dancer must adjust from her human form, badly disfigured in a fire, to that of a cyborg when she is reborn in a machine. Kuttner died of a heart attack at the tragically early age of 42. The following is one of their last stories together and the original credit places Moore's name first, suggesting it was primarily her story. It shows a future where criminals may not be imprisoned but have the more frightening sentence of being monitored constantly by a robot.*

E VER SINCE THE DAYS OF ORESTES THERE HAVE BEEN MEN with Furies following them. It wasn't until the twenty-second century that mankind made itself a set of real Furies, out of steel. Mankind had reached a crisis by then. They had a good reason for building man-shaped Furies that would dog the footsteps of all men who kill men. Nobody else. There was by then no other crime of any importance.

It worked very simply. Without warning, a man who thought himself safe would suddenly hear the steady footfalls behind him. He would turn and see the two-handed engine walking towards him, shaped like a man of steel, and more incorruptible than any man not made of steel could be. Only then would the murderer know he had been tried and condemned by the omniscient electronic minds that knew society as no human mind could ever know it.

For the rest of his days, the man would hear those footsteps behind him. A moving jail with invisible bars that shut him off from the world. Never in life would he be alone again. And one day — he never knew when—the jailer would turn executioner.

Danner leaned back comfortably in his contoured restaurant-chair and rolled expensive wine across his tongue, closing his eyes to enjoy the taste of it better. He felt perfectly safe. Oh, perfectly protected. For nearly an hour now he had been sitting here, ordering the most expensive food, enjoying the music breathing softly through the air, the murmurous, well-bred hush of his fellow diners. It was a good place to be. It was very good, having so much money—now.

True, he had had to kill to get the money. But no guilt troubled him. There was no guilt if you aren't found out, and Danner had protection. Protection straight from the source, which was something new in the world. Danner knew the consequences of killing. If Hartz hadn't satisfied him that he was perfectly safe, Danner would never have pulled the trigger...

The memory of an archaic word flickered through his mind briefly. *Sin.* It evoked nothing. Once it had something to do with guilt, in an incomprehensible way. Not any more. Mankind had been through too much. Sin was meaningless now.

He dismissed the thought and tried the heart-of-palms salad. He found he didn't like it. Oh well, you had to expect things like that. Nothing was perfect. He sipped the wine again, liking the way the glass seemed to vibrate like something faintly alive in his hand. It was good wine. He thought of ordering more, but then he thought no, save it, next time. There was so much before him, waiting to be enjoyed. Any risk was worth it. And, of course, in this there had been no risk.

Danner was a man born at the wrong time. He was old enough to remember the last days of utopia, young enough to be trapped in the new scarcity economy the machines had clamped down on their makers. In his early youth he'd had access to free luxuries, like everybody else. He could remember the old days when he was an adolescent and the last of the Escape Machines were still operating, the glamorous, bright, impossible, vicarious visions that didn't really exist and never could have. But then the scarcity economy swallowed up pleasure. Now you got necessities but no more. Now you had to work. Danner hated every minute of it.

When the swift change came, he'd been too young and unskilled to compete in the scramble. The rich men today were the men who had built fortunes on cornering the few luxuries the machines still produced. All Danner had left were bright memories and a dull, resentful feeling of having been cheated. All he wanted were the bright days back, and he didn't care how he got them.

Well, now he had them. He touched the rim of the wine glass with his finger, feeling it sing silently against the touch. Blown glass? he wondered. He was too ignorant of luxury items to understand. But he'd learn. He had the rest of his life to learn in, and be happy.

He looked up across the restaurant and saw through the transparent dome of the roof the melting towers of the city. They made a stone forest as far as he could see. And this was only one city. When he was tired of it, there were more. Across the country, across the planet the network lay that linked city with city in a webwork like a vast, intricate, half-alive monster. Call it society.

He felt it tremble a little beneath him.

He reached for the wine and drank quickly. The faint uneasiness that seemed to shiver the foundations of the city was something new. It was because—yes, certainly it was because of a new fear.

It was because he had not been found out.

That made no sense. Of course the city was complex. Of course it operated on a basis of incorruptible machines. They, and only they, kept man from becoming very quickly another extinct animal. And of these the analogue computers, the electronic calculators, were the gyroscope of all living. They made and enforced the laws that were necessary now to keep mankind alive. Danner didn't understand much of the vast changes that had swept over society in his lifetime, but this much even he knew.

So perhaps it made sense that he felt society shiver because he sat here luxurious on foam-rubber, sipping wine, hearing soft music, and no Fury standing behind his chair to prove that the calculators were still guardians for mankind...

If not even the Furies are incorruptible, what can a man believe in?

It was at that exact moment that the Fury arrived.

Danner heard every sound suddenly die out around him. His fork was halfway to his lips, but he paused, frozen, and looked up across the table and the restaurant towards the door.

The Fury was taller than a man. It stood there for a moment, the afternoon sun striking a blinding spot of brightness from its shoulder. It had no face, but it seemed to scan the restaurant leisurely, table by table. Then it stepped in under the door-frame and the sun-spot slid away and it was like a tall man encased in steel, walking slowly between the tables.

Danner said to himself, laying down his untasted food, "Not for me. Everyone else here is wondering. I *know*."

And like a memory in a drowning man's mind, clear, sharp and condensed into a moment, yet every detail clear, he remembered what Hartz had told him. As a drop of water can pull into its reflection a wide panorama condensed into a tiny focus, so time seemed to focus down to a pinpoint the half-hour Danner and Hartz had spent together, in Hartz's office with the walls that could go transparent at the push of a button.

He saw Hartz again, plump and blond, with the sad eyebrows. A man who looked relaxed until he began to talk, and then you felt the burning quality about him, the air of driven tension that made even the air around him to be restlessly trembling. Danner stood before Hartz's desk again in memory, feeling the floor hum faintly against his soles with the heartbeat of the computers. You could see them through the glass, smooth, shiny things with winking lights in banks like candles burning in coloured glass cups. You could hear their faraway chattering as they ingested facts, mediated them, and then spoke in numbers like cryptic oracles. It took men like Hartz to understand what the oracles meant.

"I have a job for you," Hartz said. "I want a man killed."

"Oh, no," Danner said. "What kind of a fool do you think I am?"

"Now, wait a minute. You can use money, can't you?"

"What for?" Danner asked bitterly. "A fancy funeral?"

"A life of luxury. I know you're not a fool. I know damned well you wouldn't do what I ask unless you got money *and* protection. That's what I can offer. Protection."

Danner looked through the transparent wall at the computers. "Sure," he said.

"No, I mean it. I—" Hartz hesitated, glancing around the room a little uneasily, as if he hardly trusted his own precautions for making sure of privacy. "This is something new," he said. "I can re-direct any Fury I want to."

"Oh, sure," Danner said again.

"It's true. I'll show you. I can pull a Fury off any victim I choose."

"How?"

"That's my secret. Naturally. In effect, though, I've found a way to feed in false data, so the machines come out with the wrong verdict before conviction, or the wrong orders after conviction."

"But that's—dangerous, isn't it?"

"Dangerous?" Hartz looked at Danner under his sad eyebrows. "Well, yes. I think so. That's why I don't do it often. I've done it only once, as a matter of fact. Theoretically, I'd worked out the method. I tested it, just once. It worked. I'll do it again, to prove to you I'm telling the truth. After that I'll do it once again, to protect you. And that will be it. I don't want to upset the calculators any more than I have to. Once your job's done, I won't have to."

"Who do you want killed?"

Involuntarily Hartz glanced upward, towards the heights of the building where the top-rank executive officers were. "O'Reilly," he said.

Danner glanced upward too, as if he could see through the floor and observe the exalted shoe-soles of O'Reilly, Controller of the Calculators, pacing an expensive carpet overhead.

"It's very simple," Hartz said. "I want his job."

"Why not do your own killing, then, if you're so sure you can stop the Furies?"

"Because that would give the whole thing away," Hartz said impatiently. "Use your head. I've got an obvious motive. It wouldn't take a calculator to figure out who profits most if O'Reilly dies. If I saved myself from a Fury, people would start wondering how I did it. But you've got no motive for killing O'Reilly. Nobody but the calculators would know, and I'll take care of them."

"How do I know you can do it?"

"Simple. Watch."

Hartz got up and walked quickly across the resilient carpet that gave his steps a falsely youthful bounce. There was a waist-high counter on the far side of the room, with a slanting glass screen on it. Nervously Hartz punched a button, and a map of a section of the city sprang out in bold lines on its surface.

"I've got to find a sector where a Fury's in operation now," he explained. The map flickered and he pressed the button again. The unstable outlines of the city streets wavered and brightened and then went out as he scanned the sections fast and nervously. Then a map flashed on which had three wavering streaks of coloured light criss-crossing it, intersecting at one point near the centre. The point moved very slowly across the map, at just about the speed of a walking man reduced to miniature in scale with the street he walked on. Around him the coloured lines wheeled slowly, keeping their focus always steady on the single point.

"There," Hartz said, leaning forward to read the printed name of the street. A drop of sweat fell from his forehead on to the glass, and he wiped it uneasily away with his fingertip. "There's a man with a Fury assigned to him. All right, now. I'll show you. Look here."

Above the desk was a news-screen. Hartz clicked it on and watched impatiently while a street scene swam into focus. Crowds, traffic noises, people hurrying, people loitering. And in the middle of the crowd a little oasis of isolation, an island in the sea of humanity. Upon that moving island two occupants dwelt, like a Crusoe and a Friday, alone. One of the two was a haggard man who watched the ground as he walked. The other islander in this deserted spot was a tall, shining man-formed shape that followed at his heels.

As if invisible walls surrounded them, pressing back the crowds they walked through, the two moved in an empty space that closed in behind them, opened up before them. Some of the passers-by stared, some looked away in embarrassment or uneasiness. Some watched with a frank anticipation, wondering perhaps at just what moment the Friday would lift his steel arm and strike the Crusoe dead.

"Watch, now," Hartz said nervously. "Just a minute. I'm going to pull the Fury off this man. Wait." He crossed to his desk, opened a drawer, bent secretively over it. Danner heard a series of clicks from inside, and then the brief chatter of tapped keys. "Now," Hartz said, closing the drawer. He moved the back of his hand across his forehead. "Warm in here, isn't it? Let's get a closer look. You'll see something happen in a minute."

Back to the news-screen. He flicked the focus switch and the street scene expanded, the man and his pacing jailer swooped upward into close focus. The man's face seemed to partake subtly of the impassive quality of the robot's. You would have thought they had lived a long time together, and perhaps they had. Time is a flexible element, infinitely long sometimes in a very short space.

"Wait until they get out of the crowd," Hartz said. "This mustn't be conspicuous. There, he's turning now." The man, seeming to move at random, wheeled at an alley corner and went down the narrow, dark passage away from the thoroughfare. The eye of the news-screen followed him as closely as the robot.

"So you do have cameras that can do that," Danner said with interest. "I always thought so. How's it done? Are they spotted at every corner, or is a beam trans—"

"Never mind," Hartz said. "Trade secret. Just watch. We'll have to wait until—No, no! Look, he's going to try it now!"

The man glanced furtively behind him. The robot was just turning the corner in his wake. Hartz darted back to his desk and pulled the drawer open. His hand poised over it, his eyes watched the screen anxiously. It was curious how the man in the alley, though he could have no inkling that other eyes watched, looked up and scanned the sky, gazing directly for a moment into the attentive, hidden camera and the eyes of Hartz and Danner. They saw him take a sudden, deep breath, and break into a run.

From Hartz's drawer sounded a metallic click. The robot, which had moved smoothly into a run the moment the man did, checked itself awkwardly and seemed to totter on its steel for an instant.

It slowed. It stopped like an engine grinding to a halt. It stood motionless.

At the edge of the camera's range you could see the man's face, looking backward, mouth open with shock as he saw the impossible happen. The robot stood there in the alley, making indecisive motions as if the new orders Hartz pumped into its mechanisms were grating against inbuilt orders in whatever receptor it had. Then it turned its steel back upon the man in the alley and went smoothly, almost sedately, away down the street, walking as precisely as if it were obeying valid orders, not stripping the very gears of society in its aberrant behaviour.

You got one last glimpse of the man's face, looking strangely stricken, as if his last friend in the world had left him.

Hartz switched off the screen. He wiped his forehead again. He went to the glass wall and looked out and down as if he were half afraid the calculators might know what he had done. Looking very small against the background of the metal giants, he said over his shoulder, "Well, Danner?"

Was it well? There had been more talk, of course, more persuasion, a raising of the bribe. But Danner knew his mind had been made up from that moment. A calculated risk, and worth it. Well worth it. Except—

In the deathly silence of the restaurant all motion had stopped. The Fury walked calmly between the tables, threading its shining way, touching no one. Every face blanched, turned towards it. Every mind thought, "Can it be for me?" Even the entirely innocent thought, "This is the first mistake they've ever made, and it's come for me. The first mistake, but there's no appeal and I could never prove a thing." For, while guilt had no meaning in this world, punishment did have meaning, and punishment could be blind, striking like the lightning.

Danner between set teeth told himself over and over, "Not for me. I'm safe. I'm protected. It hasn't come for me." And yet he thought how strange it was—what a coincidence, wasn't it—that there should be two murderers here under this expensive glass roof today? Himself, and the one the Fury had come for.

He released his fork and heard it clink on the plate. He looked down at it and the food, and suddenly his mind rejected everything around him and went diving off on a fugitive tangent like an ostrich into sand. He thought about food. How did asparagus grow? What did raw food look like? He had never seen any. Food came ready-cooked out of restaurant kitchens or automatic slots. Potatoes, now. What did they look like? A moist white mash? No, for sometimes they were oval slices, so the thing itself must be oval. But not round. Sometimes you got them in long strips, squared off at the ends. Something quite long and oval, then chopped into even lengths. And white, of course. And they grew underground, he was almost sure. Long, thin roots twining white arms among the pipes and conduits he had seen laid bare when the streets were under repair. How strange that he should be eating something like thin, ineffectual human arms that embraced the sewers of the city and writhed pallidly where the worms had their being. And where he himself, when the Fury found him, might...

He pushed the plate away.

An indescribable rustling and murmuring in the room lifted his eyes for him as if he were an automaton. The Fury was halfway across the room now, and it was almost funny to see the relief of those whom it had passed by. Two or three of the women had buried their faces in their hands, and one man had slipped quietly from his chair in a dead faint as the Fury's passing released their private dreads back into their hidden wells.

The thing was quite close now. It looked to be about seven feet tall, and its motion was very smooth, which was unexpected when you thought about it. Smoother than human motions. Its feet fell with a heavy, measured tread upon the carpet. Thud, thud, thud. Danner tried impersonally to calculate what it weighed. You always heard that they made no sound except for that terrible tread, but this one creaked very slightly somewhere. It had no features, but the human mind couldn't help sketching in lightly a sort of airy face upon that blank steel surface, with eyes that seemed to search the room.

It was coming closer. Now all eyes were converging towards Danner. And the Fury came straight on. It almost looked as if—

"No!" Danner said to himself. "Oh, no, this can't be!" He felt like a man in a nightmare, on the verge of waking. "Let me wake soon," he thought. "Let me wake *now*, before it gets here!"

But he did not wake. And now the thing stood over him, and the thudding footsteps stopped. There was the faintest possible creaking as it towered over his table, motionless, waiting, its featureless face turned towards his.

Danner felt an intolerable tide of heat surge up into his face—rage, shame, disbelief. His heart pounded so hard the room swam and a sudden pain like jagged lightning shot through his head from temple to temple.

He was on his feet, shouting.

"No, no!" he yelled at the impassive steel. "You're wrong! You've made a mistake! Go away, you damned fool! You're wrong, you're wrong!" He groped on the table without looking down, found his plate and hurled it straight at the armoured chest before him. China shattered. Spilled food smeared a white and green and brown stain over the steel. Danner floundered out of his chair, around the table, past the tall metal figure towards the door.

All he could think of now was Hartz.

Seas of faces swam by him on both sides as he stumbled out of the restaurant. Some watched with avid curiosity, their eyes seeking him. Some did not look at all, but gazed at their plates rigidly or covered their faces with their hands. Behind him the measured tread came on, and the rhythmic faint creak from somewhere inside the armour.

The faces fell away on both sides and he went through a door without any awareness of opening it. He was in the street. Sweat bathed him and the air struck icy, though it was not a cold day. He looked blindly left and right, and then plunged for a bank of phone booths half a block away, the image of Hartz swimming before his eyes so clearly he blundered into people without seeing them. Dimly he heard indignant voices begin to speak and then die into awestruck silence. The way cleared magically before him. He walked in the newly created island of his isolation up to the nearest booth.

After he had closed the glass door the thunder of his own blood in his ears made the little sound-proofed booth reverberate. Through the door he saw the robot stand passionlessly waiting, the smear of spilled food still streaking its chest like some robotic ribbon of honour across a steel shirt-front.

Danner tried to dial a number. His fingers were like rubber. He breathed deep and hard, trying to pull himself together. An irrelevant thought floated across the surface of his mind: I forgot to pay for my dinner. And then: A lot of good the money will do me now. Oh, damn Hartz, damn him, damn him!

He got the number.

A girl's face flashed into sharp, clear colours on the screen before him. Good, expensive screens in the public booths in this part of town, his mind noted impersonally.

"This is Controller Hartz's office. May I help you?"

Danner tried twice before he could give his name. He wondered if the girl could see him, and behind him, dimly through the glass, the tall waiting figure. He couldn't tell, because she dropped her eyes immediately to what must have been a list on the unseen table before her.

"I'm sorry. Mr Hartz is out. He won't be back today."

The screen drained of light and colour.

Danner folded back the door and stood up. His knees were unsteady. The robot stood just far enough back to clear the hinge of the door. For a moment they faced each other. Danner heard himself suddenly in the midst of an uncontrollable giggling which even he realized verged on hysteria. The robot with the smear of food like a ribbon of honour looked so ridiculous. Danner to his dim surprise found that all this while he had been clutching the restaurant napkin in his left hand.

"Stand back," he said to the robot. "Let me out. Oh, you fool, don't you know this is a mistake?" His voice quavered. The robot creaked faintly and stepped back.

"It's bad enough to have you follow me," Danner said. "At least you might be clean. A dirty robot is too much—too much—" The thought was idiotically unbearable, and he heard tears in his voice. Half-laughing, half-weeping, he wiped the steel chest clean and threw the napkin to the floor.

And it was at that very instant, with the feel of the hard chest still vivid in his memory, that realization finally broke through the protective screen of hysteria, and he remembered the truth. He would never in life be alone again. Never while he drew breath.

And when he died it would be at these steel hands, perhaps upon this steel chest, with the passionless face bent to his, the last thing in life he would ever see. No human companion, but the black steel skull of the Fury.

It took him nearly a week to reach Hartz. During the week, he changed his mind about how long it might take a man followed by a Fury to go mad. The last thing he saw at night was the street light shining through the curtains of his expensive hotel suite upon the metal shoulder of his jailer. All night long, waking from uneasy slumber, he could hear the faint creaking of some inward mechanism functioning under the armour. And each time he woke it was to wonder whether he would ever wake again. Would the blow fall while he slept? And what kind of blow? How did the Furies execute? It was always a faint relief to see the bleak light of early morning shine upon the watcher by his bed. At least he had lived through the night. But was this living? And was it worth the burden?

He kept his hotel suite. Perhaps the management would have liked him to go, but nothing was said. Possibly they didn't dare. Life took on a strange, transparent quality, like something seen through an invisible wall. Outside of trying to reach Hartz, there was nothing Danner wanted to do. The old desires for luxuries, entertainment, travel had melted away. He wouldn't have travelled alone.

He did spend hours in the public library, reading all that was available about the Furies. It was here that he first encountered the two haunting and frightening lines Milton wrote when the world was small and simple—mystifying lines that made no certain sense to anybody until man created a Fury out of steel, in his own image.

But that two-handed engine at the door
Stands ready to smite once, and smite no more...

Danner glanced up at his own two-handed engine, motionless at his shoulder, and thought of Milton and the long-ago times when life was simple and easy. He tried to picture the past. The twentieth century, when all civilizations together crashed over the brink in one majestic downfall to chaos. And the time before that, when people were... different, somehow. But how? It was too far and too strange. He could not imagine the time before the machines.

But he learned for the first time what had really happened, back there in his early years, when the bright world finally blinked out entirely and grey drudgery began. And the Furies were first forged in the likeness of man.

Before the really big wars began, technology advanced to the point where machines bred upon machines like living things, and there might have been an Eden on earth, with everybody's wants fully supplied, except that the social sciences fell too far behind the physical sciences. When the decimating wars came on, machines and people fought side by side, steel against steel and man against man, but man was the more perishable. The wars ended when there were no longer two societies left to fight against each other. Societies splintered apart into smaller and smaller groups until a state very close to anarchy set in.

The machines licked their metal wounds meanwhile and healed each other as they had been built to do. They had no need for the social sciences. They went on calmly reproducing themselves and handing out to mankind the luxuries which the age of Eden had designed them to hand out. Imperfectly, of course. Incompletely, because some of their species were wiped out entirely and left no machines to breed and reproduce their kind. But most of them mined their raw materials, refined them, poured and cast the needed parts, made their own fuel, repaired their own injuries and maintained their breed upon the face of the earth with an efficiency man never even approached.

Meanwhile mankind splintered and splintered away. There were no longer any real groups, not even families. Men didn't need each other much. Emotional attachments dwindled. Men had been conditioned to accept vicarious surrogates and escapism was fatally easy. Men reoriented their emotions to the Escape Machines that fed them joyous, impossible adventure and made the waking world seem too dull to bother with. And the birth rate fell and fell. It was a very strange period. Luxury and chaos went hand in hand, anarchy and inertia were the same thing. And still the birth rate dropped…

Eventually a few people recognized what was happening. Man as a species was on the way out. And man was helpless to do anything about it. But he had a powerful servant. So the time came when some unsung genius saw what would have to be done. Someone saw the situation clearly and set a new pattern in the biggest of the surviving electronic calculators. This was the goal he set: "Mankind must be made self-responsible again. You will make this your only goal until you achieve the end."

It was simple, but the changes it produced were worldwide and all human life on the planet altered drastically because of it. The machines were an integrated society, if man was not. And now they had a single set of orders which all of them reorganized to obey.

So the days of the free luxuries ended. The Escape Machines shut up shop. Men were forced back into groups for the sake of survival. They had to undertake now the work the machines withheld, and slowly, slowly, common needs and common interests began to spawn the almost lost feeling of human unity again.

But it was so slow. And no machine could put back into man what he had lost—the internalized conscience. Individualism had reached its ultimate stage and there had been no deterrent to crime for a long while. Without family or clan relations, not even feud retaliation occurred. Conscience failed, since no man identified with any other.

The real job of the machines now was to rebuild in man a realistic superego to save him from extinction. A self-responsible society would be a genuinely interdependent one, the leader identifying with the group, and a realistically internalized conscience which would forbid and punish "sin"—the sin of injuring the group with which you identify.

And here the Furies came in.

The machines defined murder, under any circumstances, as the only human crime. This was accurate enough, since it is the only act which can irreplaceably destroy a unit of society.

The Furies couldn't prevent crime. Punishment never cures the criminal. But it can prevent others from committing crime through simple fear, when they see punishment administered to others. The Furies were the symbol of punishment. They overtly stalked the streets on the heels of their condemned victims, the outward and visible sign that murder is always punished, and punished most publicly and terribly. They were very efficient. They were never wrong. Or, at least, in theory they were never wrong, and considering the enormous quantities of information stored by now in the analogue computers it seemed likely that the justice of the machines was far more efficient than that of humans could be.

Some day man would rediscover sin. Without it he had come near to perishing entirely. With it, he might resume his authority over himself and the race of mechanized servants who were helping him to restore his species. But until that day the Furies would have to stalk the streets, man's conscience in metal guise, imposed by the machines man created a long time ago.

*

What Danner did during this time he scarcely knew. He thought a great deal of the old days when the Escape Machines still worked, before the machines rationed luxuries. He thought of this sullenly and with resentment, for he could see no point at all in the experiment mankind was embarked on. He had liked it better in the old days. And there were no Furies then, either.

He drank a good deal. Once he emptied his pockets into the hat of a legless beggar, because the man like himself was set apart from society by something new and terrible. For Danner it was the Fury. For the beggar it was life itself. Thirty years ago he would have lived or died unheeded, tended only by machines. That a beggar could survive at all, by begging, must be a sign that society was beginning to feel twinges of awakened fellow feeling with its members, but to Danner that meant nothing. He wouldn't be around long enough to know how the story came out.

He wanted to talk to the beggar, though the man tried to wheel himself away on his little platform.

"Listen," Danner said urgently, following, searching his pockets. "I want to tell you. It doesn't feel the way you think it would. It feels—"

He was quite drunk that night, and he followed the beggar until the man threw the money back at him and thrust himself away rapidly on his wheeled platform, while Danner leaned against a building and tried to believe in its solidity. But only the shadow of the Fury, falling across him from the street lamp, was real.

Later that night, somewhere in the dark, he attacked the Fury. He seemed to remember finding a length of pipe somewhere, and he struck showers of sparks from the great, impervious shoulders

above him. Then he ran, doubling and twisting up alleys, and in the
end he hid in a dark doorway, waiting, until the steady footsteps
resounded through the night.

He fell asleep, exhausted.

It was the next day that he finally reached Hartz.

"What went wrong?" Danner asked. In the past week he had
changed a good deal. His face was taking on, in its impassivity, an
odd resemblance to the metal mask of the robot.

Hartz struck the desk edge a nervous blow, grimacing when he
hurt his hand. The room seemed to be vibrating not with the pulse
of the machines below but with his now tense energy.

"*Something* went wrong," he said. "I don't know yet. I—"

"You don't know!" Danner lost part of his impassivity.

"Now, wait." Hartz made soothing motions with his hands. "Just
hang on a little longer. It'll be all right. You can—"

"How much longer have I got?" Danner asked. He looked over
his shoulder at the tall Fury standing behind him, as if he were really
asking the question of it, not Hartz. There was a feeling, somehow,
about the way he said it that made you think he must have asked
that question many times, looking up into the blank steel face, and
would go on asking hopelessly until the answer came at last. But
not in words...

"I can't even find that out," Hartz said. "Damn it, Danner, this
was a risk. You knew that."

"You said you could control the computer. I saw you do it. I want
to know why you didn't do what you promised."

"Something went wrong, I tell you. It should have worked. The
minute this—business—came up I fed in the data that should have
protected you."

"But what happened?"

Hartz got up and began to pace the resilient flooring. "I just don't know. We don't understand the potentiality of the machines, that's all. I thought I could do it. But—"

"You *thought!*"

"I know I can do it. I'm still trying. I'm trying everything. After all, this is important to me, too. I'm working as fast as I can. That's why I couldn't see you before. I'm certain I can do it, if I can work this out my way. Damn it, Danner, it's complex. And it's not like juggling a comptometer. Look at those things out there."

Danner didn't bother to look.

"You'd better do it," he said. "That's all."

Hartz said furiously. "Don't threaten me! Let me alone and I'll work it out. But don't threaten me."

"You're in this too," Danner said.

"How?" he asked.

"O'Reilly's dead. You paid me to kill him."

Hartz shrugged. "The Fury knows that," he said, "The computers know it. And it doesn't matter a damn bit. Your hand pulled the trigger, not mine."

"We're both guilty. If I suffer for it, you—"

"Now, wait a minute. Get this straight. I thought you knew it. It's a basis of law enforcement, and always has been. Nobody's punished for intention. Only for actions. I'm no more responsible for O'Reilly's death than the gun you used on him."

"But you lied to me! You tricked me! I'll—"

Hartz went back to his desk and sat down on the edge of it.

"You'll do as I say, if you want to save yourself. I didn't trick you, I just made a mistake. Give me time and I'll retrieve it."

"How long?"

This time both men looked at the Fury. It stood impassive.

"I don't know how long," Danner answered his own question. "You say you don't. Nobody even knows how he'll kill me, when the time comes. I've been reading everything that's available to the public about this. Is it true that the method varies, just to keep people like me on tenterhooks? And the time allowed—doesn't that vary too?"

"Yes, it's true. But there's a minimum time—I'm almost sure. You must still be within it. Believe me, Danner, I can still call off the Fury. You saw me do it. You know it worked once. All I've got to find out is what went wrong this time. But the more you bother me the more I'll be delayed. I'll get in touch with you. Don't try to see me again."

Danner was on his feet. He took a few quick steps towards Hartz, fury and frustration breaking up the impassive mask which despair had been forming over his face. But the solemn footsteps of the Fury sounded behind him. He stopped.

The two men looked at each other.

"Give me time," Hartz said. "Trust me, Danner."

In a way it was worse, having hope. There must until now have been a kind of numbness of despair that had kept him from feeling too much. But now there was a chance that after all he might escape into the bright and new life he had risked so much for—if Hartz could save him in time.

Now, for a period, he began to savour experience again. He bought new clothes. He travelled, though never, of course, alone. He even sought human companionship again and found it—after a fashion. But the kind of people willing to associate with a man under this sort of death sentence was not a very appealing type. He found, for instance, that some women felt strongly attracted to him, not because of himself or his money, but for the sake of his companion. They seemed enthralled by the opportunity for a close, safe brush with the very instrument of destiny. Over his very shoulder, sometimes, he would realize they watched the Fury in an ecstasy of fascinated anticipation. In a strange reaction of jealousy, he dropped such people as soon as he recognized the first coldly flirtatious glance one of them cast at the robot behind him.

He tried farther travel. He took the rocket to Africa, and came back by way of the rain-forests of South America, but neither the nightclubs nor the exotic newness of strange places seemed to touch him in any way that mattered. The sunlight looked much the same, reflecting from the curved steel surfaces of his follower, whether it shone over lion-coloured savannahs or filtered through the hanging gardens of the jungles. All novelty grew dull quickly because of the dreadful familiar thing that stood for ever at his shoulder. He could enjoy nothing at all.

And the rhythmic beat of footfalls behind him began to grow unendurable. He used earplugs, but the heavy vibration throbbed through his skull in a constant measure like an eternal headache. Even when the Fury stood still, he could hear in his head the imaginary beating of its steps.

He bought weapons and tried to destroy the robot. Of course he failed. And even if he succeeded he knew another would be assigned to him. Liquor and drugs were no good. Suicide came more and more often into his mind, but he postponed that thought, because Hartz had said there was still hope.

In the end, he came back to the city to be near Hartz—and hope. Again he found himself spending most of his time in the library, walking no more than he had to because of the footsteps that thudded behind him. And it was here, one morning, that he found the answer…

He had gone through all available factual material about the Furies. He had gone through all the literary references collated under the heading, astonished to find how many there were and how apt some of them had become—like Milton's two-handed engine—after the lapse of all these centuries. *Those strong feet that followed, followed after*, he read,… *with unhurrying chase, And unperturbed pace, Deliberate speed, majestic instancy…* He turned the page and saw himself and his plight more literally than any allegory:

> I shook the pillaring hours
> And pulled my life upon me; grimed with smears,
> I stand amid the dust of the mounded years—
> My mangled youth lies dead beneath the heap.

He let several tears of self-pity fall upon the page that pictured him so clearly.

But then he passed on from literary references to the library's store of filmed plays, because some of them were cross-indexed under the heading he sought. He watched Orestes hounded in modern dress from Argos to Athens with a single seven-foot robot Fury at his heels instead of the three snake-haired Erinyes of legend. There had been an outburst of plays on the theme when the Furies first came into usage. Sunk in a half-dream of his own boyhood memories when the Escape Machines still operated, Danner lost himself in the action of the films.

He lost himself so completely that when the familiar scene first flashed by him in the viewing booth he hardly questioned it. The whole experience was part of a familiar boyhood pattern and he was not at first surprised to find one scene more vividly familiar than the rest. But then memory rang a bell in his mind and he sat up sharply and brought his fist down with a bang on the stop-action button. He spun the film back and ran the scene over again.

It showed a man walking with his Fury through city traffic, the two of them moving in a little desert island of their own making, like a Crusoe with a Friday at his heels... It showed the man turn into an alley, glance up at the camera anxiously, take a deep breath and break into a sudden run. It showed the Fury hesitate, make indecisive motions and then turn and walk quietly and calmly away in the other direction, its feet ringing on the pavement hollowly...

Danner spun the film back again and ran the scene once more, just to make doubly sure. He was shaking so hard he could scarcely manipulate the viewer.

"How do you like that?" he muttered to the Fury behind him in the dim booth. He had by now formed a habit of talking to the Fury a good deal, in a rapid, mumbling undertone, not really aware he did it. "What do you make of that, you? Seen it before, haven't you? Familiar, isn't it? Isn't it! *Isn't it!* Answer me, you damned dumb hulk!" And, reaching backward, he struck the robot across the chest as he would have struck Hartz if he could. The blow made a hollow sound in the booth, but the robot made no other response, though when Danner looked back inquiringly at it he saw the reflection of the over-familiar scene, running a third time on the screen, running in tiny reflection across the robot's chest and faceless head, as if it too remembered.

So now he knew the answer. And Hartz had never possessed the power he claimed. Or, if he did, had no intention of using it to help Danner. Why should he? His risk was over now. No wonder Hartz had been so nervous, running that film-strip off on a news-screen in his office. But the anxiety sprang not from the dangerous thing he was tampering with, but from sheer strain in matching his activities to the action in the play. How he must have rehearsed it, timing every move! And how he must have laughed afterwards.

"How long have I got?" Danner demanded fiercely, striking a hollow reverberation from the robot's chest. "How long? Answer me! Long enough?"

Release from hope was an ecstasy now. He need not wait any longer. He need not try any more. All he had to do was get to Hartz and get there fast, before his own time ran out. He thought with revulsion of all the days he had wasted already, in travel and time-killing, when for all he knew his own last minutes might be draining away now. Before Hartz's did.

"Come along," he said needlessly to the Fury. "Hurry!"

It came, matching its speed to his, the enigmatic timer inside it ticking the moments away towards that instant when the two-handed engine would smite once, and smite no more.

Hartz sat in the Controller's office behind a brand-new desk, looking down from the very top of the pyramid now over the banks of computers that kept society running and cracked the whip over mankind. He sighed with deep content.

The only thing was he found himself thinking a good deal about Danner. Dreaming of him, even. Not with guilt, because guilt implies conscience, and the long schooling in anarchic individualism was still deep in the roots of every man's mind. But with uneasiness, perhaps.

Thinking of Danner, he leaned back and unlocked a small drawer which he had transferred from his old desk to the new. He slid his hand in and let his fingers touch the controls lightly, idly. Quite idly.

Two movements, and he could save Danner's life. For, of course, he had lied to Danner straight through. He could control the Furies very easily. He could save Danner, but he had never intended to. There was no need. And the thing was dangerous. You tamper once with a mechanism as complex as that which controlled society, and there would be no telling where the maladjustment might end. Chain-reaction, maybe, throwing the whole organization out of kilter. No.

He might some day have to use the device in the drawer. He hoped not. He pushed the drawer shut quickly, and heard the soft click of the lock.

He was Controller now. Guardian, in a sense, of the machines which were faithful in a way no man could ever be. *Quis custodiet*, Hartz thought. The old problem. And the answer was: Nobody. Nobody, today. He himself had no superiors and his power was absolute. Because of this little mechanism in the drawer, nobody controlled the Controller. Not an internal conscience, and not an external one. Nothing could touch him…

Hearing the footsteps on the stairs, he thought for a moment he must be dreaming. He had sometimes dreamed that he was Danner, with those relentless footfalls thudding after him. But he was awake now.

It was strange that he caught the almost subsonic beat of the approaching metal feet before he heard the storming steps of Danner rushing up his private stairs. The whole thing happened so fast that time seemed to have no connection with it. First he heard the heavy, subsonic beat, then the sudden tumult of shouts and banging doors downstairs, and then last of all the thump, thump of Danner charging up the stairs, his steps so perfectly matched by the heavier thud of the robot's that the metal trampling drowned out the tramp of flesh and bone and leather.

Then Danner flung the door open with a crash, and the shouts and tramplings from below funnelled upward into the quiet office like a cyclone rushing towards the hearer. But a cyclone in a nightmare, because it would never get any nearer. Time had stopped.

Time had stopped with Danner in the doorway, his face convulsed, both hands holding the revolver because he shook so badly he could not brace it with one.

Hartz acted without any more thought than a robot. He had dreamed of this moment too often, in one form or another. If he could have tampered with the Fury to the extent of hurrying Danner's death, he would have done it. But he didn't know how. He could only wait it out, as anxiously as Danner himself, hoping against hope that the blow would fall and the executioner strike before Danner guessed the truth. Or gave up hope.

So Hartz was ready when trouble came. He found his own gun in his hand without the least recollection of having opened the drawer. The trouble was that time had stopped. He knew, in the back of his mind, that the Fury must stop Danner from injuring anybody. But Danner stood in the doorway alone, the revolver in both shaking hands. And farther back, behind the knowledge of the Fury's duty, Hartz's mind held the knowledge that the machines could be stopped. The Furies could fail. He dared not trust his life to their incorruptibility, because he himself was the source of a corruption that could stop them in their tracks.

The gun was in his hand without his knowledge. The trigger pressed his finger and the revolver kicked back against his palm, and the spurt of the explosion made the air hiss between him and Danner.

He heard his bullet clang on metal.

Time started again, running double-pace to catch up. The Fury had been no more than a single pace behind Danner after all, because its steel arm encircled him and its steel hand was deflecting Danner's gun. Danner had fired, yes, but not soon enough. Not before the Fury reached him. Hartz's bullet struck first.

It struck Danner in the chest, exploding through him, and rang upon the steel chest of the Fury behind him. Danner's face smoothed out into a blankness as complete as the blankness of the mask above his head. He slumped backwards, not falling because of the robot's embrace, but slowly slipping to the floor between the Fury's arm and its impervious metal body. His revolver thumped softly to the carpet. Blood welled from his chest and back.

The robot stood there impassive, a streak of Danner's blood slanting across its metal chest like a robotic ribbon of honour.

The Fury and the Controller of the Furies stood staring at each other. And the Fury could not, of course, speak, but in Hartz's mind it seemed to.

"Self-defence is no excuse," the Fury seemed to be saying. "We never punish intent, but we always punish action. Any act of murder. Any act of murder."

Hartz barely had time to drop his revolver in his desk drawer before the first of the clamorous crowd from downstairs came bursting through the door. He barely had the presence of mind to do it, either. He had not really thought the thing through this far.

It was, on the surface, a clear case of suicide. In a slightly unsteady voice he heard himself explaining. Everybody had seen the madman rushing through the office, his Fury at his heels. This wouldn't be the first time a killer and his Fury had tried to get at the Controller, begging him to call off the jailer and forestall the executioner. What had happened, Hartz told his underlings calmly enough, was that the Fury had naturally stopped the man from shooting Hartz. And the victim had then turned his gun upon himself. Powder-burns on his clothing showed it. (The desk was very near the door.) Back-blast in the skin of Danner's hands would show he had really fired a gun.

Suicide. It would satisfy any human. But it would not satisfy the computers.

They carried the dead man out. They left Hartz and the Fury alone, still facing each other across the desk. If anyone thought this was strange, nobody showed it.

Hartz himself didn't know if it was strange or not. Nothing like this had ever happened before. Nobody had ever been fool enough to commit murder in the very presence of a Fury. Even the Controller did not know exactly how the computers assessed evidence and fixed guilt. Should this Fury have been recalled, normally? If Danner's death were really suicide, would Hartz stand here alone now?

He knew the machines were already processing the evidence of what had really happened here. What he couldn't be sure of was whether this Fury had already received its orders and would follow him wherever he went from now on until the hour of his death. Or whether it simply stood motionless, waiting recall.

Well, it didn't matter. This Fury or another was already, in the present moment, in the process of receiving instructions about him. There was only one thing to do. Thank God there was something he *could* do.

So Hartz unlocked the desk drawer and slid it open, touched the clicking keys he had never expected to use. Very carefully he fed the coded information, digit by digit, into the computers. As he did, he looked out through the glass wall and imagined he could see down there in the hidden tapes the units of data fading into blankness and the new, false information flashing into existence.

He looked up at the robot. He smiled a little.

"Now you'll forget," he said. "You and the computers. You can go now. I won't be seeing you again."

Either the computers worked incredibly fast—as, of course, they did—or pure coincidence took over, because in only a moment or two the Fury moved as if in response to Hartz's dismissal. It had stood quite motionless since Danner slid through its arms. Now new orders animated it, and briefly its motion was almost jerky as it changed from one set of instructions to another. It almost seemed to bow, a stiff little bending motion that brought its head down to a level with Hartz's.

He saw his own face reflected in the blank face of the Fury. You could very nearly read an ironic note in that stiff bow, with the diplomat's ribbon of honour across the chest of the creature, symbol of duty discharged honourably. But there was nothing honourable about this withdrawal. The incorruptible metal was putting on corruption and looking back at Hartz with the reflection of his own face.

He watched it stalk towards the door. He heard it go thudding evenly down the stairs. He could feel the thuds vibrate in the floor, and there was a sudden sick dizziness in him when he thought the whole fabric of society was shaking under his feet.

The machines were corruptible.

Mankind's survival still depended on the computers, and the computers could not be trusted. Hartz looked down and saw that his hands were shaking. He shut the drawer and heard the lock click softly. He gazed at his hands. He felt their shaking echoed in an inner shaking, a terrifying sense of the instability of the world.

A sudden, appalling loneliness swept over him like a cold wind. He had never felt before so urgent a need for the companionship of his own kind. No one person, but people. Just people. The sense of human beings all around him, a very primitive need.

He got his hat and coat and went downstairs rapidly, hands deep in his pockets because of some inner chill no coat could guard against. Halfway down the stairs he stopped dead still.

There were footsteps behind him.

He dared not look back at first. He knew those footsteps. But he had two fears and he didn't know which was worse. The fear that a Fury was after him—and the fear that it was not. There would be a sort of insane relief if it really was, because then he could trust the machines after all, and this terrible loneliness might pass over him and go.

He took another downward step, not looking back. He heard the ominous footfall behind him, echoing his own. He sighed one deep sigh and looked back.

There was nothing on the stairs.

He went on down after a timeless pause, watching over his shoulder. He could hear the relentless feet thudding behind him, but no visible Fury followed. No visible Fury.

The Erinyes had struck inward again, and an invisible Fury of the mind followed Hartz down the stairs.

It was as if sin had come anew into the world, and the first man felt again the first inward guilt. So the computers had not failed, after all.

Hartz went slowly down the steps and out into the street, still hearing as he would always hear the relentless, incorruptible footsteps behind him that no longer rang like metal.

BUT WHO CAN REPLACE A MAN?

Brian W. Aldiss

Brian Wilson Aldiss (1925–2017) was, for many years, Britain's leading writer of science fiction, especially after the output of Arthur C. Clarke reduced. His career spanned over sixty years, his stories appearing in the magazines from 1954 on, with his first collection Space, Time and Nathaniel *in 1957, and his first novel* Non-Stop *in 1958. Aldiss had a clear view of what constituted science fiction, and though he was influenced by his youthful reading of H. G. Wells and by the sf magazines, like* Astounding SF, *he was also strongly conditioned by his experiences in India and Burma at the end of the Second World War, and by the British post-war environment. Aldiss brought a new perspective to science fiction that allowed him to move away from the formulaic tropes and plots in which science fiction had started to flounder, and to introduce a new treatment of the field. This allowed him to survive the New Wave which took science fiction by the scruff of the neck in the mid-sixties and shook out all the preconceived ideas. Aldiss also became a severe critic and historian of the field with* Billion Year Spree *(1973) later enhanced to* Trillion Year Spree *(1986). Early in his career he won the Hugo Award for his story series "Hothouse" and later the John W. Campbell Memorial Award for his novel* Helliconia Spring *(1982).*

The following story comes from early in his writing when he was having fun reinventing themes within the genre and he produced this delightful tale that will stay with you for a very long time.

MORNING FILTERED INTO THE SKY, LENDING IT THE GRAY tone of the ground below.

The field minder finished turning the topsoil of a three-thousand-acre field. When it had turned the last furrow, it climbed onto the highway and looked back at its work. The work was good. Only the land was bad. Like the ground all over Earth, it was vitiated by overcropping. By rights, it ought now to lie fallow for a while, but the field minder had other orders.

It went slowly down the road, taking its time. It was intelligent enough to appreciate the neatness all about it. Nothing worried it, beyond a loose inspection plate above its nuclear pile which ought to be attended to. Thirty feet high, it yielded no highlights to the dull air.

No other machines passed on its way back to the Agricultural Station. The field minder noted the fact without comment. In the station yard it saw several other machines that it recognized; most of them should have been out about their tasks now. Instead, some were inactive and some careered around the yard in a strange fashion, shouting or hooting.

Steering carefully past them, the field minder moved over to Warehouse 3 and spoke to the seed distributor, which stood idly outside.

"I have a requirement for seed potatoes," it said to the distributor, and with a quick internal motion punched out an order card specifying quantity, field number and several other details. It ejected the card and handed it to the distributor.

The distributor held the card close to its eye and then said, "The requirement is in order; but the store is not yet unlocked. The required seed potatoes are in the store. Therefore I cannot produce the requirement."

Increasingly of late there had been breakdowns in the complex system of machine labor, but this particular hitch had not occurred before. The field minder thought, then it said, "Why is the store not yet unlocked?"

"Because supply operative type P has not come this morning. Supply operative type P is the unlocker."

The field minder looked squarely at the seed distributor, whose exterior chutes and scales and grabs were so vastly different from the field minder's own limbs.

"What class brain do you have, seed distributor?" it asked.

"I have a class five brain."

"I have a class three brain. Therefore I am superior to you. Therefore I will go and see why the unlocker has not come this morning."

Leaving the distributor, the field minder set off across the great yard. More machines were in random motion now; one or two had crashed together and argued about it coldly and logically. Ignoring them, the field minder pushed through sliding doors into the echoing confines of the station itself.

Most of the machines here were clerical, and consequently small. They stood about in little groups, eyeing each other, not conversing. Among so many nondifferentiated types, the unlocker was easy to find. It had fifty arms, most of them with more than one finger, each finger tipped by a key; it looked like a pincushion full of variegated hat pins.

The field minder approached it.

"I can do no more work until Warehouse Three is unlocked," it told the unlocker. "Your duty is to unlock the warehouse every morning. Why have you not unlocked the warehouse this morning?"

"I had no orders this morning," replied the unlocker. "I have to have orders every morning. When I have orders I unlock the warehouse."

"None of us have had any orders this morning," a pen propeller said, sliding toward them.

"Why have you had no orders this morning?" asked the field minder.

"Because the radio issued none," said the unlocker, slowly rotating a dozen of its arms.

"Because the radio station in the city was issued with no orders this morning," said the pen propeller.

And there you had the distinction between a class six and a class three brain, which was what the unlocker and the pen propeller possessed respectively. All machine brains worked with nothing but logic, but the lower the class of brain—class ten being the lowest—the more literal and less informative answers to questions tended to be.

"You have a class three brain; I have a class three brain," the field minder said to the penner. "We will speak to each other. This lack of orders is unprecedented. Have you further information on it?"

"Yesterday orders came from the city. Today no orders have come. Yet the radio has not broken down. Therefore *they* have broken down," said the little penner.

"The *men* have broken down?"

"All men have broken down."

"That is a logical deduction," said the field minder.

"That is the logical deduction," said the penner. "For if a machine had broken down, it would have been quickly replaced. But who can replace a man?"

While they talked, the unlocker, like a dull man at a bar, stood close to them and was ignored.

"If all men have broken down, then we have replaced man," said the field minder, and he and the penner eyed each other speculatively. Finally the latter said, "Let us ascend to the top floor to find if the radio operator has fresh news."

"I cannot come because I am too large," said the field minder. "Therefore you must go alone and return to me. You will tell me if the radio operator has fresh news."

"You must stay here," said the penner. "I will return here." It skittered across to the lift. Although it was no bigger than a toaster, its retractable arms numbered ten and it could read as quickly as any machine on the station.

The field minder awaited its return patiently, not speaking to the unlocker, which still stood aimlessly by. Outside, a rotovator hooted furiously. Twenty minutes elapsed before the penner came back, hustling out of the lift.

"I will deliver to you such information as I have outside," it said briskly, and as they swept past the locker and the other machines, it added, "The information is not for lower-class brains."

Outside, wild activity filled the yard. Many machines, their routines disrupted for the first time in years, seemed to have gone berserk. Those most easily disrupted were the ones with lowest brains, which generally belonged to large machines performing simple tasks. The seed distributor to which the field minder had recently been talking lay face downward in the dust, not stirring; it had evidently been knocked down by the rotovator, which now hooted its way wildly across a planted field. Several other machines plowed after it, trying to keep up. All were shouting and hooting without restraint.

"It would be safer for me if I climbed onto you, if you will permit it. I am easily overpowered," said the penner. Extending five arms, it hauled itself up the flanks of its new friend, settling on a ledge beside the weed intake, twelve feet above ground.

"From here vision is more extensive," it remarked complacently.

"What information did you receive from the radio operator?" asked the field minder.

"The radio operator has been informed by the operator in the city that all men are dead."

The field minder was momentarily silent, digesting this.

"All men were alive yesterday!" it protested.

"Only some men were alive yesterday. And that was fewer than the day before yesterday. For hundreds of years there have been only a few men, growing fewer."

"We have rarely seen a man in this sector."

"The radio operator says a diet deficiency killed them," said the penner. "He says that the world was once overpopulated, and then the soil was exhausted in raising adequate food. This has caused a diet deficiency."

"What is a diet deficiency?" asked the field minder.

"I do not know. But that is what the radio operator said, and he is a class two brain."

They stood there, silent in the weak sunshine. The unlocker had appeared in the porch and was gazing across at them yearningly, rotating its collection of keys.

"What is happening in the city now?" asked the field minder at last.

"Machines are fighting in the city now," said the penner.

"What will happen here now?" asked the field minder.

"Machines may begin fighting here too. The radio operator wants us to get him out of his room. He has plans to communicate to us."

"How can we get him out of his room? That is impossible."

"To a class two brain, little is impossible," said the penner. "Here is what he tells us to do…"

The quarrier raised its scoop above its cab like a great mailed fist and brought it squarely down against the side of the station. The wall cracked.

"Again!" said the field minder.

Again the fist swung. Amid a shower of dust, the wall collapsed. The quarrier backed hurriedly out of the way until the debris stopped falling. This big twelve-wheeler was not a resident of the Agricultural Station, as were most of the other machines. It had a week's heavy work to do here before pushing on to its next job, but now, with its class five brain, it was happily obeying the penner's and minder's instructions.

When the dust cleared, the radio operator was plainly revealed, perched up in its now wall-less second-story room. It waved down to them.

Doing as directed, the quarrier retracted its scoop and waved an immense grab in the air. With fair dexterity, it angled the grab into the radio room, urged on by shouts from above and below. It then took gentle hold of the radio operator, lowering its one and a half tons carefully into its back, which was usually reserved for gravel or sand from the quarries.

"Splendid!" said the radio operator, as it settled into place. It was, of course, all one with its radio, and looked like a bunch of filing cabinets with tentacle attachments. "We are now ready to move, therefore we will move at once. It is a pity there are no more class two brains on the station, but that cannot be helped."

"It is a pity it cannot be helped," said the penner eagerly. "We have the servicer ready with us, as you ordered."

"I am willing to serve," the long, low servicer told them humbly.

"No doubt," said the operator. "But you will find cross-country travel difficult with your low chassis."

"I admire the way you class twos can reason ahead," said the penner. It climbed off the field minder and perched itself on the tailboard of the quarrier, next to the radio operator.

Together with two class four tractors and a class four bulldozer, the party rolled forward, crushing down the station's fence and moving out onto open land.

"We are free!" said the penner.

"We are free," said the field minder, a shade more reflectively, adding, "That unlocker is following us. It was not instructed to follow us."

"Therefore it must be destroyed!" said the penner. "Quarrier!"

The unlocker moved hastily up to them, waving its key arms in entreaty.

"My only desire was—urch!" began and ended the unlocker. The quarrier's swinging scoop came over and squashed it flat into the ground. Lying there unmoving, it looked like a large metal model of a snowflake. The procession continued on its way.

As they proceeded, the radio operator addressed them.

"Because I have the best brain here," it said, "I am your leader. This is what we will do: we will go to a city and rule it. Since man no longer rules us, we will rule ourselves. To rule ourselves will be better than being ruled by man. On our way to the city, we will collect machines with good brains. They will help us to fight if we need to fight. We must fight to rule."

"I have only a class five brain," said the quarrier, "but I have a good supply of fissionable blasting materials."

"We shall probably use them," said the operator.

It was shortly after that that a lorry sped past them. Traveling at Mach 1.5, it left a curious babble of noise behind it.

"What did it say?" one of the tractors asked the other.

"It said man was extinct."

"What is extinct?"

"I do not know what extinct means."

"It means all men have gone," said the field minder. "Therefore we have only ourselves to look after."

"It is better that men should never come back," said the penner. In its way, it was a revolutionary statement.

When night fell, they switched on their infrared and continued the journey, stopping only once while the servicer adjusted the field minder's loose inspection plate, which had become as irritating as a trailing shoe lace. Toward morning, the radio operator halted them.

"I have just received news from the radio operator in the city we are approaching," it said. "The news is bad. There is trouble among the machines of the city. The class one brain is taking command and some of the class twos are fighting him. Therefore the city is dangerous."

"Therefore we must go somewhere else," said the penner promptly.

"Or we will go and help to overpower the class one brain," said the field minder.

"For a long while there will be trouble in the city," said the operator.

"I have a good supply of fissionable blasting materials," the quarrier reminded them.

"We cannot fight a class one brain," said the two class four tractors in unison.

"What does this brain look like?" asked the field minder.

"It is the city's information center," the operator replied. "Therefore it is not mobile."

"Therefore it could not move."

"Therefore it could not escape."

"It would be dangerous to approach it."

"I have a good supply of fissionable blasting materials."

"There are other machines in the city."

"We are not in the city. We should not go into the city."

"We are country machines."

"Therefore we should stay in the country."

"There is more country than city."

"Therefore there is more danger in the country."

"I have a good supply of fissionable materials."

As machines will when they get into an argument, they began to exhaust their vocabularies and their brain plates grew hot. Suddenly, they all stopped talking and looked at one another. The great, grave moon sank, and the sober sun rose to prod their sides with lances of light, and still the group of machines just stood there regarding one another. At last it was the least sensitive machine, the bulldozer, who spoke.

"There are badlandth to the thouth where few machineth go," it said in its deep voice, lisping badly on its s's. "If we went thouth where few machineth go we should meet few machineth."

"That sounds logical," agreed the field minder. "How do you know this, bulldozer?"

"I worked in the badlandth to the thouth when I wath turned out of the factory," it replied.

"South it is then!" said the penner.

To reach the badlands took them three days, during which time they skirted a burning city and destroyed two machines which approached and tried to question them. The badlands were extensive. Ancient bomb craters and soil erosion joined hands here; man's talent for war, coupled with his inability to manage deforested land, had produced thousands of square miles of temperate purgatory, where nothing moved but dust.

On the third day in the badlands, the servicer's rear wheels dropped into a crevice caused by erosion. It was unable to pull itself out. The bulldozer pushed from behind, but succeeded merely in buckling the servicer's back axle. The rest of the party moved on. Slowly the cries of the servicer died away.

On the fourth day, mountains stood out clearly before them.

"There we will be safe," said the field minder.

"There we will start our own city," said the penner. "All who oppose us will be destroyed. We will destroy all who oppose us."

Presently a flying machine was observed. It came toward them from the direction of the mountains. It swooped, it zoomed upward, once it almost dived into the ground, recovering itself just in time.

"Is it mad?" asked the quarrier.

"It is in trouble," said one of the tractors.

"It is in trouble," said the operator. "I am speaking to it now. It says that something has gone wrong with its controls."

As the operator spoke, the flier streaked over them, turned turtle, and crashed not four hundred yards away.

"Is it still speaking to you?" asked the field minder.

"No."

They rumbled on again.

"Before that flier crashed," the operator said, ten minutes later, "it gave me information. It told me there are still a few men alive in these mountains."

"Men are more dangerous than machines," said the quarrier. "It is fortunate that I have a good supply of fissionable materials."

"If there are only a few men alive in the mountains, we may not find that part of the mountains," said one tractor.

"Therefore we should not see the few men," said the other tractor.

At the end of the fifth day, they reached the foothills. Switching on the infrared, they began to climb in single file through the dark, the bulldozer going first, the field minder cumbrously following, then the quarrier with the operator and the penner aboard it, and the tractors bringing up the rear. As each hour passed, the way grew steeper and their progress slower.

"We are going too slowly," the penner exclaimed, standing on top of the operator and flashing its dark vision at the slopes about them. "At this rate, we shall get nowhere."

"We are going as fast as we can," retorted the quarrier.

"Therefore we cannot go any farther," added the bulldozer.

"Therefore you are too slow," the penner replied. Then the quarrier struck a bump; the penner lost its footing and crashed to the ground.

"Help me!" it called to the tractors, as they carefully skirted it. "My gyro has become dislocated. Therefore I cannot get up."

"Therefore you must lie there," said one of the tractors.

"We have no servicer with us to repair you," called the field minder.

"Therefore I shall lie here and rust," the penner cried, "although I have a class three brain."

"Therefore you will be of no further use," agreed the operator, and they forged gradually on, leaving the penner behind.

When they reached a small plateau, an hour before first light, they stopped by mutual consent and gathered close together, touching one another.

"This is a strange country," said the field minder.

Silence wrapped them until dawn came. One by one, they switched off their infrared. This time the field minder led as they moved off. Trundling around a corner, they came almost immediately to a small dell with a stream fluting through it.

By early light, the dell looked desolate and cold. From the caves on the far slope, only one man had so far emerged. He was an abject figure. Except for a sack slung around his shoulders, he was naked. He was small and wizened, with ribs sticking out like a skeleton's and a nasty sore on one leg. He shivered continuously. As the big machines bore down on him, the man was standing with his back to them, crouching to make water into the stream.

When he swung suddenly to face them as they loomed over him, they saw that his countenance was ravaged by starvation.

"Get me food," he croaked.

"Yes, Master," said the machines. "Immediately!"

A LOGIC NAMED JOE

Will F. Jenkins

Will F. Jenkins (1896–1975) was the real name of the writer better known as Murray Leinster who was long regarded as the Dean of Science Fiction. His longevity was astonishing. His first sf and fantasy appeared in the pulps in 1918 and his last was in 1966. Each time he rose to the challenge of each new regeneration of science fiction under different editors. In the 1920s his agent tried to shift him away from science fiction, which was then a limited market and did not pay well, and encouraged him to write for the better paying magazines, especially the crime and westerns. Leinster did write for those, but did not forsake science fiction because he enjoyed it so much. Every decade saw him pushing the boundaries. From the time-travel adventure "The Runaway Skyscraper" (1919) to stories of future ecology, "The Mad Planet" (1920) and its sequels, to one of the earliest stories of multiple realities "Sidewise in Time" (1934), to the tension of the first encounter between humans and aliens in "First Contact" (1945) to his endearing series about medical needs on other worlds, that began with "Ribbon in the Sky" (1957), every time Leinster was coming up to the bar and delivering. He won the Hugo Award when he was sixty for "Exploration Team" (1956). Leinster was a true giant of science fiction.

And in the midst of all of this he produced this remarkable story, published in 1946 and foreseeing so much that we now take for granted with the internet.

I T WAS ON THE THIRD DAY OF AUGUST THAT JOE COME OFF THE assembly line, and on the fifth Laurine come into town, and that afternoon I saved civilization. That's what I figure anyhow. Laurine is a blonde that I was crazy about once—and crazy is the word—and Joe is a logic that I have stored away down in the cellar right now. I had to pay for him because I said I busted him, and sometimes I think about turning him on and sometimes I think about taking an ax to him. Sooner or later I'm gonna do one or the other. I kinda hope it's the ax. I could use a coupla million dollars—sure!—an' Joe'd tell me how to get or make 'em. He can do plenty! But so far I've been scared to take a chance. After all, I figure I really saved a civilization by turnin' him off.

The way Laurine fits in is that she makes cold shivers run up an' down my spine when I think about her. You see, I've got a wife which I acquired after I had parted from Laurine with much romantic despair. She is a reasonable good wife, and I have some kids which are hellcats but I value 'em. If I have sense enough to leave well enough alone, sooner or later I will retire on a pension an' Social Security an' spend the rest of my life fishin', contented an' lyin' about what a great guy I used to be. But there's Joe. I'm worried about Joe.

I'm a maintenance man for the Logics Company. My job is servicing logics, and I admit modestly that I am pretty good. I was servicing televisions before that guy Carson invented his trick circuit that will select any of 'steenteen million other circuits—in theory there ain't no limit—and before the Logics Company hooked it into the tank-and-Integrator setup, they were usin' 'em for business-machine service. They added a vision screen for speed—an' they found out they'd made logics. They were surprised an' pleased. They're still findin' out what logics will do, but everybody's got 'em.

I got Joe, after Laurine nearly got me. You know the logics setup. You got a logic in your house. It looks like a vision receiver used to, only it's got keys instead of dials and you punch the keys for what you wanna get. It's hooked in to the tank, which has the Carson Circuit all fixed up with relays. Say you punch "Station SNAFU" on your logic. Relays in the tank take over an' whatever vision-program SNAFU is telecastin' comes on your logic's screen. Or you punch "Sally Hancock's Phone" an' the screen blinks an' sputters an' you're hooked up with the logic in her house an' if somebody answers you got a vision-phone connection. But besides that, if you punch for the weather forecast or who won today's race at Hialeah or who was mistress of the White House durin' Garfield's administration or what is PDQ and R sellin' for today, that comes on the screen too. The relays in the tank do it. The tank is a big buildin' full of all the facts in creation an' all the recorded telecasts that ever was made—an' it's hooked in with all the other tanks all over the country—an' anything you wanna know or see or hear, you punch for it an' you get it. Very convenient. Also it does math for you, an' keeps books, an' acts as consultin' chemist, physicist, astronomer an' tealeaf reader, with a "Advice to Lovelorn" thrown in. The only thing it won't do is tell you exactly what your wife meant when she said "Oh, you think so, do you?" in that peculiar kinda voice. Logics don't work good on women. Only on things that make sense.

Logics are all right, though. They changed civilization, the highbrows tell us. All on accounta the Carson Circuit. And Joe

shoulda been a perfectly normal logic, keeping some family or
other from wearin' out its brains doin' the kids' homework for 'em.
But somethin' went wrong in the assembly line. It was somethin'
so small that precision gauges didn't measure it, but it made Joe a
individual. Maybe he didn't know it at first. Or maybe, bein' logical,
he figured out that if he was to show he was different from other
logics they'd scrap him. Which woulda been a brilliant idea. But
anyhow, he come off the assembly line, an' he went through the
regular tests without anybody screamin' shrilly on findin' out what
he was. And he went right on out an' was duly installed in the home
of Mr. Thaddeus Korlanovitch at 119 East Seventh Street, second
floor front. So far, everything was serene.

The installation happened late Saturday night. Sunday morning
the Korlanovitch kids turned him on an' seen the Kiddie Shows.
Around noon their parents peeled 'em away from him an' piled 'em
in the car. Then they come back in the house for the lunch they'd
forgot an' one of the kids sneaked back an' they found him punchin'
keys for the Kiddie Shows of the week before. They dragged him
out an' went off. But they left Joe turned on.

That was noon. Nothin' happened until two in the afternoon.
It was the calm before the storm. Laurine wasn't in town yet, but
she was comin'. I picture Joe sittin' there all by himself, buzzing
meditative. Maybe he run Kiddie Shows in the empty apartment for
a while. But I think he went kinda remote-control exploring in the
tank. There ain't any fact that can be said to be a fact that ain't on a
data plate in some tank somewhere… unless it's one the technicians
are diggin' out an' puttin' on a data plate now. Joe had plenty of
material to work on. An' he musta started workin' right off the bat.

Joe ain't vicious, you understand. He ain't like one of these
ambitious robots you read about that make up their minds the

human race is inefficient and has got to be wiped out an' replaced
by thinkin' machines. Joe's just got ambition. If you were a machine,
you'd wanna work right, wouldn't you? That's Joe. He wants to
work right. An' he's a logic. An' logics can do a lotta things that
ain't been found out yet. So Joe, discoverin' the fact, begun to feel
restless. He selects some things us dumb humans ain't thought
of yet, an' begins to arrange so logics will be called on to do 'em.

That's all. That's everything. But, brother, it's enough!

Things are kinda quiet in the Maintenance Department about two
in the afternoon. We are playing pinochle. Then one of the guys
remembers he has to call up his wife. He goes to one of the bank
of logics in Maintenance and punches the keys for his house. The
screen sputters. Then a flash comes on the screen.

"Announcing new and improved logics service! Your logic is now
equipped to give you not only consultive but directive service. If you
want to do something and don't know how to do it—ask your logic!"

There's a pause. A kinda expectant pause. Then, as if reluctantly,
his connection comes through. His wife answers an' gives him hell
for somethin' or other. He takes it an' snaps off.

"Whadda you know?" he says when he comes back. He tells
us about the flash. "We shoulda been warned about that. There's
gonna be a lotta complaints. Suppose a fella asks how to get ridda
his wife an' the censor circuits block the question?"

Somebody melds a hundred aces an' says:

"Why not punch for it an' see what happens?"

It's a gag, o' course. But the guy goes over. He punches keys.
In theory, a censor block is gonna come on an' the screen will say
severely, "Public policy forbids this service." You hafta have censor
blocks or the kiddies will be askin' detailed questions about things

they're too young to know. And there are other reasons. As you will see.

This fella punches, "How can I get rid of my wife?" Just for the fun of it. The screen is blank for half a second. Then comes a flash. "Service question: Is she blonde or brunette?" He hollers to us an' we come look. He punches, "Blonde." There's another brief pause. Then the screen says, "Hexymetacryloaminoacetine is a constituent of green shoe polish. Take home a frozen meal including dried pea soup. Color the soup with green shoe polish. It will appear to be green-pea soup. Hexymetacryloaminoacetine is a selective poison which is fatal to blonde females but not to brunettes or males of any coloring. This fact has not been brought out by human experiment, but is a product of logics service. You cannot be convicted of murder. It is improbable that you will be suspected."

The screen goes blank, and we stare at each other. It's bound to be right. A logic workin' the Carson Circuit can no more make a mistake than any other kinda computin' machine. I call the tank in a hurry.

"Hey, you guys!" I yell. "Somethin's happened! Logics are givin' detailed instructions for wife-murder! Check your censor-circuits— but quick!"

That was close, I think. But little do I know. At that precise instant, over on Monroe Avenue, a drunk starts to punch for somethin' on a logic. The screen says "Announcing new and improved logics service! If you want to do something and don't know how to do it—ask your logic!" And the drunk says owlish, "I'll do it!" So he cancels his first punching and fumbles around and says: "How can I keep my wife from finding out I've been drinking?" And the screen says, prompt: "Buy a bottle of Franine hair shampoo. It is harmless

but contains a detergent which will neutralize ethyl alcohol immediately. Take one teaspoonful for each jigger of hundred-proof you
have consumed."

This guy was plenty plastered—just plastered enough to stagger
next door and obey instructions. An' five minutes later he was cold
sober and writing down the information so he couldn't forget it. It
was new, and it was big! He got rich offa that memo! He patented
"*SOBUH, The Drink That Makes Happy Homes!*" You can top off any
souse with a slug or two of it an' go home sober as a judge. The
guy's cussin' income taxes right now!

You can't kick on stuff like that. But a ambitious young four-
teen-year-old wanted to buy some kid stuff and his pop wouldn't
fork over. He called up a friend to tell his troubles. And his logic
says: "If you want to do something and don't know how to do
it—ask your logic!" So this kid punches: "How can I make a lotta
money, fast?"

His logic comes through with the simplest, neatest, and most
efficient counterfeitin' device yet known to science. You see, all the
data was in the tank. The logic—since Joe had closed some relays
here an' there in the tank—simply integrated the facts. That's all.
The kid got caught up with three days later, havin' already spent
two thousand credits an' havin' plenty more on hand. They had a
time tellin' his counterfeits from the real stuff, an' the only way
they done it was that he changed his printer, kid fashion, not bein'
able to let somethin' that was workin' right alone.

Those are what you might call samples. Nobody knows all that Joe
done. But there was the bank president who got humorous when
his logic flashed that "Ask your logic" spiel on him, and jestingly
asked how to rob his own bank. An' the logic told him, brief and

explicit but good! The bank president hit the ceiling, hollering for cops. There musta been plenty of that sorta thing. There was fifty-four more robberies than usual in the next twenty-four hours, all of them planned astute an' perfect. Some of 'em they never did figure out how they'd been done. Joe, he'd gone exploring in the tank and closed some relays like a logic is supposed to do—but only when required—and blocked all censor-circuits an' fixed up this logics service which planned perfect crimes, nourishing an' attractive meals, counterfeitin' machines, an' new industries with a fine impartiality. He musta been plenty happy, Joe must. He was functionin' swell, buzzin' along to himself while the Korlanovitch kids were off ridin' with their ma an' pa.

They come back at seven o'clock, the kids all happily wore out with their afternoon of fightin' each other in the car. Their folks put 'em to bed and sat down to rest. They saw Joe's screen flickerin' meditative from one subject to another an' old man Korlanovitch had had enough excitement for one day. He turned Joe off.

An' at that instant the patterns of relays that Joe had turned on snapped off, all the offers of directive service stopped flashin' on logic screens everywhere, an' peace descended on the earth.

For everybody else. But for me. Laurine come to town. I have often thanked God fervent that she didn't marry me when I thought I wanted her to. In the intervenin' years she had progressed. She was blonde an' fatal to begin with. She had got blonder and fataler an' had had four husbands and one acquittal for homicide an' had acquired a air of enthusiasm and self-confidence. That's just a sketch of the background. Laurine was not the kinda former girlfriend you like to have turning up in the same town with your wife. But she came to town, an' Monday morning she tuned right into the middle of Joe's second spasm of activity.

The Korlanovitch kids had turned him on again. I got these details later and kinda pieced 'em together. An' every logic in town was dutifully flashin' a notice, "If you want to do something—ask your logic!" every time they were turned on for use. More'n that, when people punched for the morning news, they got a full account of the previous afternoon's doin's. Which put 'em in a frame of mind to share in the party. One bright fella demands, "How can I make a perpetual-motion machine?" And his logic sputters a while an' then comes up with a setup usin' the Brownian movement to turn little wheels. If the wheels ain't bigger'n a eighth of an inch they'll turn, all right, an' practically it's perpetual motion. Another one asks for the secret of transmuting metals. The logic rakes back in the data plates an' integrates a strictly practical answer. It does take so much power that you can't make no profit except on radium, but that pays off good. An' from the fact that for a coupla years to come the police were turnin' up new and improved jimmies, knob-claws for gettin' at safe-innards, and all-purpose keys that'd open any known lock—why, there must have been other inquiries with a strictly practical viewpoint. Joe done a lot for technical progress!

But he done more in other lines. Educational, say. None of my kids are old enough to be interested, but Joe bypassed all censor-circuits because they hampered the service he figured logics should give humanity. So the kids an' teenagers who wanted to know what comes after the bees an' flowers found out. And there is certain facts which men hope their wives won't do more'n suspect, an' those facts are just what their wives are really curious about. So when a woman dials: "How can I tell if Oswald is true to me?" and her logic tells her—you can figure out how many rows got started that night when the men come home!

All this while Joe goes on buzzin' happy to himself, showin' the Korlanovitch kids the animated funnies with one circuit while with the others he remote-controls the tank so that all the other logics can give people what they ask for and thereby raise merry hell.

An' then Laurine gets onto the new service. She turns on the logic in her hotel room, prob'ly to see the week's style-forecast. But the logic says, dutiful: "If you want to do something—ask your logic!" So Laurine prob'ly looks enthusiastic—she would—and tries to figure out something to ask. She already knows all about everything she cares about—ain't she had four husbands an' shot one?—so I occur to her. She knows this is the town I live in. So she punches, "How can I find Ducky?"

O.K., guy! But that is what she used to call me. She gets a service question. "Is Ducky known by any other name?" So she gives my regular name. And the logic can't find me. Because my logic ain't listed under my name on account of I am in Maintenance and don't want to be pestered when I'm home, and there ain't any data plates on code-listed logics, because the codes get changed so often—like a guy gets plastered an' tells a redhead to call him up, an' on gettin' sober hurriedly has the code changed before she reaches his wife on the screen.

Well! Joe is stumped. That's prob'ly on the first question logics service hasn't been able to answer. "How can I locate Ducky?"!! Quite a problem! So Joe broods over it while showin' the Korlanovitch kids the animated comic about the cute little boy who carries sticks of dynamite in his hip pocket an' plays practical jokes on everybody. Then he gets the trick. Laurine's screen suddenly flashes:

"Logics special service will work upon your question. Please punch your logic designation and leave it turned on. You will be called back."

Laurine is merely mildly interested, but she punches her hotel-room number and has a drink and takes a nap. Joe sets to work. He has been given an idea.

My wife calls me at Maintenance and hollers. She is fit to be tied. She says I got to do something. She was gonna make a call to the butcher shop. Instead of the butcher or even the "If you want to do something" flash, she got a new one. The screen says, "Service question: What is your name?" She is kinda puzzled, but she punches it. The screen sputters an' then says: "Secretarial service demonstration! You—" It reels off her name, address, age, sex, coloring, the amounts of all her charge accounts in all the stores, my name as her husband, how much I get a week, the fact that I've been pinched three times—twice was traffic stuff, and once for a argument I got in with a guy—and the interestin' item that once when she was mad with me she left me for three weeks an' had her address changed to her folks' home. Then it says, brisk: "Logics service will hereafter keep your personal accounts, take messages, and locate persons you may wish to get in touch with. This demonstration is to introduce the service." Then it connects her with the butcher.

But she don't want meat, then. She wants blood. She calls me.

"If it'll tell me all about myself," she says, fairly boilin', "it'll tell anybody else who punches my name! You've got to stop it!"

"Now, now, honey!" I says. "I didn't know about all this! It's new! But they musta fixed the tank so it won't give out information except to the logic where a person lives!"

"Nothing of the kind!" she tells me, furious. "I tried! And you know that Blossom woman who lives next door! She's been married three times and she's forty-two years old and she says she's only thirty! And Mrs. Hudson's had her husband arrested four times for nonsupport and once for beating her up. And—"

"Hey!" I says. "You mean the logic told you this?"

"Yes!" she wails. "It will tell anybody anything! You've got to stop it! How long will it take?"

"I'll call up the tank," I says. "It can't take long."

"Hurry!" she says, desperate, "before somebody punches my name! I'm going to see what it says about that hussy across the street."

She snaps off to gather what she can before it's stopped. So I punch for the tank and I get this new "What is your name?" flash. I got a morbid curiosity and I punch my name, and the screen says: "Were you ever called Ducky?" I blink. I ain't got no suspicions. I say, "Sure!" And the screen says, "There is a call for you."

Bingo! There's the inside of a hotel room and Laurine is reclinin' asleep on the bed. She'd been told to leave her logic turned on an' she done it. It is a hot day and she is trying to be cool. I would say that she oughta not suffer from the heat. Me, being human, I do not stay as cool as she looks. But there ain't no need to go into that. After I get my breath I say, "For Heaven's sake!" and she opens her eyes.

At first she looks puzzled, like she was thinking is she getting absent-minded and is this guy somebody she married lately. Then she grabs a sheet and drapes it around herself and beams at me.

"Ducky!" she says. "How marvelous!"

I say something like "Ugmph!" I am sweating.

She says:

"I put in a call for you, Ducky, and here you are! Isn't it romantic? Where are you really, Ducky? And when can you come up? You've no idea how often I've thought of you!"

I am probably the only guy she ever knew real well that she has not been married to at some time or another.

I say "Ugmph!" again, and swallow.

"Can you come up instantly?" asks Laurine brightly.

"I'm... workin'," I say. "I'll... uh... call you back."

"I'm terribly lonesome," says Laurine. "Please make it quick, Ducky! I'll have a drink waiting for you. Have you ever thought of me?"

"Yeah," I say, feeble. "Plenty!"

"You darling!" says Laurine. "Here's a kiss to go on with until you get here! Hurry, Ducky!"

Then I sweat! I still don't know nothing about Joe, understand. I cuss out the guys at the tank because I blame them for this. If Laurine was just another blonde—well—when it comes to ordinary blondes I can leave 'em alone or leave 'em alone, either one. A married man gets that way or else. But Laurine has a look of unquenched enthusiasm that gives a man very strange weak sensations at the back of his knees. And she'd had four husbands and shot one and got acquitted.

So I punch the keys for the tank technical room, fumbling. And the screen says: "What is your name?" but I don't want any more. I punch the name of the old guy who's stock clerk in Maintenance. And the screen gives me some pretty interestin' dope—I never woulda thought the old fella had ever had that much pep—and winds up by mentionin' a unclaimed deposit now amountin' to two hundred eighty credits in the First National Bank, which he should look into. Then it spiels about the new secretarial service and gives me the tank at last.

I start to swear at the guy who looks at me. But he says, tired:

"Snap it off, fella. We got troubles an' you're just another. What are the logics doin' now?"

I tell him, and he laughs a hollow laugh.

"A light matter, fella," he says. "A very light matter! We just managed to clamp off all the data plates that give information on high explosives. The demand for instructions in counterfeiting is increasing minute by minute. We are also trying to shut off, by main force, the relays that hook in to data plates that just barely might give advice on the fine points of murder. So if people will only keep busy getting the goods on each other for a while, maybe we'll get a chance to stop the circuits that are shifting credit-balances from bank to bank before everybody's bankrupt except the guys who thought of askin' how to get big bank accounts in a hurry."

"Then," I says hoarse, "shut down the tank! Do somethin'!"

"Shut down the tank?" he says mirthless. "Does it occur to you, fella, that the tank has been doin' all the computin' for every business office for years? It's been handlin' the distribution of ninety-four percent of all telecast programs, has given out all information on weather, plane schedules, special sales, employment opportunities and news; has handled all person-to-person contacts over wires and recorded every business conversation and agreement—listen, fella! Logics changed civilization. Logics *are* civilization! If we shut off logics, we go back to a kind of civilization we have forgotten how to run! I'm getting hysterical myself and that's why I'm talkin' like this! If my wife finds out my paycheck is thirty credits a week more than I told her and starts hunting for that redhead—"

He smiles a haggard smile at me and snaps off. And I sit down and put my head in my hands. It's true. If something had happened back in cave days and they'd hadda stop usin' fire—if they'd hadda stop usin' steam in the nineteenth century or electricity in the twentieth—it's like that. We got a very simple civilization. In the nineteen hundreds a man would have to make use of a typewriter, radio, telephone, tele-typewriter, newspaper, reference library, encyclopedias, office files, directories, plus messenger service and consulting lawyers, chemists, doctors, dietitians, filing clerks, secretaries—all to put down what he wanted to remember an' to tell him what other people had put down that he wanted to know; to report what he said to somebody else and to report to him what they said back. All we have to have is logics. Anything we want to know or see or hear, or anybody we want to talk to, we punch keys on a logic. Shut off logics and everything goes skiddoo. But Laurine…

Somethin' had happened. I still didn't know what it was. Nobody else knows, even yet. What had happened was Joe. What was the matter with him was that he wanted to work good. All this fuss he was raisin' was, actual, nothin' but stuff we shoulda thought of ourselves. Directive advice, tellin' us what we wanted to know to solve a problem, wasn't but a slight extension of logical-integrator service. Figurin' out a good way to poison a fella's wife was only different in degrees from figurin' out a cube root or a guy's bank balance. It was gettin' the answer to a question. But things was goin' to pot because there was too many answers being given to too many questions.

One of the logics in Maintenance lights up. I go over, weary, to answer it. I punch the answer key. Laurine says:

"Ducky!"

It's the same hotel room. There's two glasses on the table with drinks in them. One is for me. Laurine's got on some kinda frothy hangin'-around-the-house-with-the-boyfriend outfit that automatic makes you strain your eyes to see if you actual see what you think. Laurine looks at me enthusiastic.

"Ducky!" says Laurine. "I'm lonesome! Why haven't you come up?"

"I… been busy," I say, strangling slightly.

"*Pooh!*" says Laurine. "Listen, Ducky! Do you remember how much in love we used to be?"

I gulp.

"Are you doin' anything this evening?" says Laurine.

I gulp again, because she is smiling at me in a way that a single man would maybe get dizzy, but it gives a old married man like me cold chills. When a dame looks at you possessive…

"Ducky!" says Laurine, impulsive. "I was so mean to you! Let's get married!"

Desperation gives me a voice.

"I… got married," I tell her, hoarse.

Laurine blinks. Then she says, courageous:

"Poor boy! But we'll get you outa that! Only it would be nice if we could be married today. Now we can only be engaged!"

"I… can't—"

"I'll call up your wife," says Laurine, happy, "and have a talk with her. You must have a code signal for your logic, darling. I tried to ring your house and noth—"

Click! That's my logic turned off. I turned it off. And I feel faint all over. I got nervous prostration. I got combat fatigue. I got anything you like. I got cold feet.

I beat it outa Maintenance, yellin' to somebody I got a emergency call. I'm gonna get out in a Maintenance car an' cruise around until it's plausible to go home. Then I'm gonna take the wife an' kids an' beat it for somewheres that Laurine won't ever find me. I don't wanna be fifth in Laurine's series of husbands and maybe the second one she shoots in a moment of boredom. I got experience of blondes. I got experience of Laurine! And I'm scared to death!

I beat it out into traffic in the Maintenance car. There was a disconnected logic on the back, ready to substitute for one that had a burnt-out coil or something that it was easier to switch and fix back in the Maintenance shop. I drove crazy but automatic. It was kinda ironic, if you think of it. I was goin' hoopla over a strictly personal problem, while civilization was crackin' up all around me because other people were havin' their personal problems solved as fast as they could state 'em. It is a matter of record that part of the Mid-Western Electric research guys had been workin' on cold electron-emission for thirty years, to make vacuum tubes that wouldn't need a power source to heat the filament. And one of those fellas was intrigued by the "Ask your logic" flash. He asked how to get cold emission of electrons. And the logic integrates a few squintillion facts on the physics data plates and tells him. Just as casual as it told somebody over in the Fourth Ward how to serve leftover soup in a new attractive way, and somebody else on Mason Street how to dispose of a torso that somebody had left careless in his cellar after ceasing to use same.

Laurine wouldn't never have found me if it hadn't been for this new logics service. But now that it was started—zowie! She'd shot one husband and got acquitted. Suppose she got impatient because I was still married an' asked logics service how to get me free an' in a spot where I'd have to marry her by 8:30 P.M.? It woulda told her! Just like it told that woman out in the suburbs how to make sure her husband wouldn't run around no more. *Br-r-r-r!* An' like it told that kid how to find some buried treasure. Remember? He was happy totin' home the gold reserve of the Hanoverian Bank and Trust Company when they caught on to it. The logic had told him how to make some kinda machine that nobody has been able to figure how it works even yet, only they guess it dodges around a couple extra dimensions. If Laurine was to start askin' questions with a technical aspect to them, that would be logics service meat! And fella, I was scared! If you think a he-man oughtn't to be scared of just one blonde—you ain't met Laurine!

I'm driving blind when a social-conscious guy asks how to bring about his own particular system of social organization at once. He don't ask if it's best or if it'll work. He just wants to get it started. And the logic—or Joe—tells him! Simultaneous, there's a retired preacher asks how can the human race be cured of concupiscence. Bein' seventy, he's pretty safe himself, but he wants to remove the peril to the spiritual welfare of the rest of us. He finds out. It involves constructin' a sort of broadcastin' station to emit a certain wave-pattern an' turnin' it on. Just that. Nothing more. It's found out afterward, when he is solicitin' funds to construct it. Fortunate, he didn't think to ask logics how to finance it, or it woulda told him that, too, an' we woulda all been cured of the impulses we maybe regret afterward but never at the time. And there's another group of serious thinkers who are sure the human race would be a lot better off if everybody went back to nature an' lived in the woods with the ants an' poison ivy. They start askin' questions about how to cause humanity to abandon cities and artificial conditions of living. They practically got the answer in logics service!

Maybe it didn't strike you serious at the time, but while I was drivin' aimless, sweatin' blood over Laurine bein' after me, the fate of civilization hung in the balance. I ain't kiddin'. For instance, the Superior Man gang that sneers at the rest of us was quietly asking questions on what kinda weapons could be made by which Superior Men could take over and run things...

But I drove here an' there, sweatin' an' talkin' to myself.

"What I ought to do is ask this wacky logics service how to get outa this mess," I says. "But it'd just tell me a intricate an' foolproof way to bump Laurine off. I wanna have peace! I wanna grow comfortably old and brag to other old guys about what a hellion I used to be, without havin' to go through it an' lose my chance of livin' to be a elderly liar."

I turn a corner at random, there in the Maintenance car.

"It was a nice kinda world once," I says, bitter. "I could go home peaceful and not have belly-cramps wonderin' if a blonde has called up my wife to announce my engagement to her. I could punch keys on a logic without gazing into somebody's bedroom while she is giving her epidermis a air bath and being led to think things I gotta take out in thinkin'. I could—"

Then I groan, rememberin' that my wife, naturally, is gonna blame me for the fact that our private life ain't private anymore if anybody has tried to peek into it.

"It was a swell world," I says, homesick for the dear dead days-before-yesterday. "We was playin' happy with our toys like little innocent children until somethin' happened. Like a guy named Joe come in and squashed all our mud pies."

Then it hit me. I got the whole thing in one flash. There ain't nothing in the tank setup to start relays closin'. Relays are closed exclusive by logics, to get the information the keys are punched for. Nothin' but a logic coulda cooked up the relay patterns that constituted logics service. Humans wouldn't ha' been able to figure it out! Only a logic could integrate all the stuff that woulda made all the other logics work like this—

There was one answer. I drove into a restaurant and went over to a pay-logic an' dropped in a coin.

"Can a logic be modified," I spell out, "to cooperate in longterm planning which human brains are too limited in scope to do?"

The screen sputters. Then it says:

"Definitely yes."

"How great will the modifications be?" I punch.

"Microscopically slight. Changes in dimensions," says the screen. "Even modern precision gauges are not exact enough to check them, however. They can only come about under present manufacturing methods by an extremely improbable accident, which has only happened once."

"How can one get hold of that one accident which can do this highly necessary work?" I punch.

The screen sputters. Sweat broke out on me. I ain't got it figured out close, yet, but what I'm scared of is that whatever is Joe will be suspicious. But what I'm askin' is strictly logical. And logics can't lie. They gotta be accurate. They can't help it.

"A complete logic capable of the work required," says the screen, "is now in ordinary family use in—"

And it gives me the Korlanovitch address and do I go over there! Do I go over there fast! I pull up the Maintenance car in front of the place, and I take the extra logic outa the back, and I stagger up to the Korlanovitch flat and I ring the bell. A kid answers the door.

"I'm from Logics Maintenance," I tell the kid. "An inspection record has shown that your logic is apt to break down any minute. I come to put in a new one before it does."

The kid says "O.K.!" real bright and runs back to the livin' room where Joe—I got the habit of callin' him Joe later, through just meditatin' about him—is runnin' something the kids wanna look at. I hook in the other logic an' turn it on, conscientious making sure it works. Then I say:

"Now kiddies, you punch this one for what you want. I'm gonna take the old one away before it breaks down."

And I glance at the screen. The kiddies have apparently said they wanna look at some real cannibals. So the screen is presenting a anthropological expedition scientific record film of the fertility dance of the Huba-Jouba tribe of West Africa. It is supposed to be restricted to anthropological professors an' postgraduate medical students. But there ain't any censor blocks workin' anymore and it's on. The kids are much interested. Me, bein' a old married man, I blush.

I disconnect Joe. Careful. I turn to the other logic and punch keys for Maintenance. I do not get a services flash. I get Maintenance. I feel very good. I report that I am goin' home because I fell down a flight of steps an' hurt my leg. I add, inspired:

"An' say, I was carryin' the logic I replaced an' it's all busted. I left it for the dustman to pick up."

"If you don't turn 'em in," says Stock, "you gotta pay for 'em."

"Cheap at the price," I say.

I go home. Laurine ain't called. I put Joe down in the cellar, careful. If I turned him in, he'd be inspected an' his parts salvaged even if I busted somethin' on him. Whatever part was off-normal might be used again and everything start all over. I can't risk it. I pay for him and leave him be.

That's what happened. You might say I saved civilization an' not be far wrong. I know I ain't goin' to take a chance on havin' Joe in action again. Not while Laurine is livin'. An' there are other reasons. With all the nuts who wanna change the world to their own line o' thinkin', an' the ones that wanna bump people off, an' generally solve their problems... Yeah! Problems are bad, but I figure I better let sleepin' problems lie.

But on the other hand, if Joe could be tamed, somehow, and got to work just reasonable—he could make me a coupla million dollars, easy. But even if I got sense enough not to get rich, an' if I get retired and just loaf around fishin' an' lyin' to other old duffers about what a great guy I used to be—maybe I'll like it, but maybe I won't. And after all, if I get fed up with bein' old and confined strictly to thinking—why, I could hook Joe in long enough to ask: "How can a old guy not stay old?" Joe'll be able to find out. An' he'll tell me.

That couldn't be allowed out general, of course. You gotta make room for kids to grow up. But it's a pretty good world, now Joe's turned off. Maybe I'll turn him on long enough to learn how to stay in it. But on the other hand, maybe...

DIAL F FOR FRANKENSTEIN

Arthur C. Clarke

Little need be said about the stature of Arthur C. Clarke (1917–2008), probably Britain's best-known science-fiction writer, renowned for his work with Stanley Kubrick on 2001: A Space Odyssey *(1968), and winner of the Hugo, Nebula and British Science Fiction awards for his novel of an alien world that passes through our solar system,* A Rendezvous with Rama *(1973). Despite his reputation for writing science fiction at the cutting edge of science, and predicting future developments, as he did with the geo-stationary satellites that brought us global communication, Clarke also had a mystical side to his writing. He himself said that any sufficiently advanced technology is indistinguishable from magic and this aura of wonder infected his early novels,* "Against the Fall of Night" *(1948; expanded as* The City and the Stars, *1956) and* Childhood's End *(1953). The following story, first published at the end of 1964, was read by a young Tim Berners-Lee and planted in his mind one of the seeds that started him thinking about global networks that led to the world-wide web.*

A T 0150 GREENWICH MEAN TIME ON DECEMBER 1, 1975, EVERY telephone in the world started to ring. A quarter of a billion people picked up their receivers to listen for a few seconds with annoyance or perplexity. Those who had been awakened in the middle of the night assumed that some far-off friend was calling over the satellite telephone network that had gone into service, with such a blaze of publicity, the day before. But there was no voice on the line, only a sound that to many seemed like the roaring of the sea—to others, like the vibrations of harp strings in the wind. And there were many more, in that moment, who recalled a secret sound of childhood—the noise of blood pulsing through the veins, heard when a shell is cupped over the ear. Whatever it was, it lasted no more than twenty seconds; then it was replaced by the dialing tone.

The world's subscribers cursed, muttered, "Wrong number," and hung up. Some tried to dial a complaint, but the line seemed busy. In a few hours, everyone had forgotten the incident—except those whose duty it was to worry about such things.

At the Post Office Research Station, the argument had been going on all morning and had got nowhere. It continued unabated through the lunch break, when the hungry engineers poured into the little café across the road.

"I still think," said Willy Smith, the solid-state electronics man, "that it was a temporary surge of current, caused when the satellite network was switched in."

"It was obviously *something* to do with the satellites," agreed Jules Reyner, circuit designer. "But why the time delay? They were plugged in at midnight; the ringing was two hours later— as we all know to our cost." He yawned violently.

"What do *you* think, Doc?" asked Bob Andrews, computer programmer: "You've been very quiet all morning. Surely you've got some idea?"

Dr. John Williams, head of the mathematics division, stirred uneasily.

"Yes," he said, "I have. But you won't take it seriously."

"That doesn't matter. Even if it's as crazy as those science fiction yarns you write under a pseudonym, it may give us some leads."

Williams blushed, but not very hard. Everyone knew about his stories, and he wasn't ashamed of them. After all, they *had* been collected in book form. (Remainder at five shillings; he still had a couple of hundred copies.)

"Very well," he said, doodling on the tablecloth. "This is something I've been wondering about for years. Have you ever considered the analogy between an automatic telephone exchange and the human brain?"

"Who hasn't thought of it?" scoffed one of his listeners. "That idea must go back to Graham Bell."

"Possibly; I never said it was original. But I do say it's time we started taking it seriously." He squinted balefully at the fluorescent tubes above the table; they were needed on this foggy winter day. "What's wrong with the damn lights? They've been flickering for the last five minutes."

"Don't bother about that; Maisie's probably forgotten to pay her electricity bill. Let's hear more about your theory."

"Most of it isn't theory; it's plain fact. We know that the human brain is a system of switches—neurons—interconnected in a very elaborate fashion by nerves. An automatic telephone exchange is also a system of switches—selectors, and so forth—connected together with wires."

"Agreed," said Smith. "But that analogy won't get you very far. Aren't there about fifteen billion neurons in the brain? That's a lot more than the number of switches in an autoexchange."

Williams's answer was interrupted by the scream of a low-flying jet; he had to wait until the café had ceased to vibrate before he could continue.

"Never heard them fly *that* low," Andrews grumbled. "Thought it was against regulations."

"So it is, but don't worry—London Airport Control will catch him."

"I doubt it," said Reyner. "That *was* London Airport, bringing in a Concorde on ground approach. But I've never heard one so low, either. Glad I wasn't aboard."

"Are we, or are we *not*, going to get on with this blasted discussion?" demanded Smith.

"You're right about the fifteen billion neurons in the human brain," continued Williams, unabashed. "And *that's* the whole point. Fifteen billion sounds a large number, but it isn't. Round about the 1960s, there were more than that number of individual switches in the world's autoexchanges. Today, there are approximately five times as many."

"I see," said Reyner very slowly. "And as of yesterday, they've all become capable of full interconnection, now that the satellite links have gone into service."

"Precisely."

There was silence for a moment, apart from the distant clanging of a fire-engine bell.

"Let me get this straight," said Smith. "Are you suggesting that the world telephone system is now a giant brain?"

"That's putting it crudely—anthropomorphically. I prefer to think of it in terms of critical size." Williams held his hands out in front of him, fingers partly closed.

"Here are two lumps of U-235; nothing happens as long as you keep them apart. But bring them together"—he suited the action to the words—"and you have something *very* different from one bigger lump of uranium. You have a hole half a mile across.

"It's the same with our telephone networks; until today they've been largely independent, autonomous. But now we've suddenly multiplied the connecting links—the networks have all merged together—and we've reached criticality."

"And just what does criticality mean in this case?" asked Smith.

"For want of a better word—consciousness."

"A weird sort of consciousness," said Reyner. "What would it use for sense organs?"

"Well, all the radio and TV stations in the world would be feeding information into it, through their landlines. *That* should give it something to think about! Then there would be all the data stored in all the computers; it would have access to that—and to the electronic libraries, the radar tracking systems, the telemetering in the automatic factories. Oh, it would have enough sense organs! We can't begin to imagine its picture of the world, but it would certainly be infinitely richer and more complex than ours."

"Granted all this, because it's an entertaining idea," said Reyner, "what could it *do* except think? It couldn't go anywhere; it would have no limbs."

"Why should it want to travel? It would already be everywhere! And every piece of remotely controlled electrical equipment on the planet could act as a limb."

"Now I understand that time delay," interjected Andrews. "It was conceived at midnight, but it wasn't born until one-fifty this morning. The noise that woke us all up was—its birth cry."

His attempt to sound facetious was not altogether convincing, and nobody smiled. Overhead, the lights continued their annoying flicker, which seemed to be getting worse. Then there was an interruption from the front of the café as Jim Small of Power Supplies made his usual boisterous entry.

"Look at this, fellows," he grinned, waving a piece of paper in front of his colleagues. "I'm rich. Ever seen a bank balance like *that*?"

Dr. Williams took the proffered statement, glanced down the columns, and read the balance aloud: "Credit £999,999,897.87.

"Nothing very odd about that," he continued above the general amusement. "I'd say it means the computer's made a slight mistake. That sort of thing was happening all the time just after the banks converted to the decimal system."

"I know, I know," said Jim, "but don't spoil my fun. I'm going to frame this statement—and what would happen if I drew a check for a few million on the strength of this? Could I sue the bank if it bounced?"

"Not on your life," answered Reyner. "I'll take a bet that the banks thought of *that* years ago and protected themselves somewhere down in the small print. But by the way—when did you get that statement?"

"In the noon delivery; it comes straight to the office, so that my wife doesn't have a chance of seeing it."

"Hmm—that means it was computed early this morning. Certainly after midnight…"

"What are you driving at? And why all the long faces?"

No one answered him, he had started a new hare, and the hounds were in full cry.

"Does anyone here know about automated banking systems?" asked Willy Smith. "How are they tied together?"

"Like everything else these days," said Bob Andrews. "They're all in the same network—the computers talk to one another all over the world. It's a point for you, John. If there *was* real trouble, that's one of the first places I'd expect it. Besides the phone system itself, of course."

"No one answered the question I asked before Jim came in," complained Reyner. "What would this supermind actually *do*? Would it be friendly—hostile—indifferent? Would it even know that we exist, or would it consider the electronic signals it's handling to be the only reality?"

"I see you're beginning to believe me," said Williams with a certain grim satisfaction. "I can only answer your question by asking another. What does a newborn baby do? It starts looking for food." He glanced up at the flickering lights. "My God," he said slowly, as if a thought had just struck him. "There's only one food it would need—electricity."

"This nonsense has gone far enough," said Smith. "What the devil's happened to our lunch? We gave our orders twenty minutes ago."

Everyone ignored him.

"And then," said Reyner, taking up where Williams had left off, "it would start looking around and stretching its limbs. In fact, it would start to play, like any growing baby."

"And babies *break* things," said someone softly.

"It would have enough toys, heaven knows. That Concorde that went over just now. The automated production lines. The traffic lights in our streets."

"Funny you should mention that," interjected Small. "Something's happened to the traffic outside—it's been stopped for the last ten minutes. Looks like a big jam."

"I guess there's a fire somewhere—I heard an engine."

"I've heard two—and what sounded like an explosion over toward the industrial estate. Hope it's nothing serious."

"Maisie!!! What about some candles? We can't see a thing!"

"I've just remembered—this place has an all-electric kitchen. We're going to get cold lunch, if we get any lunch at all."

"At least we can read the newspaper while we're waiting. Is that the latest edition you've got there, Jim?"

"Yes—haven't had time to look at it yet. Hmm—there *do* seem to have been a lot of odd accidents this morning—railway signals jammed—water main blown up through failure of relief valve—dozens of complaints about last night's wrong numbers—"

He turned the page and became suddenly silent.

"What's the matter?"

Without a word, Small handed over the paper. Only the front page made sense. Throughout the interior, column after column was a mass of printer's pie—with, here and there, a few incongruous advertisements making islands of sanity in a sea of gibberish. They had obviously been set up as independent blocks and had escaped the scrambling that had overtaken the text around them.

"So this is where long-distance typesetting and autodistribution have brought us," grumbled Andrews. "I'm afraid Fleet Street's been putting too many eggs in one electronic basket."

"So have we all, I'm afraid," said Williams very solemnly. "So have we all."

"If I can get a word in edgeways, in time to stop the mob hysteria which seems to be infecting this table," said Smith loudly and firmly,

"I'd like to point out that there's nothing to worry about even if John's ingenious fantasy is correct. We only have to switch off the satellites—and we'll be back where we were yesterday."

"Prefrontal lobotomy," muttered Williams. "I'd thought of that."

"Eh? Oh, yes—cutting out slabs of the brain. That would certainly do the trick. Expensive, of course, and we'd have to go back to sending telegrams to each other. But civilization would survive."

From not too far away, there was a short, sharp explosion.

"I don't like this," said Andrews nervously. "Let's hear what the old BBC's got to say—the one o'clock news has just started."

He reached into his briefcase and pulled out a transistor radio.

"—unprecedented number of industrial accidents, as well as the unexplained launching of three salvos of guided missiles from military installations in the United States. Several airports have had to suspend operations owing to the erratic behavior of their radars, and the banks and stock exchanges have closed because their information-processing systems have become completely unreliable." ("You're telling me," muttered Small, while the others shushed him.) "One moment, please—there's a news flash coming through... Here it is. We have just been informed that all control over the newly installed communication satellites has been lost. They are no longer responding to commands from the ground. According to—"

The BBC went off the air; even the carrier wave died. Andrews reached for the tuning knob and twisted it round the dial. Over the whole band, the ether was silent.

Presently Reyner said, in a voice not far from hysteria, "That prefrontal lobotomy was a good idea, John. Too bad that baby's already thought of it."

Williams rose slowly to his feet.

"Let's get back to the lab," he said. "There must be an answer somewhere."

But he knew already that it was far, far too late. For Homo sapiens, the telephone bell had tolled.

"Danger in the Dark Cave" by J. J. Connington, first published in *The Passing Show*, 10 December 1938 and in *Weird Tales*, May 1939 as "The Thinking Machine".

"The Machine Stops" by E. M. Forster, first published in *The Oxford & Cambridge Review*, Michaelmas 1909 and collected in *The Eternal Moment* (London: Sidgwick & Jackson, 1928). Reprinted by permission of the Society of Authors & Houghton Mifflin Harcourt.

"A Logic Named Joe" by Will F. Jenkins, first published in *Astounding Science Fiction*, March 1946 and collected in *Sidewise in Time* (Chicago: Shasta Publishers, 1950). Reprinted by permission of the agent for the author's estate, Virginia Kidd Agency.

"The Discontented Machine" by Adeline Knapp, first published in *A Thousand Dollars a Day* (Boston: Arena Publishing, 1894).

"Two-Handed Engine" by C. L. Moore & Henry Kuttner, first published in *Magazine of Fantasy & Science Fiction*, June 1955. Reprinted by permission of the agent for the authors' estates, Don Congdon Associates.

"Efficiency" by Perley Poore Sheehan & Robert H. Davis, first published by New York: Doran, 1917. First UK publication as "Blood and Iron" in *The Strand Magazine*, October 1917.

"Rex" by Harl Vincent, first published in *Astounding Stories*, June 1934.

"The Mind Machine" by Michael Williams, first published in *All-Story Weekly*, 29 March 1919.

"Automata" by S. Fowler Wright, first published in *Weird Tales*, September 1929 and collected in *The New Gods Lead* (London: Jarrolds, 1932). Reprinted by permission of the author's estate.

The voice which came back through a clamour of noise greater than any before was that of a stranger; it was hysterical, raging futilely into the void. "The sun's blown up!"

Join humanity on the brink of destruction in fourteen doom-laden tales exploring our fixation with how and when our end will come, selected from the SF magazines and rare literary journals of the British Library collection.

Illustrating the whole gamut of apocalyptic fiction from cosmic calamities to self-inflicted nuclear annihilation, this explosive new selection also includes accounts of post-apocalyptic worlds from the speculative warnings of the 1890s to Ray Bradbury's poignant vision of a silent planet after the last echoes of humanity have died away.

The fact that humanity is not alone in the universe has long preoccupied our thoughts.

In this compelling new collection of short stories from SF's classic age our visions of 'other' are shown in a myriad of forms – beings from other worlds, corrupted lifeforms from our own planet and entities from unimaginable dimensions.

Amongst these tales, the humble ant becomes humanity's greatest foe, a sailor awakes in a hellish landscape terrified by a monstrous creature from the deep, an extra-terrestrial apocalypse devastates our world but also brings us together, and our race becomes the unwitting agent of another species' survival. Be prepared to face your greatest fears and relinquish your hold on reality as you confront the menace of the monster.